sp

ma

mantic, Marlowe's story is an uplifting celebration of how failure never has to define us. The romance is sizzling hot, the commentary on the drawbacks of exposure in the age of social media is on point, and the writing is the perfect mix of humorous and poignant. But my favorite thing about *Marlowe Banks, Redesigned* is the setting: it's clear that Jacqueline Firkins knows the world of costume design, and she wove millions of fascinating details into a uniquely sensory experience. A sparkling, charming novel everyone should read!"

—Ali Hazelwood, author of *The Love Hypothesis*

"Reading this book feels like spending time with a dear friend. A smart, sexy treasure of a romance stitched together with warmth, flair, and compassion. Jacqueline Firkins is an author to watch."

—Rachel Lynn Solomon, author of *The Ex Talk*

"*Marlowe Banks, Redesigned* is ready for its close-up. It's delightfully fun, thoughtfully charming, and poignantly honest. The cast of characters is genuine and diverse, the love story raw and sweet, while the themes of friendship, expectations, and perception versus reality are relatable. I truly enjoyed this book."

—Sophie Sullivan, author of *How to Love Your Neighbor*

"Smart, sweet, and utterly charming, *Marlowe Banks, Redesigned* is a delicious enemies-to-lovers tale about finding the inner strength to pursue your dreams. I couldn't stop turning the pages and loved every moment!" —Sara Desai, author of *The Singles Table*

"As comforting as the perfect pair of jeans, this sweet, funny, and sexy book is filled with memorable characters and a swoony, slow-burn romance. I loved the glimpse into the world of Hollywood TV sets and costume designers. Marlowe and Angus's connection seemed so real, despite the Tinseltown setting, and it was so satisfying to see their connection grow. This book is such a delight!"
—Farah Heron, author of *Kamila Knows Best* and *Tahira in Bloom*

"Firkins delivers on every front—sweet, smart, and utterly satisfying, *Marlowe Banks, Redesigned* is a treat for romance readers everywhere." —Elizabeth Everett, author of *A Perfect Equation*

"With sparkling banter, incisive humor, and an authoritative glimpse of television's controlled behind-the-scenes chaos, *Marlowe Banks, Redesigned* is a slow-burn love story about taking chances and the exhilarating feeling of finally being truly seen. The chemistry between the leads is tangible, and the supporting cast is relatable and real. I loved it—five shining Hollywood stars!"
—Jen Devon, author of *Bend Toward the Sun*

ALSO BY JACQUELINE FIRKINS

How Not to Fall in Love

Hearts, Strings, and Other Breakable Things

Marlowe Banks, Redesigned

A NOVEL

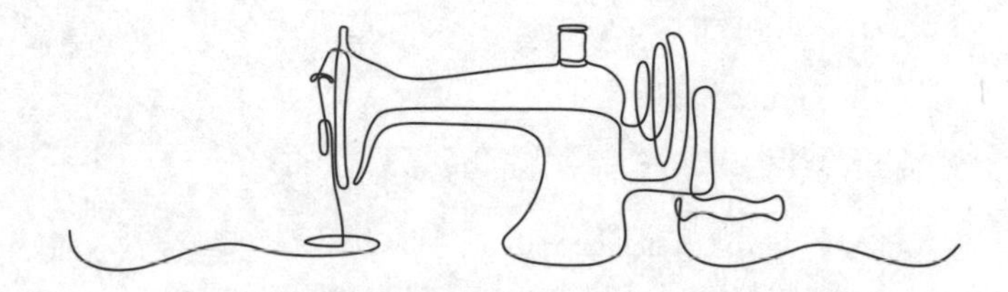

Jacqueline Firkins

ST. MARTIN'S
GRIFFIN
NEW YORK

This is a work of fiction. All of the characters, organizations, and events portrayed in this novel are either products of the author's imagination or are used fictitiously.

First published in the United States by St. Martin's Griffin, an imprint of St. Martin's Publishing Group

Designed by Jen Edwards

www.stmartins.com

Library of Congress Cataloging-in-Publication Data

Names: Firkins, Jacqueline, author.
Title: Marlowe Banks, redesigned: a novel / Jacqueline Firkins.
Description: First edition. | New York: St. Martin's Griffin, 2022.
Identifiers: LCCN 2022020130 | ISBN 9781250836502 (trade paperback) | ISBN 9781250836519 (ebook)
Subjects: LCGFT: Romance fiction. | Novels.
Classification: LCC PS3606.I734 M37 2022 | DDC 813/.6—dc23/eng/20220502
LC record available at https://lccn.loc.gov/2022020130

First Edition: 2022

10 9 8 7 6 5 4 3 2 1

For the worriers and the wonderers. For the wrestlers with imposter syndrome, pointless comparisons, or persistent fear of failure. And for Timothy Olyphant, who I once took shopping for jeans and who will have absolutely no memory of that day.

Marlowe Banks, Redesigned

Chapter One

Marlowe Banks never dreamed that an MFA from Yale would earn her a job organizing hangers, picking crusted insoles out of an old pair of Top-Siders, and busting every last fingernail in an attempt to resize a watchband using only a safety pin and the force of her formidable will. The title Costume Production Assistant had sounded so glamorous. More commonly referred to as a PA, she was a cog in a machine. Nothing more.

"Just great," she muttered as the safety pin slipped and blood beaded on her finger for the third time. "Amazing opportunity. Spectacular learning experience. Dream job." The words strained to emerge but if she said them often enough maybe she'd start to believe them. After all, unambitious cogs didn't have to watch reviewers and competitive industry professionals pick apart their creative work. They didn't feel like imposters for calling themselves artists. In fact, most people didn't even notice them, which was precisely what Marlowe had hoped for when she shelved her nascent design career in New York City and flew out to Los Angeles: city of dreams, sandy beaches, delicious tacos, and so many insanely beautiful people anyone ordinary was basically invisible.

The wristwatch finally set to the actress's size, Marlowe began unpacking a large order of novelty socks, the next item on her list of Tasks No One Else Wanted to Do. As a lowly PA, Marlowe spent a lot of time with such lists. No one used that phrasing, of course, but everyone knew. She was slicing open the first box when the clatter of excessive bangle bracelets reached her from the trailer entrance, followed by sharp heels clicking on linoleum and the telltale aroma of sandalwood and well-cultivated disdain.

"How are we only on episode three?" Babs Koçak sank into a canvas chair beside Marlowe, turning toward the nearby mirror and smoothing out her perfectly arched eyebrows, jet black above slightly pinched gray eyes. She was petite in stature but large in personality, always impeccably dressed and coifed, her means of ensuring that others trusted her to style them. "I feel like I've been picking out velveteen blazers and silk boxer shorts since tyrannosauruses dreamed of kidskin gloves for their tiny hands."

Marlowe fluttered a polite smile as she set aside the box cutter.

"Maybe it seems that long because you're on season six?" she offered.

Babs groaned. "They were supposed to stop at five, but apparently if you put enough hot young actors on the screen, people will tune in until every last one of them has slept with all of the others." She let out a put-upon sigh and smoothed the faintest of wrinkles from her crisp silk pedal pushers. "Did you get through those receipts?"

"All set. I left the invoice with production this morning."

"Contact Calvin Klein?"

"The samples will be ready for me to pick up tomorrow."

"Reschedule my chiropractor appointment?"

"You're on for next Tuesday. Eleven A.M."

"Find me a seaweed salad without sesame seeds?"

"Holy Rolls is making it to order. I'll grab it at noon."

"And Edith Head?"

"Is doing fine at the new doggy daycare. She's even sharing her squeaky bone."

Babs tipped an eyebrow and glanced around the trailer as if looking for something to criticize, having come up short with her initial inquiries. Marlowe continued her task at hand, sorting the socks with llamas and sloths from the ones with rainbow stripes or catchy phrases. The department had ordered almost a hundred pairs, though the chances that any of them would be seen on camera were about as high as tyrannosauruses wearing kidskin gloves. TV work was so different from Marlowe's first few theater jobs, where the entire budget for twenty or thirty period costumes was less than the cost of this one sock order. She'd been on the costume team for *Heart's Diner* for ten weeks now, so she was past the initial mouth-agape, Dorothy-lands-in-Oz phase, though sometimes she still half-expected a munchkin with a lollipop to walk into the trailer. In Hollywood, anything was possible.

"Are you really drinking that?" Babs asked.

Marlowe paused, both fists full of banana-print socks. "Drinking what?"

Babs nodded at a canned beverage on the counter near Marlowe. "It's not even ten A.M."

"It's only sparkling water." Marlowe set down the socks and picked up the can, searching for toxicity warnings or ingredients beyond the obvious.

Babs mumbled a vaguely disapproving *hmm*. "All that carbonation can wreak havoc on your digestive system. You confuse your body's natural signals and next thing you know . . ." She mimed inflating like a balloon. "At least wait until lunch or dinner."

Marlowe tucked the sparkling water can behind a pile of crumpled packaging, mentally noting that no self pep talk would make her situation ideal. Problem one: living in L.A. didn't suit her. The city demanded an attention to brands and health culture, maybe not for everyone, but for anyone working in a fashion-related field, or at least for anyone working with Babs Koçak. Despite Babs's frequent "helpful suggestions," Marlowe hated gyms and she considered super foods decidedly un-super. Except for blueberries, and maybe broccoli, as long as cheese was nearby to mask its more viridescent qualities. She jogged every week so she wasn't totally sedentary, but no sparkling water? Seriously?

Babs peered over at the socks Marlowe was stacking on the counter.

"I should've been more specific about the order." She picked up a pair printed with cats talking on telephones. "Keep the stripes and general patterns. Send the rest of this nonsense back. We're supposed to be in Middle America. Not *Jumanji*." She examined a few more pairs while Marlowe started repacking the box. "Do you think Idi could pull these off with his McQueen suit?" She held up a pair with blue and black stripes.

"McQueen?" Marlowe asked, mouth agape. "Doesn't his character work at a gas station?"

"This isn't one of your little Chekhov plays, dear. This is television. People want style and glamor." Babs tossed the socks aside. "You're so new, but you'll learn."

Marlowe offered up her usual placid smile while noting problem two: the job. Not that being a PA on a major TV show was all bad. The pay was good. Marlowe was well suited to the tasks: organized, efficient, detail-oriented, and uncomplaining. She was effectively avoiding her harshest critics and those schmoozy opening-night parties where she never knew what to say besides, "Great working with you!" She even had celebrity gossip to sneak to her friends back in New York. However—and it was a big *however*—she hadn't totally managed to shut down her designer brain and career ambitions. She had opinions about story, world, and character. She was bursting with thoughts on symbolic color palettes or ways to deliver information about alliances and antagonisms, sometimes by simply changing out a tie or adjusting the part in someone's hair. But she'd come to L.A. to hide, and hiding required a minimization of opinions. Ditto for ambitions.

The trailer door swung open and Cherry Cho walked in, dressed in her usual uniform of tight black jeans, black designer blazer, and ironic T-shirt. Today's logo read BINARY IS FOR COMPUTER PROCESSORS ONLY. She was slim and striking with long black hair she'd twisted into the kind of messy bun Marlowe often attempted but quickly gave up on, lacking Cherry's ability to make "messy" appear intentional.

"I ran into Angus over at craft services," Cherry told Babs. "He wants a word about his leather jacket."

"What about it?" Babs stood, tugging the hem of her blouse, perhaps to straighten it, perhaps to reveal a hint of cleavage, a habit she often succumbed to when Angus Gordon's name was invoked. "Isn't it the same one he wore last week?"

"Apparently there's an issue with the fit. Again." Cherry rolled her eyes. "He's been hitting the weights harder than usual lately. Now he needs more shoulder room. I told him the jacket looked fine but he demanded a second opinion."

"How many leather jackets can one actor go through in a season?" Babs flicked a pointed finger at Marlowe and Cherry. "Don't answer that. I don't want to know." She dabbed at her eye makeup and smoothed her hair before exiting the trailer.

The second the door closed behind her, Cherry crumpled to the floor, lolling about like a restless cat, one torn between stretching and going straight to sleep.

"I'm sooooooo tired," she moaned.

"Work late?" Marlowe asked, still sorting the remaining socks.

"My ex finally came to get the last of her crap from my apartment. Should've taken an hour, two max. Then we got to talking, which was fine at first but before long we were rehashing every argument about my tendency to prioritize work and her jealousy issues and why the hell do I assume a woman I've been assisting for four goddamned years is suddenly going to recommend me for my own design gig but I can't give up now when I'm so close to a big break and you're deluded, no, *you're* deluded, and next thing I know it's six A.M. and we're practically screaming at each other." She yawned into a fist, long and slow, blinking through dense lash extensions before going limp again. "I'm making so many mistakes today. I don't function on zero sleep. Something's going to go horribly wrong and it'll be my fault." Never one to rest on ceremony about unnecessary conventions such as using chairs, she rolled onto her side and smothered another yawn.

Marlowe polished off her sparkling water while she could do so without censure.

"Anything I can do to help?" she offered.

"Any chance you can keep our friend Babs away from me today? She practically bit my head off this morning when I missed her text about picking up gluten-free, sugar-free scones with her coffee order. As if we don't have a catering truck for all that."

"Are their scones gluten-free and sugar-free?"

"Would anyone here eat them if they weren't?" Cherry swiveled around and hauled herself to a seated position, darting a quick glance at the door. "Sometimes I swear Babs invents reasons to be pissed off, just so she can remind the rest of us she's in charge. She was in our shoes once. Now it's her turn to dole out pain. The film industry is basically an endless hazing loop." She stretched her neck and danced her fingers along her spine, performing a self-massage.

At twenty-eight, Cherry was only three years older than Marlowe but she'd been working in the industry since she was eighteen: two years as a PA, four as a shopper and stitcher, and another four as Babs Koçak's design assistant. As Cherry had explained to Marlowe, assisting was one of the best ways to land a design job. Not only did directors and producers get to know you, but if the designer was offered a film or series they couldn't take, they might pass the job to their assistant. So far Cherry's aspirations had proven merely . . . aspirational. Despite the long slog, and despite all of her complaints about the industry, she was determined to make it to the top. Marlowe admired Cherry's drive. She also wondered how it reflected on her own.

She leaned toward Cherry and lowered her voice. "Do you think something's going on between Babs and Angus?"

Cherry made a gagging motion. "God, I hope not. I mean, the guy's a man-whore, so maybe, but she's twice his age and he has waaaaay better options. I'm pretty sure the supermodel who snuck out of his trailer this morning was *not* the one I saw yesterday."

Marlowe frowned in the general direction of Angus's trailer, curious which girl—or rather, girls—he'd been pursuing most recently. He was one of six lead cast members, in his mid-to-late twenties with red hair too bright to be considered auburn and too dark to be called ginger, though it suited him by any name. He played the town bad boy, always getting into trouble, with a shady past and a hefty chip on his shoulder.

Of all the celebrities Marlowe had encountered over the past few months, Angus was the one her friends in New York had been most eager to hear about. She couldn't blame them. She'd been curious, too. His face had been plastered on tabloids and film fan sites for years, first as a teen heartthrob from a popular Disney show, more recently beside a rotating roster of beautiful actresses. He had the kind of rugged, square-jawed good looks that made girls stammer and blush in his presence, centering him in countless fantasies. He'd even maintained a high position on Marlowe's Top Ten Imaginary Love Interests list throughout her adolescence, and she'd entertained a few steamy thoughts back when *Heart's Diner* first aired, but that was before she met the man and realized he was the most self-involved human being on the planet. Now she avoided him, which was easily done as a PA whose tasks seldom included direct interaction with the central cast.

Her phone buzzed in her back pocket. She pulled it out and checked the screen without opening it.

Kelvin: How's La-La Land treating you, Lowe?

Marlowe's frown deepened. Problem number three: loneliness, and its annoyingly frequent companion, regret. Kelvin's question was innocuous enough but the nickname still tugged at Marlowe's heart in ways she *really* wished it wouldn't. Relationships were funny that way. People built a private language together. When the relationship ended, no one else knew the words and symbols so the language had to die, too.

Cherry clambered up and dusted herself off. "S'up?"

"Apparently it's ex day."

"He's *still* texting you? He knows you broke up, right?"

"Yeah. No mixed messages there." Marlowe tucked her phone back into her pocket. "We're trying to work through the fallout so we can stay friends."

Cherry eyed her sideways. "What, exactly, does 'staying friends' mean?"

"So far it means he texts me a random question every week or so. I answer, because I'm compelled by the gods of good manners to never *ever* leave a question hanging. Then I ask him a question. He does not answer it."

Cherry leaned toward the mirror and prodded the shadows under her eyes.

"I hate that benching shit," she said. "All those little feelers that make sure you're still there if someone decides they want you. As soon as you give them even the slightest hint that they have your attention, they vanish. You should seriously block him already."

"Maybe. I don't know." Marlowe wrapped a hand around her ring finger, twisting at the base, a nervous tic she hadn't yet managed to overcome. "A few friendly texts won't kill me. I miss him. And I still feel like an asshole for bailing the way I did."

"So, are you staying in touch because you're friends or because you feel bad?"

"Both, I guess?" Marlowe's voice came out small and meek. She hated that.

"Just be careful." Cherry spun around and leaned back on the counter, drumming the edge with her turquoise lacquered fingernails. "Make sure he's adding something positive to your life, like actively making an effort to see that you're happy. If he's only making you unhappy, call People Disposal Services, stat."

Cherry's words hit home, calling into question Marlowe's inability to let go and move on. She shifted on her feet as her phone pressed into her backside, demanding her attention. Scrambling for a distraction, she tidied stacks of socks. She'd barely begun when Cherry grabbed her by the arms and pivoted her toward the mirror.

"What do you see?" she asked.

Marlowe blinked at her reflection. Before her stood an awkward girl/woman, tall and angular with a reedy figure, a too-long neck, a too-sharp nose, and lank brown hair that fell almost to her waist as though it'd tried to do something more interesting but gave up in despair. She slouched, a habit she hadn't shaken since she outgrew most of her classmates at age thirteen, even though she topped out at five-ten while a lot of the boys kept growing. She had a few lingering acne scars and she hadn't yet succumbed to L.A. staples like eyebrow waxing and chemical peels. Also, she was clearly indoors-y.

"I don't know what I see," she said. "Someone still trying to figure it all out?"

"Fair." Cherry stepped to her side. "But I bet you just logged ten things you hate about yourself instead of ten things you like."

Marlowe cringed. "Maybe? How did you know?"

"It's kind of your trademark. Also, it's what the world teaches women to do. Take in the negative and ignore the positive. It's bullshit, but no one can tune out *all* the noise. Besides, I think Kevin—"

"Kelvin."

"Whatever. Bench Boy. I think he doesn't help matters." Cherry swept Marlowe's hair off her shoulders and started loosely plaiting it. "I know you loved him but he sounds like an emotional predator. Didn't he say you'd never find someone as good as him?"

"I shouldn't have told you that. He was angry and upset. He didn't mean it."

"You sure about that?"

Marlowe opened her mouth to argue the point but nothing came out. Those awful words still haunted her. *You'll never find someone else as good as me.* Whether or not Kelvin meant them, he knew she'd take them to heart. He always knew. He'd never physically harmed her, but he had a knack for making her feel . . . what? Diminished? Small? Unworthy? Grateful for every attention? Still, he was smart, funny, talented, attractive. He cheered on her artistic aspirations. He was generous with little gifts that said, "I'm thinking of you." She fit perfectly in the crook of his arm when they slept together. What if Marlowe never did find someone better? What if she'd made the wrong choice when she booked her flight and gave back the ring? What if she wasn't worth more?

Cherry yanked a rubber band off her wrist, untangling it from several others. She met Marlowe's gaze in the mirror as she bound the end of the braid.

"From what you've told me, it sounds like he kept making you feel lucky to be with him. Don't you want to be with someone who feels lucky to be with you?"

"Yes, but—"

"But nothing. You are hereby ordered to accept nothing less." Cherry gave her a militant nod before turning to the far corner of the trailer. "Now help me get all of these shoeboxes over to background before Babs returns and catches us idling."

Marlowe and Cherry stacked up as many shoes at they could carry: brand-name sandals and sneakers in every size, ready to replace whatever flip-flops the background actors arrived in. Babs's attention to "style and glamor" included every stud earring, every belt buckle, and every last piece of footwear that would end up on the cutting room floor.

"You're right," Marlowe said as she stepped out of the trailer.

"I'm always right." Cherry flashed her a smile. "But what am I right about now?"

"I *can* do better. I loved Kelvin as a person but I didn't love how he made me feel as part of a couple. I wasn't his partner. He was always in the driver's seat, making the decisions. I was like"—she searched for the right extension of her metaphor. Navigator? Copilot? Floor mat?—"his sidecar passenger, one who lost more of myself with every ride." She adjusted her hold on the shoes, rethinking how many she could carry.

"Damned straight you can do better," Cherry said, her boxes perfectly stacked.

"No more narcissists. No more emotional predators. No more men who expect a woman to revolve around them. I just have to hold out until I find a guy who—" She slammed into what was either a brick wall or a broad chest, halting her thoughts. Her shoeboxes scattered, spilling out sparkly sandals and tissue paper. With a hasty apology, she knelt to gather everything, eye level with the worn-out knees in a pair of faded jeans.

"Walk much?" a low, angry voice barked above her.

"I'm *so* sorry, I . . ." Her eyes trailed up.

Low-slung jeans, cinched by a weathered leather belt. A plain white T-shirt soaked with what looked like coffee, forcing the folds against a Michelangelo-level sculpted chest. A sharply chiseled jaw speckled with warm stubble. Full lips turned into a frown. Wide-set amber eyes, curtained with pale lashes and brimming with irritation.

As recognition dawned, Marlowe scrambled for a proper apology but other words emerged instead.

"Oh, shit."

Chapter Two

Marlowe clambered to her feet, utterly mortified. As she stood, Angus Gordon handed his coffee cup to a jittery member of his entourage, a gangly girl in her early twenties with a tightly pulled French twist that made her look as if she'd had a facelift. Then again, this being L.A., a facelift might've made her look as if she'd had a facelift. Beside her, a hipster in rolled-up jeans and a pinstriped suit vest whipped out a napkin. Angus used it to pat at his wet T-shirt, frowning below his not-quite-auburn/not-quite-ginger brows.

"Nice greeting," he huffed out. "Let me guess. You're new?"

Marlowe managed a wry smile. "If ten weeks counts as new."

"Close enough. I've never seen you."

Naturally, Marlowe thought. *Because, of course.*

She gestured toward the wardrobe office trailer. "Should I get you a towel?"

"I have towels in my trailer. What I don't have, apparently, is a way to get there without requiring a towel." He paused his shirt-drying efforts to give Marlowe a head-to-toe scan. The look wasn't sexual or predatory. It was direct, almost clinical, as if he was cataloguing information, taking in her shifting stance, her anxious expression, her off-brand clothes, noting each as support for his low estimation of her character.

While he handed his soaked napkin to the jittery girl who carried his mug—because didn't everyone have people waiting around to carry their crap?—Cherry stepped forward.

"Do you need time to shower?" she asked. "I can let Ravi know over in makeup."

He checked his phone. "I'll be on schedule. Just introduce your helper girl to a tote before she takes out half the crew."

Marlowe opened her mouth, a retort ready, but Cherry set a hand on her arm.

"On it," she said. "Sorry about the spill. We'll get everything cleaned for you."

He flapped a hand and carried on, sauntering across the lot with the jittery girl, the hipster, a security guard, and two other people whose roles Marlowe could only guess at.

"'Your helper girl'?" she squeaked once Angus was out of earshot.

"Whatever." Cherry stacked shoeboxes in Marlowe's waiting arms. "He's a douche but arguing with him won't change that and you don't want to risk pissing him off even further. Once an actor's face is on camera, they're set. The show can't continue without them. You and I, however . . . our jobs are a little less secure."

Marlowe watched Angus's retreating back as she balanced the last of the shoeboxes, ensuring she could see over the top, and ensuring her improved shoe-carrying capabilities were on display, on the off-chance Angus turned around to see if his orders were being followed. While she wasn't crazy about her job, she was determined to hold onto it through the end of her contract. And as her mom had so often drilled into Marlowe's head: there was no point doing a thing unless she could do it well.

"Do you think people who are born beautiful naturally evolve into assholes?" she asked as she and Cherry carried the shoes toward the background tent. "Especially if they get famous when they're young? Like, if you grow up surrounded by people desperate to please or impress you, maybe you can't help being entitled."

"That's bullshit." Cherry neatly skirted a cluster of lighting gear. Marlowe followed with far less grace but at least her stack of shoeboxes remained upright. "Janie, Kamala, and Idi are all hot and famous and they're super nice. Most of the cast is. Kindness is a choice, not a default or an exclusive club for the ordinary. Besides, beauty is subjective. What you find beautiful is way different from what I'm attracted to."

Marlowe considered all this as they dropped off the shoes with a background dresser. She appreciated Cherry's point, but then why did some of the actors turn into such raging narcissists while others took all of the attention in stride?

She and Cherry were about to return to the wardrobe trailer when Elaine, the costume coordinator, pulled them aside. She was a short, stout woman with a froth of dusty-blond curls and a love of the color orange. Today the color only appeared on her sneakers and her oversized earrings, but where it appeared, it made itself known.

"Please tell me you sorted out the spare waitress uniforms," she begged.

"They didn't come over from the shop with everything else?" Cherry asked.

"I thought you were grabbing them from the dyer."

"From the—?" Cherry blanched, planting a palm against her forehead. "Oh, god. The color matching. I was supposed to follow up on that this morning, wasn't I?"

Elaine's brows shot up. "'Supposed to'?"

"Long night. I'm so sorry. What can I do?"

With a full complement of brusque gesticulations, Elaine explained that the background performer who was supposed to play the waitress in today's shoot called in sick. Casting sent someone new who was supposedly the same size, but the girl was significantly larger than her measurements had claimed. Not a problem if Cherry had ensured that the other uniforms were on set as scheduled, but in her sleep-deprived state, she'd forgotten all about them. While she got on the phone and started tracking them down, Marlowe searched a nearby rack as though they'd magically appear before her.

"What happens if Cherry can't get the uniforms here?" she asked Elaine.

"We'll have to find someone who fits the one we have."

"You can't swap it out with something else?"

"Not now that we already shot with it. Continuity's a bitch." Elaine extracted the sole existing uniform from the rack. It was a lemon-yellow shirtwaist dress with a white piqué collar and cuffs. The show was set in modern day but the design had a 1950s feel with a comic book color palette and punchy details that required building a lot of pieces from scratch rather than shopping them off the rack. Marlowe remembered the dress from a recent shoot. She also remembered the actress who wore the dress. Narrow-waisted, small-chested, long in the torso, hips that were almost as nonexistent as her own.

She looked over at the dozen or so background actors who were sipping coffee and scrolling through their phones on the other side of the tent. The actors were all fit, sun-kissed, and conventionally attractive, from the twentysomething girl with the impossible-to-ignore cleavage to the sixtysomething guy with the impressive silver pompadour.

"Surely someone here fits," she said.

"If only." Elaine put the dress back on the rack. "It's a non-speaking role, so any of the background actors can do it, but only those few are called in today, none of them are the right size, and our alteration time's limited. Casting can call in someone else, but the clock's ticking. If filming gets held up and everyone knows it's our fault, production will come down hard on Babs, and Babs will come down hard on Cherry."

Marlowe went still. "How hard?"

Elaine pursed her lips and cast a sympathetic glance at Cherry, who was bent over in a chair, muttering sharply, her phone pressed to her ear and a fist knotted in her hair.

"She wouldn't," Marlowe whispered to Elaine.

"She might. Especially if she's looking for a scapegoat."

"Cherry's worked way too hard all these years to get fired over a stupid uniform. The situation's not even her fault. Not entirely. And it's one simple mistake."

"Yes, but in film and TV, mistakes are expensive. If the cameras are waiting, so are a lot of people being paid by the hour."

Marlowe peered toward an opening in the tent as though Babs was about to burst in on cue, waving a fistful of hot-pink termination notices. God, Marlowe missed theater. If an item wasn't perfect, people fixed it when they could get to it, not always right away. Production companies weren't hemorrhaging millions on A-list actors and massive crews and the need to get the angle of a collar positioned *precisely* the same way every time.

As she wilted beside Elaine, Cherry launched herself off the chair.

"They're not *done*!" She shot an agonized look at Marlowe.

Marlowe spun toward Elaine. "Give me the dress." She whisked it from Elaine's outstretched hands and held it up against her chest. "If I fit, can I go on?"

Elaine eyed her skeptically. "Do you act?"

"I'm no Meryl Streep but I took a few classes as an undergrad theater major. I'm sure I can handle pouring coffee and handing out menus. Or do I need to be union?"

"Exceptions are made, but Babs must be running you ragged with other tasks."

"Today it's mostly paperwork." Marlowe flicked open the dress buttons. "I can multitask from set. Anything I don't finish, I'll take home with me tonight." She slipped the dress on over her shirt and trousers and buttoned it up, smoothing the front as she backed away from Elaine. "Does it work? Close enough?"

Cherry marched over, phone in hand. "What are you doing?"

"What does it look like?" Marlowe spun around, making the skirt splay out as if she was Cinderella in her ball gown, though her current attire lacked the requisite wow factor, especially with her corduroys and sneakers poking out below the dress hem.

"You can't," Cherry said.

Elaine laughed to herself. "Actually, I think she can."

Chapter Three

Two hours after first donning the uniform, Marlowe stepped into the wardrobe trailer, bubbling with anticipation. Her brows had been plucked, her makeup done, and her hair cut and styled, now with blunt bangs and a perfect, shiny corkscrew ponytail that stopped at the nape of her neck. She wore cute little white sneakers and folded ankle socks, plus a light crinoline that kicked out the skirt of the uniform. Cherry sat at a desk at the far end of the trailer, her eyes glued to a laptop. Babs perched by a makeup counter, scowling at a seaweed salad. Neither of them noticed her.

"Well?" Marlowe asked. "What do you think?"

Babs looked up, offering Marlowe a light but perceptible sneer. "I think you owe me two hours of work," she said.

Marlowe held out the skirt, trying not to deflate. "I meant about the costume."

Babs's expression didn't budge. "The receipts won't tally themselves, you can't sort fabric samples while on set, and I had to get my lunch delivered. They were late, you know. They still expect such high tips *and* they forgot the chopsticks."

"Sorry about the lunch." Marlowe caved in on herself, a habit she was trying but failing to stem. "I'll get the receipts done today. I promise. I'll take the samples home with me tonight and return with them sorted and labeled tomorrow. I'll also bring you chopsticks from catering before I head to set." She stepped up to Cherry's desk and grabbed a thick accordion file that contained the paperwork she had to complete.

Cherry finally looked up from her screen. A grin instantly broke across her face.

"Wow! Look at you, sassy, sexy waitress girl!" She leapt from her chair and gave Marlowe a full appraisal. "Way to sneak a great haircut onto the company dime."

Marlowe tipped her head side to side, letting her ponytail swing.

"I didn't realize they'd want to cut it when I volunteered, but Patrice said my usual style only worked if I was playing Rapunzel or a Pre-Raphaelite drowning victim."

Babs let out a derisive little snort while Cherry snuck Marlowe a quick eye-roll.

"Your brows are stellar. And you should get the number on that lipstick."

"Good grief!" Babs huffed from halfway down the trailer. "No one needs their ego stroked simply for having the right measurements to carry a pot of coffee."

"Sorry," Marlowe said again, this time with slightly less caving. "It really did seem like the easiest solution. It's one day. Everything will be back to normal tomorrow."

"Whatever." Babs flicked a hand as she stood and *click-click-click*ed her way to the door. "I'll go get my own chopsticks. You're obviously too busy admiring yourself."

Marlowe stepped forward, ready to halt Babs with yet another apology, but Cherry set a hand on her wrist and shook her head, mouthing *Let her go*. Marlowe cringed, uncomfortable neglecting her boss's request, but she trusted Cherry's judgment. She also suspected that even if she got the chopsticks, Babs would find another way to prove she wasn't doing her job. Earlier that day, all of the necessary parties had quickly approved Marlowe's casting, whisking out waivers for her to sign and shuffling her to hair and makeup, but Babs had been prickly from the first suggestion.

"Ignore her," Cherry said once Babs was long gone. "She's jealous that you're getting attention instead of stuck behind a laptop or in a car all day. She'll get over it."

"Let's hope so." Marlowe nodded at the laptop that'd held Cherry's rapt gaze. "Everything okay? You seemed worried when I got here. Not another catastrophe?"

"Just the usual drama. Nothing you need to see." Cherry slammed the laptop shut and practically sat on it, so obviously attempting to mask it from view, she might as well have taped a giant *Whatever you do, don't look here* sign on it.

Marlowe couldn't help but laugh. "You do realize that now I *have* to see?"

"Okay, fine. But promise me you won't take it seriously." Cherry waited for Marlowe's nod before opening the laptop. The screen showed Angus's Instagram account, with a photo of him from the hips up, posing in his dampened T-shirt. The hem of his shirt rode up as though his hand just *happened* to get caught in the fabric, revealing several inches of his sculpted abs. His stance was casual, his expression pensive, while the whole image was carefully filtered to look like a high-end cologne ad.

"Guess I shouldn't feel so bad about soaking him if he got eight thousand likes out of it." Marlowe shrugged, unsure what Cherry had been so protective about. She skimmed a few comments, most of which were written in emojis, some more suggestive than others. Then her eyes snagged on the caption. *Wardrobe Malfunction.* Innocuous enough on the surface, but Cherry had hidden the post for good reason.

"Clever," Marlowe said flatly.

"More like plausibly deniable assholery," Cherry amended.

Marlowe slumped against her side, fully aware of what she meant. "Wardrobe" referred to their department and the malfunction was clearly Marlowe's. Spectacular. In a matter of minutes, she'd gone from Helper Girl to Malfunctioning Wardrobe Girl. If she kept up the good work, by evening she might get promoted to Vaguely Dismissible Nincompoop or maybe just That Clumsy but Largely Forgettable Person with the Hair.

She reread the caption, trying to convince herself it was innocent, but combined with the memory of Angus's pointed ire, it felt just as condescending on the second read.

"It was only a T-shirt," she said. "And nothing says *I humbly accept your apology* like immediately shaming someone on social media."

Cherry reached for the laptop and pivoted the screen out of Marlowe's view.

"It's not really about you. He's seizing a chance to show off the Great Gordon Chisel-fest." She peeked at the screen and scoffed. "Man muscles are so overrated."

"Eight thousand people—and counting—would argue otherwise." Not wanting to belabor the subject, Marlowe stepped away to gather everything she needed for work: the accordion file, a department laptop, a thick stack of scratch paper, two rolls of tape, a handful of spare file folders, and a giant shopping bag filled with Babs's unsorted receipts. Still, her mind buzzed. Truthfully, she wasn't convinced that a well-toned male body was overrated. She understood the stream of heart-eyed emojis beneath Angus's photo, but his post reminded her too much of her relationship with Kelvin. Small mistakes had so often led to such large doses of shame. How did guys do that? And why?

Cherry held open the trailer door, eyeing Marlowe suspiciously as she passed.

"You promised you wouldn't take it seriously," she said.

"I'll let it go as fast as I can." Marlowe shifted the bag and tightened her hold on the files, hoping to avoid two accidents in one day. "And you? You hanging in there?"

"I'll make it through the day." Cherry straightened Marlowe's collar where it had bunched up under her purse strap. "You're a lifesaver for doing this. Any plans Friday?"

"Let me check my busy social calendar." She shifted slightly while looking at nothing in particular. "Imagine that. I'm wide open."

"Drinks on me after work that night?"

"Thanks. Sounds perfect." Marlowe perked up, grateful to anticipate her first social event since moving to L.A. After living with three roommates in New York, and sharing any free time with her boyfriend, the endless nights alone had been wearing on her. The sheer lack of activity made her want to text Kelvin, which made her reopen every wound, seeking evidence that their relationship really had been bad enough for her to walk away. Some days—hell, some moments—the *yes* was harder to find than others.

She headed to the background tent, her arms laden. For the better part of an hour, she parked herself at a folding table, cross-checking invoices, but soon enough, she was setting aside her work to head inside the diner. There, an assistant director gave her a pot of fake coffee (aka flat diet Coke) and explained her blocking. She walked the path and performed her business. Once the AD was satisfied that she understood the camera placements and stopping points, he asked her to stay put until they were ready to roll.

Marlowe took advantage of her position by anchoring herself to the counter and watching the crew. Though this wasn't her first time on set, she was still dazzled by the size of the operation. The cameras, lights, sound equipment, monitors, snaking cords and gearboxes, and all of the people. It was so strange after years of watching TV to realize that just outside the frame was a crowd of crewmembers. In this particular case, that crowd numbered over thirty, though she'd previously seen it reach more than fifty.

"Keep a firm grip on that thing," said a low voice behind her, possibly teasing but probably not. "You wouldn't want to spill on anyone."

Marlowe spun around to see Angus standing a few feet away, fanning the pages of a worn paperback. Lacking the patience to pander to him, she held up the coffeepot.

"I asked if I could put this in a tote, but Lex said no." She nodded at the director, a portly, bearded guy who was scowling at a nearby trio of monitors.

Angus studied her, impenetrably serious. She let her gaze drift to his costume, assuming he'd made his jibe, she'd made hers, and they had nothing further to say to one another. Over his usual jeans and T-shirt, he wore the leather jacket Cherry had mentioned earlier. It was custom built with aged brown leather, a cross between a classic motorcycle jacket and a pre-war aviator style. It did look tight in the shoulders. Also, he wasn't walking away yet.

"What?" she asked when she couldn't stand his scrutiny any longer.

"The hair." He mimed flicking bangs off his forehead. "You have a face."

"Turns out it's a standard amenity with the whole being-born thing. I hit the jackpot. I got a full set of limbs and organs, too. Oh, and also a name."

"Yeah. Marlowe. My assistant tracked it down. Though I didn't think to inquire about limbs and organs." Still failing to reveal even a hint of a smile, he tucked a thumb into his leather belt, all James Dean swagger with an easy stance and a chin that rested a *little* higher than necessary, covered with a carefully cultivated three-day shadow.

"Why did your assistant want my name?" she asked.

"I figured I should find you and apologize after being so rude this morning. All those people. They can be so—There was a—They want me to—Never mind. It's not your problem. Anyway. I was mad at everyone. I probably said some things I shouldn't."

Marlowe softened at that, though his apology confused her after the Instagram post. If he was truly sorry, wouldn't he have kept their interaction to himself?

"What are you doing here, anyway?" he asked. "I thought you were in wardrobe."

"I am. There was a mix-up. I'm the solution." She spread her arms in a limp voilà motion, displaying a full view of the yellow shirtwaist dress and a cute little apron.

He kept his eyes on hers while lazily tipping an eyebrow. "Must've been a pretty serious mix-up to warrant putting someone like you on camera."

At that, she tensed right back up, tightening her grip on the coffeepot.

"Could've been worse," she said with exaggerated civility. "At least no one required a towel. Apparently that indicates a real tragedy."

He huffed. She flashed him a brief but insincere smile. They squared off as the hum of activity continued buzzing around them. Grips angled reflective umbrellas while props artists dropped plastic ice cubes into tumblers of water. A makeup artist dusted an actress's cheeks with powder. An AD arranged background players in one of the booths. The crew was obviously shooting soon. And *still*, Angus didn't walk away.

"You're the one who swore at me," he said.

"I swore *near* you. And I couldn't help it."

"Because 'I'm sorry I crashed into you' was too many syllables?"

"Because you looked like you wanted to murder me."

"I told you. I was . . . having a day."

"Having a day or being a jerk?"

"I had a right to be pissed."

"Pissed? Yes. Condescending? Questionable."

"You scalded my chest."

"Scalded?"

"The coffee was hot, okay?"

"Like, sunburn hot or cozy-tub-water hot?"

"It was"—his lips twitched as his eyes narrowed—"inconvenient."

Marlowe forced herself to take a slow breath. People were watching them. That wasn't good. Especially after what Cherry had said about job security in the industry.

"Generally speaking," she said, lowering her tone this time, "an apology is considered acceptable recompense for an inconvenience."

"Generally speaking." Finally, *finally* his lips tipped up in what could almost be called a smile. The hint of amusement in his eyes had taken so long to emerge it only increased her irritation. He didn't seem to notice. He just amped up the swagger, crossing his arms and shaking his head at her. "You know, you have a lot of attitude for a PA."

"Maybe, but I think it's spot-on for a helper girl." With that, she turned and walked away, even if it meant an AD had to track her down and put her back in position.

Cherry was right. Arguing with an actor was a dumb idea. Angus's derisive remarks weren't even that bad, and Marlowe was no stranger to contempt. Her mom was constantly sending her motivational articles and picking at her for not being more aggressive with her career. Her dad could dole out shame with the best of them as a cancer researcher who liked to remind her that shopping for shoes all day was a hobby, not a job. She'd also heard far worse from Babs. So what if Angus thought she was worthless? But Marlowe had spent the last three years with a guy who made her question her worth and she was really, *really* tired of it. She was also tired of all the ways so many guys assumed they had a right to attention, jobs, money, praise, love, respect, and admiration, while most of the women she knew struggled to feel like they'd earned a good burger.

An AD soon wrangled everyone on set. Angus and three of his female costars sat in a corner booth with the dozen or so background players scattered throughout the diner, fake-eating. In the scene, Angus's character, Jake Hatchet, discussed his numerous failed relationships while his friends teased him about how he was too busy chasing an elusive ideal to accept anything real. He stuck to his principles—a character trademark—declaring he'd know what he wanted when he saw it. Marlowe stepped into frame and poured the coffee, allowing a perfect pause for a few subtext-laden looks between Jake and the girls. Then they carried on with their conversation while she walked away.

The shot took twelve takes to get right. First Angus's gaze lingered too long on one actress, then on another, with Lex trying to build the perfect amount of suspense about which girl he might pursue over the course of the season. Twelve takes meant Marlowe had to pour his coffee twelve times, which also meant feeling Angus's eyes on her twelve times, watching her hands as if waiting for an inevitable spill, or watching her face as if still wondering where she'd picked up her "attitude." She told herself to think of him as a cardboard cutout, to release the resentment she'd built up that morning, to focus on the coffeepot and the quartet of mugs on the table, but sometimes she couldn't help herself. Her gaze crept to his. As she caught him studying her, weighing her value, she imagined pouring something besides room-temperature soda into his lap. Something that might not create the perfect photo op for his zillions of followers. Something that might sting, *just* a little.

The scene complete, Marlowe remained on set so she was available for two more quick shots: a menu drop-off that took three takes and an arrival with an order pad that took seven. The number of takes, even for such simple moments, gave her pause. She had it easy. She only had to walk from point A to point B with a designated prop. The cast had to re-create the tension and humor every time, building her respect for them not just as pretty faces and walking fashion plates, but as skilled workers, an assessment she even applied to Angus. He might be a frontrunner for president of the Entitled Egomaniac's Society, but he was a good actor, and she could give credit where credit was due.

Between setups, Marlowe plowed through Babs's paperwork, or rather, she tried to get through the paperwork but she was battling a growing awareness that Angus kept staring at her. The attention grated on her nerves. She didn't understand it. He wasn't sneaking flirty glances or trying to catch her eye or doing anything to indicate the slightest hint of attraction. Her best guess was that he was sizing her up, using the information to tweak his definition of "someone like you." God, that was an awful phrase, so innocuous on the surface, and complimentary in the right context, but so biting with even the slightest investigation into its possible meaning. Someone ugly? Awkward? Talentless? Not worth being classified as an individual? Or just someone . . . less?

The requisite shots finally captured to the director's content, Marlowe was released while the lead actors remained for close-ups. Babs halted her on her way to the background tent. She offered Marlowe a smattering of praise for her professionalism on set—a nice gesture since she rarely paid a compliment to anyone but the cast. Then she followed it up with a reminder that Marlowe had promised to make up the time she'd lost during her "little acting stint" by taking work home with her that night. With a smile that strained to emerge, Marlowe agreed to have everything ready by morning.

She changed into her own clothes and found Cherry at the wardrobe trailer.

"Looked like it went pretty well from where I was standing," Cherry said.

"I guess." Marlowe wilted into a chair, dropping the accordion folder on the counter beside her. "Everyone was really nice. Well, almost everyone."

Cherry laughed softly. "I noticed some simmering there."

"I can't help it. He's just so"—she balled up her fists—"you know?"

"Yeah. I know." Cherry stepped up behind Marlowe, wrapping her in a loose embrace. "Don't worry. I doubt you'll ever need to talk to him again. I also squared away the other uniforms. They'll be ready for pickup tomorrow morning." Cherry straightened up and pinched her lapels, adopting a haughty air. "Miss Banks, we appreciate your commitment to prompt coffee service but consider this your notice of termination from the waitstaff at Heart's Diner."

"Thank god."

Chapter Four

For the next three months, Marlowe kept her head down and did her job. As Cherry had predicted, avoiding Angus took no effort at all. Marlowe was barely on set. Babs always had a long list of errands for her to run: picking up and dropping off loaned samples at fashion houses, liaising between the crew on set and the shop personnel at headquarters, shopping for elusive bits of trimming and notions, and performing an increasing number of personal tasks Marlowe doubted were within her job description.

So far, Marlowe saw no reason to complain. She enjoyed spending a large portion of each day with her car stereo blasting and the ubiquitous L.A. sun pouring through her windshield. She even liked her car, a thirty-year-old hatchback with a mismatched fender and a peeling hood. Whoever had owned it before her had taken great pains to upgrade the sound system and no pains at all to preserve the exterior. It ran and Marlowe could afford it. It was perfect.

In the last week of August, as soon as Marlowe's episode was streamable, she FaceTimed with her friends in New York. Chloe, Nat, and Heather gathered in their hip repurposed Williamsburg warehouse space while Marlowe stretched out in her shabby Westwood basement apartment. The decor was a depressing medley of beiges. The only exceptions were a rusty water stain on her living room ceiling and a chenille sofa the color of moldy pears. The most recent piece of furniture had likely been purchased around 1975 and everything smelled vaguely of feet. However, the apartment was cheap, and it came furnished. It was also across the street from the Los Angeles National Cemetery, so most of the neighbors were quiet. Since Marlowe worked fourteen-hour days and she never invited anyone over—not yet knowing anyone besides her coworkers—the apartment was adequate for her daily needs. If she decided to stay in L.A. past her year's lease, she'd upgrade to a space with more light. She'd also buy some new furniture. She might even put up art that didn't feature creepy owls.

With giddy anticipation and plenty of popcorn, Marlowe and her friends settled in to watch her episode, hitting play at the same time to synchronize their viewing. The action on-screen followed three interwoven plotlines. A long-term couple dealt with the aftermath of a brief affair. Another character battled extortion by an ex-lover. Angus's character, Jake, sought revenge against a scheming woman who'd wronged his father. It was all the usual drama, which the girls accompanied with ample commentary.

When the scene in the diner finally came on, they all went quiet. Marlowe watched, her popcorn bowl tucked in her lap atop her penguin-print pajama bottoms, a gift from Kelvin she hadn't quite talked herself into giving up. On-screen, Angus/Jake said his line about knowing what he wanted when he saw it. Marlowe stepped into view and poured the coffee. Her friends cheered through her phone but the cheering dropped off when the wide shot was followed by a close-up of Angus looking her way, burning through the screen with his intense amber eyes. Another shot followed of

Marlowe looking back at him, long and direct, the coffeepot raised and waiting. Neither look could accurately be called withering, but the sense of mutual challenge was palpable.

"What was *that*?" Chloe asked, her tone aghast.

"Did you just—?" Nat started.

"She totally did," Heather interjected.

"I did what?" Marlowe asked, already wishing she hadn't.

"You had eye sex," her friends answered in unison.

"What?! No!" Marlowe slammed the pause button and snatched her phone off the table. "More like *You're a jerk and I hope they write you into a coma so you finish the season in the world's least-flattering hospital gown and with tubes shoved up your nose.*"

"Not what I saw," Chloe argued.

"Me, neither," Nat said.

"That was hot," Heather finished.

Marlowe argued the point but to no avail. She and her friends replayed the scene several times, speculating on the reasons behind the editing choice. Surely after so many retakes, the crew had footage that didn't involve Marlowe at all, or if it did involve her, she was smiling serenely while gliding away to fetch menus, serve pie, or do other bland waitress-y things. Was she misremembering that day? She'd been angry, yes, but so angry she couldn't pour a cup of coffee without looking pissed? And had he felt the same? Or were *angry* and *pissed* the wrong words entirely?

After watching the episode all the way through, the group concluded that the editors had crafted the exchange of glances to illustrate Jake's tendency to scope out new options, even when he was surrounded by old ones, sure ones, and really, *really* attractive ones. It made sense, but the exchange was still weird, like a glimpse into Marlowe's real feelings. Not the eye sex, of course. That was totally, utterly, completely, and a hundred percent without question in her friends' imaginations. But Marlowe had felt something when she sparred with Angus, something that might be more complicated than pure loathing. Until she figured out what that something was, she wanted to keep it to herself.

The subject was eventually dropped as Marlowe's friends filled her in on recent events in their own lives. Chloe had landed her first off-Broadway set design. It was a small show with a tight budget, but the playwright, Adrienne Achebe, was getting a lot of national attention for her other works. If the new production did well, it might move to Broadway. Nat was still assisting their costume professor on the next big Disney musical, a job that could last for years if the show went on tour or got picked up at additional non-Broadway theatres. Heather was directing part of a series of new one-acts downtown. No money but great art. All three women were moving forward in their chosen careers, even if they weren't skyrocketing to Tony Awards. Meanwhile, Marlowe was organizing sock returns.

"We don't have a costume designer yet for the Achebe play," Chloe said. "My director asked if anyone had suggestions. The producing organization doesn't have the budget for flights and housing so they have to hire local, but . . ."

"But my sister's only using your old room through October," Heather hinted.

"And you'll be finished on *Heart's Diner* by then," Nat added unnecessarily.

"Without another gig lined up after," Heather volleyed even more unnecessarily.

"Any chance you'll be back by the time rehearsals start in December?" Chloe asked. "Should I give my director your name and info?"

"I don't know." Marlowe traced a smiling penguin on her PJ bottoms, feeling her uncertain future stretch out before her, with no plan beyond the remaining six weeks of her current PA contract. A design job in New York would solve that problem, even if she had to pick up non-costume-related work in order to support herself for a while. However . . . "There are so many great designers in the city. They don't need me."

Marlowe's friends ignited with a chorus of passionate reassurance, begging her to at least throw her hat in the ring. Her mind raced as her stomach roiled with equal parts excitement and dread. Off-Broadway. Opening in mid-January. Less than five months away. Reviewed in the same papers and on the same sites that'd shredded her last design.

"My lease here isn't up until the end of March," she hedged.

"Screw the lease," Nat said through a laugh. "We miss you!"

"I miss you, too, but . . ." Marlowe ran through every excuse she could think of. She didn't know the artistic team. She wasn't familiar with the script. She couldn't give up her first sunny L.A. winter. She couldn't give up the tacos. She'd decided to quit costumes and sell Star Maps for a living. She'd become an antisocial, creatively stunted spinster and was only available for menial tasks, pandering to patronizing bosses, and long bouts of self-doubt. Her friends would hear none of it, so Marlowe eventually caved and agreed that Chloe could pass along her name and also forward a script she could read. Just in case. In the meantime, at least she had a future as a simmering waitress.

The following morning, as Marlowe finally stopped hitting snooze and rolled out of her lumpy, depressing bed, she found two texts waiting.

Kelvin: Miss you, Lowe. Find the perfect taco yet?

Cherry: Stay off social. See you on set

Marlowe didn't answer either text. Kelvin's irritated her too much with its ever-present, ever-beckoning question mark, sent every time she stopped thinking about him for ten goddamned seconds. Cherry's text was too ominous to answer, even though Marlowe had little reason to worry. She made limited use of social media, uncomfortable with its performative nature, and with the ways it perpetuated a constant desire to curate and share rather than be present in a moment, embracing experience as it unfolded. She kept her personal life private, and when she did pop online, she felt safe in assuming no one would troll her for wishing a friend Happy Opening or retweeting a video of a baby hedgehog chewing on a celery stalk.

An hour or so later, she sat across from Cherry in the wardrobe office trailer, plucking at a seam on her jeans while Cherry asked her yet again if she was absolutely certain she wanted to see. When Marlowe confirmed that she was now far too curious to not look, Cherry opened the show's Twitter account and passed her phone to Marlowe.

HeartsDiner: Who do you ship with Jake Hatchet this season?

The tweet contained a poll, listing four characters from the show: two of the girls who were in the diner scene, the older woman who'd wronged Jake's father, and a sexy neighbor who was always swapping innuendo-laden glances with him when he worked on his motorcycle or she watered her roses. So far one of the girls from the diner was in the lead.

"So?" Marlowe held out the phone. "What's the problem?"

Cherry nudged the phone back her way. "Read the comments."

Marlowe took another look. At first she didn't see anything startling, but sure enough, the fifth or sixth response said #IShipTheWaitress. She kept scrolling. The hashtag appeared again a few tweets down, and again, and again as countless strangers chimed in with support for her "character" hooking up with Angus's character. There were GIFs, memes, and long conversations about the possible meaning of what people were calling "The Look."

"Oh my god," she said as she scrolled. "What the—? How? Why? The episode only went live last night. And I was in, like, five seconds of it."

"That's the power of social media for you." Cherry leaned back in her chair, absently patting the molded plastic arms. "I don't know if anything will come of it, but the producers are always looking for a hook to bring in more viewers. If they can fan the flames of the Twitter storm, you might get asked to do a cameo."

Marlowe kept scrolling, unable to look away. "But I don't act."

"You wouldn't have to do much. They'd give you a couple of lines. Some *You broke my heart, Jake* bullshit, just enough to get audiences to tune in. Jake would brood, overcome with guilt for how he treated you, like we haven't seen that scene a thousand times already. Then he'd ride off on his motorcycle, you'd leave town with one last, longing look out the back of a bus, and things would carry on as already scripted."

Marlowe finally handed the phone back. "They wouldn't."

"They might."

"They can't."

"They can. You wouldn't have to say yes, but considering the pay gap between on-screen and off, you might at least give it some thought."

"*If* they ask."

"Exactly. *If* they ask." Cherry offered her a sympathetic smile.

Marlowe dropped her head in her hands, wishing she could delete the entire Twitter thread, and anything else that used that stomach-turning hashtag. She supposed she should be flattered, but she wanted no part in a publicity stunt. L.A. was supposed to hide her, make her invisible, provide an escape from the reviews and criticism that'd eroded her confidence in New York. Now total strangers were talking about her, judging her, deciding whether or not she was worth being paired up with some guy, not even a real guy, and not even the real her. They were including her in their fantasy of what they thought a relationship should feel like, or at least look like. The idea was ridiculous. She was the last person who should exemplify romantic love. She couldn't even ignore a question mark or throw away a pair of pajama pants. And, okay, so this wasn't about her. It was about the waitress, but who the hell was the waitress? And why did people care?

"It was only a look," Marlowe muttered into her hands.

"Yeah," Cherry said, "but it was a hell of a look."

Before either of them could say more, Babs flung open the door and marched in, lips pursed, heels clicking. She flashed the girls a palm, jangling her bangles.

"I don't want to talk about it," she snapped. "The only tags I want to hear about are the ones sewn into the Prada clothes you'll pick up at ten, or the Dolce samples that'll be ready by eleven. That big party scene's coming up in episode seventeen and everyone has to look fabulous." She thrust a folded piece of paper at Marlowe.

"This should keep you busy while all that Twitter nonsense runs its course."

Marlowe unfolded the paper to read a sharply scribbled list of tasks that included stops at a dozen fashion houses, a pickup at the florist (not for the show), another at the dry cleaners (also not for the show), an appointment for Edith Head at the dog groomer, and several specialty food stores that purveyed meats, cheeses, liquor, and desserts for a party Babs was hosting tomorrow. The number of locations implied three days of work, not one, and only half of the stops were related to the costume needs for *Heart's Diner*.

She held up the list. "I'm not sure the food stuff—"

"If you do those errands, I'll have the time and energy to get my work done here, so yes, they all matter, and yes, they're part of your job, and for god's sake don't tell me you can't pick up a few flowers." Babs dropped into the desk chair and turned her attention to the computer, jabbing at the keyboard in a way that implied the conversation was over.

Marlowe looked to Cherry for guidance. Cherry inched up a tiny shrug and waggled her thumbs over her phone while mouthing *I'll text you*.

"Check in later," she said aloud. "If you're running behind, I'll see if we can get a shopper to do some of the pickups."

"Or she can finish the work tomorrow," Babs tossed off without looking up.

Marlowe prickled with annoyance. "Tomorrow's my day off."

"Then you'd better get going." Babs shooed her away with a flick of the hand.

Marlowe exchanged one last look with Cherry before slipping out the door, fighting the urge to slam it. Babs had been short-tempered with Marlowe ever since the day she donned that stupid uniform. She dropped little jabs about how nice everyone was to let Marlowe go on camera, as though they were doing her a favor that day rather than the other way around. She amped up her criticism of Marlowe's eating habits, noting that they weren't doing her figure or complexion any favors. She shut down even the slightest hint of creative input as though entertaining it would be a gross waste of everyone's time. She also kept Marlowe off set. Marlowe had been assuming Babs was punishing her for her divided attention the day of the shoot, but maybe *her* attention wasn't the issue at all.

She grabbed a coffee from craft services and sat down to plan her route, punching the destinations into her map app. As she entered the last store, a text came through.

Cherry: Sorry about that. I think it's a jealousy thing
Marlowe: So something IS going on between them?
Cherry: Doubt it. But she sure as hell wishes there was
Marlowe: She has nothing to be jealous about
Cherry: Tell that to The Look
Marlowe: It was nothing!!!!
Cherry: Whatever. LMK if you need shopping help. I'll find someone
Marlowe: Thanks. I'll update later
Cherry: Good luck
Marlowe: You too

Marlowe checked her shopping route and headed to her car. As she neared her rotting but lovable hatchback, she spotted Angus on the opposite side of the lot, signing autographs for a trio of shrieking fangirls while a security guard looked on from a few yards away. One girl held out a photo. Another bared her forearm. The third unbuttoned her shirt and indicated he should sign her cleavage. He graciously complied before encouraging a group selfie. The girls gathered in while he soaked up their adoration and held out the phone like someone well practiced in getting the angle *just right*.

With a roll of her eyes, Marlowe got into her car and drove off. She wasn't sure how she was going to deal with Babs for the last six weeks of her contract, but one thing was certain: she was *not* going to play Jake Hatchet's next relationship victim, no matter how much they offered to pay her.

Chapter Five

"A thousand dollars per episode?" Marlowe choked out.

On the other side of a long table covered in scripts and assorted papers, the showrunner leaned forward from his seat between two producers, resting his stubbled chin on his steepled fingers. Wes Quinlan was a tall, broad man of about forty, with sandy-blond hair that winged out from beneath his ever-present Oakland A's baseball cap. With his faded jeans, dingy T-shirts, flannel button-downs, and camel-colored work boots, he looked like he'd be more at home in a hardware store than on a film set, but *Heart's Diner* was his baby. He was responsible for the concept and characters, and he was still the lead writer, six years into filming. Now he was addressing Marlowe from a meeting room/workspace at headquarters, catching her up on his thinking over the weekend.

"We like the idea of three appearances," he said. "Episodes twenty to twenty-two. A little sparring, a little flirting, a moment of redemption. It'll make a good season ender for Jake's character arc, so people wonder if he'll start season seven as a nicer guy."

"If we have a season seven," the producer on his left added. Greg was one of the only people Marlowe had seen wearing a tie around set or HQ. She assumed that meant he was in charge of financial rather than creative decisions, but maybe he just liked ties.

"She also needs to pass a screen test," said Alejandra, the producer on the right, a serious-faced woman in hip green glasses and casual, layered linens. "I'm not supporting this plan if she goes flat once you put words in her mouth, no matter how many people have replayed that clip." She folded her arms and regarded her colleagues with a distinct air of skepticism.

The three of them debated the matter amongst themselves. Marlowe barely heard a word they said. She was still imagining earning three thousand dollars for only a few days of work. She could pay off her credit card and start in on her student loans. If she told her parents, maybe they'd stop asking if she needed money. She always needed money, but telling her parents that meant admitting she wasn't "living up to her earning potential." The admission led to lectures about frivolous career choices and ill-considered graduate degrees, lectures that toppled whatever self-confidence she'd managed to build up lately.

"What does Angus think?" Alejandra asked.

"Does it matter?" Greg blew a dismissive laugh through his nose. "Jake sleeps with four or five girls every season. What's one more?"

Marlowe went rigid. Alejandra caught the panic in her eyes.

"Don't worry. We wouldn't throw you into a sex scene. I'll make sure of that."

Marlowe blew out a breath, grateful that among the upper ranks—which were notably dominated by men—at least one woman held a position of power.

The trio continued tossing out ideas while Marlowe half-listened, her thoughts still hammering away. All weekend she'd tried to ignore the #IShipTheWaitress fiasco, but it was really hard to ignore. Not only did it go viral on Twitter, it also spread across other platforms. Soon talk show hosts were playing the clip, debating the meaning behind The Look. One invented an elaborate story about a dine-and-ditch episode that sent the waitress on a murderous revenge spree. A second turned it into a meme about the divided state of the current political system. Many speculated that Marlowe must be Angus's latest fling because "that kind of electricity couldn't possibly be fake." The statement was easily refuted but a *lot* of people were eager to support it, repeating the phrase *eye sex* until Marlowe wanted to track down the person who coined it and throttle them.

No matter the theory, everyone was talking about those few heated seconds, and by Sunday night, Marlowe wasn't surprised to get the call Cherry had warned her to anticipate. She'd arrived this morning fully prepared to shut down any conversation about a waitress reprise with a firm *no*, but three thousand dollars was hard to walk away from. She could handle a *little* flirting, as long as it was fake. And as long as Angus didn't offer to sign her boob.

After much debate among the higher-ups and a lot of wary silence on Marlowe's part, they put her in front of a camera and gave her a script sample to read. It was a short monologue from a recent episode, noting all the little, unseen sacrifices a woman had made to maintain her relationship, all the times she'd put her husband first while he failed to give their relationship the same attention. For the woman in the scene, the relationship was a product of hard work and constant nurturing. For the man, it was an assumption. Marlowe started off rocky, her voice trembling, but as the words began to feel all too real and the emotion behind them all too familiar, she stopped worrying about what she was doing with her hands or how she was standing or what inflection to use. She simply read.

Wes gave her a bit of direction and she read again, repeating the process twice more. Then Greg asked her to wait in a small seating area outside the meeting room so the higher-ups could confer amongst themselves. Unarmed with anything else to do, she got out her phone and opened Kelvin's latest message, sent Saturday, as yet unanswered.

Kelvin: Are you sure this is what you want?

She slid the bar over to reveal the red *delete* option. Then she slid it back again. Forward. Back. Forward. Back. Five months they'd been apart now. Chances were high he'd seen something about her TV appearance and the ensuing media chatter. One of their friends would've pointed it out if he didn't stumble into it on his own. She wanted to believe his question was about that, about getting caught up in Hollywood gossip, but she knew it wasn't true. He was asking if she was sure she wanted to be without him.

She toyed with the *delete* button again, unable to complete the gesture. Too many memories flooded her every time she tried to take that final step. Sharing pints of ice cream while snuggling close under blankets and watching scary movies. Kelvin showing up for her opening nights, flowers in hand, or stopping by her studio with takeout when she was at her busiest. He never had to ask what she wanted. He knew all of her favorites. He knew *her*. She missed being known. Five months of going home to an empty, beige-infused apartment had opened up a pit of longing that widened by the day. Marlowe wasn't entirely happy with Kelvin, but she wasn't entirely happy without him, either.

Delete? Reply? Delete? Reply?

Someone swept past, drawing her attention up from her screen.

"You guys are *not* serious," Angus said as he flung open the door of the meeting room and stormed out of view. The reply was out of earshot, though the tone was level and placating. Angus's tone was the opposite. "Christ, Greg, she's not even an actress. What's next? YouTube star? Local librarian? Costco's employee of the month?"

Marlowe sank in on herself, wondering if she should leave now or wait for further instructions/humiliation. A rumble of overlapping voices reached her, still too indistinct for her to make out any clear words. A moment later, Greg appeared in the doorway. He eked out a whispered apology and asked Marlowe to wait another minute. Then he shut the door, leaving her alone with her phone and her growing feelings of inadequacy.

Lacking sufficient fortitude to let an old wound fester while a new one began to bleed, Marlowe reread Kelvin's text one last time before punching away at her phone.

Marlowe: Yes. I'm sure. This is what I want

She hit *send* before she could continue debating the matter. The ellipses appeared almost instantly, making her jump, but no reply came. As the blank screen stared back at her and as she pictured Kelvin silently considering her reply, Marlowe's stomach knotted. Her skin itched. Her mind searched for ways to soften her text, backpedal, add a note about how she missed him or hoped he was happy. Her text wasn't even honest. She wasn't sure about anything. And what if, in her bluntness, she came across as cruel?

Overcome with guilt, Marlowe started typing a follow-up message. She stopped partway through and deleted it. It would only confuse matters or launch her into a stream of apologies she'd regret later. Cherry was right. Kelvin wasn't adding anything positive to Marlowe's life. Only guilt and doubts. Better to leave her text as is and work on believing it.

The office door eventually opened and Alejandra waved Marlowe in. Wes and Greg were seated behind the long table. A guy in a headset stood by the camera, as before. Angus leaned back on a windowsill to Marlowe's right, his ankles crossed, one hand tapping the sill, the other holding an open script. He wore what she'd come to think of as his uniform: low-slung jeans and a plain white T-shirt that made him look a lot like his character, though his own clothes were far brighter and less weathered than his costumes. A pair of aviator sunglasses was tucked into his neckline while clean white Converse replaced Jake's trademark dusty motorcycle boots.

Alejandra handed Marlowe a script and gestured to a spot in front of the camera.

"Test number two," she said. "Chemistry."

The knots in Marlowe's gut yanked tighter as she shot a nervous look at Angus. His brows inched up but the tension around his mouth remained. Marlowe had never been good at chemistry tests and she had a feeling today's performance would be no exception. Angus appeared to share her thoughts, which at least gave the two of them something in common. She considered calling the whole thing off, but if he was willing to go through with the charade, she could manage it, too.

"Page twelve," Wes instructed. "Top of the scene. You'll start. Angus will enter on his first line. You two will take it from there. Don't worry about all the backstory. We just want to see you two together. Let us know when you're ready."

Marlowe found the scene and gave the first few lines a quick skim, trying to ground herself before starting. *Ignore the camera,* she thought. *Ignore the people. Ignore the super-famous TV star who thinks you're pond scum. Get this done. Get out. Move on.*

She nodded at Wes. Wes nodded at the camera operator. And they were rolling.

"I'm sorry," she read. "It's not the way I wanted things to turn out."

"It never is." Angus's tone was clipped, impatient. Acting? Probably not.

She locked her eyes on the script but in her peripheral vision she sensed Angus moving toward her. Her palms sweated. Her throat seized. She swallowed, focused.

"I—I'm not the only one to blame," she stammered.

"You never are."

"Don't act like—"

"Like what?" His footsteps stopped beside her. She looked up, startled to see him so close. They were the same height. She hadn't noticed before. She'd had no reason to. Now she couldn't help it as he stood less than an arm's length away. Other details hit her, one right after the other: three freckles on his left cheek, another on his ear, cowlicks, a slight chin dimple, a downward curve to his nose, golden lashes, amber irises edged with russet tones like a tiger's eyes. He met her gaze, held it, used it to demand something of her, something she didn't know how to find. "Like you have no right to be mad?"

"Like . . . like I have no right to be hurt," she ad-libbed, unable to look away.

His brows flickered, barely, a fleeting moment of surprise. Then he inched closer still, holding his script low as though he already knew the words.

"I'm no villain," he said.

"You're no hero, either."

"Exactly. I'm just a man. Why can't that be enough for you?"

She blinked at him, confused. Was she talking to Jake? Angus? Kelvin?

"I, um . . ." She found her place in her script. "I can't see how it would work."

"You *can't* see how or you *don't want* to see how?"

She shook her head, struggling to keep the words fake, scripted, meaningless. A moment ago they were high melodrama, but the underlying conflict felt too real and the anger blazing from Angus's eyes reminded her too much of someone else.

"Say it," he demanded. "Say. It."

"I don't want to see it . . . with you." A lump filled her throat but she forced it down. He ran a hand over his chin, holding it there while he studied her with the kind of intensity that usually made her back away from people. This time she held still. She let herself be looked at, judged, seen, and for some reason, it felt okay.

"Are you sure?" His words filled the room, too simple, too big, too familiar.

Marlowe checked her next line before lowering her script. Angus's image blurred, warped by newly forming tears. At the sight of them, his expression shifted, softening into what seemed like real concern. He leaned closer, maybe, a hand raised toward her face Just before he caught a tear, she shook her head and whispered, "Yes. I'm sure."

His hand didn't meet her cheek. Her first tear fell, unimpeded, lodging in the corner of her lips. He lowered his hand. Took a step back. Exhaled. The tension uncoiled from his body. With another breath, he turned and walked away.

"Cut!" Wes shouted.

Marlowe blinked herself into awareness. *Window. Camera. Table. Producers.* While she adjusted to reality, Angus marched to the table and slapped down his script.

"Are we done here?" he asked through gritted teeth.

Greg, Alejandra, and Wes exchanged a series of indecipherable glances.

"Go on." Wes tipped his chin toward the door. "We'll be in touch."

"Can't wait for that call." Angus shot them one final glare before storming past Marlowe and out of the room, slamming the door behind him. Marlowe stared at it, stunned, feeling the echo in her bones. His warm regard, his almost-touch, his words had been fake. Of course they had. He was playing a part. They both were, weren't they?

Marlowe wiped away the last of her tears and handed her script to Alejandra. With great effort, she forced herself not to apologize, a habit she was trying to stem. Instead, she pasted on a polite smile, thanked everyone for their time, and assured them she enjoyed the job she already had. It was a small lie housed in a bigger truth. So Babs abused her time and most of the errands were mindless. The next gig might be better. More importantly, Marlowe didn't want to be an actress. She wanted to be a costume designer, or at least continue working in the field. She wanted to be part of the visual creation, the world and character development. New York was also calling her back, quiet but persistent. Maybe she should stop denying that call.

Babs was out on set but Cherry was shoe shopping at the laptop when Marlowe returned to the wardrobe office. Tossing out a lazy

"Hey," she trudged over to a pile of shopping bags Babs had left her to sort through for returns. A quick scan of the labels told Marlowe she'd be hitting every corner of the L.A. Basin, as usual.

"Well?" Cherry spun around in her chair. A few tendrils of hair escaped her French braid and danced across her enviably prominent cheekbones. She should've been the one to get a cameo. She'd be amazing on camera. Fierce and fabulous. "How did it go? Did you convince them you could pull a full Nicholas Sparks on cue?"

"Only if Nicholas Sparks specializes in extreme levels of humiliation." Marlowe blew out a sigh as she located an envelope of receipts and started matching them with the bags and their contents. "I didn't choke on the lines, not badly anyway, but Angus clearly thinks I'm worthless and I think he's basically an ego jammed into a great pair of jeans. Together we have as much spark as a wet match."

Cherry waggled her brows. "Wet matches can be dried and lit."

"Whatever. Bad metaphor. Suffice to say I'm still Babs's errand bitch for the next six weeks." The words caught in Marlowe's throat. Spoken aloud, *six weeks* sounded like such a short period of time in which to make a What's Next plan, one that might or might not include a return to New York. "If my waitress role has dead-ended, at least Babs will have no further motivation to punish me."

"I wouldn't count on that." Cherry pointed a thumb at the shopping bags. "I'm pretty sure she bought half that stuff knowing it would need to be returned."

"Awesome. And she probably wants it done in the next hour or she'll send me off to shop for some obscure toy for her dog again. Or more of that fig and tomatillo jam that doesn't exist." Marlowe swallowed her frustration while aligning the remaining clothes to their receipts.

As she was about to haul everything to her car, someone knocked on the door. It opened a second later as a lanky guy in a ball cap and windbreaker peeked in.

"Delivery for"—he checked a small envelope—"Marlowe Banks."

Marlowe swapped a confused look with Cherry before meeting the guy at the door. He held out a large vase of gorgeous pink-tipped white roses. Marlowe gasped, astonished that Kelvin had responded to her brusque text with such a romantic gesture, and so quickly, too. She signed for the flowers and took the vase. As she swept a thumb across a velvety petal, she reminded herself that Kelvin had always been sweet about flowers, though upon reflection, they were always offered when others could witness the gesture. Was he doing it again? Trying to look noble in front of her coworkers? Or was he simply being nice and she was warping the gesture, so determined to find peace with the breakup, she'd cling to any nuance she could classify as negative?

"For a girl who just got the most amazing bouquet of roses, you don't look very happy," Cherry said, already clearing a spot on the desk.

Marlowe set down the flowers, still frowning. "He sent out a not-so-subtle feeler about the potential to try again. I don't know if he meant it or if he was just testing to see if I'd say yes. Either way, I told him it was definitely over."

Cherry groaned. "So like a dude to want you more when you don't want him."

Marlowe slid the card out from underneath a ribbon. She turned it over in her hands, staring at her name in neatly printed block letters. This wasn't what she wanted, the push-pull, the confusion, the constant questioning about whether or not she could do better. The gesture was just enough attention to inch the needle back toward a no, or at least for Kelvin to lodge himself in her thoughts when she was trying to let go. The flowers weren't really romantic. They were a manipulation. Weren't they?

"Don't just stare at it," Cherry chided. "Open it already. Then we can burn it."

Marlowe removed the card from the envelope.

Sorry I've been such an asshole. You deserve better.
Angus

Chapter Six

Marlowe set the vase on her cracked laminate tabletop and wedged a folded napkin under the leg so the table didn't seesaw. When the surface was as stable as it was ever going to get, she sat down to enjoy the fish tacos she'd picked up on her way home, now cold but still delicious and dripping with spicy mayo. She paused between tacos to pet the rose petals yet again, drawn to touch them the way an infant might reach for crinkly paper or some other sparkly toy. Marlowe hadn't told Cherry that Angus sent the flowers. Lying felt weird but Cherry might slip and mention something while Babs was around. She also would've asked questions Marlowe didn't want to answer, ones she couldn't answer, not after his consistent irritation at her mere existence. What did *You deserve better* even mean? Better than what? And how did he know what she deserved?

Recognizing that she was obsessing about a gesture that was probably intended as a simple apology, nothing more, Marlowe distracted herself by checking her email while she finished her dinner. Student loans. Electricity bill. Credit card statement. All things she'd deal with later. The first personal message was from her mom, a physics professor at Brown who'd achieved tenure early, published widely in her field, run the New York marathon every year since she was twenty-five, established an endowment for funding rescue work with endangered rhinos in Africa, and otherwise drilled into Marlowe that everything she wanted in life could be achieved with hard work. Marlowe still struggled to fully accept that theory. Her parents had divorced when she was six, so clearly some things didn't turn out perfectly, no matter how much work was invested.

The email contained the same five questions as always, rephrased slightly with each iteration but otherwise consistent.

1. Have you made any friends yet?
2. Are you dating anyone yet?
3. Have you inquired about a promotion yet?
4. Are you taking care of yourself?
5. Do you need money?

They were reasonable questions but the *yet*s still stung, implying Marlowe was taking too long to advance her social life, her love life, and her career. Maybe she wasn't applying her mom's work ethic rigorously enough, but friendships were hard to form when most of Marlowe's hours were spent alone in her car or briefly engaging with retail clerks and administrative assistants. On the dating front, ending things with Kelvin didn't mean she was hopping onto Tinder, looking for a quick rebound. Career-wise she needed a lot more experience before she could move up the ranks in the film and TV industry. And no, eating cold tacos at 10:00 P.M. right before falling into bed exhausted probably didn't qualify as taking care of herself. Also, yes, she was flat broke, still trying to pull herself out of the debt she'd incurred in grad school. But the scent of roses . . .

She smiled at the sight of them, touched them, smelled them, wished everything was as simple, soft, and beautiful as the smooth curl of an ivory petal, tipped with a blush, embracing a slowly opening bud. Warmed by the thought, she ignored her mom's email. She didn't even open her dad's, which promised to annoy her in similar ways. Instead, she risked a look at Angus's socials, praying he hadn't posted about producers forcing him to do a screen test with a "malfunctioning wardrobe girl."

Thankfully, she found no mention of the day's events. His Twitter feed was mostly *Heart's Diner* trivia and his latest Instagram post showed him raising a beer while the sun set over the ocean behind him. Wrapped around him was Tanareve Hughes, her lips pressed into his cheek while he scrunched up his face against the pressure, half-cringing, half-laughing, and entirely happy. The caption read simply *#LifeIsGood*. The comments were mostly hearts, cheers, praise, and congrats for "getting back together."

Tanareve was Angus's on-again/off-again girlfriend of several years, and apparently the relationship was on again. She was an actress, best known for playing some superhero's imperiled love interest. Marlowe couldn't remember which superhero. After a while, they all blended together. Regardless of which spandex-clad muscleman had saved Tanareve from certain death, she was stunningly beautiful, with flawless sun-bronzed skin, bee-stung lips, impossibly thick lashes, and long, glossy chestnut hair that'd landed her an advertising contract with Clairol. She was also vegan and liked turtles. Marlowe wasn't proud of herself for knowing anything at all about Angus or Tanareve, but celebrity gossip had a way of sneaking into life's margins, especially if the subject of that gossip was the object of one's teenage fantasies. And the object of a few significantly more adult fantasies, ones far more graphic than a smattering of *MB + AG* hearts scribbled with glitter pens on colorful notebook covers.

Marlowe shut the app, reminding herself that even her most recent fantasies about Angus had ebbed years ago. Allowing the flowers to reignite her imagination would be a huge mistake. Angus had an entourage. Some assistant or other had bought the flowers and written the card. Gestures like this were probably standard procedure for celebrities, a way of tempering fallout from bad behavior. The same flowers would've been sent to hotel maids, waiters, media personnel, and anyone else Angus talked down to. Meanwhile, he was off living his glamorous, romantic, don't-you-envy-us life while Marlowe was dripping cold mayonnaise into the cracks of her tabletop, looking out her window to a sea of moonlit headstones, no longer certain which dreams to chase.

Still, the flowers were beautiful.

For the rest of Marlowe's night, that was enough.

"An orgy?" Marlowe's eyes went wide.

"Not a real one," Cherry said through a laugh. "A bit of raciness the writers have added to spice up Jane and Vivek's marriage, or rather, to spice up ratings. Sex, babies, and weddings always draw an audience. Also amnesia, but I haven't figured out why."

Marlowe spun around in the fitting room, marveling at how much lingerie had been acquired practically overnight. As Cherry explained, shooting had paused for a few days while the crew prepped for the next episode. Thanks to last-minute script changes, the episode now included a location shoot at a Beverly Hills mansion with almost two hundred background players. Elaine would start background fittings that afternoon while Cherry and Babs dealt with the leads through private appointments at a specialty store.

"What's on my list for the day?" Marlowe asked.

"Shoes," Babs said as she burst through a door on the far side of the room. A giant purse swung from her elbow while she sipped from a bottle of coconut water. "I can't believe they're only giving us three days for this nonsense. Even a real orgy takes a little planning." She marched to the desk where she thunked down her bottle and whisked off her sunglasses in dramatic fashion. "'It's only underwear,' they said. 'Should be easy.'"

Marlowe scanned the nearest rack of bras and underpants, knowing full well that "only underwear" was harder to design than office attire, evening wear, or even period clothes. Every actor's insecurity had to be managed, tattoos and body piercings had to be addressed, as well as sensitive topics like body hair. Also, with only a few elements to tell a story or create a character, every detail counted. No wonder Babs was frazzled.

"What am I looking for?" Marlowe asked as she flipped through the bras, noting colors, textures, and style choices. "Are we going full fetish or more street wear?"

"I compiled research images for you last night," Babs said. "Get the credit card from Elaine. Shop on spec where you can. Think black. Think strappy. Think sexy."

"Did someone say *sexy*?" asked a gravelly voice on the other side of the room.

Babs, Cherry, and Marlowe all spun toward the open door. Angus was leaning against the frame, arms loosely folded, ankles crossed, peering over his aviators as though he couldn't even stand in a doorway without posing for a camera, reveling in his self-declared sexiness. Hoping to avoid another blow to her already shaky confidence, Marlowe busied herself by sorting through bras that didn't require sorting.

"Angus, darling." Babs strode across the room to exchange air kisses. "What are you doing here? Aren't you off today? You should be out enjoying the sun."

"The sun'll be there tomorrow. And the next day. And the day after that." He removed his sunglasses and glanced around the room, taking in the racks Elaine and her team had set up for fittings. "Looks like you have your hands full."

"Don't even get me started." Babs flicked her dark bangs off her forehead, making her bangles jangle. "Producers think background actors show up wearing the perfect clothes from their closets and none of this takes an ounce of effort."

Angus nodded thoughtfully. "Guess this means we can't make that jeans run."

"Today?" Babs swept a hand around the room. "Not possible. I'm up to my elbows in lingerie. We'll go next week, when all of this settles down."

"Sounds good, unless . . ." He wrapped a hand over his chin, rubbing at a cheekbone with his index finger, much like he had during yesterday's screen test. "Unless one of your assistants can fill in. Did I hear you mention a shopping trip?"

Babs sighed the sigh of the deeply exhausted. "Cherry's with me all day and Marlowe's only a—Wait, I suppose you know each other now, what with all that Twitter fuss?" The last few words came out with a familiar hint of acid, one that promised to increase in days to come if Marlowe didn't address it immediately.

"We don't know each other." She spun around, knocking several bras off the rack in her haste. Because of course she did. "I poured him coffee. Or poured coffee on him. Or near him. Whatever.

There was coffee. That's all. The waitress idea was a mistake. Everyone knows that now and it's already forgotten." She picked up the fallen bras and thrust them at Cherry, sneaking in a quick fuck-my-life look before spinning back toward Babs. "If you give me that research, I'll find Elaine and head right out."

"Why don't I go with you?" Angus offered.

Marlowe froze. Cherry gaped. Babs forced a pained smile.

"The last thing you need to do is spend your day off running errands with a PA." Babs laughed lightly as she set a hand on his shoulder, stealing an admiring glance when his eyes were averted. "Surely you have better ways to spend your time."

"Nothing vital," he said. "And it'll save you having to fit me in next week."

"Not if I have to make the selection. I'm still the designer."

"True, but I'm sure—what was it, Margot? Marley?—knows your aesthetic by now." He tucked his sunglasses into his neckline, cleverly dislodging Babs's hand as he wedged them into place. "You're always so generous about training the people who work for you, imparting your wisdom, making sure your assistants learn from the best."

Cherry choked on a laugh, hiding it with a fake sneeze. Marlowe grabbed the upright pole at the end of the nearest rack, bracing for Babs to bust a gasket, but Babs remained calm, in an annoyed hostess kind of way. All smiles and la-di-da flicks of a wrist, she explained that despite her exhaustive mentoring efforts, a PA was hardly an artistic authority. Angus countered with well-orchestrated flattery, outmaneuvering her at every step.

Ten minutes later, after a quick stop in Elaine's office, Marlowe found herself heading out the door with Angus while poor Cherry was left behind to tend to Babs. As soon as they were outside the building, Marlowe spun on Angus.

"What are you doing?" she asked with more force than she'd intended.

He stumbled back a step. "You don't think I need jeans?"

"I don't think you need them in the next twelve hours." She studied him, searching for evidence of ulterior motives, finding none. He just stood there, looking impenetrably serious. As usual. "You knew Babs would be busy today, didn't you?"

He shifted a shoulder. "I wanted to talk to you."

"Not that badly if you don't even remember my name."

"You said we didn't know each other. I was playing along."

She scrambled for a retort but couldn't find one, so she pursed her lips and headed toward her car with Angus following a step behind.

"Mar-loh." He leaned toward her, watching for her reaction, as though the simple recollection of her name would impress her. "Like that actress from the sixties?"

"Like the detective. My mom's a Raymond Chandler fan." This time she watched for his reaction. He simply nodded, giving her no indication of whether or not he knew who Raymond Chandler was. It hardly mattered, but she wondered what he did like to read, a thought that irritated her to no end. "Let me guess. You're named after the beef?"

He smiled, something she'd rarely seen him do in person, only on screens or in a fake way for fans. His smile made her want to smile back but she restrained herself, not wanting to resemble one of those fans, going gooey at a glimpse of his perfect teeth.

"Angus is a family name," he said. "My family's big on tradition. Long line of Scots. We have a tartan but no cattle, and therefore no beef."

Marlowe considered asking him what his tartan looked like, but then she'd picture him in a kilt and her mind would wander in a direction she didn't want it to go. So the two of them crossed the parking lot without further conversation, stopping when they reached her rusted, flaking hatchback. Rather than find her keys, she sat back against the hood. He stood nearby, taking in the glorious splendor of her vehicle while raking a hand through the reddish hair she still couldn't accurately describe.

"You don't have to come with me," she said.

"I know, but I want to."

"In this?" She patted the corroded hood, then brushed grit off her fingertips.

He peered in, shielding his eyes. "It'll be an adventure."

"It'll be about as adventurous as individually peeling the skin off a bag of peas." She felt a scowl settle onto her face. She tried to dial it down from intense irritation to mild displeasure but it proved remarkably hard to soften. She kept picturing Angus flying out of the room yesterday, irate that he'd been forced to read with her. "Whatever you wanted to say, say it here and we can both carry on with our lives."

"What about the jeans?"

"I know your size. I'll pick some up. Babs can fit you here next week."

"What about the coffee I was going to buy you?" His smile inched up again.

She locked her arms across her chest. "I can buy my own coffee."

"I never said you couldn't."

"And I don't want to shop with you."

"How do you know you don't want to do something you've never even tried?" His eyes danced as his smile widened. This time Marlowe felt no inclination to mirror it.

"Don't flirt with me," she said.

"Was I flirting?"

"Is that rhetorical?"

"Depends how loosely you define rhetoric."

"Oh, for god's sake." She threw up her hands as she practically leapt off the car. "You strut around set like we should all feel privileged to breathe the same air as you, you show no consideration whatsoever for people who are working hard to make *you* look good, and yet you seriously think all you have to do is smile at a girl and she'll—"

"They're going to call you. That's what I wanted to talk about." The amusement faded from his eyes as he watched her, all hint of flirtation gone.

A silence stretched out, heavy and muddled.

"You're not kidding, are you?" Marlowe asked.

He shook his head, slowly, the way people do when they wish they were nodding.

"Wow," she said. "Then I guess you're coming with me after all."

Chapter Seven

Angus poked at the louvers on the air vent, leaning forward to peer into them the way people in horror movies study dark spaces right before aliens leap onto their faces.

"You seriously don't have air-conditioning?" he asked.

"I seriously don't." Marlowe eased onto the northbound highway, merging in with the slow trudge of L.A. traffic. She'd been in the car with Angus for fifteen minutes now and so far he'd remarked on the shabby vinyl upholstery, the unidentifiable stains on the dashboard, the strange device that manually rolled down the window, the cracked cup holder, the lack of leg room, and the odor he said smelled like his grandmother's pot roast, a dish he clearly thought of without fondness.

"We should've taken my car," he said.

"Do I want to know what you drive? Porsche? Ferrari? Corvette? Something low and shiny with doors that open up instead of sideways?"

"Tesla," he said. "This city has enough smog."

She snuck in a quick glance as the car crept forward. Angus was struggling to roll down his window. Despite his concerted efforts, the handle barely budged and the pane only shifted a couple of inches in its track. His concentration on the effort amused her, and also, okay, the environmentally conscious car choice was seriously decent.

"Why do you think they'll call?" she asked.

"Why wouldn't they?" He gave up on the window, leaving it open just enough for the draft to flutter his cowlicks. "The show's on its last legs. Everyone knows that. Audiences are ready for something new but the producers are hoping to squeeze one more season out of us. They'll try anything that might bring in more viewers. All that press is too good to waste. Besides, you nailed the read."

She hit the brakes, jerking the car to a stop inches from hitting an expensive-looking Mercedes. She blinked at the too-close bumper, but the second she caught her breath, she whipped around to face Angus, certain she'd heard him wrong.

"I made up my own lines," she said. "I stammered. I lost my place. I wept, for god's sake, and I made you rush from the room so fast you probably got windburn."

"*You* didn't make me rush out. The situation did."

"You mean being forced to read with someone who's 'not even an actress'?"

"Wow. No. I'm sorry you heard that. Let me explain." He rotated to face her, wedging himself against the door and drawing a hand over his chin in a way that was already becoming familiar. "How did you feel on the day that hashtag broke?"

She flashed through tweets and video clips, each one burned into her memory.

"Weird, I guess? Judged. Dissected. Like I was desperate to defend myself to total strangers but I knew engaging would only make things worse. All those assumptions. The speculation. The jokes. I hated it. I felt"—she searched for the right word—"naked."

"Now imagine feeling that way all the time."

Traffic started moving, so Marlowe returned her attention to the road. As the car inched forward, she considered Angus's point, something that hadn't crossed her mind when she was facing the prospect of three thousand dollars for a few days of work. Was any amount of money worth opening herself up to more criticism and speculation? Especially in a world where the cruelest voices were often the loudest?

"Is that how you feel?" she asked.

"Sometimes." Angus picked at the frayed edge of his seatbelt's cross strap, the motion brusque and agitated. "I'll admit the attention was addictive back when I was fourteen and I got the lead on that Disney show, but over time it messed with my head. People conflate my characters with the real me. They assume I'm vapid, or violent, or that I'm always on the make and I drive a flashy sports car."

Marlowe sank a little lower in her seat, duly chastised. "Sorry about that."

"Wasn't the first time." He yanked a loose thread off the seatbelt as though torturing the edge hadn't sufficiently satisfied his agitation. "I know people think I have no right to complain about anything, and maybe I don't. Fame provides certain comforts and opportunities. No question. But it has its downsides. I can't make a friend, date a girl, or get a job without wondering if someone's only interested in a manufactured idea of who I am, or if fame alone is the draw." He held the severed thread up toward the partially open window and watched it dance in the draft. His fascination was sweet, almost childlike, in sharp contrast to the soul-baring conversation they were having. "Also, while fans can be enthusiastic, the haters, as they say, are gonna hate."

Marlowe kept her eyes on the road but she snuck a sideways glance every few seconds, trying to align the guy beside her with the guy she'd seen around set. For months Angus had seemed impenetrable, snobbish, and spectacularly pleased with himself. He carried the air of celebrity on his shoulders everywhere he went, as if he assumed he was being watched and being wanted and he'd long since grown comfortable with that kind of attention. Now he looked so . . . human. Beautiful, yes, but still human.

"So, don't read the comments?" She made a quivering attempt at a smile.

He continued staring at the thread, neither noticing nor returning her smile.

"Definitely ignore the comments," he said. "But they're only part of the issue. The moment you get enough attention, enough influence, enough eyes on you, you become a commodity. Publicity specialists get involved. They package and sell you. Pretty soon it's hard to draw a line between who you are and who they want you to be." The thread flew from his fingers, into the exhaust-filled air and toward an SUV in the next lane over. Inside the vehicle, a group of teenage girls was conferring and pointing his way. He shielded his face with a cupped hand and turned away from them in what struck Marlowe as a well-rehearsed move. "Actors sign up for this. You didn't. That's what I meant by 'not even an actress.' It's also why I'm here. They won't just give you a few lines and walk you past a camera. They'll expect you to become part of the promotional machine. I thought you should know what you were getting into before you say yes."

Marlowe let that sink in while her hatchback crept forward,

packed in by other cars as the L.A. sunshine streamed through the windshield, bright and hot. She tried to imagine the level of public attention he was describing, but it seemed impossible.

"Wes didn't mention anything about promotion," she said.

"They'll bury it in a contract. Use language they don't expect you to understand."

"They won't want me representing the show, not once they realize I can't act."

"I wouldn't count on that realization as a foregone conclusion."

The car finally picked up a little speed and then jerked to a halt again. Such was life in L.A. Such was life in general. So how did this moment fit into that pattern? Was it a chance to speed up or a reason to hit the brakes? And was she really debating the choice with Angus Gordon, of all people? A guy who'd been smoldering on her screen since the days when she used a retainer and three kinds of acne medication, dreaming of the year she'd develop breasts?

"I don't look anything like the girls they always pair you up with," she said.

"Maybe that's the point." Angus shifted, replanting his feet as though he couldn't get comfortable all of a sudden. He probably thought she was fishing for a compliment. She wasn't, and she was glad he didn't toss one out. "People . . . audiences get perfection fatigue. It makes for a good fantasy but after a while, they want something real."

She snuck another glance his way, wondering if he meant more than he said. Before she could give that thought full consideration, her attention snagged on the girls in the SUV. They were leaning out their windows, camera phones poised while they waved and shrieked, trying to get Angus's attention. Marlowe had seen him soak up adoration so many times over the past few months, but right now, with his shoulders hunched, a hand shielding his cheek, and annoyance painted across his face, he looked as if he wanted to wither into the footwell.

"This is what you have to look forward to," he said.

"No way. Not possible. Not me. And we're only talking about a cameo."

"My first screen credit was dog walker number two. My second was Kip on *Kate and Kip Take Down Cleveland.* It's a crazy industry, as ready to make a star as it is to tear one down." He smiled a little, in a nice, natural way. No challenge, no flirting, just a moment of gentle humor shared between two people. "If it's okay to ask, why are you even considering this? You don't seem like someone who's dying to be on TV."

"I'm not." She let the traffic pull forward so she could merge in behind the screaming girls and get her car into the far-right lane, allowing Angus to sit up straight. "I know this might not make any sense to someone who probably has bicoastal mansions and a butler with a British accent, but I need the money."

He nodded as he settled into his seat.

"Then you should ask them to double it."

Chapter Eight

Marlowe spun a cart into the first aisle of women's shoes at DSW with Angus trailing close behind, still wearing his aviators. While she scanned the shelves and swept shoeboxes into the cart with her usual efficiency, he stopped to examine every item he passed, fascinated with each heel, buckle, and curved arch. His open sense of wonder made him look as if he'd never been in a store before. Someone else probably did his shopping for him. Someone else probably did pretty much everything for him.

As Marlowe sent Cherry pics of some black patent leather wedges to get her opinion, Angus scrutinized a gold gladiator sandal with a sharp stiletto heel.

"How do women walk in these?" he asked.

She motioned to her comfy sneakers. "You're asking the wrong person."

"Even though you pick this stuff out for a living?"

"I pick it out. I don't wear it. That's a very deliberate career move."

"Until someone offers you an acting gig."

"As a waitress. With three lines, flat shoes, and a definitive end date." She flashed him a *Drop it* look before continuing down the aisle, flinging shoes into the cart.

He hung back, turning the sandal over to study something on the sole. She left him to it. With the number of shoes Babs was expecting, Marlowe didn't have time to discuss the finer points of fetish footwear with Angus. Still, he was there, hovering, making her feel like she should be paying him attention she didn't have to spare. When he'd barely moved by the time she neared him one aisle over, she halted the cart.

"How many people work for you?" she asked.

He looked up from the marabou slipper he was now studying. "Like my agent?"

"Like anyone. Publicist, chef, maid." She leaned forward for emphasis. "*Driver.*"

"You're bored with me already?" He set down the shoe, flicking at the feathers.

"I appreciate everything you told me on the way here, but I think we covered it. I'll give the situation some thought, and I won't say yes without reading the fine print."

He removed his aviators as his already serious expression pinched into a pronounced frown, one that forced a pair of deep creases between his brows.

"So that's it?" he said. "Thank you, goodbye?"

"This can't possibly be how you wanted to spend your day."

"How do you know what I want to do?"

"Educated guess?"

"Or gross assumption?"

"How about educated assumption?"

"Educated how?" His chin tipped up, a gaining of ground, a hint of superiority.

Her chin remained precisely where it was. "By watching other people wait on you all the time. You don't even get a cup of coffee without an entourage. Someone's always nearby to do your bidding. You probably shop by sitting in a cozy chair, sipping cocktails with your feet kicked up while harried personal attendants display their wares for you."

"Unfortunately none of those 'attendants' are qualified to select my costume."

"I told you. I can get your jeans without you."

"And miss the opportunity to take another jab at my imaginary lifestyle?"

She opened her mouth to reply. He raised a brow. She closed her mouth. For a long moment they held a look, edged with an already familiar sense of mutual challenge. When she didn't contradict him—because, how?—he picked up a Lucite mule and turned it over as though it was the most intriguing thing ever.

"This doesn't even bend," he said.

Marlowe rolled her eyes and pushed the cart away, sensing she'd lost this battle and she should focus on the task at hand. While Angus poked around like a kid at a science exhibit, she filled the cart, texting with Cherry until they agreed on her selections. Then she met with the manager on duty to complete her purchase, requesting multiple sizes and by-end-of-day delivery so she wouldn't tax her car's limited baggage capacity.

As she slipped the extensive purchase order into her purse, the manager glanced at something over Marlowe's shoulder, something that made her eyes widen in surprise.

"Is that who I think it is?" she asked.

Marlowe turned around to see Angus frowning at a high-heeled sneaker as though he couldn't reconcile the decorative heel with the athletic style. She prepared a lie but he chose that moment to flash her a grin, one that was far too recognizable to deny.

"Yep," she said to the manager. "That's exactly who you think it is."

"Oh, my god." The woman's jaw dropped open. "And are you the waitress?"

Marlowe flinched as Angus's warnings echoed in her ears. *Enough eyes on you. Part of the promotional machine. This is what you have to look forward to.*

"I'm the shoe shopper." She backed away, hoping her lack of makeup, unstyled hair, and spectacular ordinariness would lend weight to her assertion. Fortunately the manager's attention was already back on Angus as she grabbed a nearby salesgirl.

"Look who's in aisle one," she gushed. "Patty and Carolyn are going to die."

Predictably, Patty and Carolyn did not die. Instead, they posed for a group photo with Angus and every other employee present. They giggled and fawned. They asked him about the show and Tanareve and his favorite food or role or color and if he ever thought about modeling. They might've carried on all day but Marlowe eventually caught his eye and pointed at her wrist to indicate that time was of the essence.

"You seriously don't have a chauffeur?" she asked as they belted themselves back in her car. "Or an Uber account? A teleporting phone booth? A dragon? Anything?"

He rolled his head toward her. "You really want to get rid of me, don't you?"

"I don't have time to wait while you play another round of Catch the Swooning Saleswoman." She flung a hand toward the store, assuming her window was open. It wasn't. With a sharp *thwack*, her knuckles hit the pane. She grimaced as she shook out her hand, wondering what it was about Angus that brought out her inner klutz. Fame? A subtle but persistent air of antagonism? Unnervingly steady eye contact? Really amazing bone structure? She looked up to catch him swallowing a laugh, though not discreetly enough to prevent her from flushing with embarrassment. "Forget that happened."

"Not a chance." He continued to chuckle.

She groaned as she attempted to roll down her window. When it refused to budge, he reached across her and gave the crank a good whack, setting its rotation in motion and letting the first hint of fresh air into the car. He settled back into his seat right away, but quarters were tight. His elbow brushed her arm and his shoulder bumped hers, sparking an unexpected ripple of sensation all across her skin. She flushed again, rotating to focus on the crank so he couldn't see her red cheeks. Her response was frustrating. She was reacting *way* too strongly to the barest hint of human contact. Clearly, she should think about dating again, a subject she'd revisit when she wasn't stuck in a rancid, overheated hatchback with an oddly stubborn TV star and an impossible to-do list.

"You sure I can't drop you off somewhere?" Marlowe asked as she started the car. "I need to pick up the pace. Babs will give me hell if I don't get her what she needs."

Angus slipped his aviators on, making his already impenetrable expression even harder to read. Still, she got the sense he was studying her again, the same way he studied shoes, and threads ripped off seatbelts, and anything else that drew his attention.

"What if I help with the shopping?" he asked.

"How? By flirting with more saleswomen?"

"Did you see me flirt?"

She opened her mouth to say a firm *yes* but her conviction died in her throat.

"Fine," she said instead. "Then by letting them flirt with you."

"You think we should've made a run for it?"

"No, but . . ." She stopped there. What did she expect him to do? Was taking a few photos and talking to his fans really such a stretch? Or was he simply being kind?

"Would it help if I bought you lunch?" He caught her swift intake of breath and held up both palms. "Not because you can't buy your own. Just to prove I'm capable of doing something for myself, you know, since I gave my personal wallet carrier the day off. Sick relatives in Paducah. Auntie Midge is about to kick it. I was feeling generous." The edge of Angus's lips tipped up, revealing a hint of amusement that was unfairly sexy.

As Marlowe fought back a smile of her own, she reconsidered her manic need to hit every last shoe store between Sunset Boulevard and the north edge of Burbank. Despite her attempts to downplay the situation and smother every remnant of her prior interest, Angus Gordon—*the* Angus Gordon—was offering to be her assistant for the afternoon. Screw efficiency. This would be her go-to party story for the next twenty years. Why in the hell was she trying to get rid of him?

"Okay," she said. "But I'm picking the restaurant."

Chapter Nine

The afternoon sun blazed down as Marlowe and Angus sat at a lone picnic table near a quiet street-side taco stand. A rickety umbrella provided a circle of shade but three sizable holes prevented it from doing much good. Still, it was something, and the air was cooler outside than it was in her stifling car. She and Angus had shopped for five hours together and he hadn't been entirely useless. He'd scanned boxes for alternate sizes and pushed a cart around. He'd also been so easily distracted and run into so many fans, she was moving at about half her intended pace. She would've carried on without stopping but she'd agreed to let him buy her lunch and he was determined to hold her to it.

"I could've taken you somewhere nicer," Angus said as he settled the tray between them. "We didn't have to hit the cheapest taco stand in the entire L.A. Basin."

"I'm sure these are great." Marlowe picked an unidentifiable black speck off a skimpy layer of shredded cheese. She didn't really think lunch would be great but she refused to let him spend more than a few bucks on her. A nice meal together would make her feel indebted. It was a submission, a ceding of power. A meal like this was more of a dare. "Tacos are a very forgiving food. They're also perfectly designed. You can put anything you want in them and they come with their own edible, wobbly plate."

He examined his lunch a little more closely.

"I will never think of tortillas in the same way again."

While he tucked his sunglasses into the neckline of his T-shirt, she peeled limp strands of spinach from one of her tacos and laid them on the side of her paper plate.

"You don't like spinach?" he asked.

"I'm not big on vegetables." She folded her tortilla back over the beans, rice, and other less offensive ingredients. "I blame my mom. She's a pretty serious health nut. After her divorce, she started us both on a raw diet. I was six. Until I left home at eighteen, flavor was something I only experienced on the down-low."

Angus took her idling spinach and slipped it into his taco.

"Big family, no money," he said. "We ate anything we could."

Marlowe paused with her taco halfway to her mouth.

"Didn't you say you were fourteen when you started that Disney show?"

"Yeah, and I'll admit I've grown used to having nice things, but when I was a kid, we barely got by. My mom was a factory foreman. My dad worked the fields. The paychecks didn't go far with eight kids." He peeked into her second taco and extracted the rest of her spinach as though sharing food with her was most natural thing in the world. It was weird but sort of fine. "And just so we're clear, I only have one mansion."

"Only one? However do you manage?" She rolled her eyes but he took her teasing in stride, with a self-effacing chuckle that was admittedly quite charming.

Finding her taco painfully flavorless, Marlowe tore open a plastic packet of hot sauce. The contents burst forth, splattering both her plate and his. She braced herself for a tirade, or at least a sardonic demand for a towel, but to her surprise, he didn't even flinch. He just worked the closest drops into his tacos while she mopped up the rest. It was so bizarrely familiar, easy, like they were two old friends with established routines.

"Was I at least right about the butler with the British accent?" she asked.

"Now you're confusing me with Batman."

"If you were Batman, you definitely would've had more pressing demands on your time today." As she wadded up sauce-stained napkins that looked like they came from a triage unit, she pictured Angus in a Batman mask. The image formed easily. With his ridiculously square jaw, strong features, and a chin dimple that'd be more pronounced if he shaved, he'd look a lot like the comic-book character. Maybe one day he'd play the role. His girlfriend might even play his love interest, if every other superhero hadn't already rescued her by then.

Marlowe got up to fetch more napkins, skeptical she'd make it through lunch without another mishap. She proved this prediction accurate when she licked her sticky fingers and hit a lurking glob of hot sauce. Tongue on fire, she grabbed her drink but the straw was busted, forcing her to wrench off the plastic lid and take a gulp directly from the cup. The ice cubes chose that moment to free themselves from one another and fall against her cheeks, bringing with them a wave of cold citrus soda pop. Coughing and sputtering, she made swift use of her second stack of napkins and went to fetch a third. Angus watched the entire scene play out with a dry smile tugging at his lips.

"I'm not usually this clumsy," she said as she finally settled in to eat.

His smile lingered. "Do I make you nervous?"

"I think you make me unlucky. It's a gift. Hone it." She managed a bite, pleased the tortilla held and she didn't further embarrass herself. When she looked up, Angus was watching her again in that way he had, too long and too direct. "What?"

"I don't believe in luck."

She searched his face for signs he wasn't implying what she thought he was implying, but there he sat, with his chin up and his eyes narrowed, as if he just *knew*.

"Trust me," she said. "I'm not hoping you'll sign my boob."

"You know I never offer, right? It's something women request."

"Then it's lucky you know how to write on a curved surface." She slapped a palm against her forehead. "Wait. Sorry. Forgot. You don't believe in luck."

He sat back and folded his arms, all hint of his smile gone now.

"What's your problem with me?" he asked.

"Nothing. I just . . ." She flapped a hand at him. "It's the whole 'you know you want me' vibe. I get it. You're used to that kind of attention. You've come to expect it."

"You don't know what I expect."

"Really? Try me." She set down her food and mirrored his position, crossed arms, haughty chin tilt, and all.

He leaned forward, arms still folded, eyes locked on hers.

"How about a simple thank-you after I buy a girl lunch or send her flowers? How about being treated as a person, not as an idea? How about someone getting to know me without assuming she already knows every detail about my life? *That's* what I expect." He raised a brow, otherwise unmoving. She opened her mouth to fire back a reply but she had no defense. He was right about all of it. Sure, they'd interacted a few times, but she didn't know him, and she shouldn't assume she did. He seemed to sense her thinking as his expression softened and his shoulders relaxed. "Also, while we're at it, and in case there's any confusion about the issue, I'm not hoping you'll sign my boob, either."

For a long moment she simply stared at him. Then she burst into a laugh.

"Thank god," she said through her sputters. "Thank you for the flowers. They're beautiful. I loved them." She looked down at the wreckage on her plate. "And thank you for the absolute worst taco I've tried since moving to L.A."

He met her laughter with a smile, one that looked sincere and not manufactured for a perfect photo op. Despite her intense desire to avoid being one more girl swooning over his full lips and perfect teeth, it really was one hell of a smile.

"Truce?" he asked.

"Truce," she agreed.

They raised their tacos in a sort of toast. As they ate, he told her more about his family and she related a few stories about her own. His childhood was full of noise and competition for attention. Hers was defined by a quiet undertone of disapproval. They discovered they'd both had hamsters, neither of whom had lived long and both of whom received elaborate backyard funerals. Angus had visited every continent. Marlowe had only left North America twice. He ran thirty to forty miles a week. She stuck to single digits. They both grew up near a coast, though she hadn't seen the Pacific Ocean until she abandoned her theater career for a shot in the film and TV industry (aka a place to hide from critics and angry exes). To her surprise, he displayed no judgment about anything she shared. He listened as if he was interested. She didn't know how long their truce would last, but for almost half an hour, he was no longer Angus Gordon, untouchable TV star who looked down on "people like her." He was a guy she was having lunch with. After so many months of always eating alone, she was grateful for the company.

Four more hours of shoe shopping later, Marlowe finally parked at the Hardwired Jeans store. Hardwired was Angus's favorite brand and the one Babs most often used to dress him, discounting anything custom made. The styles drew on Old West influences, though the cuts were distinctly modern and the high prices created a sense of exclusivity.

Marlowe unfastened her seatbelt, letting it bunch up on the floor when the retraction mechanism failed. Beside her, Angus faced similar challenges, but with the effort of an aquanaut escaping a giant squid, he eventually untangled the straps.

"We're tight on time," she said as they got out of the car. "Let's grab three or four pairs that might work. Then you can assure Babs we couldn't possibly make a decision without her input since I don't know a mid-wash from a vintage finish."

Angus's brows inched up above his aviators. "I'm guessing that's a lie?"

"Better not to ask or I'll regale you with a lecture on the differences between a tint, a treatment, a wash, and a finish. You don't need to hear it and Babs doesn't need to know that I know. Oh, and also, please don't mention we had lunch together."

"So we shopped all day without eating?"

"Fasting's big in L.A., right?"

"Juice fasts, maybe."

"Works for me. Shoes, jeans, and juice. That's all. Agreed?" She held out a hand.

He took it in his own and gave it a firm shake. "Agreed, as long as I can make fun of the disgusting green goo you sucked down as though it was water."

"I happen to adore green goo."

"I suspected as much by your enthusiastic spinach intake."

"And I question your excessive garnish demands."

"One can never have too many serrated strawberries."

"So I've heard."

They swapped a brief smile before releasing their handshake. It was amicable, straightforward, and precisely what it should've been, but as the two of them headed inside the store, Marlowe felt an unexpected wave of sadness wash over her. In other circumstances—like if he wasn't rich and famous with a gorgeous girlfriend, and she wasn't . . . herself—their agreement might be the start of a new private language. Next time they got together, she'd order something green. He'd pile on serrated strawberries. They might even laugh about her absurd napkin-to-food ratio or his random fascination with shoe construction. Instead, the moments were only moments. Nothing more.

She glanced down to realize she was twisting at her ring finger again. She seriously had to quit that habit. She'd find someone who'd share more than moments with her. Someone who wasn't her ex. Someone who wouldn't make her feel small.

Ten minutes later, Marlowe was parked in a chair by a trio of fitting rooms while Angus hauled in an armload of jeans, unwilling to grab a few pairs and go. Since he'd been kind enough to warn her about the potential downsides of the acting gig, and since she was too tired to argue, she humored him. His head and shoulders poked out above the saloon-style doors while his feet and calves protruded below. As he changed, she passed the time by trying yet again to describe his hair. Russet? Too brown. Burnt sienna? Too orange. Pumpkin? Squash? Carrot? Yam? Something that didn't come from a garden?

She was still debating the matter when he stepped out in a pair of dark-wash jeans, holding up his T-shirt hem to examine the fit, and also probably to show off his abs. Marlowe found the instinct humorous but she didn't totally despise it.

"What do you think?" He twisted away from her.

She stifled a laugh. "Are you asking me to check out your ass?"

"Someone has to make sure it's camera ready."

"I believe that's your job."

"Just tell me what you think of the jeans." He did a slow turn.

Marlowe stood and took a closer look. "They're a size too big in the waist, the color's too cold against your complexion, the rise is off, your legs would look longer in a boot cut, and that pocket detail's in the wrong place for your proportions."

"So you *were* looking at my ass."

"Occupational hazard. Try another pair."

Angus stepped back into the fitting room and flung the dark-wash jeans over the door. Marlowe made a Herculean effort at studying a gaslight-inspired lamp on the table beside her, but her gaze soon traveled back to the fitting room. This time it didn't land on Angus's hair. It lingered on his bare lower legs. His calves tensed as he adjusted his weight, revealing the sharp outline of each well-toned muscle. She'd always envied people with great legs, mainly because she was such a lousy runner. She had legs like broomsticks. Angus had legs like freaking Atlas. And he was on the other side of the saloon doors, shuffling pairs of jeans that were totally not on his body right now. Which meant he was only wearing—

"Can I ask you a question?" he called as he shifted behind the doors.

"Sure. I guess." Her voice came out suspiciously raspy. She cleared her throat and tried again. "I mean yes. You can. As long as I can ask you one, too."

"Totally fair. One for one." He plunged a foot into the next pair of jeans. "You obviously know what you're doing. World's most decisive shoe shopping aside, all that stuff you noticed about the jeans, Babs doesn't see all that. So why are you only a PA?"

Marlowe sighed as she sank into the chair. She'd enjoyed getting to know Angus over the course of the day, chatting about favorite bands and childhood pets, but he didn't need to know about her stunted dreams, especially not when this was probably the only time they'd ever talk to each other alone, off set, almost like equals. Almost like friends.

"Gotta start somewhere," she said with as much cheer as she could muster.

"Bullshit." He swung open the doors, dressed in faded jeans that sat low on his hips and puddled around his ankles, the hems pre-frayed. "Tell me the truth."

"Too pale, too baggy, and the outseam is set too far back."

"I don't mean about the jeans."

"I know." She scratched at a reddish spot on her pants. Hot sauce from lunch, probably. She waited for him to step back into the fitting room but he leaned against the open doorway, arms folded, awaiting her response. Did he really want to know? Did she want to tell him? Then again, did she have a good reason *not* to tell him? Unable to answer that question, she braced herself and met his eyes. "Fear of failure."

He nodded, rubbing his stubbled chin. "Yet you're not afraid to move across the country, leave behind your support network, and throw yourself into a new career?"

She pursed her lips, hoping to withhold her next admission, but out it came.

"I can't truly fail if I'm not chasing what I really want." She waited for Angus to laugh or call her a coward but the laughter didn't come. He offered no disapproval, no retorts. He barely even moved, other than to lower his hand and rest it against his chest. The silence was beautiful. It was also torture. "Stupid, right?"

He shook his head. "Refreshingly honest."

They exchanged another smile, one that was barely there, yet it pierced something inside her. It was the kind of smile that couldn't be offered. It had to be earned.

Before Marlowe could give that more thought, a pair of middle-aged women scurried over, declaring their undying love for Angus and begging for a photo. Marlowe watched as he posed with them, all swagger and easy charm, like always, but this time she noticed a hint of tightness around his eyes and mouth, and a restless twitch in his shoulders, signs he might not be reveling in the attention after all. If that was true, if she was reading him right, then maybe he wasn't chasing what he most wanted, either.

Eventually the women left him alone, thanks to the herding prowess of a laconic retail clerk who'd obviously experienced similar circumstances many times. Marlowe helped Angus select three pairs of jeans before driving back to headquarters and parking near the wardrobe building. As the evening sun stretched shadows across the pavement, she unloaded shopping bags and lined them up behind her trunk, counting them out to assess what she could carry and how many trips she'd need to haul everything inside. Angus offered to help but Marlowe suggested parting ways instead. Better not to risk running into Babs while still in his company.

Angus agreed to leave her to it, though he didn't take off right away. Instead he lingered, helping her load her forearms with bags.

"You're going to take the role, aren't you?" he asked.

"I don't know. It'll depend on what they offer. *If* they offer. But thanks for talking to me about it first. It's good to know what I might be signing up for."

"Least I could do." He handed off the last of her first load and they stepped apart from one another. "Before you go. I just realized. You never asked your question."

"My question?"

"One for one. Back at Hardwired."

"Oh. Right." She considered her options. Go deep and ask what dream he wasn't chasing? Go light and ask for a taco stand recommendation? Or take a real risk and go personal? "You probably don't remember, but that day I played the waitress, you said you were surprised they put 'someone like me' on camera. What did you mean?"

"Wow. That was a long time ago." He squinted toward the setting sun while scratching the back of his neck. "Someone who had things to do, probably. Every time I looked at you, you were pounding at a laptop or making lists or sorting out some issue with Cherry or Babs or Elaine. You seemed like someone other people relied on." He shrugged, shifted, *almost* smiled. "Sorry if what I said came out another way. It wasn't my best week. I was being kind of a dick to everyone. When I get stressed, I push people away, even people I don't know. It's something I need to work on."

"Guess we all have things to work on." With a brief smile and a failed attempt to wave, Marlowe said goodbye. Angus nodded, turned, and walked away. She watched him for a moment in case he turned around, but he didn't, and she felt kind of stupid for thinking he might. Still, as she headed inside, she was a little lighter on her feet despite the weight on her arms. Angus's answer about "someone like her" meant a lot, even if she wasn't proud of how long she'd held on to her resentment about his initial comment, or how long she'd let it feed her insecurities. Things to work on, indeed.

She was so lost in her thoughts, she practically crashed into Babs, who was still flustered about the new scenes they were prepping without sufficient lead-time. Elaine and a crew of four other costumers were busy corralling background players. Cherry was darting out of the fitting area to fetch something from the office. Marlowe did her best to stay out of everyone's way as she unpacked the shoes, lining them up in size order along with the many pairs she'd had delivered. Once her car was emptied and everything was sorted, she found Cherry in the main office, digging through files.

"Know where I can find the order forms from Under Nation?" Cherry asked.

"They're not in hard copy yet. Only online." Marlowe opened the office computer and found the file. "Want me to pull them up and print everything off?"

"Yes! You're a godsend." Cherry wiped sweat off her forehead. "Babs has been on fire today. She was *not* happy you drove off with her boy toy while we were left trying to convince one actress that no, she didn't need a body double and another that yes, she was a C cup. What was that even about this morning? Please tell me he didn't try to get into your pants. And that you ditched him right away. Fuck! What a day." She finally paused to take a breath, draping herself across the desk. "Oh, and Jerry from catering brought over your smoothie. Thanks for asking if I wanted anything."

"My smoo—?" Marlowe caught sight of a large plastic cup filled with the greenest, gooiest concoction she'd ever seen. The name on the side read *Marlowe, like the detective*. The rim was garnished with a perfectly serrated strawberry.

Chapter Ten

Marlowe sat in a small reception area in the main office building on the studio lot. A curvy blonde in a perfectly fitted sheath dress perched at a glass desk, answering calls on a headset. Beyond the desk were the offices of the show's producers. Marlowe wasn't sure which producer she was here to see, but she'd been summoned from wardrobe and here she sat, jittery, restless, and generating underarm sweat at an astonishing rate.

She'd expected the call, thanks to yesterday's conversation with Angus, but now that the role was closer to becoming a reality, his warnings about packaging and publicity rang in her ears. She also nursed a growing unease about the criticism that would come her way if she appeared on-screen again, and this time, not just as a nameless background player. Her only immediate diversion was the latest issue of *People* with a photo of Angus and Tanareve on the front under the bold yellow headline REUNITED AND IT FEELS SO GOOD. They were arm in arm, strolling down a busy sidewalk, laughing to themselves as though someone just happened to be walking in front of them and snapped the photo.

Marlowe picked up the magazine. Then she set it down again.

She didn't want to read about Angus's relationship. It did nothing to ease her current anxieties. Instead, it seemed to amplify them. It shouldn't. He was happy. End of story. It had nothing to do with her. But why couldn't someone else have spent the day shopping with her? Made her laugh? Listened? Cared? Stolen her spinach? Sent her a nauseating smoothie that melted her heart even though she could only manage a single sip without retching?

"Marlowe Banks?"

She looked up to see a woman in a sharp black suit standing on the other side of the coffee table. The woman's dark brown hair was swept into a tidy twist, her silver and stone accessories were understated, and she had the ultra-fit physique so common among L.A. residents. She looked like a runway model, though her tailored clothes and soft briefcase indicated she'd be equally at home in an office or a courtroom.

"My name's Sanaya Baqri. I'm Angus Gordon's agent." She held out a hand.

Marlowe glanced around. "He's in today, too?"

"Actually, I'm here for you." She shook Marlowe's hand and took a seat, smoothing her pencil skirt over her thighs. "Angus was in this morning. He got a sense of what was coming down the pipeline. He wanted to make sure someone was present who could explain the contract to you. I hope you don't mind the intervention?"

"It's amazing. Thank you." Marlowe flipped the *People* magazine upside down, lest Angus's image incite feelings she didn't want to entertain at present, or ever. An intense swell of gratitude was unavoidable. Anything else had to be shut down. Stat.

Marlowe and Sanaya chatted for a few minutes, but the receptionist soon ushered them down the hall to Greg's office, where Wes and Alejandra were also waiting. Greg sat behind a formidable desk, his tie askew and his TV awards covering the wall behind him. Wes stood by the door with his blond tufts winging out under his Oakland A's cap. Alejandra leaned against a windowsill on the far wall, leaving the chairs in front of the desk for Marlowe and Sanaya. After a round of introductions, Wes stepped forward.

"The writers' room convened yesterday and we have a plan." He began to pace, all fidgety excitement as he rubbed his hands and his chunky work boots clomped across the floorboards. "For five seasons we've hinted that Jake wouldn't commit to any of the women he's slept with because he'd invented an ideal girl and no one could live up to her image. We've never explained what that ideal is, but now we can. With me so far?"

"I think so?" Marlowe scanned the faces around her. Greg nodded thoughtfully while Alejandra and Sanaya were unmoving, postures rigid and expressions guarded.

"The waitress will be Jake's first love," Wes continued. "The two met on his family vacation when the kids were twelve or thirteen. A beach. Seagulls. Plenty of sun."

"As long as there aren't plenty of people," Greg interjected.

"No background, as promised. We'll do a one-day shoot with a small second unit crew in Malibu. Won't break the bank. Now. Picture it." Wes framed an imaginary shot with his thumbs and forefingers. "Two cute kids run through the waves, collect shells, watch a sunset, share cotton candy, hold hands, whatever tugs on the heartstrings. It'll be crazy adorable until Adelaide departs without warning, leaving Jake with abandonment issues." Wes flapped a hand at Marlowe. "Adelaide's you. Think sweet, wholesome, all-American girl. Gingham. Apple pie. Kittens. The whole nine."

Alejandra rolled her eyes. "More like the whole cliché."

"The day people stop tuning in for clichés, I'll stop writing them." Wes shot her a gentle dare-you-to-contradict-me look before making his frame again. "So. The kids. We'll watch a car pull away with Little Adelaide looking out the back window. Squirt tears in her eyes. Underscore the shit out of it. Violins. Cellos. Give it all the feels. Then Little Jake shows up at their usual spot on the beach to find her gone. Little Jake gets superimposed against Big Jake, sitting in the diner, seeing you again after all these years. The audience will eat. It. Up." He blew out a breath as though he'd just sprinted a mile.

"Okay?" Marlowe blinked toward him, still trying to picture everything. "So all I have to do is stand there for a moment of recognition in the diner?"

"At first. We still want three episodes. Number one." Wes held up a finger. "Jake sees you at the diner. You make a signature gesture we repeat with the kids, like tucking your hair over your ear in a notable way or chewing on your pinky. He says, 'It *is* you.' You react. He reacts. End of episode. Perfect cliffhanger. Number two." A second finger shot up. "Jake convinces Adelaide to have a conversation. They catch up on years gone by. She hasn't forgotten him, either. All that potential torn away! So tragic!" Wes's palm flew to his chest, landing with a loud *thunk* that made Marlowe flinch. "Shared longing. Flirtation. Coy looks. Potential reignited. Blah, blah, blah. As soon as we think they might kiss, she pulls out an engagement ring she wears around her neck."

"She wears the ring around her neck?" Marlowe rubbed at the finger that still felt uncomfortably naked, even after all these months.

"She's engaged," Wes said as though confused by the question. "It's why Jake and Adelaide can't get together. But we can't know until after they want each other."

"I get that, but why does *she* choose to wear the ring around her neck?"

Greg chuckled behind his desk. "Already becoming an actress. Good for you."

Marlowe stiffened at his patronizing tone. "I'm not an actress. I'm a costume designer. The ring tells a story about who Adelaide is, what she cares about, and why. Her character would have a reason for how she wears it."

Wes waved her off. "We'll figure it out later. What matters is we can film what we need. Fast. Cheap. Two locations, inside the diner and behind it. And we can fit the scenes between everything else that's already scripted." He perched on the corner of the desk, eliciting subtle looks of disapproval from Greg and Alejandra. "Still with me?"

Marlowe nodded, though the conversation unsettled her. So much of it focused on shooting schedules, budget considerations, and manipulating the audience. So little was about meaningful story and characters, the elements that initially drew her to her design career. It made her crave one of her "little Chekhov plays," as Babs called them. Chloe's show came to mind, but thoughts about Marlowe's design career would have to wait.

"And number three?" she asked warily.

"Number three." Greg flung up a third finger. "Jake almost gets it on with his neighbor, a means of distraction, but he changes his mind at the last minute, says he has to be somewhere, jumps on his motorcycle, and speeds to the church."

Marlowe went wide-eyed. "The church where Adelaide's getting married?"

"Audiences will love it. Total *Graduate* callback." Wes caught Greg opening his mouth as if to speak, halting him with a flash of his palm. "No wedding. Don't worry. Just a shot in front of a crappy little church. Adelaide's about to head inside with her bridesmaids."

"Bridesmaid, singular," Greg amended.

"Fine. Whatever." Wes sent him a light sneer before snapping back into high-drama mode. "Jake pulls up on his bike. He pleads with his eyes. You falter, step toward him, torn. He steps toward you, but no! It's too late! Do you? Don't you? You don't! You gather your conviction and head inside, leaving Jake shattered all over again, staring at the church doors. All is lost. The perfect season finale." He practically slid off the desk in his excitement but he righted himself at the last second with a quiet chuckle.

As the energy of his speech ebbed, the room went quiet. Wes adjusted his ball cap. Greg drummed his fingers on a thick stack of papers. Sanaya folded her hands, the picture of patience, while over by the window, Alejandra offered Marlowe a kind smile and a light shrug. Marlowe felt them all waiting for her to say something, but what was she supposed to say? *A couple of lines*, Cherry had told her. *Just enough to get audiences to tune in. A little sparring and a little flirting*, Wes had said last week. No one had suggested an entire character arc or a heart-wrenching season finale.

"Be thankful," Alejandra said, breaking the silence. "Wes's first idea was that you were a stripper. Why every 'wholesome, all-American girl' also has to be a stripper is beyond me. God, I can't wait until we have more women in the writers' room."

Wes got defensive and Greg jumped in to clarify the gender breakdown of the writing staff. Like a contentious but loving family, the trio worked out their differences with a few gentle jibes, leaving Marlowe to process the more immediate matter at hand.

"Three scenes?" she clarified. "And I only have to talk in one of them?"

"Piece of cake." Wes tapped Greg's stack of papers. Greg slid it forward.

Marlowe scooted her chair next to Sanaya's so they could peruse what turned out to be over twenty pages of dense legalese. No wonder Angus had called in help.

"This is the fee scale for a standard day player," Sanaya noted, flipping pages much faster than Marlowe could follow along. "From what you've described, you're asking Miss Banks to play a character who's pivotal to the storyline of the entire series."

"In theory." Greg shifted behind his desk. "But in a tangential kind of way."

"Didn't sound tangential to me." Sanaya stood and tucked the contract into her briefcase. "I'm going to review this with Miss Banks. I understand time is of the essence so we'll get back to you by end of day with an acceptance, rejection, or any proposed amendments. However"—she looked Greg square in the eye—"if this idea is to be considered, expect to come up with ten thousand or your contract is basically kindling."

With a round of handshakes, Marlowe headed out of the building with Sanaya, squinting against the late-morning sun. They grabbed coffee at the little shop on the studio lot. Under the welcome shade of an umbrella, they talked through the contract until Marlowe grasped the terms, which included clauses about nudity, the suggestion of nudity, and the potential for a stand-in's nudity. Sanaya assured her they were standard and she needn't worry. She should pay more attention to the nondisclosure section, which dictated hefty fines for leaking storylines. Marlowe wasn't allowed to tell anyone about her role until the PR department released the information. She swiftly convinced Sanaya this wouldn't be a problem. Sure, she might be tempted to tell her friends in New York, but the idea of surprising them later held more appeal. And since she didn't know anyone in L.A. who wasn't on the show, pressure to mention her role would be minimal.

"Then I think we've covered everything." Sanaya crossed out *$3,000* and wrote in *$10,000* while Marlowe tried not to gape. "You'll lose a third of that in taxes but you deserve better than cab fare for what they're asking of you. Filming might only be three days, but since this is a PR grab, you can expect some public interface."

Marlowe thought back to her conversation with Angus.

"You mean promoting the show?" she asked.

"A bit, sure, but these days it's not the official PR you have to worry about."

Right, Marlowe thought. *The Twitter storm. The talk show jokes. The uninformed judgments. The sinking feeling that people are laughing at me. All because of a look.*

While Marlowe's thoughts swam, Sanaya patted the contract.

"We made sure the essentials are in here," she said. "They can't ask you to take off your clothes, perform stunts, alter your weight or appearance, or do anything else that dramatically changes your requirements. Well, they can ask, but then you could renegotiate for more money, or you could simply say no." She held out a pen. "I don't think you have anything to worry about, not if Angus is keeping an eye on you. He can be a bit hard-edged sometimes, but he's one of the good ones, you know?"

Marlowe eked out an uncertain smile as she took the pen. She didn't know Angus well enough to rate him good, bad, or indifferent, but he'd shown signs that he was less like Jake Hatchet than she'd once believed. And while she didn't buy into the whole man-as-protector idea, she wasn't about to turn away help when it was offered, especially in an area where she was way out of her depth.

She looked through the contract again, surprised she hadn't already declined the offer and returned to the wardrobe building. But $10,000 stared up at her, willing her to sign. Admittedly, she also knew this was a once-in-a-lifetime opportunity. It was a risk, but risks brought excitement, and she'd had precious little excitement recently. So, with a few deep breaths and a prayer to the patron saint of the introverted—whoever that might be—she signed the contract and initialed Sanaya's changes. And just like that, she'd agreed to become all-American Adelaide: waitress, heartbreaker, bride.

Wait . . . bride?

As the word sank into Marlowe's brain, her eyes drifted eastward and another choice flashed through her memory. In rapid-fire snapshots, she relived conversations about guest lists, cake flavors, reception halls, flower arrangements, and invitations that'd been printed but not sent. A ring returned. A dress selected but never purchased. A date, not far from today. A parallel life not lived.

Funny the way the universe worked sometimes. As it turned out, saying a few lines on camera might end up being the least of her concerns.

Chapter Eleven

Marlowe tucked herself against the shaded side of the wardrobe building, stalling for time. The second she stepped inside, she'd be bombarded with questions about her meeting with the producers. Cherry and Elaine would be enthusiastic but Babs would be unbearable. She wouldn't fire Marlowe or openly punish her for taking the role. Such gestures would make her look ungracious, but the impossible tasks would pile up. The disdain would sharpen. One way or another, Babs would ensure Marlowe knew her place.

Marlowe bought herself a few extra minutes by checking her messages.

Nat: I met Tony Kushner! Call me tonight. My turn to gush

Chloe: Sent you the script. LMK what you think

Heather: My sister confirmed. Moving out by Halloween. Come back!!!!!

Mom: Got mail for you from Yale. Should I forward? How are those loans?

Kelvin: You know this isn't right. Can we at least talk about it?
Kelvin: sfsjhgfjadkgdhgd
Kelvin: Sorry. Butt text. Mortified

Mildly amused, Marlowe deleted the last two texts but she stopped there, staring at the familiar, insidious question mark. Half of her brain said *Let go. Delete. Move on.* The other half—or, more honestly, the other 51 percent—urged her to have the requested conversation. The bride idea had shaken her up, reminding her how much less alone she'd be now if she'd made another choice back in New York. Minutes ago, she'd signed a contract to act in a massive hit TV show, and in an actual role with a story arc. Sure, it wasn't the creative pinnacle she'd been striving for. In fact, it terrified her, but it was a big goddamned deal. Now here she was, heading straight back to work as if nothing had happened. If she hadn't broken up with Kelvin, they'd be on the phone right now, giddily sharing the secret. He'd cheer her on, full of support. He'd make her feel as if she'd accomplished something, even if all she really did was throw on a waitress outfit at an opportune moment. And accidentally cry during a screen test.

Unable to hit *delete*, Marlowe left the remaining messages to deal with later. Then she stopped stalling and returned to work. Elaine was busy fitting background actors but Cherry and Babs were sitting in the design office at a pair of opposing desks. Babs picked shredded cheese off what looked like a spinach salad while Cherry typed at a computer, probably skipping lunch entirely to attend to Babs's latest urgent requests. Both women looked up as Marlowe entered the room.

"Well?" Cherry asked. "What's the verdict?"

Marlowe bit her lip as she darted a look at Babs. Babs merely blinked, her expression placid, though somehow it also reeked of thinly veiled contempt.

"Three days of shooting," Marlowe said. "Two on set. One on location. And they'll hire a replacement PA for the days I'm not working here."

"But they made the offer," Cherry clarified. "And you took it?"

Marlowe glanced at Babs again.

"Don't look at me." Babs flicked a hand, bangles jangling. "Anyone can cover for you here. What you do in this department is hardly skilled labor. If you want to run off and pretend to be an actress for a few days, who am I to stand in your way?"

"Thanks, I think?" Marlowe turned back to Cherry. "Yeah. It's all signed."

"Woohoo!" Cherry pumped her fists into the air. "We get to costume you for real now. Did they tell you what you'd be shooting? More diner stuff in the uniform?"

Yet again Marlowe looked at Babs. Babs's brows tilted up as though she couldn't be bothered to shift more than one facial feature for anything Marlowe had to say. Unsure if that would remain the case, Marlowe braced herself against Cherry's desk.

"Two days in the uniform," she said. "One in a wedding dress."

Babs's chair ground across the floor as she stood and tugged down her jacket.

"Guess I have some calls to make. First an orgy. Now a wedding. Do they think we vomit up clothes in here?" She flashed Cherry and Marlowe a tight smile as she marched out of the room with her percussive heels and bracelets.

Marlowe dropped into a nearby chair, letting the tension in her neck uncoil.

"My character's a waitress," she said. "We can get a dress at any chain store."

Cherry broke into a laugh. "You think she's mad about the *dress*? Seriously, Banks?" She continued to chuckle. "I can't believe you have to marry that jackass."

"Right. I mean, no. I don't. I marry someone else. Angus—I mean Jake—gets ditched for another guy. Also . . . I'm not sure he's really a jackass."

Cherry's laugh cut short. "Pleeeeease tell me you didn't drink the Gordon Kool-Aid." She leaned back in her chair, splaying out her slender limbs and going limp. "What is it with straight girls? Toss an unmown square jaw and a six-pack on a guy and you all clamor for smelling salts. I thought you saw past all that."

"I did. I do."

"Then why are you blushing?"

"I'm not!" Marlowe snatched a wad of tangled paper clips off Cherry's desk and began extracting one from another. She forced herself to focus on the interlaced curves, but as Cherry stared at her, painted head to toe in disbelief, Marlowe stopped fidgeting. "Okay, so I find him attractive. Trust me when I say I wish I didn't, but that's not what I'm talking about. You know the weirdness earlier this week when he suddenly needed jeans? He wanted to explain industry expectations. He even called his agent to negotiate my contract for me. He's gone out of his way to help me deal with a situation that frankly scares the crap out of me. He also—" She halted before mentioning lunch, and the roses, and the smoothie. They weren't professional assistance. So what were they?

"He also *what*?" Cherry prompted, her voice thick with suggestion.

"Nothing. He pushed a shopping cart. Whatever." Marlowe renewed her focus on the paper clips, certain her blush had returned and at two or three times its prior heat. "My point is, he's been nice. And I don't want to pretend I don't appreciate his kindness because I'm trying to shut down my physical attraction as fast as possible."

Cherry narrowed her eyes. "You know he's back with what's-her-name? The one with the lips and the hair." She mimed flicking dense locks off her shoulders the way Tanareve did in her Clairol commercials.

Marlowe ran a hand down her own lifeless ponytail. "Yeah. I know."

"And half the day players on this show have visited his trailer. I swear the security guard who stands outside is only there to make sure one girl enters at a time."

"I'm not going anywhere near his trailer."

"And you vowed, no more narcissists."

"I *know*, and I meant it, but is he really—?"

"Yes. He *is* really." Cherry pulled up Angus's Instagram account and skimmed through pics with Marlowe. Most were filtered shots of Angus in poses that showed off his physique, twisting his torso or folding an arm behind his head so his bicep bulged. The account also included black-and-white portraits with *I dare you* looks directed at the camera, and not-quite-believably-candid shots of him laughing with friends or locked in perfect rom-com moments with Tanareve. "It's selfie central. He can't get enough of himself. Can you imagine? I think my last Insta post was a brownie I inhaled on my ten-second lunch break last week. Or those limited-edition Fluevog shoes I'll never afford."

Marlowe dropped her chin into her hand as she watched pics flash past. "My account only has about twenty followers and ten posts," she said. "A few grad school photos. Clothes I wanted my friends' opinions on but couldn't talk myself into buying. I'm pretty sure my last post was a photo of Edith Head I took the first time I dropped her off in doggy daycare. The likeness is amazing. Minus the glasses."

"You should see her in a wig." Cherry skimmed back up to Angus's most recent shots. "Whoa. What's this?" She clicked on a photo in which Angus handed off a trio of shopping bags while Marlowe stood among the other items she'd unloaded from her trunk, already holding five or six bags herself. The shot was posted Monday. The caption read: *Helping with crew errands (and sneaking in an extra lifting session).* "Dude can't hold out a bag without using the opportunity to make himself look like some kind of hero. He's hardly lifting a bus off you. And what's this 'crew errands' shit? Like he was soooooo gracious to assist us lowly crew folks with our menial tasks. You hardly went to him begging for assistance. He's the one who hijacked your workday. Who even took this shot? Does he hire staff to follow him around and snap a pic every time he flexes?"

Marlowe's stomach sank. She didn't recall seeing any of his entourage that evening, but she and Angus were hardly in a private setting. Anyone allowed on the studio lot could've passed by and taken the pic. Still, the moment had felt sweet to her, intimate, shared between two people, not something to blast out to his massive fan base.

"I thought he was just helping me out," she said.

"More like helping himself out."

"I guess." Marlowe peered closer, wondering why Angus would post a photo of the two of them together when it would only increase his fans' curiosity in their supposed connection. Unless he was trying to make sure his fans didn't view her as a romantic prospect, not like the polished version of herself people had seen on TV, but the "crew" version with her unkempt hair, lack of makeup, overwashed Target wardrobe, and car that looked one gasp away from being junked for parts. Or maybe Cherry was right. He just wanted another chance to flex. "Point taken. He's still a pompous ass."

Cherry swung an arm over Marlowe's shoulders and pulled her into a side hug.

"I know you've had a hard time of it with the guy you left in New York," she said. "If you want a rebound, I'll help you find one. I just think he should be a guy who treats you like an equal. A guy who helps because he wants to make your life easier, not so he can solicit praise from his fans. A guy who won't put a check mark next to fangirl number two hundred and twelve and then move on to number two hundred and thirteen."

Marlowe nodded against Cherry's shoulder, weighed down by the dull ache of disappointment. She already knew dating Angus wasn't an option, but she had started to wonder if he might eventually become a friend. Now she didn't know what he was.

"Don't worry," she said. "I won't be number two hundred and anything."

Chapter Twelve

Marlowe crunched down on her dry toast, wishing she'd remembered to stop for butter on her way home from work last night. She hadn't thought of it after staying at the lot until midnight to size and label all the men's dress shirts as per Babs's latest request. It was now four hours later, and the sky was dark outside her kitchen window. The street was quiet. Her call time for her first day as Adelaide was 5:00 A.M. and she wasn't a morning person. She wasn't really a night person or an afternoon person, either, but mornings were definitely the worst. Two days ago, her contract had seemed generous. Extravagant, even. Now she wished she'd pulled a diva and negotiated a sleep-in clause.

While washing down her toast with almost unbearably strong coffee, she skimmed her mom's marathon training update and her dad's announcement about his recent article in *The Scientific Journal*. How had two such consistent overachievers given birth to a girl who couldn't stock a refrigerator or fully open her eyes before 7:00 A.M.? Her friends had also started a funny text thread of memes about kicking out Heather's sister early, so Marlowe could move in when her contract ended in five weeks, five weeks that sounded like a lot less time than six weeks, for a girl without a plan.

Somehow Marlowe got herself to set, where she was installed in a trailer and assessed by no fewer than six experts who all had opinions on her complexion, her hair, the shape of her face, and how to turn her from a real ordinary girl into a fake ordinary girl. By the time a plan was in place, Marlowe realized why she'd been called to set so early. She wasn't a background player this time, able to appear on-screen as a slightly polished version of herself. She had to match the rest of the world. In order to achieve this highly ambitious goal, her hair was highlighted, cut, and styled into a more dramatic version of her previous ponytail, complete with face-framing tendrils that were carefully extracted from an elastic. Her brows were waxed and plucked. Her lashes were extended. Her nails were painted and then carefully chipped. When the assistants had completed the broader strokes, Ravi, one of the head makeup artists, spent over an hour applying liners and powders while repeatedly assuring Marlowe the goal was for her to look natural. Oh, the irony.

"You're supposed to draw attention to this," Ravi said as he drew a large freckle on her left earlobe. "That's how Jake recognizes you as the girl from his past."

Marlowe played with her earlobe, testing variations of the gesture while trying to recognize herself with her blemishes concealed and with every hair in place—except for the hair that was intentionally out of place. She was still experimenting when Cherry arrived, looking effortlessly fabulous, as always, in a sharp black blazer and with her spiky topknot brushing the doorframe. She paused in the doorway, a garment bag in one hand, the other hand pressed to her chest.

"Aww. Look at you. My baby girl's all grown up."

Marlowe gingerly patted her head. "I'm afraid to move or I'll ruin something."

"Relax." Ravi laughed while cleaning brushes. "You have nothing to worry about. We shellac you. And someone will be on set to make sure you don't shine."

He soon stepped out so Marlowe could get dressed. Cherry unpacked the garment bag and handed off the underwear Babs had picked out during the fitting a few days ago: a padded bra that turned Marlowe from barely a B cup into a rather assertive C cup, and contoured underpants that amplified her hips and butt. Marlowe put them on and assessed her reflection in the trifold mirror at the end of the trailer.

"Don't you think audiences will notice the difference?" She turned sideways, marveling at her profile. "I had no boobs at all in the other episode. No butt, either."

"With so many episodes between your appearances, most people won't catch on. Anyone who does will talk about it on Twitter. Hashtag waitress got a boob job."

"It's ridiculous." Marlowe took the uniform from Cherry and slipped it on. "We're perpetuating a myth that only girls with hourglass figures deserve male attention. We're also making the bar for looking 'natural' completely out of reach for anyone without a six-person crew and hundreds of dollars of hair and make-up products. Why can't a small-town, middle-America, minimum-wage waitress look like a real woman?"

Cherry flicked her wrists and adopted a dramatic, Babs-like tone. "You foolish girl! You know *nothing* about working in television. You and your little theater career. What do they even teach you at Yale?! Watch and learn, dear. Watch and learn."

Marlowe laughed as she fastened her buttons, but soon she was shaking her head at her lowered neckline and shortened hem. Babs had a good eye for fit. The changes were flattering on Marlowe's figure—her fake figure. They were also unnecessary.

With an odd sense of nostalgia for the old uniform, Marlowe sat down to complete the outfit with white ankle socks and canvas sneakers.

"At least Babs didn't put me in heels," she said.

"Only because you're tall. You think the hourglass myth is prevalent? I dare you to name a single hetero on-screen couple where the guy's shorter than the girl."

Marlowe thought about it as she laced up the sneakers. Such couples had to exist, but Cherry was right, she couldn't name a single one off the top of her head.

"Oh, shit!" Cherry dug through an accessory bag. "I almost forgot. Babs would kill me if she found you on set without this." She pulled out a silver chain linked through an impressive rhinestone ring. "That fiancé of yours is quite the big spender."

Marlowe slipped the chain over her neck. The ring was cold, hard, and sharp against her chest. Though it bore little resemblance to the simple engraved band Kelvin had given her, it stirred up enough feelings to make it seem like an exact replica.

Cherry set a hand on her arm. "You're thinking about Bench Boy, aren't you?"

"If I was a real actress, I'd say no and you might actually believe me." Marlowe pressed the ring against her breastbone. Still cold. Still hard. Still sharp.

"You *are* a real actress. They made you audition. You earned the role." Cherry drew Marlowe's hand away from the ring. "This calls for an intervention. Since we have the weekend off and we can sleep in as late as we want tomorrow, let's go out dancing tonight. We'll celebrate your first day as a 'real actress.' We can even work on that rebound plan. I'll gather a group."

"Anyone particular in that group?" Marlowe hinted, already knowing the answer.

"Oh, just some of the girls from the costume shop. Ravi and Patrice will probably be game. But if the new script supervisor also *happens* to make an appearance, I won't complain."

"If she shows, the first round of drinks is on me."

One of the ADs led Marlowe into the diner when they were ready for her. Introductions were made with the other actors who were part of the scene, including Angus, Idi, Kamala, Janie, Meg, and Whitman. Together the six of them made up the core cast, playing a group of lifelong friends who fought and loved each other in equal measure. Some of the cast recalled Marlowe from fittings or other costume-related business. Others mentioned the #IShipTheWaitress tweets and videos while she tried to hide her embarrassment, cringing at every reenacted punch line.

Angus stayed notably quiet through it all, standing to the side in dark jeans, a thin gray T-shirt, and Jake's trademark leather jacket. His costume was similar to his personal wardrobe but the fit was tighter. The colors were darker. The textures were dirty and gritty. Everything had hard edges, from the sculpted jacket to the square-toed motorcycle boots to the gelled-back hairstyle that held on to the grooves from a comb. The differences added up, made even more noticeable by his unexpected remove. Marlowe might've questioned his lack of friendliness, but Lex—the same director who was on Marlowe's earlier episode—wandered over and called the group to order.

As the six leads tucked into their corner booth, surrounded by lights, sound equipment, cameras, and crew, Lex talked Marlowe through the action. The dialogue would unfold in the booth. Marlowe would drop off pie or beverages on cue. Angus would track her movement, building a sense of recognition as the scene transpired.

"You know who Jake is," Lex told Marlowe. "But you hope he doesn't know who you are. You're curious, anxious. You're about to be married. You don't want to ruin your relationship by holding on to what-ifs about some other guy. But also"—he tipped his chin at Angus, who was listening from his seat at the edge of the booth—"you want to tear off Jake's clothes. That sense of desire has to reach straight through the camera."

Marlowe's face ignited. She risked a glance at Angus, who made no attempt to hide an amused smirk. The *You know you want me* look was back. Ironically, it was the look that made her want nothing to do with him at all.

For the next two hours, Lex and his crew shot the scene he'd described, capturing take after take with slight variations and careful attention to continuity. Marlowe played her role as instructed, acting more by instinct than by an ability to embrace and express everything Lex had asked of her. Curious and anxious? No problem. Not wanting to get involved with the hot guy in the leather jacket? Check. Wanting to tear his clothes off anyway? Harder, but not a complete stretch of the imagination.

It wasn't his toned body or his pretty face that drew her in. It was the way he looked at her, studying her as though he wouldn't be content until he understood some key secret about her. Three months ago, that look had made her uncomfortable. It was too intense. Too direct. Too long and unwavering. Now that she'd seen Angus study severed threads and marabou slippers in a similar way, his stare was no longer intimidating. He wasn't judging. He just wanted to know. And maybe, buried under umpteen layers of defense mechanisms, she wanted to be known.

When the crew took their first break, Marlowe headed outside and tucked herself behind the diner where she could escape into her phone. Her friends in New York had a group text going about a trashy but entertaining reality show they were all watching, one Marlowe hadn't found time for past the pilot episode. She hadn't found time to read Chloe's script, either. She usually got home with just enough time to eat, sleep, and get up to return to work. Days off were about laundry and groceries and tracking down the landlord so he'd fix the pipes or whatever else had broken. Besides, her friends were all watching the show together. She'd be watching it alone. Like everything else she did.

With that thought, she pulled up another text that tugged at her heart.

Kelvin: You know this isn't right. Can we at least talk about it?

The text was *still* haunting her. She shouldn't let it. He was doing what he always did: telling her what she should think rather than asking. She'd said it was over. She'd said she was sure. So why couldn't she delete the text and block him already?

"If I give you my number, will you quit ignoring me?" a deep voice asked to her left. It was Angus, walking toward her, rubbing at his chin in that already familiar way. Maybe he was drawn to the stubble. It was probably softer than it looked and it made him want to pet himself, though that thought conjured another image entirely.

Marlowe pocketed her phone, stuck between one conundrum and another.

"I'm supposed to ignore you," she said. "Lex told me Adelaide—"

"I'm not talking about Adelaide." He stopped a few feet away and leaned a shoulder against the pebbled wall. "I thought you might let me know you took the role. I had to hear about your meeting from Sanaya. You're welcome, by the way."

"Right. Sorry. Thank you. Getting her to help with my contract was amazing. Beyond amazing. I should've said something. But how would I even—?"

He cut her off with a look. One that said she knew damned well how. They worked on the same lot. She got a call sheet every day. She knew where he'd be and when. She could've knocked on his trailer, swung by the set, or left a note with his security guard. She could've passed a message through Cherry or Elaine, who attended most of his fittings while Babs kept Marlowe as far away as possible. She could've sent him a massive order of serrated strawberries. It would've reached him.

"I had a good time the other day," he said. "It was a nice break from all of this." He flapped a hand toward the front of the diner, roughly indicating the milling crew and vast sprawl of electrical equipment. "It felt normal, in a good way, even though you bought, like, four hundred pairs of shoes. I guess I didn't realize that was it."

She eyed him sideways. "Why wouldn't that be it?"

"Because you still think I'm an asshole?"

"Because we lead *completely* different lives."

"Maybe they're not as different as you think."

"Are you kidding?" She choked out a laugh. "I spend fourteen hours a day hauling shopping bags or taping receipts to eight-and-a-half-by-eleven sheets of paper so they can be copied in triplicate as though we don't have budget apps for this stuff. I take actresses shopping for six-hundred-dollar shoes because one of them found out hers only cost half as much as her costar's and now she demands equal treatment. I track down black fabric to replace blue fabric because a director looked at Xeroxed research instead of a colored costume sketch and we have to rebuild a ball gown so it matches his mistaken vision. I pick sesame seeds off my boss's hamburger bun even though she hasn't eaten a bread product in years. I grovel. I bury my passion and opinions. I 'pay my dues.'"

Angus crossed his arms and dropped the casual lean.

"And you think everything in life is easy for me?" he asked.

"No. I know you have your own crap to deal with, but it's different. You show up and doors open for you. You don't have to prove anything to anyone."

"Apparently I have to prove something to you."

Marlowe rotated to face him straight on, prickling with defensiveness.

"Don't act like you don't know what I mean. You're rich. You're famous. You're also"—she frowned, regarded him, searched for the right word—"confusing."

His brows shot up. "Confusing how?"

"I don't know." She blew out a breath, wishing she'd kept her mouth shut. But now that she'd started . . . "Flowers. Lunch. Your agent. The smoothie. I can't tell if you're being friendly or flirting or expecting me to return the favors somehow. But also, all that stuff on social media. The manufactured perfect lifestyle. The idyllic couple shots. The look-how-hot-I-am selfies. The self-congratulatory or condescending Instagram captions. It's not my scene. I think it makes other people feel shitty about their own lives, which is a task most of us manage well enough without help."

His jaw shifted as his shoulders squared with hers. Everything about him seemed to ratchet a notch tighter. Marlowe braced for a rebuke, but Angus didn't make one. Instead, he threw back his head and rubbed his face with both hands.

"Of course," he muttered into his hands. "Of fucking course."

Marlowe took a step back, buying herself space.

"What?" she asked. "What did I say?"

For a painfully long moment he just stood there, running his hands over his face and shaking his head skyward, but eventually he rolled his head forward to look at her.

"I'm such an idiot," he said. "I had this crazy notion that because you were a costumer you knew the difference between reality and appearances. 'She does this for a living,' I thought. 'She knows you're not Jake or Kip or some bullshit version of yourself publicity people invent to build a fan base. She knows what's fake.'" He backed away from her, still shaking his head as though he was trying to rid himself of a painful but persistent thought. "I thought you'd judge me based on who I was when I was right in front of you. I thought you'd give me a chance. Turns out you're just like everyone else." He threw up his hands as he spun away and headed toward the front of the diner.

Marlowe watched him, open-mouthed, torn between wanting to defend herself and wondering if she had a right to do so. Before she could even begin to sort through the possibilities, he whipped around and marched toward her.

"Just so we're totally clear," he said, "the flowers were a sincere and deserved apology. The offer to buy you lunch was an attempt to do something nice for someone who spent her whole day taking care of other people. An attempt you foiled by trying to prove I was a food snob, which I'm not. Sending in my agent was an act of basic human decency. The producers were hovering like vultures after that hashtag broke. I don't care who you are. No one deserves to be treated like carnage to pick at. And the smoothie"—he pressed his lips together, locked his eyes on hers—"*that* was flirting."

He held her gaze a moment longer.

Then he turned and walked away.

Chapter Thirteen

A strident techno beat pounded in Marlowe's ears as she trudged through the crowded club behind Cherry and the other crewmembers. Pink and blue neon tubes framed every wall, giving the space a 1980s jukebox feel. A pair of DJs spun tracks on a balcony at the opposite end of the room while a tight mass of at least three hundred people bounced to the beat on a dance floor. Countless kitschy toys dangled from above, completely obscuring the ceiling. Rusted jack-in-the-boxes hung limply from their cubes while creepy dolls with matted hair ogled the dancers. Tricycles hung down between Slinkys and stuffed animals. The panoply of lost childhood was an odd design choice against the neon and techno, but few people present had their eyes trained upward.

Marlowe was one of those few. She took in the scenery as she dodged elbows and attempted to keep up with the rest of her group. After fighting with Angus and then filming for three more hours as though everything was fine between them, she was in no mood to go dancing. She'd said as much, but Cherry had already laid the groundwork for her crush to consider coming. Marlowe didn't need to dance, but she did need to be here.

"First round's on me!" Cherry shouted over the noise, collecting orders while the group claimed squatter's rights on a high top that was vacating.

As Cherry's spiky topknot disappeared into the crowd, Ravi fled to the dance floor with two of the other makeup artists. Marlowe grabbed napkins and wiped spilled beer off the table. Patrice, one of the key hairstylists, found a chair they could pile with shed clothing or personal belongings. The gesture was barely necessary since everyone had carpooled over from the studio and most had shed their extra layers back in the parking lot. Marlowe was the only who didn't know the drill. Her last club outing had involved a subway ride, several layers of winter gear, and no convenient trunks in which to store anything. Score one for L.A.

Already sweating from the sheer mass of bodies around her, Marlowe shimmied out of the bland linen blouse she'd thrown on early that morning, leaving her in a white spaghetti-strap tank top and a short black skirt she'd bought for its ample cargo pockets. If she ever gave up costuming and went into fashion, she'd crusade for more pockets on women's clothing, and not the decorative pockets, but the ones that could actually hold stuff.

Cherry soon returned with a tray of cocktails and a round of tequila shots for anyone who wanted one and wasn't driving. Marlowe was not driving. Her car was back at the studio lot, where she planned to leave it for the weekend. After a quick survey of drinking plans and Uber or Lyft options for returning to the studio as needed, Ravi and Cherry had volunteered to drive everyone that night. Marlowe had also volunteered, but with one look at her dilapidated vehicle, the group took up Cherry's and Ravi's offers instead.

Now that they were all at the club, Marlowe was glad no one

had wanted her to drive. Dancing might have lost its appeal, but drinking had not. Not that she was much of a drinker. She was a lightweight, but the week had exhausted her, she wasn't home alone to drink herself into a puddle of extreme loneliness, and she was desperate to loosen the tension that'd coiled up inside her on set. So she grabbed one of the shots and braced for the burn.

Cherry held up her soda glass. "To the waitress!"

Everyone joined in the toast and tipped back their drinks. Marlowe shook off the initial sting and let the warm, jelly-like feeling settle into her joints. Damn, it felt good. As if she'd been gripping the edge of a cliff for days and she could finally let go and fall.

Cherry glanced around the room. "So, who are we looking at?"

Marlowe located her whiskey sour, using it to cut the tequila burn.

"Who are we looking at for what?" she asked.

"Your rebound. He has to be hot enough for you to enjoy gawking at him naked but dull enough to make you want to ditch him once you're done."

Marlowe practically spat out her drink. Before she could form a coherent reply, the rest of the group leapt on board, scanning the crowd and pegging three possible targets: a hipster with a waxed moustache and a vest that showed off his fit arms, the tallest member of an oxford-clad quartet that seemed to have arrived straight from the office, and a heavily tattooed guy busting moves on the corner of the dance floor.

Mid-debate about Marlowe's best plan of attack, Cherry grabbed her arm.

"Holy shit. She showed."

Marlowe followed Cherry's gaze to see a short, smiling woman in a rayon dress elbowing her way through the crowd. She wore pearl earrings and her dense black curls were twisted up in a red scarf, making her look like she'd stepped out of an old painting.

"She's cute," Marlowe said.

"Cute?" Cherry shook her head. "She's more than cute. Her name is Maria Louisa Sofia Liliana and I want to whisper every last one of those names against her perfect ear."

With some effort, Maria made it to the table. Everyone introduced themselves while Cherry and Maria exchanged just enough coy looks to suggest Cherry might get her wish, maybe not that night, but in time. The thought filled Marlowe with joy. No matter what happened with her own love life—or lack thereof—Cherry deserved to be happy. From the looks of things so far, that achievement had already been unlocked.

Marlowe purchased the next round of drinks, as promised. By the time she'd emptied her glass, she was ready to surrender to the energetic club vibe. The people. The throbbing music. The adrenaline. The total lack of beige. Patrice let down Marlowe's ponytail and gave her hair a professional fluff. Cherry helped her apply a fresh coat of red lipstick and rubbed away her smudged mascara. With a chorus of encouragement from the group, Marlowe plunged into the crowd on the dance floor, where she quickly spotted Ravi and the other makeup artists. They welcomed her into their circle with more cheers.

She started off timid, barely moving, but soon she was bouncing along with everyone else, arms swinging, hips swaying, lost in a feeling of pure release. When she accidentally spun into a buff guy in a black dress shirt and he started grinding against her, she didn't resist. She leaned into the motion. The contact felt good, a strong body pressed against hers. The friction of thighs against thighs. Heat. Sweat. Touch. A hand set low on her back, drawing her close.

Her skirt hem inching higher. Bare, wet skin. An unexpected moment of eye contact. A sucked-in breath. A jolt of anticipation.

Hmm, Marlowe thought. *Maybe Cherry's right. A rebound isn't such a terrible idea.*

The music shifted. A heavy downbeat. Machines pumped out smoke. Lights flashed in hot magenta and icy blue. Marlowe felt herself get passed from one guy to another. Someone tall. Lanky. A tousled tuft of black curls. One hand on her waist, the other gripping her hand, spinning her away and drawing her back again, hips against hips. Dark brown eyes. Parted lips, dewy with moisture. A salsa step. Maybe. Face-to-face. Another turn. Backing against him, arms raised as his fingertips skimmed from her wrists to her elbows, carrying on to her waist and hips, igniting a sharp sense of want she'd been trying to bury for months. He held her against him, his breath hot against the side of her neck. He stepped forward, back, and then spun her away again. Only to pull her in.

God, she'd missed this. No wonder her entire body had tingled when Angus brushed past her in her car last week. No matter how many times she'd told herself she didn't need a man in her life, the days without physical connection added up, hollowing her, leaving her feeling a little less real, a little less solid, until she might as well be a ghost. Now, with every hand on her back, her hip, her neck, she became more herself.

Or so she thought until a leering creep with a toothy grin grabbed her ass.

Marlowe stopped short and shot the guy a violent glare, willing him to wither and vanish. When he continued to hover as though her glare was an indication of her interest rather than her repulsion—seriously, where did men get their confidence?—she decided she had two options: punch him or slip away and go pee.

The restroom was cramped and dark, with black cinderblock walls covered in graffiti and cheaply printed posters. Marlowe caught a glimpse of her reflection as she stepped up to a sink to wash her hands. She'd forgotten about the highlights, lash extensions, and other upgrades she'd received that morning. Admittedly, she liked the changes, even if they were far too glamorous for her character. She felt a little less invisible, in a good way, though maybe she was riding endorphins from the dance floor. And maybe the guy in the black dress shirt was still back there.

"Oh, my god," came a light, breathy voice behind her. "You're the waitress."

Marlowe stiffened as she spun around, madly preparing a lie, but the lie fell away as soon as she saw the woman before her. She was about Marlowe's age, with an athletic build and flawless tanned skin. Her pink chiffon halter dress was obviously couture and she wore the kind of strappy high heels Marlowe would've toppled over in the second she tried to stand. Marlowe might've recognized the woman's face, even in a grungy public restroom, but it was the thick, chestnut hair that cemented her as Tanareve Hughes.

"The waitress, yeah. I guess so." Marlowe looked down, newly self-conscious of her cheap, sweat-soaked tank top and thrifted cargo skirt. Clearly, the universe hated her. Right when she'd stopped stressing about the day's events, she had to run into Angus's girlfriend. Angus's gorgeous, fit, perfectly coifed, amazingly dressed girlfriend.

Marlowe was about to say she recognized Tanareve, but before she got the words out, Tanareve's arms circled her shoulders and pulled her into a tight hug.

"I knew it! Marlowe, right? I'm Tanareve, or Tan, whichever you prefer. I'm not a creepy stalker fan, I swear. We have some mutual friends." She released her hold and took a breath, giving Marlowe a second to appreciate that Tanareve didn't assume her fame preceded her. "Sorry. I'm a lot. I know. I'm just so excited to meet you! It was your first day today, right? I bet it was crazy. Angus said you did great. A total pro. Didn't even seem nervous. You must be celebrating. Funny that we all ended up here. The Hollywood club scene is so tiny everyone bumps into everyone else. Am I right?"

"Sure, I guess?" Marlowe faltered, this being her first time in a Hollywood club. Also, what did Tanareve mean by *we ALL ended up here*? And Angus said *what*?

"I'm celebrating just because," Tanareve continued, speaking so quickly Marlowe had to strain to keep up. "With the right company, anything's a party. We're playing Shot in the Dark. Have you played? Idi and Whitman are playing with me. Angus is here, too, but he leaves the drinking games to the rest of us. His body is his temple. It's amazing I dragged him out tonight. This is *so* not his scene, but now we can all celebrate together. You *have* to join us." She let out a little squeal of excitement as she washed her hands.

Marlowe edged toward the door. "I'm not sure that's such a good idea."

"Don't be silly. You at least have to come say hi. Who knows when we'll get the chance to hang out again? I want to hear *everything*. How many takes? Did they stick to the script? Did Angus behave himself? I bet he stared a lot. God, the staring! What is that about?" She laughed in a bright, impossibly cheerful way and Marlowe couldn't help but laugh with her. Tanareve's energy was a lot to take in, but she was like a bulldozer made of pinwheels and twinkle lights, one that suggested getting run over might feel okay.

Despite a continued protest, Tanareve was soon dragging Marlowe by the wrist through the crowd, rattling on blithely while 90 percent of her words got lost in the din. As the two of them eased out of the tight swarm of bodies, Marlowe spotted Idi and Whitman standing at the bar, lining up shot glasses. Around the corner from them, facing away from her, was a guy with a familiar head of red—or whatever color it was—hair and a broad back packed into a snug white T-shirt. Marlowe tensed but she continued to stumble onward, lacking a viable escape plan. Lacking any escape plan.

Idi was the first to spot her, breaking into an easy smile with gentle eyes and deep dimples in both cheeks. He was friendly both on camera and off, and the bright red toque that pressed his dreads downward gave him an almost childlike appearance.

"Look who you found!" he called as they reached the bar.

Whitman offered up a warm greeting but as Angus turned around and caught Marlowe's eye, his lips pressed together and he settled into a pronounced glower.

"Of all the gin joints . . ." he pushed through clenched teeth.

"I tried." Marlowe tipped her head at Tanareve, who still had hold of her wrist.

His glower brightened a little as if in recognition of the unstoppable force that was his girlfriend. Then he turned away and gulped down a tall glass of what Marlowe hoped was water. It had to be water. Anything harder would've knocked him flat.

"How are you feeling about your first day?" Whitman called over the rumble of the crowd and the thumping music. He was blond and blue-eyed, quick with a laugh or a smile. He wore a faded black concert T-shirt, though Marlowe was used to seeing him in crisp button-downs or cashmere sweaters as the privileged rich kid on the show. "Tired of delivering fake pie while Lex tells you to smolder harder?"

"I think I can manage two more days. I'm probably done with

pie, anyway. And smoldering." Marlowe felt her wrist free up so she took a step back. "I just came to say hi. Great to see you all. Don't let me interrupt your game." She took a second step back, ready to turn and bolt, but Idi, Whitman, and Tanareve all encouraged her to stay, while Angus remained silent, his back to Marlowe, his attention glued to his glass.

"I'm here with friends." She pointed over her shoulder. "I should really—" Her third step caught on someone's foot. She teetered, leaning hard on the guy behind her. They almost toppled together, but somehow they righted themselves. As she apologized, she backed into a woman sipping a beer, causing the beer to spill down the woman's front. With a second round of apologies, Marlowe gave up trying to flee. She planted her feet and mustered a self-effacing smile. "I'm not drunk. Just clumsy."

Angus eyed her over his shoulder. "Or unlucky?"

Her smile went flat. "Or cursed."

His shoulders juddered but she couldn't tell if he was laughing with her or at her. It didn't really matter. Tanareve was already drawing her into another conversation with more rapid-fire chatter. She described her acting debut at age ten, how overwhelmed she was, and how long she took to adjust to the Hollywood scene. She even plugged her private number into Marlowe's cell in case industry questions arose and Marlowe wanted advice or a sympathetic ear. Idi and Whitman shared their own stories about their first roles. Idi recalled a vampire film that was plagued with so many natural disasters they eventually canned the whole enterprise. Whitman laughed about a minor stunt gone wrong. Marlowe tried to listen, and she loved how quickly everyone had embraced her as part of the group, but she was too aware of Angus brooding to her left, drumming his fingers on his glass and looking anywhere but at her.

Eventually she couldn't stand it anymore, so she sidled up beside him and murmured, "I'm sorry I was so judgy earlier today."

He shifted a shoulder. "Better to know now, I guess."

She frowned at that. "As opposed to?"

"After I started those garnish classes."

"Big plans with serrated strawberries?"

"Thought I'd start with carrot curls. Balsamic drizzles. The occasional olive."

"I've always had a soft spot for an occasional olive."

"I had a feeling." His lips twitched but he didn't quite smile. His posture also remained rigid while his eyes stayed locked on his glass.

Marlowe turned her attention to her right where Tanareve was deep in conversation with Idi and Whitman, her eyes bright and her gestures animated, a stark contrast with Angus's quiet and stillness. What an odd pair they made, though perhaps that was their strength. Then again, if they were so strong as a couple, why had they broken up so many times over the years? And why had he flirted?

Actually, that one was easy. Flirting was part of Angus's well-honed fan interface charm. It was probably subconscious by now, like a default switch getting flipped when female attention was available. He'd turned it on for Babs and the women in the shoe stores. Why not turn it on for Marlowe, too?

While she shook off that thought, Tanareve rallied everyone to play Shot in the Dark. Marlowe had never heard of the game, but she quickly grasped that it was a variation on Truth or Dare—mostly Dare—with the dares provided by strangers and collected in a basket to draw from. There were also plenty of opportunities to drink. Marlowe avoided the drinking while enjoying the dares. Idi belted out the refrain from a Taylor Swift song, a song half the nearby crowd was singing by the time he'd finished. Whitman swapped shirts with a stranger, much to the stranger's delight. Tanareve made a pyramid out of sixteen shot glasses but failed to balance them all and had to drink. Others got into the game, cheering each other on, but eventually all eyes were on Marlowe.

"I'm only watching," she said.

Whitman slid three shot glasses her way. "That's the skipping toll."

Marlowe eyed the shots, unsure she could manage three and remain upright.

"Angus doesn't have to pay a toll," she argued.

He raised a fresh glass of water. "Driver's privilege."

Marlowe stammered out more excuses but she wasn't at her most articulate with a few drinks already buzzing through her system and so many people watching her. She'd always floundered when under observation, and this was no exception. The voices rose and the pressure mounted until she caved and drew a slip of paper from the basket. She unfolded it and read the dare to herself. Before anyone else could read it, she crumpled it up, grabbed the nearest shot, and tossed it back.

"Looks like I lost," she said, which, of course, was when she dropped the paper.

Tanareve snatched it up and flattened it out before Marlowe could stop her.

"*Dance with the person on your left*," she read. "You can't forfeit this one. It's too easy. Anyone can manage a dance."

"Yeah, but I haven't really, and he's not, and we don't—" Marlowe backed up, rotated her body, tried desperately to ensure someone else—*anyone* else—was on her left, but the club was too crowded and she didn't get far. Idi and Whitman were already chanting for Angus to stop sulking, others joined in, and before Marlowe knew what was happening, a hand slipped around hers and she was being dragged onto the dance floor.

"You don't have to do this," she said as Angus pivoted around to face her, both of them jostled by the throng of sweaty bodies bouncing all around them.

His chin tipped up, as it so often did. "Think you can't handle it?"

"I'll 'handle it' just fine, thank you very much."

"Figured I should ask. I can't always tell what 'vibe' I'm giving off."

She rolled her eyes. Were they really going to fight again? Here? Now?

"Let's call it an *I'd rather be anywhere but here* vibe," she said.

"Bad call and untrue. I could be in a pit of snakes. Shark tank. Gulag."

"Then I'm grateful I can spare you the pain." She shot him a light sneer before closing her eyes and focusing on the downbeat, letting her body settle into just enough movement to officially complete the dare. If Angus was willing to dance with her, she could manage a few minutes of swaying in his presence. Especially with her eyes shut.

As before, the music found its way in. The crowd. The heat. The noise. The rhythm. The raw power of lost inhibitions that sparked from person to person as they pulsed en masse. Also, that last tequila shot felt amazing. Marlowe should hang out with rich people more often. They bought the good stuff. It coursed through her veins, freeing her body to twist and thrust as her arms rose over her head and she stopped holding back.

A knee grazed hers. Then another. Accidental, surely, with the crowd pressing in on all sides, but when a hand brushed her waist, her eyes popped open. Her breath caught at the sight of Angus dancing closer now, his elbows bent and his hands hovering near the waistband of her skirt. He was watching her in that way he had, as though he didn't give a damn if he got caught staring, as though there was no shame in looking at something—or someone—that piqued his curiosity. And it was . . .

Hot. Really hot. Knee-weakening, skin-tingling, how-much-did-I-drink-again hot.

Angus registered her intake of breath, leaving her three options. One: let him know he'd flustered her. Two: act like something else had unsettled her and step away to regain space. Three: pretend she was totally unfazed that he was touching her, fitting himself against her, matching her movement. The first was out of the question. The second demanded acting skills beyond her reach. Also—did she *really* want space?

As his hand settled on her waist and stayed there, she set her hands on his shoulders. Played along. That's what they were doing, right? Playing a game? Fulfilling a dare? Except his shoulders were like a dare unto themselves. Good lord.

"Tanareve seems great," Marlowe said, using the name like a shield.

"She is great." Angus inched closer, swaying with an even rhythm centered in his hips. "We've known each other for ages. She gets the whole scene. The pressures. The paparazzi. The lack of privacy. The way people think they know you from what they see on a screen." He gave Marlowe a pointed look.

She stiffened at his jibe but the tension didn't last long, not with the heat and the motion and the tequila. Also, both of Angus's hands were on her waist now and they felt good there. They probably felt good a lot of places. A thought she instantly aborted.

"So I'm not allowed to draw any conclusions about you?" she asked, a little breathless now. "Even from what you *choose* to put out into the world?"

"That's the trick, isn't it? Knowing what I've chosen." His breath gusted faster, too, laced with spearmint or peppermint. Toothpaste, probably. Clean and unpretentious.

"Why do I get the feeling you're not going to tell me?"

"Because I've wasted way too much energy defending myself to people who didn't bother getting to know me. It got me nowhere. I don't do it anymore. So you can pick through what you find on the Internet, crafting whatever version of me suits your purpose, or you can ignore all the noise and judge the person in front of you. Your call."

The person in front of me, she thought. The one with the tiger's eyes and the full lips and the strong hands gripping her waist. The one with his thumbs rubbing circles so faint she could almost convince herself they weren't moving at all. Almost.

It was all too much. After half a year of sleeping alone, showering alone, never holding a hand or snuggling on a sofa or even leaning a head on a shoulder to watch the clouds go by, Marlowe's body took over. Every warning light sputtered and went out. Every wall crumbled. Her hands laced together behind Angus's neck. Her thighs wedged more tightly against his. His hips met hers. And still, it all felt so good, so right. Maybe it shouldn't, but it was only a dance. She might as well enjoy the hell out of it.

Lights strobed. Beats overlapped as DJs blended two tracks, one loud and driving, the other softer, lower, more like the *thunk-thunk-thunk* of a heartbeat. Swaying turned into grinding. Angus's hand slid to the center of Marlowe's lower back, fingers splayed open. She arched against them, bringing her chest to his as her hands rode upward into his hair. It was softer than she'd expected, like the silken threads that dangled off cut satin. He found her skin beneath the hem of her tank top, barely, but enough to send a shiver rippling to her toes and back. Again, he registered the way she responded to him. It wasn't fair, the way he saw, the way he knew, but she didn't pull away, couldn't pull away, not when he was right there, so close and so strong and so beautiful.

That sense of desire has to reach straight through the camera, Lex had said hours earlier. The cameras were off now, and halfway across L.A., but damn if Marlowe wasn't nailing her performance. Angus wasn't exactly the picture of indifference, either. His cheeks were flushed, his eyes were glassy, and his chest was rising and falling rapidly. An effect of dancing or of something else entirely?

He skated a hand around her ear and she nearly imploded.

"You left the freckle," he said, a low, delicious, breathy rumble. "An ironic choice for Adelaide, since you have a real freckle on your ear."

"You noticed that?"

"Occupational hazard."

"Bullshit." His smile quirked up, familiar by now and yet not. Amusement? Check. Smugness? A little. But also that knowing quality, as though the time he'd spent studying her had yielded answers. The thought was terrifying. It was also exhilarating. Or it would be, if they weren't playing a game while his girlfriend waited back at the bar.

Right. His girlfriend.

Marlowe blinked herself into awareness and backed away.

"I think we can safely say I completed the assigned task," she said.

His brows lifted. "I don't think we can *safely* say much of anything right now."

"Stop flirting with me. It's not funny."

"It's not meant to be funny."

"Don't say that. If you mean it for real it's even worse."

"Wow. Seriously?" His forehead furrowed as his smile flattened.

She continued backing up, letting the crowd swallow her.

"I can't deal with this right now," she said. "I should . . . I'm going to go."

"Marlowe, wait!" He reached toward her but she was already on her way.

She elbowed her way through the crowd, mortified she'd let lust, alcohol, and latent teenage fantasies override her common sense. Maybe it was only a dance, but she couldn't claim she didn't want it to be more, and that was where her transgression lay. It wasn't right. It wasn't her. At least, it wasn't who she wanted to be. Fangirl number two hundred and whatever, drooling over a guy who was way out of her league. A guy who turned a private conversation into a social media ego boost. A guy who treated flirtation like light entertainment. A guy with a girlfriend. A really, *really* nice girlfriend.

Marlowe avoided the bar area, darting straight to the table where the *Heart's Diner* crew was still gathered, their table packed with half-empty glasses in every size and shape. She grabbed her blouse off the chair back and edged her way over to Cherry.

"I'm heading out," she said. "Thanks for the celebration."

Cherry held her at arm's length. "Whoa. Wait a sec. You okay?"

"Yeah. No. Sort of. I'm ready to go. That's all."

"Let me drive you. Just give me a minute to make sure everyone's covered."

Marlowe almost laughed. The cars that'd been so convenient a few hours ago were now a liability as drivers and rides needed sorting in a city without a subway. Score one for New York. And speaking of scores . . . She glanced across the table. Maria was laughing at something with Patrice, sneaking a sideways glance at Cherry. So cute.

"Seriously. Stay," Marlowe said. "I'll grab a Lyft. We'll catch up on Monday."

After a quick round of hugs and goodbyes, she made her exit, found a bench outside, and booked a ride. She tried to wait patiently, staring out at a sea of parked cars, but her buried wants and needs had exploded on the dance floor and they demanded her attention. She wanted to be held. To be kissed. To be touched in tender places that made her shudder and moan. Instead she was on her way home alone to face the creepy owls and the beige emptiness. She knew Angus wasn't really a possibility, only a fantasy stoked by alcohol and too much eye contact, so she opened her phone.

Kelvin: You know this isn't right. Can we at least talk about it?

She started typing a reply but her phone was whisked from her hand.

"Friends don't let friends drunk-text exes." Cherry held Marlowe's phone out of reach, staring down at her like an angry schoolmarm.

"How did you know?" Marlowe asked.

"Because you have 'bone me now' written all over you. Which

would be fine if you were leaving with a hot and charming dude who was super aware of the rules of consent. But you disappeared for over an hour so you were obviously connecting with someone, only now you're bolting on your own." She lowered the phone.

Marlowe took it and jammed it into a skirt pocket. "Am I that obvious?"

"You're that human." Cherry sat down beside Marlowe. "Look, I get it. I've wanted to reach out to my ex, too. But our relationship ended for good reason. So did yours. If having a boyfriend is important to you, find someone new. Someone better."

Marlowe chewed on that thought as Kelvin's parting words rang in her ears for the thousandth time. *You'll never find someone else as good as me.* She hated that she still gave that statement any credence at all, but thus far, she couldn't prove it wrong.

"I can't bear Tinder." She slumped forward, dropping her head in her hands. "I can't start a relationship knowing a guy met me because he swept a thumb over my face."

"What about speed dating?"

"What about a nunnery?"

"You can't join a nunnery. Too much polyester and zero waist definition." Cherry laughed a little. Marlowe tried to join in but she couldn't quite manage it.

"Maybe I should adopt a kitten," she muttered into her hands. "Get a head start on the crazy-cat-lady thing. Though I should probably ensure I have an income before I accumulate dependents. I don't even know what I'm doing after the season wraps."

"There, I might be able to help." Cherry fixed something on Marlowe's collar, patting down the point and lining up the edges, gifted as always in bringing order to chaos. "Let me talk to Babs. See if she'll bring you with us on our next project. It's a film set in a girls' rock camp. A nerdy group of underdog tweens learns the power of punk. Should be cool. *If* you can deal with Babs for another six months."

Marlowe sat up a bit straighter, grateful for a solution to *one* of her problems.

"Would Babs deal with me?" she asked. "Even after the waitress stuff? The time I'm taking off from wardrobe and the . . . whatever with Angus?"

Cherry fluttered her fingertips together like an evil villain.

"I have my ways," she said. "I may never convince Babs to recommend me for my own design job, but she trusts my judgment. Besides, she'll cool off about Angus once shooting stops and we're doing wrap. She knows how hard you work. You also make smart choices, you're super efficient, and you know this show almost as well as she and I do. She basically gets a second assistant at a PA rate. So if you're staying in L.A. . . ."

Marlowe looked eastward, or what she hoped was eastward, past the palm trees, the full parking lot, and the low, tiled roofs. Past the smoggy night sky. She thought of her friends, and her theater work, and a city where no one cared if she drank seltzer in the morning or if she had as much muscle definition as a baked potato. She thought of the script waiting on her laptop, and the possibility of walking into a theater again. Then she thought about all the ways she still felt like a failure. After all, she was stupid enough to lust after an unavailable TV star. It was not a sign of brilliance.

"Thanks," she said to Cherry. "Getting me work on that film would be great."

Chapter Fourteen

Bright morning light streaked through the vacant spots in Marlowe's busted metal blinds. With a grumpy moan, she dragged her phone off the nightstand and squinted at the time. Nine twenty-three A.M., the latest she'd slept in months. Her head ached and her mouth felt like a hedgehog had climbed in and died there. The slightest movement also launched waves of nausea. She'd forgotten about the misery of hangovers since her social life had diminished to virtual nonexistence. Still, a night out was worth a little discomfort, except for those last ten minutes or so. *That*, she could do without repeating.

Wiping sleep from her eyes, she hauled herself up and checked her messages.

Dad: Cancer Prevention Foundation Gala next month. Want to come?

Babs: New scenes added. Need you to work today

Babs: Yes, I know it's your day off

Babs: The girl who replaced you yesterday was excellent

Babs: LMK if you're no longer interested in your position

Babs: Otherwise meet at HQ ASAP

Babs: Wear comfortable shoes

Babs: Never mind. You always do

Cherry: Have you heard from Babs? I'm heading in now. Take some Advil. Drink lots of water. EAT SOMETHING YOU SKINNY BITCH! Hugs. See you soon

Mom: 18 miles this morning! Feeling great. Are you still running?

Chloe: OMG!!!!! We're dying here. Call immediately!!!!!!!

Following Chloe's punctuation explosion was a link to a gossip site called *Star Spotting*, which was well known for posting unauthorized photos of celebrities going about their business at stores or on vacations. The site particularly liked pointing out cellulite or belly fat on anyone in a bathing suit. Marlowe supposed this was intended to make people who didn't have perfect bodies feel better, but really it perpetuated the idea that all bodies were targets for judgment. It was gross. It was also insanely popular.

Prickling with curiosity, Marlowe ignored the other texts and clicked on the link. A headline popped into view: IS ON-AGAIN OFF AGAIN FOR ANGUS GORDON AND TANAREVE HUGHES? WAITRESS DELIVERS MORE THAN MENUS AT L.A. NIGHTCLUB. Following the headline were three photos. 1.) Tanareve leaning against the bar with Idi and Whitman while Marlowe and Angus stood nearby, their heads bowed together, probably during the only thirty seconds in which they were speaking to each other. 2.) Marlowe and Angus wrapped around each other on the dance floor, lips parted, eyes locked, looking like a sexy still from *Dirty Dancing*. 3.) Tanareve screaming at Angus, her finger prodding his chest, his hands held up in surrender. A few lines followed, claiming that Tanareve had caught Angus out with "the waitress," leading to a giant public blowout.

Marlowe read the article over and over, trying to make sense of it. Who had even taken those photos? And hadn't Tanareve *encouraged* Angus and Marlowe to dance? It was part of the game. Nothing happened. How had it turned into a screaming match?

Also, that photo of Marlowe with Angus was crazy hot. Was that really what they looked like together? No wonder *Heart's Diner* fans had shipped them.

Crap. Scratch that. Back to more important matters . . .

Marlowe: Was there a fight at the club last night?
Cherry: Thank god you're up. Put some pants on
Cherry: Also, no. Not while I was there. What did I miss?

Marlowe sent Cherry the link and waited, chewing a fingernail. Then she remembered her nail polish had been carefully chipped to look chewed, and increasing the damage would disrupt continuity. As she lowered her hand, a reply came.

Cherry: THAT'S who you were with when you disappeared last night?
Marlowe: Only for one dance. We did it on a dare. Part of a game his friends were playing. Yes, Tanareve was among those friends
Cherry: And she saw you two together?
Marlowe: Not sure but she's the one who pushed us to dance

Cherry: Unless you've been Photoshopped, that was more than a dance

The screen went blank for another minute. Marlowe sank back into her pillows, or rather, pillow—singular. She didn't even do much sinking. Her pillow was as flat as a tortilla. She seriously had to invest in some basic comforts. If she was going to stay in L.A. and keep working with Babs and Cherry, she could at least buy decent sheets. Maybe a fork or two that still had all of their tines.

Cherry: Skimmed the article. It's probably clickbait. But Maria and I left not long after you caught your Lyft. She says hi by the way ☺

Marlowe: Congratulations!

Cherry: Prepare for insane amounts of gushing

Marlowe: Can't I call in sick? Panic attack imminent

Cherry: Welcome to multitasking. Panic while you shop

Marlowe: I'd rather panic while I panic

Cherry: Let it go. A and T break up more often than mediocre white men get unearned promotions. If they split again it's not your fault. Even if you dry humped him

Marlowe: I'm only coming in today if you promise never to say dry hump again

Cherry: Dry hump. Dry hump. Dry hump. See you soon!

Marlowe set aside her phone and squinted toward the sunlight. If she did invest in her living space, curtains would come first. Three hundred and sixty-five days a year of sunshine had its perks, but not when the light felt like an interrogation bulb, amplifying her guilt and anxiety. It *was* only a dance. Wasn't it??????

Unable to answer that question with any real conviction, Marlowe dealt with the hedgehog in her mouth and the crusted sweat on her skin. She was out of clean work attire, so she put on a faded Yale T-shirt and smell-checked a pair of cropped jeans she'd worn earlier in the week. Until she had time for laundry, they'd have to do.

Over a strong cup of coffee, she blearily browsed through her mom's marathon training blog and looked up her dad's fundraising gala. She could probably attend his event if she really wanted to. Her dad would even pay for the flight and buy her a nice dress, but she didn't love being surrounded by people who were saving the world when her daily anxieties still included zip code dissociation and combination skin. Though apparently her anxieties now included breaking up Hollywood's It Couple.

She fired off three texts. One to her mom (*Great job! Yep, still running, though not 18 miles*), one to her dad (*Thanks for the invite. Can't make it to NY next month. Work*), and one to her friends' group thread (*Weird article. Went out with cast and crew last night. Everyone got along great. Headed to work. More later*). The final text was a touch on the evasive side, but it was true and it was all she could handle at the moment.

Half an hour later, Marlowe stepped out of her Uber and trudged into the wardrobe office at the studio, still fighting her hangover. Babs and Cherry were conferring over something on Cherry's computer, while over at Babs's desk, a sleek Weimaraner sat in a chair, blinking at Marlowe with a distinctly guilt-ridden expression. Marlowe knew that expression well, having picked up and dropped off Edith Head many times over the past five months. The first few times, she swore the dog had done something wrong. Now she knew the lowered snout and upturned eyes were Edith's default, even when she was seated at a desk as though she ran the place.

"Finally!" Babs threw up her hands. "Edith's daycare was closed for repairs today and I didn't know where else to take her. Cherry and I will be in fittings for the next eight hours, but Edith can go with you. Just don't leave her in the car. She hates that."

"Okay?" Marlowe glanced back and forth between Babs and the dog. "Where am I going today and will people mind if I bring a dog inside?"

"They won't mind if you convince them it won't be a problem."

"Convincing people isn't my strength."

"Nonsense. All that untapped acting talent shouldn't go to waste." Babs offered up a smile that was *just* credible enough to prevent Marlowe from treating her comment like the dig that it was. It was one of Babs's greatest talents. One among many.

While Marlowe petted Edith's silky ears, Babs explained that the new scenes involved two dozen background players and three of the leads. Whitman and Janie could wear pieces pulled from prior looks, but Kamala would fall into a pond and get soaked. Since the shot would require several takes, several identical costumes were also needed. The initial outfit—a crisp black wrap blouse and pair of dark denim pedal pushers—had already been shopped and fit. Fortunately the items came from a chain store, though they'd been modified to make them less recognizable. Now Marlowe had to track down as many doubles as possible by end of day so the stitchers and dyers could make them all match and the clothes would be ready to shoot by Monday. Marlowe wondered how anyone working in film and TV had a personal life, but she didn't ask. Instead, she took down the necessary information, leashed up Edith Head, and promised to do her best.

Cherry walked her out into the parking lot.

"You holding up?" she asked as Edith made use of the nearest flowerbed.

"Hungover. Tired. Freaked out. Desperately want to crawl into a hole. You?"

An irrepressible grin broke over Cherry's face. "Same. Totally."

Marlowe laughed. "If I didn't like you so much, I might say something really unpleasant right now. But I'm happy you're happy."

Cherry's grin somehow managed to widen. "Thanks. I'm happy I'm happy, too. And stop freaking out. No matter what's going on with Tanagus or Angareve or whatever people are calling them these days, it'll blow over. It always does."

Marlowe spun in a circle, unwinding the leash that was wrapped around her legs.

"Ever notice telling someone not to freak out never makes them freak out less?"

"Yeah, but telling you thousands of people probably hate you now seems worse."

"Excellent point."

They exchanged a hug before Cherry went back inside and Marlowe found a shady spot where she tied up Edith Head and called around to every branch of Luscious Popsicle in drivable distance, asking them to check their inventory and hold the blouses and pedal pushers for her. She found seven stores that had at least one of the pieces and she was determined to hit them all before closing. As she mapped out a route, her phone approximated that the trip would take her eight hours, and that didn't count time spent in the stores or dealing with the dog. If she was lucky, she'd get home around eight or nine, after her local Laundromat had closed. The day was going to exhaust her, especially with that article plaguing her.

Though maybe she could sneak in one more stop . . .

Chapter Fifteen

Tanareve flung her arms around Marlowe's shoulders, drawing her into an enthusiastic hug, which appeared to be her standard greeting. Her thick chestnut hair brushed against Marlowe's nose, smelling of pear or guava or some other fancy fruit. She wore a cute rayon romper that looked like something she'd just tossed on, even though it probably cost several hundred dollars. Ditto for her hoop earrings and embroidered espadrilles.

"Sweet dog," she said. "And I'm so glad you texted."

"You are?" Marlowe tugged on Edith Head's leash, narrowly preventing the dog from stealing a scone off a nearby table. They were at a small sidewalk café near Rodeo Drive. Marlowe had asked if Tanareve could chat at some point that afternoon. Tanareve responded with the time and place. Marlowe confirmed and worked the café into her route. Now here they were, and Marlowe's big *Nothing happened* speech no longer seemed quite so pressing. "I thought you might be upset about last night."

"Because you left without saying goodbye?"

"Um . . . no." Marlowe hooked Edith's leash to a chair and sat down opposite Tanareve. The dog fussed and spun in circles, refusing to settle until Marlowe pulled up another chair and let Edith hop up. Then she found the article and showed Tanareve.

"Oh, lord. They're at it again." Tanareve flapped a dismissive hand. "You can't take this stuff seriously, though they're getting better at Photoshop. That last photo was taken years ago. I can't even remember what I was mad about. Funny. It really does look like I'm wearing the same dress." She passed Marlowe's phone back with an easy smile.

Marlowe examined the shots more closely. Sure enough, in the pic of Tanareve yelling at Angus, her dress was slightly different, though the color match was spot-on.

"Then you didn't fight last night?" she asked.

"I gave him grief for being a grouch, but that's nothing new. You should've known him when he was a teenager. Total brooder. I'd take him to a party and he'd spend the whole night examining bookshelves or parked in a corner discussing some obscure branch of philosophy with people who were way too stoned to do anything but blink at him. God! And the staring! The guy can still examine a saltshaker for, like, half an hour. I've called him out on the habit but he swears he has no idea he's doing it."

A waiter came by and asked Marlowe to remove the dog from the chair. Tanareve intervened. As recognition dawned, the waiter shifted from scolding to fawning, offering to bring the dog a bowl of water. He left without asking if Marlowe wanted anything.

She leaned onto her elbows, ready to wither onto the tabletop after nursing high anxiety for the last few hours while driving all over L.A. and dragging Edith Head in and out of stores with stringent No Pets policies. Also, hangovers had serious staying power.

"So you and Angus are still together?" she asked, daring to hope. "Like, *together* together?"

"I guess?"

"God, no." Tanareve laughed, all brightness and sparkles. "We dated for, like, four months when we first met. Realized pretty quickly that we were a terrible match. We're perfect as friends, though. He keeps me grounded. I push him to get a little more adventurous." She tore off a piece of her biscotti and fed it to Edith, who gobbled it up with crumbs flying out both sides of her floppy lips. "We hang out a lot. The press can't decide what to do with us. Saying we're just friends doesn't get clicks. We both leave it in the hands of our publicists now. They know when a few cozy photos will help build ratings. But *that* crap"—she gestured at Marlowe's phone—"*that*, you learn to ignore."

Marlowe pocketed her phone, still feeling ten steps behind. After seeing photos of Angus and Tanareve splashed across magazines and websites for the last few weeks—and the last ten years—the idea that they'd only ever dated for a few months as teenagers seemed impossible.

Before she could form another question, the waiter returned with a bowl of water. He set it on the table without requesting that the dog drink from the ground, which was good because Edith was already lapping up the water, splashing in all directions. The waiter turned to go but Tanareve halted him by pointedly asking if Marlowe wanted anything. He took in her stretched-out T-shirt and sloppy ponytail, raising a droll brow. Marlowe brushed aside his obvious disdain as she ordered a latte, requesting it to go. As grateful as she was for Tanareve's company and candor, she still had to make it to four more stores before they closed.

"So how do you learn to ignore what people say about you?" she asked, a question that was simple enough on the surface, but one that resonated bone deep.

"You build a thick skin. You get a good therapist. And you find the humor in the situation. *Hollywood Reporter* once ran a piece about how I stole a monkey from the zoo. *BuzzFeed* claimed I'd auctioned off my underwear. People will say anything for clickbait. Now if a monkey auctions off my underwear, *that* will be worth clicking on." She laughed again, making her hair-model waves fall forward over her perfectly tanned and sculpted shoulders. Marlowe used to dream of having shoulders like that. Then she learned that exercise was involved. Tanareve clearly didn't share Marlowe's athletics aversion. She probably liked vegetables, too. Even kale. "If the chatter really bothers you, you could do what Angus does and avoid the Internet altogether. He has email and he reads the news or orders stuff online, but he has pretty much anything else blocked."

"Ah . . ." Marlowe's chin dropped onto her palm again as the full weight of Tanareve's revelation sank in. "So he doesn't run his Instagram account?"

Tanareve shook her head, sending up another waft of her fruity shampoo.

"It's a fan account run by a PR pro. She has a backlog of photos and she's never without her phone to sneak a new shot. Angus lets her do what she wants with the account as long as it means he never has to see the trolls."

Marlowe let that information sink in for another minute. Everything made so much more sense now—all of those discrepancies between who Angus was in person versus who he was online—but what a weird life, to have one's entire public persona not only curated, but completely manufactured by someone else.

As she pondered that idea, Edith Head turned in circles on her chair, precariously balancing on her skinny legs before settling again on her bony butt and adopting her usual guilt-ridden expression.

Marlowe suspected her own expression was similar. No wonder Angus got so angry when she criticized his social media use. Though how could she have known someone else ran his account? In her world, people didn't have PR pros at their command, which was obvious by the amount of insanely boring food and flower photos they posted, yet another reason she barely touched social media. Still, if her friends put something out there, it was because they wanted others to see it.

"I had no idea," she said. "I guess I misjudged him."

"Easily done. He's a hard read and he doesn't let many people in." Tanareve fed Edith another bite of her cookie. "He's a good actor so he knows how to 'turn on the friendly' with his fans. He's a grade-A flirter, obviously. He's also tight with his closest friends, like, once you're in, you're *really* in. But you probably noticed by now that he's a hardcore introvert. It's why Idi, Whitman, and I pushed so hard to get him to dance."

"Right. The dance." Marlowe slumped forward, nearly sagging into Edith's water bowl.

Tanareve studied her, eyes welling with concern.

"I don't know if something's going on between you two or not," she said. "But if you're interested in more than a dance, he just takes a little patience. He puts up a lot of walls. Like most guys, he hides his soft underbelly, but all that impenetrable confidence is an act." She caught the surprise in Marlowe's eyes and chuckled in response. "Don't get me wrong. He knows a lot of women find him attractive, but he doesn't consider himself 'relationship material.' Most women don't bother getting to know him. They just want a story to tell their friends." She paused to take a sip of her tea, giving Marlowe a moment to realize she'd thought of Angus in precisely that way on the shoe-shopping day. Not *I'd like to get to know him better* or *I enjoy his company*. Her thought had been, *This will be my go-to party story for years*. But she'd also seen him with fans.

"He doesn't seem to mind that kind of attention," she said.

Tanareve shrugged her amazing shoulders. "To some degree he does enjoy it, but he leans into it more by habit than by any real intention. It's all so superficial. Most fans want to meet the characters they've grown to love from a show, not the people who play those characters, and they don't always understand the vast difference between the two." Tanareve smiled as though she'd learned this through experience, and Marlowe recalled Angus saying something similar in her car the other day. "The truth is, Angus is lonely. He'd kill me for telling you that, but it sucks to know people prefer the fake version of you to the real version. It's not exactly a morale boost."

While Tanareve sipped her tea and finished her biscotti, Marlowe reframed every interaction she'd had with Angus, from the Instagram posts she'd taken as egotism to the flirting she'd commanded him to stop to the anger he'd expressed over her frequent assumptions. *Maybe our lives aren't as different as you think,* he'd said. And maybe something had sparked between them, but what then? After only one dance, Marlowe was the center of a new wave of gossip.

She'd tried not to look but she couldn't help herself. Between stores, she'd Googled *Angus Gordon + Tanareve Hughes + waitress*. The *Star Spotting* article had bled onto other sites and the #IShipTheWaitress hashtag was trending on Twitter again, this time with fans split between declaring they "knew something was up" and tweeting about all the ways Marlowe "didn't deserve him." She couldn't even deal with reviews of her creative work back in New York. How was she supposed to handle criticism that was so much more personal, so much more vitriolic, and so much less informed?

Answer: she couldn't.

"Nothing's going on between us," she said. "Though I owe Angus an apology."

"It's as good a place to start as any." Tanareve shined her million-dollar smile on Marlowe, making her feel as though maybe everything would be okay. It was that warm, and that powerful. No wonder Tanareve's career had taken off when she was ten. And no wonder fans were furious about Angus and Marlowe's supposed indiscretion.

The waiter soon returned. Marlowe bought her latte and wrangled Edith Head to depart. Tanareve gave them both earnest hugs and encouraged Marlowe to text anytime. Marlowe thanked her sincerely, at which point Edith squatted for a pee right there among the café tables. Marlowe was mortified. She scrambled for napkins, but Tanareve shooed her off, laughing in her infectious, joyful way.

"Go!" she said. "I'll smooth things over with Mr. Snootypants."

"Thank you!" Marlowe skirted the puddle and stepped away. "And next time, I don't think you should play the girl in peril. I think you should play the superhero."

"Damned straight I should!" Tanareve called after her.

As Marlowe clambered into her stinky, overheated car and forced her window ajar—as much for Edith's sake as for her own—she promised herself she'd stop making so many assumptions, even ones she had a reasonable right to make. Then she shoved aside thoughts of Angus and Tanareve and gossip sites that treated real people like chicken feed to peck at. It was all beside the point. Marlowe had a job to do and an impatient boss to please. For the next few hours, nothing else mattered.

Chapter Sixteen

Marlowe: The wardrobe building's locked
Cherry: We finished background two hours ago. We're with Whitman now
Marlowe: Where do I leave everything?
Cherry: Kamala's trailer should be open. Babs and I are about to wrap up. We'll meet you by wardrobe in 20 to collect the dog. You're my hero

Marlowe started a reply but she dropped her phone. With seven shopping bags, the organic Thai food Babs had asked her to pick up, and a restless dog, she was lucky she'd managed to text at all. She wasn't in the best mood, either. The headache from her hangover lingered. Her wrist was chafed from the leash. Her brain was replaying mean comments from strangers. Her muscles were sore from last night's dancing. Her skin was covered in goose bumps now that night had fallen. She also had vanilla shake in her hair, thanks to an angry *Heart's Diner* fan who'd recognized her as the waitress, called her a man-stealing bitch, and tossed the contents of a McDonald's cup at her face. Now Marlowe was totally spent and out of patience with the world. All she wanted to do was shower, crawl into her lumpy bed, and pray Babs let her take Sunday off.

She picked up her phone and pocketed it while Edith circled her with the leash. Unwinding herself and tightening her hold on the bags, Marlowe stumbled across the lot toward the actors' trailers. She was almost there when Edith darted after a tiny little mouse that ran across their path. Marlowe lurched to her right, dropped several shopping bags, and watched the contents spill out.

"Come *on*!" she shouted at the sky. "Cut me a little slack here!"

"Clumsy, unlucky, or cursed?" asked a deep voice behind her.

Marlowe turned around slowly, or at least she tried to turn slowly until Edith practically leapt at Angus, nuzzling his hands for a pet. He was in his usual low-slung jeans and plain white tee, though he'd added a light jacket because he knew how to dress for L.A. weather. Also, he probably got dressed without a hangover.

"What are you doing here?" she asked, far too exhausted for pleasantries.

"A bit of voiceover work. It could've waited, but I was free." He extended a hand.

Inferring his intent, Marlowe gave him the leash. Then she crouched to gather the clothes, brushing off each piece and praying nothing was stained or damaged.

"Babs made you work today?" Angus asked as he also took the Thai food, sweeping it out of Edith's reach.

"A water scene got added. We needed multiples, though they're hardly necessary since Babs chose black percale and dark denim." Marlowe huffed out a breath as she folded a pair of cropped jeans into a bag with several others. "You can't tell they're wet on camera. A light cotton dress would make the moment clear. Even pale denim would indicate *something* to the viewer. A peasant blouse.

Voile. Chiffon. Anything without stabilizers. But this is pointless." She gathered her bags and reached out for the leash.

Angus shook his head. "I've got it. Where are we headed?"

"The clothes go to Kamala's trailer. The food and the dog stay with me until Babs emerges from her last fitting and blames me for letting her dinner get cold."

"Go on." Angus nodded toward the nearest trailer. "We'll wait here."

Marlowe opened her mouth to protest but this wasn't a moment to deny help.

"Thanks," she said. "I'll be right back."

She dropped off the clothes. While still in the trailer, she paused to check her reflection. Her ponytail was barely holding on to its elastic. Her T-shirt was speckled with fake dairy product. Her face had a dull glaze of dog spit from where Edith had licked away a good portion of the shake. She felt about as attractive as her mom's compost bin. Unable to do much about that feeling, or about what led to that feeling, she stepped outside, where Angus was feeding Edith a spring roll.

"That's not going to make my night any easier," Marlowe said.

"She looked hungry."

"She's a dog. Dogs always look hungry." Marlowe took the leash while Edith polished off the spring roll and Angus folded down the top of the takeout bag.

"Where are you waiting?" he asked.

"In front of the wardrobe building."

"You sure?" He glanced at her bare arms. "You're welcome to wait in my trailer."

Marlowe looked past him toward his trailer. *The security guard who stands outside is only there to make sure one girl enters at a time,*

Cherry had said. *I'm not going anywhere near his trailer,* Marlowe had responded, later noting, *I won't be number two hundred and anything.*

"Nah," she said. "I'm good."

"I'm not trying to seduce you."

"Awesome. I'm not trying to seduce you, either."

He gave her a quick scan as the barest hint of a smile dented his cheeks.

"No kidding," he teased.

She snatched the takeout bag from him. "Nice. Really nice. Like I need to feel even worse about myself right now." She spun away and started off toward the wardrobe building, but he followed close by.

"Why are you so determined to misinterpret everything I say to you?" he asked.

"So you meant that 'no kidding' as a compliment?"

"I meant it as a joke. A bad one, apparently."

"I definitely preferred the garnish banter."

"Duly noted." He dodged out of Edith's way as she crossed in front of him to sniff the corner of a building. "Seriously, why don't we ever just talk to each other?"

Marlowe stopped and spun toward him. "You want to talk? Okay. How about starting with 'I don't do my own social media and I don't have a girlfriend.'"

His not-quite-red brows knitted. "You thought I had a girlfriend?"

"*Everyone* thinks you have a girlfriend!"

"So that's why . . ." He dragged a hand over his chin, slow and thoughtful.

"Yeah. That's why." Marlowe gave the leash a light tug, reining Edith in. "I know I owe you an apology. A big one. I made a lot of assumptions I shouldn't have, but it isn't a huge stretch of the imagination to think you had at least *some* awareness of what was being shared on *your* accounts in *your* name." She stopped there and braced for a rebuttal.

Angus continued stroking his stubble, deep in thought, but no rebuttal came. Marlowe had no idea how to respond to his silence, so she tightened her hold on Edith's leash and carried on to her meeting point by the wardrobe building. After a moment's pause, Angus followed, sitting down beside her on the railroad ties that bound in a row of palm trees and a cluster of scrubby underbrush.

When the silence continued, growing more awkward by the second, Marlowe's instinct to backpedal kicked in. This was the point in a conversation where Kelvin would question her right to criticize, or one-up her criticism with his own, or ask what had happened to make her so "crabby," or—

"You're right," Angus said. "It's my name. It's my responsibility."

Marlowe gaped at him, realized she was gaping, and shut her mouth. While she marveled at the simplicity of his reply, Angus picked up a bit of gravel and turned it over in his hands, scrutinizing it as though it held the great mysteries of the universe.

"I used to be more involved," he said, "but I wasn't good at filtering. Checking social media was like walking into a party full of people who weren't invited, people who were all talking over each other, fighting for attention by being the biggest, loudest, most volatile voice in the room, and somehow, I kept wanting to engage with the vitriol, to explain or defend myself. So I left the party. And locked the door on my way out." He skimmed the gravel bit across the mostly empty parking lot, watching it skid to a stop.

Marlowe followed his gaze, no longer angry. Just kind of . . . sad.

"But it's *your* party," she said, softly, quietly, as if she was delivering bad news.

"I know." He skimmed another gravel bit across the lot, like skipping stones on a lake. "I'll remove the blocks when I get home. Take a look. Talk to my PR rep."

"Or I can save you the wait." Marlowe pulled up the shot of the two of them by her car and handed her phone to Angus. "I thought we were alone. Talking like friends."

Angus frowned at the photo. "Alone. Yeah. Me too. I'm so sorry. I should've set clearer boundaries." He squinted at the screen as he scrolled through more pics. Cute couple shots. Group photos with other cast members, all of them looking glamorous, flawless, and beautiful. Black-and-white close-ups that displayed Angus's ridiculously fit body to best advantage. "I have no idea how you got the impression I was conceited."

"Another stretch of the imagination."

"And all the stuff about Tan."

"It's not exactly subtext."

Angus nodded before shutting off her phone and handing it back. They sat quietly for several seconds, though this time the silence didn't feel so fraught.

"I understand the instinct to walk away," Marlowe said. "And I get why you're tired of defending yourself, but a few basic truths shouldn't be too much to ask."

"How many is a few?"

"Truths? I don't know. Five?"

He considered, nodding again. "Okay. Five for five. Go ahead."

"I can ask you anything and you'll answer without an evasion?"

"I'll do my best." He propped an elbow on his thigh and rested his cheek on a loose fist, watching her sideways. His posture was wonderfully ordinary, slightly slouched and lacking bravado. He was just a guy, having a chat. Then again, maybe his posture was irrelevant. Maybe he looked like "just a guy" because Marlowe was finally doing what he'd asked her to do back on set: seeing him as a person instead of as an idea.

"Favorite color?" she asked.

"Gray. Dark gray. Like pebbles in a riverbed. How badly do you hate your job?"

Marlowe flinched. "*That's* your first question?"

"I only get five. I don't give a shit about your favorite color."

"I was being polite."

"Your loss." His smile quirked up again, not a lot, but enough to call it a smile.

Marlowe drew Edith Head to her side and made her sit. Edith grumbled and shifted, much preferring chairs, but her fussing bought Marlowe time to form a thought.

"I'm learning a lot," she said. "It's . . . eye-opening."

"You're setting the 'no evasions' bar pretty low there."

"Fine." Marlowe glanced in all directions to ensure they were alone. "I despise my job. Most of the tasks could be accomplished by anyone with a car and a credit card. The tasks that do require my skills also require me to ensure my boss thinks they only require *her* skills. I'm not telling an inspiring story. I'm not making interesting art. But at least the job's temporary, and it'll lead to the next gig, which might be better." She grimaced at that, unsure that a film with Babs would be less painful than a TV series with Babs. Of course, Chloe's script was still waiting to be read, but the offer was a long shot. Even if Marlowe did get the design, she wasn't sure she could handle it. And speaking of things she wasn't sure she could handle . . . "How many women have you had sex with?"

Angus burst into nervous laughter that took a long time to dissipate.

"Okay. Not so polite then." He scratched at his neck while his eyes darted left, right, and everywhere in between. "Wow. Right. Um . . . more than ten, less than twenty."

Marlowe almost fell off the railroad tie. "That's all?"

He laughed again, still breathy and unsure. "Why? What's your number?"

"It doesn't matter."

"No way. I told you mine."

"I thought it would be a lot higher." She draped an arm over Edith, anchoring her attention to the less complicated of her current companions. The dog was soft, warm, and cozy, even though she never sat still. While Marlowe snuggled in closer, Angus plucked a blade from a spiky shrub near his shoulder. He twisted and toyed with it as though maybe he also needed an anchor for his attention.

"I know what people think," he said. "They're not shy about saying so. It's part of why I left social. Truth is, I've tried casual. It has its perks, but only if it's what both people want. Otherwise it leads to disappointment and resentment."

"So the women you slept with got attached too quickly?"

He shook his head as he ran the blade between his thumb and forefinger. She watched him, baffled at how far off the mark some of her assumptions had been. For a long moment, neither of them spoke. Then he gave her a little nudge with his knee.

"Right. My turn." She sent a fuck-my-life look toward the hazy night sky. "Three." She waited for a burst of astonishment but it didn't come. "My adolescence wasn't marked by attention the way yours was. I was awkward. Quiet. Friend to many, love interest to none. College was no easier. I spent most of it studying or at a sewing machine, envying beautiful, fun, outgoing girls practically every guy had a crush on."

"I've dated that girl. It's exhausting." He let the blade fall, toeing at it with his white Converse.

Marlowe pictured him sitting across the bar from Tanareve last night, with their polar-opposite energies. Most of Marlowe's dating attempts had ended with some iteration of her not being "fun enough." The few times she'd logged onto a dating site, that was the word that punctuated every profile. *Looking for someone fun. Just want to have fun. Must be fun.* Even Kelvin had criticized her for wanting to stay in and cuddle sometimes instead of seeking out a grand adventure together. The evidence had seemed pretty clear. Guys wanted girls who didn't get sad, or angry, or struggle, or need to retreat from the world. They wanted smiles and effervescence. But maybe not all guys.

As the quiet stretched on, Angus tipped his chin at Marlowe's T-shirt.

"You went to Yale?" he asked.

"Yeah. Grad school. Best three years of my life. You? Where was college?"

"Nowhere. I stopped going to school when I was fourteen. Everything past that was private tutoring or reading whatever books I picked up on my own." He glanced sideways at her as though he was waiting for her judgment, but she didn't have any to offer. He shifted and toed at the greenery bits anyway, a quieter, smaller version of the guy she'd seen strutting around set for the past few months. "This industry's tough. The hours and travel make it hard to have a normal life, not that I need to tell you that since you're at work at nine P.M. on a Saturday with a dog and a takeout bag."

"Maybe this is how I like to spend my Saturday nights."

"Funny. You struck me as more of a vegan cooking classes girl."

"Nailed it." She tipped her head onto Edith's back, growing more and more sleepy by the second now that she wasn't on the go anymore. "What are we on, number four? How do you really feel about all the fan photos and autographs?"

He shrugged and plucked another blade from the underbrush.

"I think it's amazing that people want to connect with me, or at least that they want to connect with whoever they think I am. Without fans, I'd still be playing dog walker number two." He peered past Marlowe to smile at Edith. "So I appreciate the energy. If signing my name or taking a photo makes someone happy, it's the least I can do. But"—he leaned toward Edith as though he was addressing her personally—"given the choice, I'd slide through the world unrecognized. No photos. No autographs. No one posting diatribes about what a raging dick I am if I didn't stop and smile for them."

"Mmm," Marlowe mumbled, still sinking closer to sleep.

"My turn. I've got a tough one for you."

"Fire away."

"What in the hell is in your hair?"

"Oh. That." Marlowe straightened up, patting a crusted patch over her right ear. "An article about us went up this morning. Apparently I lured you away from Tanareve. Not sure how I managed it, but wow, some of your fans are *pissed*."

Angus went still, watching her melt against the dog again.

"I'm so sorry," he said.

"You did try to warn me."

"I'm still sorry." His forehead rippled with concern. "Can I make it up to you?"

She shook her head in a lazy, lolling way. Then the question sank in. "How?"

"What are you doing after work?"

"Is that your last question?"

"Sure, if that's yours."

"Works for me." Her eyes glazed over as she stared out at the parking lot. "Number one, shower. Number two, locate a Laundromat that's open late on weekends since I'm completely out of clean clothes, and thus, my current attire. I'd wait until tomorrow but Babs might knock down my door, waving another impossible to-do list. Number three, mute my phone. Number four, sleep until the end of time."

He squinted at her and she was struck once again by how beautiful he was, though if she hadn't thought so, she wouldn't have been caught in that dance and her hair would be shake-free right now. Damn, pheromones were a bitch.

"You don't have your own washer and dryer?" Angus asked.

"You're out of questions. And that one smacks of privilege."

"I'll take that as a no." He held out a palm. Marlowe frowned at it, unsure what he was getting at. He inched his palm closer. "Your phone. I know a place that's open all night. They also have amazing showers, comfortable beds, and Do Not Disturb signs."

"You mean a hotel with laundry services?"

"Something like that."

"I doubt it's in my budget."

"It's cheaper than you might think."

Marlowe continued frowning at his hand, trying to picture the place he'd described, but she was out of energy for questions and answers. So she handed off her phone. He plugged something into it and handed it back.

"Thanks," she said. "Now, at the risk of being a total jerk, can you please leave?"

He flinched, but an amused smile flickered into place. "What did I do this time?"

"Nothing. Babs will be here any second. She'll forgive me for 'forgetting' her spring roll. She won't forgive me for hanging out here with you."

"Got it." He stood and brushed off his butt, maybe to draw attention to it, but probably not. "Can I at least leave you my jacket?"

"Better not. Besides, if she knows I'm cold and miserable, she's less likely to give me grief about her dinner." Marlowe remained seated, drooping against Edith.

Angus backed away. "Seriously. I mean it. Check out that place I recommended."

"I will." She smiled up at him. It was a weak effort but a sincere one. "Thanks for talking. And for being honest. Especially about the color gray. Total shocker."

"See you around, Marlowe like the detective."

"See you around, Angus not like the beef."

He grinned at that. Goddamn, he was pretty. A thought that drifted away as quickly as it arose.

In the next moment, he was gone. His timing was good, since Babs and Cherry showed up only a few minutes later. Cherry was full of apologies. Babs mostly inquired about the state of her dog. When Marlowe handed off the food and apologized for "forgetting the spring roll," Babs assured her it didn't matter since she'd changed her mind about what she wanted and ordered delivery over an hour ago.

Straining for patience, Marlowe described the clothes she'd purchased, confirmed she wouldn't be needed tomorrow, and drove home with loud, angry music that kept her awake. She kicked off her sneakers and stripped off her shirt on the way to the shower, not wasting a single second. She was peeling off her jeans when she turned the knob on the tub, only to have it creak and groan as the faucet produced precisely two drops of water.

"Fuuuuuuuuuuuuuuuck," Marlowe moaned to the ceiling.

After trying her kitchen tap with the same predictable results, she recalled Angus's recommendation. It was probably a luxury spa that would cost an entire week's salary, but she was ready to splurge if it meant she could wash her hair and her clothes. Also: working blinds.

She found her phone and checked Angus's entry. It didn't include the name of a business. Only his name, a phone number, and a street address. She plugged the address into a map app, which opened up to an exclusive residential neighborhood in Bel Air. Suspecting the neighborhood didn't have a public spa or hotel, but curious enough to pursue the matter one step further, Marlowe texted to inquire about the possibility of booking a room.

Chapter Seventeen

Half an hour after booking her room for the night, Marlowe pulled into a curving driveway in the hills of Bel Air, just north of the L.A. Basin. She announced herself using a little speaker box beside the driveway. A moment later, a pair of wrought-iron gates swung open, allowing her to drive through and park in front of Angus's house.

She gaped as she got out of her car, taking in the façade. The house was made almost entirely of glass, two long, low stories, stacked like a pair of askew books with Japanese-inspired details in dark wood and white marble. Shades had been drawn in the upper floor but the ground level was open all the way through to the other side, revealing a sparsely furnished living room, another wall of windows, and an unobstructed view of the night sky. Angus didn't actually live in a house or even in a mansion. He lived in a magical skybox.

Marlowe was hauling her laundry bag from her trunk when Angus stepped out through the front door and joined her by her car.

"You found the place okay?" he asked.

"Your directions were great. Also, GPS."

"Right. Good." He tugged at a tie on the ski hat she was wearing. "You can lose the disguise now. This is a safe zone."

Marlowe removed her hat and tossed her sunglasses into it. She'd considered the precautions excessive when he'd suggested them earlier that night, but she'd complied, dredging out a vintage pair of cat-eye sunglasses and the only hat she could find in her closet. It was densely knitted in a snowflake pattern with earflaps, tasseled ties, and a bushy pom-pom. Hardly L.A. chic. Still, she was grateful she'd worn both the hat and the glasses when she'd passed a trio of black SUVs parked about half a mile back. The SUVs were no big deal, but the people sitting inside them, snapping photos of passing cars, were less innocuous. The last thing Marlowe needed was another round of public speculation about her supposed love affair with a guy who was simply loaning her a bed and a shower.

She blinked up at the house again. "You really live here, right? This isn't a hoax where I find out you're house-sitting when a snooty producer chases us out the door while my laundry's still in the dryer?"

"Your laundry will be safe. Though we should let the butler handle it from here." Angus took the bag from her and swung it over his shoulder. "Jeeves!" he called toward the open door. "Mind coming to lend a hand?"

Marlowe rooted herself to the driveway. "Your butler's name is Jeeves?"

Angus laughed as he spun toward her. "You bought that?"

She sucker-punched his arm. "Jerk."

"Guilty as charged, but you knew that already." He headed inside with her following close behind, eyes wide in unconcealed astonishment. "I don't have a butler. Though I've been known to hire a yard crew, a housekeeper, and a pool guy."

"Yeah, well, we all have a pool guy." She shook her head in an eye-roll kind of way, unsure how to take Angus's lifestyle in stride. She'd grown up middle class, so she wasn't without privilege, but she'd been scraping by ever since she graduated from college and started supporting herself. None of her friends lived even remotely like this. Most of them were trying to make it as artists while working odd jobs to cover bills and eke out student-loan payments. They didn't *hire* housekeepers. They *were* housekeepers.

Angus showed Marlowe to the laundry room, a tidy, spa-like space complete with glass jars of fancy-looking soaps and perfectly rolled towels nestled in cozy nooks. The room was in the corner of a basement level that also included a home gym and a private guest suite, both of which faced out to a glittering pool in the backyard.

"I left a clean T-shirt and some boxers on the bed," Angus said. "In case you need something to sleep in. Towels and toiletries are in the bathroom. I know you're exhausted so I'm going to leave you to it. This floor's all yours. Make yourself at home. Sleep as late as you like. I'll try to stay quiet so I don't wake you."

"Thanks. Really. This is insanely nice of you."

"It's not. But I'm glad I can do something to make your day a little bit better."

They exchanged a warm smile. As he rested a hand on the balustrade, her eyes traced the line of his bent wrist and tensed forearm. He had really nice arms, not bulky but fit and strong, with a light dusting of freckles that suited his complexion. He was probably a great hugger. Marlowe missed hugs, maybe even more than she missed sex. She considered asking for a hug but it felt too intimate for their short acquaintance. Even if she was about to get naked, use his shower, put on his clothes, and slip into his bed.

Yeah. That. All of that.

She didn't ask for a hug. He didn't offer. Instead, he did precisely what he'd said he was going to do and left her alone to make herself comfortable. Despite a tiny flicker of disappointment,

Marlowe was grateful. No ulterior motives. No who's-thinking-what games. No additional confusion. Just a kind gesture. One she really appreciated.

She started a load of laundry, grateful she didn't have to keep an eye on it like she did at the Laundromat. The guest suite was across the hall, a bedroom the size of her entire apartment and a bathroom decorated in creamy marble and spotless glass. Without hesitation, she stripped down and stepped into a shower with ten times the water pressure she was used to. Hours, days, months of stress seemed to wash away as she lingered in the rush of hot water, letting steam fill the room. She enjoyed generous amounts of luscious-smelling shampoo and conditioner, as well as handmade soap balls scented with lemongrass and something floral she couldn't identify. She took her time. She savored every second. Or, almost every second. Until . . .

Until she realized she was checking the closed door for the tenth or twelfth time, not because she was worried Angus would burst in on her, but because she kind of wanted him to. Not in a creepy, invasive way, but slowly, carefully. The door would inch ajar. His voice would find her, deep, low, and breaking ever so slightly with nerves.

Marlowe, he'd say, her name like velvet on his tongue. *Do you want company?*

Yes, she'd say. *I've been hoping you'd ask.*

I've been hoping you were hoping, he'd volley back.

He'd step into the bathroom, drawing his T-shirt over his head, slowly coming into focus as he neared the glass shower stall through the steam. He'd take her in with his eyes. She'd do the same, following his example, finding no shame in looking, or in appreciating what she saw. He was so damned beautiful, with his downturned nose and his angular bone structure and a faint trail of freckles that crossed his cheeks and nose like footprints left behind by a dancing fairy. God, and his body. All that strength she wanted to not care about but found herself drawn to. She was so tired of trying to be strong on her own. Of holding herself up. Of hiding her weaknesses. Was it so wrong to want—for the briefest moment—to rely on someone else's strength? And to enjoy the way the light painted his contours as though it was as drawn to him as she was?

I want you, she'd say.

You have no idea, he'd return.

He'd already be hard as he stepped into the shower, a display of desire that matched the gentle throbbing between her thighs, the undeniable craving that pulsed through her, opened her, urged her to part for him. Again she and Angus would only look at each other, asking silent questions with their eyes, answering each one with little more than a ragged breath. The spray from the shower would darken his hair and run down his sculpted chest and abs. She'd trace a single drop on its journey, down, down, down, until it met a tangle of damp hair. He'd reach forward and cup her breast, gently. Then he'd circle her nipple with the side of his thumb, watching it harden the way he watched everything else, as though her body fascinated him, as though he needed to know.

His kisses would be hungry but sure. His hands would find every spot that made her writhe and buck against him. He'd spin her around and take her from behind, his mouth hot against her neck, his chest hard against her back. He'd find a rhythm that jolted her entire body, slipping deeper into her as his groin hit her ass and he reached around to stroke her, circling, teasing, drawing her toward climax. Thrusting faster. Harder. Palms pressing against steamed-up glass. Water rushing down. Teeth tugging at her ear. Her name gasped out, maybe. His touch so certain, so aware of her response, finding the perfect spot, the perfect pressure, the perfect—

Yes, she thought. *There. Yes. Fuck. Yes.*

She'd arch against him, her head thrown back as a shudder overtook her and—

The shampoo and conditioner toppled from their shelf. Marlowe tripped on one of the bottles and fell flat on her ass, letting out a groan so unsexy she might as well have been a giant sow rolling onto its side. Spilled shampoo spiraled into the drain while splattered conditioner ran down the wall, as though the ghost of Jackson Pollock was having his way with the shower stall. As a final touch, a soap ball rolled off the shelf and hit Marlowe's forehead. She flinched, but otherwise sat dead still for what must've been a full minute, praying Angus hadn't heard her fall.

Thankfully, he didn't knock and ask if she was okay. She wasn't sure how she'd answer. Sure, her backside was only mildly bruised. She'd recover quickly enough, but goddammit! She'd *just* started getting along with Angus and she was already masturbating about him??? She was hardly okay.

Blaming her steamy fantasies on fatigue, she climbed into bed without further incident. She didn't even bother waiting up so she could switch her first load of laundry into the dryer. Clean clothes no longer seemed that essential, not with such a comfortable bed to snuggle into.

Angus's sheets were crisp and cool. His clothes were cozy and smelled of nondescript detergent. His pillow cradled her head, so soft and plush, all other thoughts vanished. Sleep beckoned. She willingly obeyed, certain she could face Angus in the morning with no sign whatsoever that her thoughts had strayed . . .

Chapter Eighteen

Marlowe turned at the top of the stairs, already blushing.

"That you?" Angus called from the living room. "You up?"

"Yeah. Um. Forgot. Thing. Dryer. Second. Clothes. Check." She scurried back down the stairs and into the laundry room, where her clothes were spinning away, her first load in the dryer and her second in the washer, as they should be since that was precisely where they were ten seconds ago. She was still wearing Angus's T-shirt and boxers, lacking any other clean clothes until the dryer cycle finished. She splashed cold water on her face and gave herself yet another pep talk. Angus had no way of knowing about her shower fantasy, or any other steamy thoughts she'd entertained over the years. He'd offered her refuge and she'd accepted. Simple. Straightforward. No big deal.

She found him seated on a gray velveteen sofa that was reminiscent of mid-century modern styles but with enough padding to sink into. His sock-clad feet were kicked up on a wood-block coffee table that was pieced together from at least a dozen different woods, giving it an Escher-like appearance. It looked handcrafted and probably cost more than an entire year of Marlowe's rent. Its value didn't seem to faze Angus as he flipped through a paperback while a mug steamed on a side table near his shoulder.

"You sleep okay?" he asked as he lowered the book.

"Great. Yeah. Obviously." She nodded at the floor-to-ceiling windows that opened out to sun-dappled hills and the ocean beyond. It was a little after 10:30 A.M., meaning she'd slept for almost eleven hours. "Let me guess, you already ran ten miles."

"Fifteen, but who's counting?"

Marlowe rolled her eyes. "My mom would love you."

Angus's cheeks reddened as he scratched at the back of his neck.

"I didn't mean that the way it sounded," Marlowe backpedaled, even though it was cute that he blushed. "I'm not frantically plotting for you to meet my parents simply because you let me use your shower and laundry room. I was referring to the running. My mom's a marathoner. She's on number fortysomething now. I lost track years ago."

"Easily done if she's run that many." He stood and stretched his arms over his head while she lingered by the top of the stairs, clinging to the newel post. The hem of his T-shirt rode up, revealing a peek of his impossibly smooth abs and hipbones, which she definitely did not notice. "You hungry? I snuck out to the market in case you wanted to stay for brunch. I bought lots of green things, knowing how much you love the color."

"Kermit should've copyrighted it before anyone tried to make kale drinkable."

"Leave it to a frog to neglect the legalities." He smiled, subtle but easy, as though he was totally relaxed having her in his home and in his clothes while he planned to cook with her. She didn't notice that, either. "Let me get you a sweater first. I have the A/C cranked.

You look a little cold." He mimicked her posture by hunching his shoulders. Then he disappeared down a hallway, leaving her to ease her way into the room.

She cleared her mind by perusing the packed bookshelves that divided the living room from the kitchen beyond. The shelves contained mostly paperbacks with a few scattered hardbacks in no particular order. Popular fiction, literary fiction, a few classics, some sci-fi and fantasy titles, philosophy, sociology, essay collections, humor. The spines were creased. The edges were worn. There were no carefully positioned Shakespeare or Dickens sets, bound in embossed leather like the ones her dad displayed, even though he hadn't read any of them. Angus's collection was eclectic and without pretense. Never once had Marlowe seen an article mention that he was an avid reader, giving even more weight to his comments about packaged celebrity. His sexually charged bad-boy image was a brand, a means of baiting audiences and followers. He didn't spend all of his weekends out partying or luring supermodels into his trailer. He stayed home, alone, reading.

He returned with a mushy cable-knit cardigan Marlowe wanted to snuggle in forever, though she tried not to pet it while he was watching. After a bit of small talk, he led her into the kitchen. Like the living room, the kitchen had a high ceiling and open views to the surrounding hills. The cabinetry was finished in off-white brushstrokes, providing brightness and texture in a space that was otherwise punctuated with stainless steel and dark, sleek granite, perhaps in Angus's favorite gray. The room felt like him: a blend of hard and soft Marlowe hadn't fully worked out yet. She contemplated the matter while she parked herself at the island and watched him scan the contents of his fridge.

"How do you feel about omelets?" he asked.

"I feel great about omelets, though I haven't had one in ages."

"What do you usually eat for breakfast?"

"Coffee. Toast. With butter if I remember to get to the grocery store. I've also been known to eat handfuls of Cheerios from the box when I forget to pick up milk."

He shook his head without looking at her. "Okay. Maybe I am a food snob. At least it'll be easy to impress you." He lined up tomatoes while she tried not to wonder if she wanted to be impressed. Probably not. Definitely not. But also . . . maybe?

"I have way too much cheese in here." He drew out a shallow drawer and set it on the counter. "Pick one. Or two or three. I'm good with any of them."

Marlowe studied the drawer with caution. Feeling out of her depth as someone who usually purchased cheese in individually wrapped slices with bright orange discount stickers, she dug around and held up something labeled in French.

"How about this one?" She faced the label toward him.

His eyes widened. "That one? Really? For an omelet?"

"Wow. Sorry." She started to put it back.

"I'm kidding." He laughed as he took it from her, setting it beside a growing pile of fresh herbs and vegetables. "I need to work on my comic timing."

"Or I need to work on my sarcasm radar."

"I suspect it's pretty acute already. You wouldn't tolerate me otherwise."

"I don't tolerate you. I'm only here for the free laundry."

"Then we'd better cook fast." He flashed her another smile, one that included a glint of mischief in his amber eyes, a glint she added to her growing list of things she didn't notice. Also included: the way he tested the ripeness of each tomato with a gentle squeeze and brushed soil off mushroom caps with the edge of his thumb. *That* thumb.

Unable to control her wandering thoughts without an activity, Marlowe asked Angus to put her to work. He set her up chopping herbs while he cracked eggs. The task was perfect. Without it she'd be fidgeting nonstop. He'd ask her why she was nervous. She'd claim she wasn't nervous. He'd tease her about being unlucky, flirting his way through her defenses until she accidentally blurted out that she came in his shower last night. For . . . reasons. Definitely better to chop herbs.

"I looked up that article this morning," Angus said as he whisked a splash of fresh cream in with the eggs. "I should've seen it coming. I overestimated the darkness of the club and the density of the crowd. I'm sorry I put you in that situation."

She shifted a shoulder. "Not much we can do about it now."

He stopped scrambling. "It won't be the only article. Your episodes won't stream for another three months. Now that a story's been planted, the PR department will run with it, use the time to build a 'did they or didn't they' debate. I made an appointment to meet with my personal rep on Monday. We'll find a way to pivot the narrative about Tan, and I've already deleted that shot of you and me, but I don't have much control over what the studio puts out. They'll use whatever will make people tune in."

A tremor of anxiety rippled through Marlowe, prickling like pins and needles.

"In other words, I can expect more frozen beverages in my hair?"

"Hopefully not, but you can expect more speculation, and some of the people speculating will cast you as a villain." He fluttered an apologetic smile. "I've been there. It's hard to avoid. You're either loved or hated. There's very little in-between. While it's all building, you might consider how you filter your media intake."

"You mean leave the party?"

"I mean figure out how to attend in a way that works for you. Obviously easier said than done." He retrieved a small metal bowl and helped Marlowe sweep chopped basil into it. "The gossip circus can be hard to take, especially if you haven't figured out how to tune some of it out yet." He took her hand, plucking off stray bits of basil and flicking them into the bowl. He didn't seem to notice the physical contact, but she watched every flick of his fingers. "People are hungry for clickbait. Anything you've ever put online is now fair game. Personal pics, offhand comments that can be taken out of context, prior relationships, any possible evidence that you're not perfect. People love a good love story, but they'll tune in even faster for a total train wreck."

Marlowe slumped against the counter, letting her hand slide from his hold as she flashed through tabloid headlines skimmed at grocery store checkouts or in the margins of websites, sensationalized tales of drugs, stalking, coercion, abuse, alcoholism, sex addiction. The Twitter buzz about her had been uncomfortable enough. The accusation that she'd broken up Angus's relationship was worse. What was next? Would someone dig into her past? Find embarrassing party photos from grad school? Solicit an angry rant from Kelvin? Pull up the reviews of her design work and mock her failed career?

As if reading her thoughts, Angus set aside the bowl of basil.

"Go get your phone," he said. "Omelets can wait. Let's get you started."

Marlowe ran downstairs and returned with her phone. On Angus's instructions, she opened the Instagram account she hadn't checked in months. Her follower count was now in the hundreds and several comments had been added to her meager photos. Some comments were simple emoji chains or encouraging *You go, girl!*–type phrases. Others berated her for being a cheap, ugly bitch who didn't deserve Angus Gordon's attention, or anyone else's. Everyone had an opinion and they shared it freely. People criticized her clothes, her haircut, her complexion, her body. They called her a slut, a whore, a—

"Stop reading them." Angus shielded her screen with his hand. "Just lock down your account as private. Better yet, delete it entirely. If you'd rather keep it, I can get my media assistant to go through and clean it up for you, delete anything the trolls have taken over, block anyone who lashed out."

Marlowe rapidly changed her settings to private, following suit with her Facebook and Twitter accounts, neither of which she used often but both of which had received a similar influx of activity over the last forty-eight hours.

"Why are people so mean?" she asked. "They don't even know me."

"Cruelty and ignorance aren't mutually exclusive. More often the opposite. This is why I've been steering clear of social media. It has its place as a venue for sharing and connecting. It's also an open invitation for any wounded soul to question your values or shred your sense of self-worth from behind the safety of their screen. Not worth it."

Marlowe let her eyes skim over a few tagged Twitter comments. *Get your own man, you skanky bitch. How drunk was he? Did you get that dance through the Make-A-Wish Foundation? You must give good head.* With a defeated groan, she closed the app and agreed to let Angus's media assistant handle the cleanup. As a marginal social media user whose interaction usually topped out at a heart-eyed face or a thumbs-up, she hadn't expected so much random outrage.

Granted, her public image was currently that of a sexually charged boyfriend stealer—hardly a magnet for likes—but still . . .

"Anything else I should check?" she asked.

"Do you have a website? One with personal contact info on it?"

"Oh, god." She typed the address and pulled up her home page. Her contact form hid all personal information, but her address was on her downloadable résumé. As fast as she could, she pulled her résumé off the site. She'd edit and repost it later, when she and Angus weren't performing Internet triage. "I can't believe all of this started with a look."

"Funny what the camera picks up." His eyes flicked to hers for the briefest instant before they both looked away. Their mutually diverted attention didn't prevent her cheeks from flaring, so she circled the island and made a show of setting her phone out of the way. He watched her without moving, other than a slight uptick of his lips she wasn't entirely sure was really there. "You're not going to let me see your costumes?"

She tensed, looked at her phone, looked back at Angus, and shook her head.

"I can't take more criticism right now," she said.

"Who says I'd criticize?"

"Other people sure have. It's not out of the question. You might think my work is boring or amateur. You might suggest I stick to arranging bulk shoe deliveries."

"C'mon." He joined her on the other side of the island. "Show me. Please?"

"Okay, fine. But if you say anything mean, I'm calling Jeeves and the two of us are working out a truly sadistic revenge plan." She opened her home page and handed Angus her phone. While she picked at her chipped nail polish, he scrolled through photos and sketches from elaborate Shakespeare productions, modernized Greek tragedies, mid-century classics with tight color palettes and carefully selected accessories, as well as new plays in simple, contemporary dress. Her designs ranged from detailed realism to bold, high abstraction, some shows mostly scavenged and others highly polished with everything built from scratch.

"This is what you really want to be doing?" he asked.

"Yes. And no." She pulled up the *New York Times* review of her last show and let Angus read it. The play was an expressionist piece she'd costumed in a mix of period styles, exaggerated in shape and all made from metallic fabrics. The *Times* had said she missed the mark, too focused on making something that looked cool while completely neglecting the humanity of the characters. "That's not the only one. *Everyone* hated the costumes. The show completely flopped. No one on the team directly blamed me, but we all knew I'd contributed to the show's failure. My choices brought everyone else's down. I hated that feeling. I never want to go through it again."

Angus nodded to himself while typing something into the search bar.

"*In the rare instances when Gordon keeps his shirt on for an entire scene*," he read, "*his performance leaves little to remark upon.*" He scrolled down. "*Given Jake Hatchet's penchant for arson, how does Gordon create so little heat with his costars?*" He scrolled again. "*Every time Gordon appears on-screen, I count the seconds until he drives off on his motorcycle and the real actors can take over.*" He let out a breathy laugh as his eye caught on something else. "Here's a real winner. *Angus Gordon is what you get if you cross a rotten carrot with a terrible actor.*"

Marlowe grabbed her phone and read the last comment for herself.

"That doesn't even make sense," she said.

"It doesn't have to. Like I said, open invitation."

"Also, you're a really good actor."

"And you're a really talented designer." He took her phone and set it facedown, out of her reach. "We live in a world of constant criticism. Some of it's thoughtful and insightful. Most isn't. But it shouldn't stop you from doing what you love."

Marlowe took a deep breath as she gave her phone serious side-eye. *I know,* she thought. *I know, I know, I know.* But she couldn't quite make herself believe it.

"Maybe that one show was terrible," Angus continued. "Maybe it was only terrible to some people. You can't please everyone, but the cool thing about what I do or what you do"—he nodded toward her phone—"is that we get to try again tomorrow, and the next day, and the day after that. We grow. We get better. We toughen up. We take a stab at something new and see if it works. If it doesn't work, we don't make that choice again. Fortunately we can make hundreds of other choices."

"By 'other choices,' I assume you don't mean pursuing a job that limits my creativity to selecting flat or round shoelaces?" She flashed him a painfully forced grin.

He didn't return it, forced or otherwise. He simply waited while her grin faded.

"Failure sucks. I don't mean to diminish that, but it's only an endpoint if we let it define us." He nudged her phone further from her reach as if he could sense it haunting her. With his hip pressed against the counter and his hand planted a few inches away, the slightest lean would bring her against his chest. She was dying to make that lean, to find comfort in being close to him. It would be so easy. Until, of course, it wasn't. One dance had caused enough problems. She didn't have a thick skin or a good therapist. So she drew Angus's sweater more tightly around her body. It was like a hug. Only . . . not.

"Anyone ever tell you you're pretty smart?" she asked.

"Not once. Not ever. High praise coming from a Yalie." He slid his hand across the counter and gave her waist a little nudge with his knuckles. She added it to her list of things she didn't notice. "Jury's out on my intelligence and I may be half carrot, but after seeing your website, I can tell you with all due authority that you shouldn't run errands for Babs Koçak for the rest of your career. You have a creative voice. Use it."

"Wow. Thank you." Marlowe swallowed, struggling not to cry. Angus hadn't said anything new. She'd been telling herself the same things for months, but the words sounded different when spoken aloud and in someone else's voice. Stronger, maybe, because it wasn't as easy to argue herself into believing she was wrong.

As the moment settled, she and Angus eased back into cooking. He browned butter in a skillet while she sliced cheese, sneaking a bite and wondering why she bought the tasteless stuff. Budget, of course, but also habit. When faced with options, Marlowe almost always convinced herself she didn't deserve nice things. It was a constant battle. A low drone of not-good-enough-yet messages had underscored her upbringing. Her relationship with Kelvin amplified that message tenfold. Meanwhile, like everyone else, she was weeding through a complex system of societal influences she couldn't even begin to unpack. Amid all that, simply enjoying something nice often felt wrong.

"What about you?" she asked as she sliced. "What's your dream job?"

"Cattle tycoon."

"Seriously."

"Garnish whiz."

"Once more. This time with feeling."

"Right. A real answer." He poured the eggs into the skillet and rotated the pan with a practiced twist of his wrist. "I feel like I should say I want to play Hamlet on Broadway or earn an Oscar as a harrowed war vet. Or I want to stop acting altogether so I can produce documentaries about climate change or world poverty. I should be chasing a big, heroic dream, but the truth is, I enjoy what I do, and I think entertainment has value. I just hate the game that comes with fame, the constant filtering, the focus not on actions but on the potential perception of those actions." He lowered the pan, studying the contents with a furrowed brow.

"It's great that you already do what you love," she said, wishing she could offer him a fraction of the encouragement he'd given her.

"I *mostly* do what I love. I've played a lot of jerks and egotists." He wagged a spatula at her. "Do *not* say typecasting." He paused as if bracing for the inevitable. She mimed zipping her lips, eliciting a wry, sexy smile not unlike the earlier one she didn't notice. "One day I'd like to play a nice guy. Someone who's important enough to move a story forward but who's out of the spotlight so no one bothers to speculate about what's real and what's performance. Then maybe I can live my life without all the noise." He returned his attention to the eggs, carefully loosening the edges with the spatula.

This time it was Marlowe's turn to watch him, to see a crease form between his brows and a twitch quiver near his jaw. What she'd interpreted for so long as arrogance was now so obviously something else entirely. Impatience. Exhaustion. Frustration with a constant demand to be "on" for others. An inability to be in his own skin, in his own way.

"You think I'm ungrateful," he said, not quite forming a question.

"No, I think you're brave."

"Brave? You must be referring to that other guy." Angus leaned toward the living room. "Jeeves? You in there? Our guest has something to say to you!"

"Stop it." She gave him a halfhearted scoldy look. "I'm serious. Listen."

While helping finish the omelets, Marlowe described her childhood, how she'd bounced between two highly ambitious parents, both of them pushing a constant message to do more, be more, say more. Try harder. Get smarter. Work faster. Speak up. Lean in. Make a mark. Change the world. Always be reaching, striving, improving, producing something vital. She discussed her conflicted relationship with social media: the way it had the potential to connect her with friends but at the cost of feeling left out of events she wasn't invited to or present for, and the ways it encouraged members to engage in a relentless competition for followers, likes, and influence. Added to that was the competitive nature of the entertainment industry, the ambition required to meet the right people and promote oneself. Trying to meet the productivity bar was exhausting. And impossible.

"You're the first person I've met who wants his life to be quieter," she said. "In a world filled with messages to be louder and bigger, to take up more space, to garner more attention, denying those messages seems pretty brave to me."

"Interesting theory." Angus shuffled the omelets onto a set of plates, taking his time to sprinkle basil on top of each one, arranging it *just so*. Maybe his sudden onset of fastidiousness was due only to the basil, a means of extending their running joke about garnishes, but Marlowe got the impression her comment had made him uncomfortable. For a guy so quick to accept a compliment about his looks, he seemed completely stymied by praise about his brain or his heart.

"Hey." She set her hand on his arm, drawing his attention up. "How about we scrap everything I said and I just tell you I think you're pretty cool."

"I can't be cool *and* brave?" he joked.

"I suspect you can be anything you want to be," she said, not joking at all.

This time when he smiled, he simply looked happy.

That, she noticed.

Chapter Nineteen

While Angus set up for breakfast outside, Marlowe ran downstairs and swapped her laundry so her final load was in the dryer and she could put on something of her own. She slipped into a pair of cotton shorts, a bra, and a scoop-neck tank top that almost made her look like she had cleavage. The clothes were nothing special, but they saved her from thinking about his clothes and his scent and how his body would look in the boxer shorts she'd been wearing. And how he'd look out of those boxer shorts.

She stepped onto the patio to find Angus already seated, ankles stacked, hands laced behind his neck, gazing out past a tranquil pool to the sunlit hills. His outdoor space was as tidy as his indoor space, defined by spare décor, clean lines, and earthy textures like dark stones and polished wood. His environment was comfortable but purposeful. Every piece of furniture was carefully selected for efficient use and high-quality craftsmanship. Except, perhaps, for the books. There, content triumphed.

"It's a lot warmer outside than inside," Marlowe said, already sweating.

Angus straightened up as he turned toward her. "Welcome to L.A."

"I've lost track of seasons since I moved here." She sat down opposite him, folding her legs beneath her, a habit she'd retained from childhood when she used to worry about taking up too much space. "Does L.A. even have seasons? Ones that have nothing to do with film awards or TV listings?"

"Tired of the sunshine already?"

"I shouldn't complain. My friends in New York are hauling out warmer clothes even though we're barely into September." Her voice caught as her mind jolted into overdrive. *September*. The month printed on two hundred wedding invitations that never got sent. A canceled reservation. A simple dress in ivory organza. A rich chocolate cake, tasted but never ordered.

"Question for a question?" Angus asked, jarring Marlowe from her thoughts.

"Yes, the food smells amazing, even with the green stuff."

"Not what I was going to ask." He picked up his fork but he didn't put it to use. "What happened with your fiancé? Or was he your husband?"

She flinched so sharply she almost fell off her chair.

"How did you know?" she asked.

"You play with your ring finger a lot. I'm betting it wasn't always naked."

Marlowe glanced down to find one hand wrapped around the other, while she did exactly what he'd said she was doing. She shook out both hands and took a drink of her orange juice. Slowly. Really, *really* slowly. When Angus was still watching her as she set down her glass, she decided there was no point evading the question. He didn't seem like he'd judge her and she was obviously preoccupied.

"We were together for three years, engaged for two months. When he proposed, I didn't even have to think about it. I said yes and I meant it. We loved each other. We also knew each other.

Everything else was so uncertain. Launching careers. Moving into the city. Meeting new people. Trying to make ends meet. Amid the chaos, we had each other. That mattered."

Angus lowered his fork, leaning forward with interest. "But?"

"That's a big question. Might require a big answer."

"I have big ears." He flicked at his freckled earlobe. "Perfect for big listening."

"All right, but don't say I didn't warn you."

While they ate, Marlowe told Angus about the parties Kelvin insisted they attend together, only so he could vanish right away to hang with his friends, leaving her at sea in a room full of strangers. If she asked to leave before he was ready, he criticized her for not letting him have more fun, or for not trying to have more fun herself. Everything was on his terms. Leaving separately was unacceptable. It would make people think they were having problems. They needed to appear to be together, even if they spent the entire night in separate rooms. Then there were the date nights he hijacked by inviting friends along without asking her first. If she got even the slightest bit upset about it, he called her needy (one of her least favorite words), selfish, or insecure. Did she have issues with sharing? Why shouldn't they hang out with friends? In public he was all smiles and sweet affection, but when they were alone, he was full of criticism about her behavior, her choices, her work, her personality. Her way of approaching things was always wrong, his was right, and there was no room for compromise. Eventually Marlowe realized that to Kelvin, the appearance of a relationship was more important than the relationship itself.

"Every date was organized around who saw us together, not who we were with each other," she said as she wound melted cheese around her fork. "I think I always knew it was a problem, but we were good together in other ways, so I convinced myself the bad parts didn't matter. Until I realized they did."

"Because you got engaged?"

"I think so." She used the melted cheese to pick up bits of basil and oregano, smiling to herself at Angus's sly gambit with the inclusion of green ingredients, ones she was actually enjoying. "Once the engagement ring was on, I started picturing myself at thirty, forty, fifty, fake-smiling through parties and acting like everything was fine while growing more and more ashamed of wanting anything for myself. And then being ashamed for being ashamed since I was complicit in silencing myself."

Angus struggled to spear a slice of tomato. The effort was cute, and it made her feel less like the one who was always dropping and spilling things around him.

"So you left?" he asked as he finally managed his task.

"I did everything at once before I could talk myself out of it. Found the apartment online, set up job interviews, and bought a plane ticket. As soon as all that was locked in, I gave back the ring and had the worst conversation of my life. *Then* I left."

They ate quietly for a moment while Marlowe realized how long she'd been talking about herself, and to a guy she didn't even know very well.

"I can't believe I just told you all that," she said.

"I asked." He scraped up the last of his omelet, unceremoniously using a finger to jam a mushroom onto his fork. "I'm getting to know who Marlowe Like the Detective is. You're getting to know Angus Not Like the Beef. Next time we shoot a scene together, maybe we won't look like we want to throttle each other. Besides, no one actually enjoys small talk about the weather, especially in L.A. Seventy-two and sunny. Done."

Marlowe scanned the desert hills and the elegant mansions that perched on each outcropping, glinting in the smog-filtered sun. Angus was right. Small talk was boring. Also, having someone besides Cherry to talk to—to *really* talk to—was nice. Cherry was amazing but she was so quick to vilify Kelvin, which often made Marlowe want to defend him. The worse he seemed, the worse she felt about staying with him for so long. If Angus judged her, he didn't show it. He didn't even default to problem-solving or offering unsolicited advice like so many guys Marlowe knew. He simply listened.

"My turn to learn more about you," she said. "You know, to help with that throttling problem you mentioned."

"If Lex could see us now." He flashed her a teasing smile as he settled back in his chair, lacing his hands over his stomach. "Do your worst. What do you want to know?"

Marlowe considered asking him about his dating history but she suspected he'd long since grown tired of answering questions about who he was or wasn't with and why. She'd even read some of those articles, though she put a lot less stock in them now.

"You said you had a big family. Can you tell me more about them?"

"*That* I can do." He started with descriptions of his seven siblings. Most were living nearby, or at least somewhere on the West Coast. One of his sisters was a doctor in San Diego. Another was a tattoo artist in the Bay Area. Two of his brothers had recently launched a tech start-up together while another was training to become a pastry chef. His dad worked at the same farm that'd employed him when Angus was a kid, though he'd taken on a management role several years ago. His mom had left her factory job to run a foundation that helped immigrant laborers find employment.

They lived about an hour north of L.A. in a bright white ranch they referred to as "The House that Disney Built," a piece of information that made Angus redden slightly as he related it.

As he unfolded tales of raucous childhood antics and recent family get-togethers, he got out his phone and scrolled through photos, pausing to describe the people or events within. Marlowe's favorite shot was one of his whole family, taken on Halloween about twenty years ago. Angus was about eight at the time, the second youngest in the family. All eight kids had reddish hair, ranging from the full ginger of his younger brother to the dark auburn of his oldest sister. The kids were dressed in a motley assortment of plaid wraps and peasant shirts. Angus's dad stood beside them, dressed as William Wallace while the rest of the family played his band of rebels, blue faces and all. Apparently he spoke with a heavy Scottish brogue that elicited countless references to *Braveheart*. Though it annoyed him in general, he'd decided to embrace the association for a night.

Following that image was a sweet photo of Angus with his maternal grandmother in front of a little stone house in the harbor village of Avoch, just north of Inverness. Their arms were wrapped around each other while the wind whipped their clothes and hair. Angus also showed Marlowe shots of weddings, Thanksgiving feasts, backyard barbecues, family hikes, and vacations he'd taken with one or more of his siblings. Together the photos and stories painted a picture of a loving family that teased each other mercilessly—the source of Angus's sarcasm—but still gathered at holidays and kept in close touch. That picture helped Marlowe round out her idea of who Angus Gordon was, not the haughty TV star in the tabloids, but the thoughtful, understated guy who was sitting across from her with his cowlicks askew and his flip-flops kicked off.

The stories also shed an interesting light on her own quiet upbringing, being shuttled between her always-preoccupied parents, with no siblings or relatives around. She'd often worried about her tendency to attach so strongly to others, blurting out *I love you*s to boys who didn't feel the same way, urging her three best friends to room with her after grad school, and staying with Kelvin despite a hundred warning signs. But no wonder she got so attached to the people she cared about, and no wonder she'd gravitated to a collaborative industry. She was trying to build the family she didn't grow up with.

"I thought you were going to ask me the same question I asked you," Angus said as he wedged his phone into the back pocket of his frayed and faded jeans.

"You mean you also ditched your fiancée in a freak panic about your future?"

"No fiancée. No freak panic." He gestured for Marlowe's plate as he stood and started clearing the table. "My last relationship is a pretty ordinary tale. We met through work. She was a director. Did a couple of episodes on season two, even though pulpy, serial dramas weren't really her thing. Our relationship was good for about six months, or as good as a relationship can be when both people are working crazy hours and barely see each other. Then she left to shoot a BBC series that was basically her dream job. I stayed in L.A. After a while, the calls weren't enough."

Marlowe followed Angus into his kitchen with the empty juice glasses.

"So if you guys didn't have jobs in different cities, you might still be together?"

"Maybe, but I doubt it." He rinsed each dish before setting it in a fancy-looking dishwasher. Marlowe didn't currently have a dishwasher, but for some reason she liked knowing that Angus was also a pre-rinser. "I blamed everything on the distance at the time. We both did. It was easier than blaming each other, or blaming ourselves, but we had other issues. For one, she thought *Heart's Diner* was total crap and she wasn't shy spouting off about it. I know it's not high art, but audiences enjoy watching it, and I like the people I work with. It's a good job. I don't want to feel ashamed of what I do because Richard Attenborough isn't narrating my show and no one's wearing a frock coat."

Marlowe bit back a smile. "You know what a frock coat is?"

He fluttered a hand by his hip. "Whatever those fancy dudes wear."

"Close enough." She grabbed a washcloth and wiped the granite counters while he scrubbed the frying pan, falling into an easy cooperation as they cleaned up. She'd never minded cleaning, not like this, not after making a meal together. Even assembling simple omelets was a form of collaboration, an act of joint creation. The thought made her miss designing. It also made her miss sharing a home. The movie nights, the quickly drained bottles of wine divided four ways, the rotation of shoulders to cry on, the near-constant bustle of activity. Clearly, she should stop stalling and read Chloe's script. Soon.

The clatter of the frying pan being stowed in a cabinet renewed Marlowe's attention to the conversation—and the company—at hand.

"Season two," she said as the detail registered. "That was a few years ago now."

"Three and a half." Angus glanced over his shoulder as though he was expecting her to express astonishment. Admittedly, she was surprised he'd been single for so long, not because being single for a few years was that unusual, but because she'd seen him in so many tabloids, working through a parade of hot actresses, though she had a different perspective about those photos now. Despite her not speaking those thoughts aloud, he caught something in her expression that made his brow furrow. "This industry is hard on relationships. The hours, the travel, the media exposure. Then there's the inevitable disappointment when a girl realizes I'm not Jake Hatchet, gunning a motorcycle and lighting shit on fire, but boring, hides-in-his-trailer-and-reads-a-book Angus Gordon."

Marlowe couldn't help but laugh.

"*That's* why you keep a guard posted? So you can read without interruption?"

"Don't even tell me what you thought the guard was there for."

"To keep your precious towels from being stolen. Obviously."

He whisked a hand towel off the counter and flicked it at her hip. She darted out of reach, laughing. Soon he was laughing, too, flashing her the grin she liked so much. It wasn't fair. He had to have a flaw somewhere. A mole or pock mark? A fungal toe?

"God, I was a dick to you that day," he said.

"Yeah, but not as much of a dick as I thought you were."

He pressed a hand to his heart. "Wow. You *almost* admitted you like me."

"Almost. Though you should be highly skeptical of any flattery I offer you. I may have ulterior motives, like finagling another offer to sleep in your bed."

His brows shot up. "Oh, really?"

"Not *that* bed." She rolled her eyes while cursing her persistent blushing habit. "I should. Laundry. Check. Done. Probably. Yeah. Okay." Swearing under her breath, she spun away and fled down the stairs to the lower floor, trailed by Angus's laughter.

She folded her clothes into her duffel bag, making a quick sweep of the bathroom to ensure she didn't leave anything behind, especially girl-sized dents in the shower floor. Her blushes already gave enough away. He didn't need to know the full extent of her attraction. Or her clumsiness. Or the apparent link between the two.

When she'd fully collected her belongings and her wherewithal, she headed upstairs and set her bag by the front door.

"Leaving already?" Angus asked as he joined her in the foyer.

"I don't want to overstay my welcome. Also, I have these biweekly phone calls with my parents. Mom at two. Dad at three. I have to fit in a solid helping of parental disapproval before I can enjoy another week of professional disapproval." She sat on a leather bench and put on her sneakers. Then she found her sunglasses and ski hat.

"Hang on. Before you go." Angus opened a coat closet, took out a well-worn ball cap, and handed it to her. She melted a little when she saw the logo. New York Yankees. "The winter hat's a dead giveaway. Besides, this one suits you better."

"This one suits anyone better." She wedged the cap onto her head and tucked her hair behind her ears, adding her sunglasses and pausing to admire her new disguise in a nearby mirror. "Those SUVs are going to be out there again, aren't they?"

"Probably. The story's hot right now. Drive the speed limit. Don't slow down. Look straight ahead. Unless they've tracked your plates, you don't have to worry."

Her chest tightened. "People do that?"

"It's been known to happen."

"Forget what I said about wanting another sleepover offer." She let out a nervous laugh, one that came out juddering and breathy. It died away when she caught the lack of laughter in Angus's eyes. His lips were pressed together and a familiar crease had formed between his brows. Suddenly his magical skybox didn't seem so magical. It felt more like an essential safe house. "This was nice, though, getting to know each other better."

He nodded as he reached forward and plucked a bit of lint off her hat brim.

"You going to ignore me again on set?"

"I didn't—" She caught the challenge already rising in his eyes. "All right. I sort of did. But I have your phone number now, so if you sweep in with more heroic gestures, I promise to at least say thank you." She slung her bag onto her shoulder.

He walked her out to her car. "Ah, your unique but pungent adventure-mobile."

She reeled in faux offense. "I love my car."

"I love my grandmother. Doesn't mean I want to spend hours in her company, especially if cramped spaces are involved."

Marlowe smiled at that, struggling to make her key work in the hatchback lock.

"I did try to warn you," she said.

"Apparently we're both rather gifted at ignoring warnings."

"Sounds like a dangerous combination."

"Totally lethal." His voice came out with a dead-sexy rumble, one that made her pivot away from him so she didn't get caught up in what was pretty clearly flirtation now. She wasn't trying to flirt but he was *really* hard to not flirt with.

With a shove of her hip, she got the hatch open and tossed her bag inside. Then she unlocked the car door and forced it open with a deafening creak.

"Thanks for the hospitality," she said as she toyed with her key ring, suddenly incapable of standing still, a malady Angus appeared to share. "I'd offer to return the favor, but you won't want to sleep on a sofa that smells like dead yak, attempt to squeeze three drops of water out of my showerhead, or limit your breakfast to dry toast. Also, my apartment is decorated with creepy owls. No one should cross the threshold. Ever."

"I'll pass on the owls. And the dead yak. But I don't suppose . . ." He scratched at the back of his neck before jamming his hands into his pockets. "Sorry. Never mind."

"What?" She let out a nervous laugh at his odd shift in demeanor. "Tell me."

"It's a dumb idea. All things considered."

"All *what* things considered?"

"The media. My supposed relationship status. Propelled milkshakes."

She eyed him sideways. "You do realize you're only making me more curious."

"Right. Okay. Fair point." He slid his hands partway out of his pockets and tapped his thumbs against his weathered belt, grimacing as though he couldn't quite force the words out. Marlowe was about to press him again when he finally spoke up. "There's a benefit next week at the L.A. County Museum of Art. I have tickets. Tan's going. Idi'll be there, too, so I wouldn't be the only person you know."

Marlowe backed against the side of her car, using it to hold herself up.

"You're asking me to a museum benefit?" she choked out.

"I believe that's the suggestion on the table."

"As your"—she swallowed. Hard.—"date?"

"As whatever you'd be comfortable with. Date. Friend. Mutual warning ignorer."

"To a red-carpet event? With limousines and couture gowns?"

"Unless frock coats fit the dress code."

"And the woman everyone thinks is your girlfriend?"

"I texted Tan first thing this morning. We're working on it."

"And lots of cameras?"

"Like I said. Dumb idea."

"It's not dumb, but . . ." She sucked in a breath, nearing panic just picturing the event. All of those people. All of those eyes on her. "I can't."

Angus nodded to himself as his expression clouded over.

"I had a feeling." He backed away, his hands still shoved in his pockets.

"I'm sorry." Her shoulders inched up and a knot tightened in her gut. "I'm insanely flattered you asked, but I don't understand your world. You've had years to figure it out. I've had, what, a week? Two? Every mean comment still etches itself in my brain. I have a hard enough time liking myself. I can't show up at a public event with you. Especially if Tanareve's there. You know what people would say."

"I thought maybe we could tell them they're wrong."

"And they'd believe us? It's that easy? Tell a few reporters nothing salacious is going on and they'll never print another word about us? No more astonishment about what a guy like you would be doing with a girl like me? No more fury from the fans who still want you and Tanareve to live happily ever after together? No more being called an ugly bitch or a trashy whore who should fuck off and die?" Her throat tightened and she worried tears weren't far off. She fought them back as Angus drooped before her.

"You're right," he said. "We can't guarantee any of that."

They both went quiet, shuffling awkwardly as if neither of them could decide if they should discuss the matter further or simply say goodbye. Marlowe didn't want to do either. Instead, she wanted to throw her arms around Angus and ask if she could stay here forever. They could cook again and dream about the future. They could enjoy his pool, and maybe even his shower. They could forget anything existed outside his glass walls. But Marlowe knew that wouldn't really last forever. When the fantasy ended, they'd be here again. No point delaying the inevitable.

Before Marlowe could second-guess herself, she stepped forward and slipped her arms around Angus, drawing him into a hug. His hands pressed against her back as he laid his cheek against hers and returned her embrace. His stubble was surprisingly soft against her cheek. His body was unsurprisingly solid in her arms, and she felt more solid in his. As she drew him closer still, holding and being held for the first time in many months, she confirmed that Angus was, in fact, a good hugger.

He gave her a final, affectionate squeeze before dropping his embrace. She got into her car and rolled down the window, or at least she tried to roll it down, inching it open far enough to peek out above the dusty glass. She offered him one last smile, tinged with regret. He mirrored it as he stepped back and flashed her a wave.

"Guess I'll see you at the diner, Adelaide."

"That, you can count on."

Chapter Twenty

"Do you think it's possible to be in love with someone you've only known for a few days?" Cherry asked Marlowe as they left the studio coffee shop and wandered toward the wardrobe building. Monday morning had come early. They both needed caffeine. "I don't mean some here-and-gone infatuation, but a profound sense of connection."

"I guess?" Marlowe hedged, pretty sure she was leaning toward yes.

"Me too." Cherry skipped a step, practically bouncing. "Sometimes you hit it off, right? Everything falls into place where her strengths balance your weaknesses and vice versa? And you like some of the same things but not all of the same things. You make each other laugh. You're good with mutual silences. You can't stop thinking about her. Also, she's the most amaaaaaazing kisser."

"Sounds great." Marlowe forced a smile, frustrated at her tendency to default to the world's least descriptive words when she was tired, uncertain, or preoccupied. A little enthusiasm shouldn't have been hard to muster. However . . .

Did Angus really ask me out? she thought. *Did I really say no?*

"You and Maria got together again yesterday?" she asked aloud.

"I went straight to her place after work Saturday night. I couldn't stay away. Yesterday we lounged around in bed most of the day. Soapy binging on Netflix. Ice cream. *Lots* of fooling around. Total heaven." Cherry stumbled again and paused to check her clothes for coffee damage. She was in her usual skinny black jeans and black designer jacket, but her baby-blue T-shirt added a pop of color. Puffy letters read *UNICORNS ONLY POOP RAINBOWS IF THEY EAT LEPRECHAUNS*. It was one of Marlowe's favorites, though she couldn't say why. "What did you do on your day off?"

"Um . . ." Marlowe sniffed her coffee, buying a second to decide how much to divulge. Cherry had always been so anti-Angus, and Marlowe didn't really want to get into it. "Nothing exciting. Laundry, of course. I finally got my landlord to fix the broken plumbing. And I had the usual *Yes, Mom and Dad, I'm failing as an adult* talks."

"Do they know about your role on the show?"

"God, no." Marlowe snorted out a laugh as she pictured the conversation. "Even if I hadn't signed an NDA, my mom would leap to inquiries about income management or how the choice might impact potential progress with my career. My dad would question the societal value of the enterprise. I was lucky he even fit me in yesterday. He had to squeeze me between a meeting with his lab and a conference call with development teams in France and India. At least he only had fifteen minutes to question my life choices. My mom ran the full gamut. Career. Health. Finances. Social life. Love life."

"Guess that means she didn't see the dirt about you and Red MacMuscles."

Marlowe felt a prickle of defensiveness for Angus but she shook it off.

"My parents don't follow celebrity gossip," she said. "Their intellectual elitism often annoys me, but this week, it's helpful. What they don't know can't hurt me."

"Boy, I know that feeling." Cherry edged out of the way of two girls wheeling a rack of coveralls and a guy driving a golf cart full of plastic flamingos. As the sidewalk cleared, she elbowed Marlowe. "That club photo, though? Smoking. You should send it to Bench Boy. Hashtag yes I can do better, you presumptuous toad."

"Presumptuous toad?"

"I kind of ran out of steam there, but you get my point." Cherry tossed back a long gulp of coffee. Marlowe never knew how she did it. The coffee was always scalding for at least ten minutes. "Seriously. You got shat on by the Tanagus fan club this weekend. Might as well use the prime gloat-to-your-ex material you got handed."

Marlowe considered the idea, but not for long.

"I can't," she said. "It feels weird. If I'm worth missing, I'm worth it when I'm on my own. Not because someone famous is willing to smile at me."

"More than smile at you." Cherry waggled her slender brows. "If you can bring that much heat to the diner, Wes will write you into more than a weepy wedding scene." She laughed as if both impressed and amused, but Marlowe trudged along, unsmiling.

Did Angus really ask me out? she thought again. *Did I really say no?*

"Do you think Babs saw the article?" she asked.

"We'll know soon enough." Cherry tipped her chin toward the nearby parking lot. Between two rows of rust-free convertibles and SUVs, Babs flung out an arm to lock her car while marching toward the wardrobe building, her arms laden with shopping bags. "The militant stride says yes, but she's not stress-eating yet, so maybe not?"

Marlowe and Cherry gave Babs a solid head start before they followed her to the main wardrobe office. Elaine was calmly typing away at her computer, dressed in an orange shirt so vivid even a crossing guard would've squinted. On the other side of the room, wearing an immaculate silk pantsuit, Babs crunched her way through a packet of sunflower seeds while manically flipping magazine pages on a gently faded sofa. Each page snapped as she turned it. Then she licked her thumb and yanked the next one over. Judging by the number of sunflower seed shells that were already accumulating, Babs had seen—or at least gotten wind of—the gossip about Marlowe and Angus.

She looked up and spotted the girls entering. With a momentary arch of an ebony eyebrow, she continued torturing the magazine. Marlowe exchanged a wary look with Cherry before easing into "How was your weekend" small talk with Elaine. While Elaine recounted a cute story about her kids, Cherry joined Babs on the sofa.

"How soon do fittings start?" she asked. "Are we still prepping the classroom scenes this morning or did they shift the shoot schedule again?"

"We're on schedule," Elaine called over from her desk. "But we got the script changes for next week. I'm running fittings today. You three have a more exciting task."

Babs quietly harrumphed as she thwacked another page into position.

Cherry cautiously peered over Babs's shoulder. "Wedding gowns?"

"Given more notice, we could've set up appointments at Dior, Givenchy, Vera Wang, Elie Saab. Better yet, we could've ordered something custom. Mask all those figure flaws." Babs flapped an impatient hand at Marlowe. "With this new church scene shooting next week, we should probably cut our losses and head straight to Hattie's."

Cherry grinned at Marlowe, her lash extensions fluttering with excitement.

"Hattie's?" Marlowe gasped out, knowing it to be one of the most expensive and exclusive bridal outlets in town. "Are you sure that's necessary? For a waitress?"

Babs lowered the magazine, glaring at Marlowe the way someone might peer over the top rim of their glasses, only Babs didn't wear glasses. Just pure annoyance.

"It's the season finale, for heaven's sake, possibly the end of the entire run. Your little character may be a virtually nameless plot device, but audiences will tune in by the droves to find out about Jake. I can't toss you into a polyester meringue with a scrap of cheap tat at the neckline." She pursed her lips and puffed out a breath through her nose. "If we get the look right, everyone will talk about it, cover it, copy it. You're no Meghan Markle, but I'll work with what I've got." She bit into another sunflower seed and extracted the shell with her deep maroon fingernails. When Marlowe continued to gape, newly freaked out about how much attention her scene could get, Babs nudged a nearby shopping bag with her toe. "No point just standing there. You might as well get these clothes hung up. But don't assume you're getting paid as a PA for today."

An hour later, Marlowe was parked on a plush loveseat at Hattie's, sorting Babs's latest receipts and staying out of the way while Cherry trailed Babs through the boutique, closely shadowed by a trio of impeccably polite saleswomen. Cherry mostly served as a sounding board for Babs's opinions, displaying a shrewd ability to gauge when her input might or might not be welcome. She also had a good eye for fit and proportion. She really did deserve a chance to be a designer in her own right, rather than continuing on as Babs's assistant year after year, but the more Marlowe learned about the workings of the film industry, the less likely it seemed that Babs would be the source of Cherry's big break. It wasn't impossible, but giving an assistant a leg up turned that assistant into direct competition. Thus far Babs hadn't demonstrated much patience for competitors.

As she made her selections, the saleswomen carried them into a large and elegantly decorated fitting room. Marlowe tried to focus on the paperwork Babs had dumped in her lap, but she kept getting distracted by passing swaths of white and ivory. Since audiences wouldn't get a glimpse of the wedding, Babs had to pack the spectacle into a single gown. It was the sort of design challenge Marlowe used to love. How could she tell a full story with a single costume? What did the dress say about the world behind the church doors? About the bride? About the groom the audience would never meet? About the life that lay behind the couple, and the one that lay ahead? Babs didn't seem to be asking these questions. She wanted something enviably stylish with a lot of "wow factor." Even better if the label could lead to promotional opportunities.

With the first round of selections made, a saleswoman hooked Marlowe into a corset-like bustier. She assessed the fit before handing off four silicone pouches disgustingly but appropriately referred to in the industry as chicken cutlets. Marlowe had always been thin—not surprising since she'd been raised to not actually enjoy food—but the bustier reduced her figure to a size two. Everyone but her seemed elated about this fact, especially once she installed her fake boobs. Yet again, she questioned the notion of staying in L.A. any longer than necessary. Of course, New York had its own pressures about appearances, but at least she could hide her lack of muscle definition in baggy sweaters nine months out of the year. She could also order from menus that weren't half vegan.

The first dress she tried on had a satin bodice with a plunging neckline and a halter neck that tied in a generous bow. Tulle spilled out from the waistline, yards and yards of it. The color was gradated from ivory to a barely discernable pink, cut in choppy sections that lengthened toward the floor and trailed behind her as she stepped into the main room for inspection. Cherry gasped with delight but Babs simply tipped her head to the side and tapped her lips with a single finger, quietly *hmm*-ing.

Marlowe tried to stand still as saleswomen pointed out the gown's features or suggested shoe styles, but soon enough she was twisting at her ring finger. Despite a monumental effort at compartmentalizing, her memories refused to stay buried. An earnest proposal and an eager acceptance. Early wedding discussions. In the city or just outside? How many guests? What would "their song" be? Should they write their own vows? Video or still photography? Seated meal or buffet? What about flowers?

The lights grew a little too bright, the temperature a little too warm. Marlowe shifted foot to foot, counting as she inhaled. *One, one thousand. Two. Three. Four.*

Cherry held two veils out to Babs. Babs selected the longer one.

More memories burst into view. Handing back the ring. Kelvin's face. The hurt. The anger. The questions Marlowe couldn't answer. *Why now? What changed? What do you think you're going to find out there?* Closing the door on her New York apartment. Opening the door on the one in L.A. The quiet. The stillness. The smell.

The lack of anything familiar. Night after night alone. A trash can filled with takeout boxes. A side of the bed that never got rumpled. Empty chairs at the kitchen table. A single mug in the sink. A single fork. A single toothbrush. A single towel. Always one. Only one.

"We'd have to trim it," Babs said from far, far away.

"And lose the edging?" Cherry suggested, also oddly distant.

Marlowe breathed. Counted to four. Pressed a hand against her uneasy stomach. Were the lights getting brighter? Why was she sweating so profusely? The long-line bra was probably hooked too tightly. The halter at the back of her neck also pinched. While she plucked at it, Cherry secured the veil on Marlowe's head. It was just enough weight to tip Marlowe's balance, forcing her to stagger sideways a step.

Cherry reached out and steadied her. "Are you okay?"

"Yeah, I'm just a little . . . um . . ." She caught her full view in a three-sided mirror: a bride, in white, ready for her wedding.

She took a breath. Then she fainted.

Marlowe awoke slowly, blinking up at a pebbled ceiling with a quartet of baroque chandeliers that caused hot spots in her vision. She patted a hand around to discover she was lying on a carpeted floor and still wearing the tulle wedding dress, though by the free movement of her rib cage, she guessed both the dress and the bustier had been unfastened. As she shifted, a slippery silicone cutlet slid into her armpit, confirming her assessment.

She started to sit up. "I'm so sorry."

A firm hand rested against her shoulder, holding her in place.

"Stay there," said a calm and soothing voice. "Get your bearings. Don't rush."

"She could rush a *little*," said a far less soothing voice. "We're only costuming a new season finale with a week's notice, but by all means, lie around as long as you like."

Marlowe rolled her head to the side to see Cherry kneeling beside her, holding out a glass of water. Behind Cherry, Babs was seated on the corner of a gilded sofa with her legs tucked up and her eyes glued to her phone. She was perfectly coifed with her swoop of black hair, perfectly attired in her crisp silk suit, and perfectly unconcerned with the girl half-clad in a couture gown, lying on the floor, newly returned to consciousness.

"When you're ready." Cherry snuck a little side-eye at Babs. "Not before."

Two saleswomen scurried over. One carried a pillow she tucked under Marlowe's head. The other handed off a damp cloth Marlowe laid across her forehead.

"Was the dress too tight?" the first woman asked.

"Low blood sugar?" asked the other. "We can get you some juice. Or cookies."

"I'm okay," Marlowe murmured. "Just, you know, overactive brain issues."

Cherry slumped forward, her expression pained. "Bench Boy?"

"Bingo." Marlowe plucked the remaining cutlets from her bra and set them aside. When her brain fog cleared, she dragged her body upright and wedged herself against a sofa leg, tipping back her head to keep the cool, wet cloth there. As if sensing they were no longer needed, the saleswomen returned to the front desk area, slyly observing the action from a polite distance. Grateful to not be fussed over, Marlowe took the glass from Cherry and sipped at the cold water within. "This is so embarrassing. All of these doubts and questions. I keep thinking I've put him behind me. Then *bang!* There he is again."

Cherry flicked at the mountain of tulle. "The date's coming up soon, isn't it?"

"This weekend." Marlowe smoothed her ruffles, making order from chaos. "For a second I saw myself in another life, the one I didn't choose, wondering where I'd be now, wondering if I'd always wonder, and if I'd ever shed the last of my regrets."

"It's pretty natural that you'd feel some anxiety right now," Cherry said.

"Is it?" Marlowe glanced over her shoulder and confirmed that Babs's attention was still locked on her phone. Babs didn't look up but Marlowe scooted closer to Cherry, just in case. "My parents made ending a relationship seem so easy. When they divorced, my dad moved closer to New York, grateful to focus more attention on his job. My mom gleefully redecorated every room in our Providence house. She reupholstered furniture, changed carpeting, switched out artwork, and painted every wall. He started dating right away. She amped up her exercise routine. They both treated the transition as a glorious fresh start. They moved on. They focused on other things."

Cherry scoffed. "You know those are coping strategies, right? Not showing your pain doesn't mean you don't feel it."

"I guess." Marlowe let her eyes glaze over at the pink-and-white froth in her lap, wondering if her parents' "coping strategies" had left her ill-equipped to deal with loss, change, and even hurt feelings. Her parents rarely showed emotions, so she never knew what to do with her own, except feel ashamed of them. But hearts couldn't be painted over like walls, primed and freshened up with bold colors that masked old marks. Some of the marks stuck around for a really long time. Some probably stuck around forever.

After Marlowe emptied the glass, she set it aside and adjusted the front of the gown where it dangled from her neck, gaping over her chest before spilling into an unruly mass of tulle. It really was a beautiful dress, far nicer than the one she'd selected for herself. The one she hadn't quite bought, which was probably a sign in itself.

"Guess I wasn't ready to see myself in a wedding gown," she said. "Not unless it was one I was wearing to a real altar with a real groom. I don't even know why I care. Kelvin was the one who was dying to get married, who wanted a big ceremony with lots of guests. I made theater every day. I didn't need to center myself in it."

Cherry took Marlowe's hand and gave it a reassuring squeeze.

"You care because marriage is about more than a ceremony," she said. "It's about companionship and mutual support. It's about two people promising to shield each other from loneliness until the day they die. That's a powerful fucking offer."

Babs let out a quiet but harsh bark of laughter. Marlowe and Cherry craned around to face her. Babs eyed them with raised brows, pursed lips, and a general air of superiority, as though they were ignorant little children and she was put out by their simplistic babbling. She pocketed her phone as she stood, pausing to scan the shop, taking in the décor and merchandise, the gowns, the veils, the shoes and jewelry.

"Saying *I do* doesn't guarantee that love will last," she said as if she was addressing the veil display and not the girls seated on the floor. "It doesn't erase any relationship problems you had before your marriage. It doesn't make both partners put in the same effort after marriage. And it doesn't stop your husband from leaving you twenty years later for a woman half your age."

Marlowe's jaw dropped open as Cherry's eyes widened. Babs looked down on them both, her expression the usual combination of strained patience and mild disdain.

"The world we live in offers men more choices than it offers to women. Might as well seize the ones we *are* offered." She met Marlowe's gaze for the briefest of seconds, a fleeting moment of understanding that bordered on encouragement without *quite* reaching it. Then she marched away and joined the saleswomen near the main desk.

Marlowe continued gaping, unable to turn her head or avert her eyes.

"Did you know she'd been married?" she whispered.

Cherry shook her head, still wide-eyed. "She's never mentioned a husband. I thought she'd always been single, perhaps by choice, perhaps . . . not by choice."

Marlowe stifled a smile at that. She knew as well as anyone that Babs wasn't the easiest person to get along with, but maybe she hadn't always been so abrasive and dictatorial. Maybe her relationship scars couldn't be painted over, either. Whether those scars ran shallow or deep, her irritability about Angus had a whole new dimension now, and Marlowe had new motivation to stop lingering in unknowable what-ifs about Kelvin.

While Marlowe continued reeling, Cherry snuck her a wink.

"Conversation for our next night out." She clambered up and assisted Marlowe to her feet. Marlowe pressed the gaping gown and bustier to her chest while smoothing out the worst of the wrinkles in the tulle. Cherry lent a hand, though the dress needed a proper steaming after being crumpled on the floor. "You going to be okay?"

"Eventually," Marlowe said. "The timing on all of this isn't ideal. It's too bad. Anyone else would be thrilled to be trying on couture wedding gowns."

"Not anyone." Cherry grabbed the gelatinous cutlets from the floor. "And don't forget, you're not trying on gowns. You're trying on costumes. Costumes are magical. What we do is magical. It's about fantasy and make-believe. With the right costume, a girl can be a princess or a warrior or the queen of the goddamned intergalactic alliance. So go with it. Seize the fantasy." She slung an arm over Marlowe's shoulders and ushered her toward the dressing room. "Next week you'll enter a church where your imaginary groom will be waiting. He can be anyone at all. Knowing that, do you really want him to be a guy who *tells* you what you know instead of asking you? Or who only does nice things when other people can see? Hell, no." She flung out her free arm, practically beaning a nearby saleswoman. "Put Prince Fucking Charming at that altar. Make him whoever you want him to be. Dream it. Own it. You with me?"

Marlowe glanced over her shoulder to see Babs watching her, brows raised. *Might as well seize the choices we're offered,* she'd said, and Marlowe had heard her, loud and clear. She took in the racks of gorgeous dresses, the amazing friend by her side, and the boss she hated a little bit less than she used to. This wasn't a moment for looking back. It was a time to look forward.

"Yeah." She leaned into Cherry's embrace. "I'm with you."

Chapter Twenty-one

On Wednesday morning, after packing her entire Tuesday checking off items on Babs's most menial and extensive task list to date, Marlowe *finally* read the Adrienne Achebe play Chloe had emailed. Taking advantage of her second day as an actress—or, more notably, of her time away from her punishing PA duties—she carefully flipped pages while Ravi did her Adelaide makeup and an assistant touched up her nails.

The story revolved around a group of young women who disappeared on a nameless road in a timeless place. They wandered as ghosts, searching for someone who'd record their stories, as told in languages that were no longer spoken. The dialogue was complicated and dense, delving into issues about gender, race, privilege, power, generational trauma, the flaws of the legal system, and the malleability of language.

The script provided little concrete information about the world of the play, so the team producing the work would have a lot of freedom with the design. The thought was both frightening and inspiring. Mostly the latter. By the time Marlowe finished the last page, her mind was racing with images of colorful art about the

Great Migration, early daguerreotypes of glassy-eyed women, news articles about the Highway of Tears, and the hidden text that asylum inmates used to embroider into their clothing, lacking paper and ink. *This* was why she'd pursued her design career. *This* was what she craved. Art. Symbols. History. Identity. Meaning.

"Better than *Heart's Diner*, season six, episode twenty-one?" Ravi handed Marlowe a tissue. She used it to dab at the tears she didn't even realize had formed.

"It depends on your taste, but to me, yeah, way better." She fanned the corners of the script, buzzing at the sheer possibility of working on the production. If not this play, something similar, and soon.

With only a month left on her contract, Marlowe could head east sometime in October. If her old room with her friends wasn't available yet, she could visit her parents for a week or two. Sure, she'd voiced interest in working on Babs's film gig, but a lot had happened over the past few days. Between her conversations with Angus, her pep talk from Cherry, and Babs's unexpected advice to seize her choices, Marlowe was ready to stop running away from what she really wanted to do, and where she really wanted to be.

In fact, she was so ready to build forward momentum, she'd texted Kelvin last night. The text had taken her ages to compose, to ensure it was kind and clear and honest, but once she hit *send*, she was pleased to note that she wasn't overcome with her usual swell of guilt and doubt. She'd said what she needed to say. No regrets. No backpedaling.

Kelvin: You know this isn't right. Can we at least talk about it?

Marlowe: It is right. Messy and complicated but right.

I'm sorry I hurt you and that the end felt so sudden. I should've realized sooner. I should've handled things better once I did realize. We were good in some ways but not in enough ways. Thank you for all the times you were there for me. I'll always be grateful for what we had but it's over. I'm moving on. You should too. There's nothing more to talk about. I think it's best if we don't text for a while. I need some time on my own. Take care of yourself.

Setting aside thoughts of big futures for more immediate stresses, Marlowe drew the TV script from beneath the play script and reread her scene for the umpteenth time. It was only three pages long. Reconnect with Jake. Reveal the ring. Look tortured. Walk away. That was it. She knew the words. She'd been in front of a camera already. She was even getting along with Angus now. It was all going to be fine. Totally, utterly fine.

Ravi set a hand on her shoulder. "Stop shaking. It'll be over before you know it."

"What if I can't make the words sound real?"

"Just do your best. No one expects perfection on the first take, and editors can work wonders, though don't tell them I told you to rely on their mastery." He touched up a smudged spot at the corner of her eye before immersing her in a mist of setting spray.

Cherry came by a few minutes later to ensure Marlowe was in costume and ready to go. Babs even peeked in this time and double-checked everything: the lapel line on the uniform, the roll of the ankle socks, the length of the chain that held the wedding ring, the placement of the freckle on Marlowe's ear. In true form, once she'd approved Marlowe's look, she noted that Marlowe should start the next round of returns first thing tomorrow morning. The invoices were also stacking up and Elaine needed a hand organizing next week's background costumes. And by the way, the wedding gown would be ready to pick up next Tuesday. Marlowe might've imagined it, but she swore Babs hid a smile as she doled out this last errand. The fitting at Hattie's had lasted for over eight hours. Marlowe had tried on more than thirty gowns, but when she exited the dressing room in the right one, everybody knew. And *everybody* smiled. Even Babs. Even Marlowe.

While she waited to be called to set, she checked her phone. Thankfully, Kelvin hadn't replied. The only new text was on the group thread with her friends. It read *Tell your new boyfriend hi from us*, along with a link to a YouTube montage of shots in which Jake Hatchet took off his shirt, dropped his jeans, or otherwise stripped down during one of his many sex scenes. Marlowe had forgotten how often Angus took off his clothes for the show, though he never went full frontal. She inched her thumb toward the exit button but she decided the video was useful as research. If another director asked her to imagine tearing off Angus's clothes, she should make that image as vivid as possible. Also . . .

Did he really ask me out? she thought for the millionth time now. *And did I really say no?*

Angus was already on set when Marlowe was finally escorted there by one of the ADs. The crew had captured the necessary interior shots last week, including a quick interchange in which Adelaide responded to Jake's recognition by scurrying out of the building. Today they were filming the exterior behind the diner. Angus was chatting with Fritz, the episode director, a guy in his midforties with a soul patch and an unruly mop of black hair. While Fritz made a series of sharp gesticulations, Angus ran a hand over his chin and nodded. His hair looked brighter than usual today, painted by morning sunshine that flickered through nearby palm fronds. In some moments, his hair looked more like caramel. In others it was closer to cinnamon, though neither descriptor seemed accurate.

Marlowe gave up speculating when Fritz beckoned her over. She approached cautiously, uncertain if the weekend had created any awkwardness. To her relief, Angus greeted her warmly while Fritz barely snuck in a *hello* before leaping straight to business.

"We're going to try shooting the scene in order. Give you a chance to build a connection. Wes's idea, since you're new to all this." He tipped his chin at a group of people clustered around the monitors, deeply immersed in conversation. Among those present was Wes, in his flannel shirt and Oakland A's cap. While Fritz was responsible for directing the episode, the show was and always had been Wes's baby. "Once we have a full take that works, we'll break the scene into smaller sections and also reset for alternate angles." He looked to Marlowe.

She nodded, tucking her hands into her pockets so she wouldn't chew on her nails and ruin the continuity. Ten seconds on set and she was already sweating buckets. As if sensing her anxiety, Angus set a calming hand on her lower back.

Fritz clapped his hands together in response. "Oh, good. You're already comfortable with each other. That'll help. Should we do a dry run?"

Marlowe nodded as she glanced around at the flurry of activity that surrounded her: camera operators, sound guys, grips, Maria with her script in hand, ADs in headsets, Babs, Wes and his colleagues, hair and makeup people, set decorators. The list went on and on, and every person present would be waiting for her to get the scene right. The scale of it all gave her a whole new respect for the actors. The pressure was insane.

Fritz led Marlowe to a stack of milk crates that'd been carefully painted to look dingy. Trash and cigarette butts speckled the ground while an upturned oil drum served as a side table with a rolled-up magazine and the leftovers from someone's fake lunch.

"Adelaide, you're already here, having escaped the diner after realizing that Jake recognized you." Fritz gestured at the crates. Marlowe took a seat and faced the direction he indicated. "Also, if you sit, we don't have to put Angus on an apple box."

"What's an apple box?" Marlowe asked.

Angus laughed as he sauntered over. "I'm too short to fit the acceptable model of manhood. Bane of my career. They like to give me something to stand on."

Marlowe couldn't help but smile at that. With the height of her perch, she was about eye level with Angus's chin, a clever way to make him appear taller than she was on screen, especially in close-ups. What a weird world, where she couldn't be filmed without hours of plucking and padding, and where he needed a booster box or a deliberately seated costar.

Fritz framed the two of them, making L shapes with his thumbs and forefingers.

"Remember, Adelaide, your goal is to get through this conversation without becoming attached. You want to put your tie to Jake behind you. Jake, you've been waiting for this moment for over a decade. You'll do anything for another chance. You're both private people, so you don't come out and say all of that, but we have to feel it." Fritz talked through the blocking, including the path of Jake's entrance at the start of the scene and Adelaide's exit at the end. They discussed a few nuances in the dialogue. Then Fritz left the pair alone for a moment as he checked in with his crew.

Angus stepped in front of Marlowe, gripping her gently by the shoulders.

"You doing okay?" he asked.

"If one step away from a panic attack is considered okay."

"It's better than no steps." He massaged her shoulders as she tried to exhale her stress. "The trick is to forget all of these people. Use whatever feels real for you. Pretend I'm your ex if it helps. Or think of me as the asshole who opened your life up to a media frenzy because he didn't keep his hands off you at a club."

She smiled a little at the memory of their dance, but her joy quickly faded, smothered by the disappointment that their dance wouldn't lead to anything more, though that disappointment was smothered by the near-panic that kept creeping in.

"What will you be thinking?" she asked.

"Exactly what Fritz said. That I'll do anything for another chance." He snuck her a hint of a smile before moving his hands to the back of her neck.

She let her head drop forward to give him more room. His thumbs pressed along either side of her spine, slow and deliberate. He was such a calming presence, so solid and steady and confident. Also, his dark jeans fit him really well, slung low on his hips with a thin gray T-shirt that barely lapped the waistband. She shouldn't be staring at his jeans from this particular angle, but that video montage was fresh in her mind. Then again, so was the LACMA benefit she wouldn't attend with him, and the feel of vanilla shake sliding down her face and neck, and all of those ugly words . . .

Her thoughts broke off as Fritz started the rehearsal. They ran the scene while he observed, consulting with Wes and making adjustments before running it again. When they had a shape everyone was happy with, the crew set up to record.

"Remember," Angus said as he gave Marlowe's shoulder a reassuring squeeze. "Forget all of these people. No one else is here. Just you and me. Fighting over that second chance." He waited for her nod. Then he returned it and ducked out of sight.

Despite his advice about forgetting the people, a parade of preparation ensued. A makeup assistant powdered Marlowe's face. Patrice from the hair department adjusted Marlowe's ponytail and combed every last flyaway into place, with the exception of two tendrils that awaited a well-timed tuck behind her ear. Elaine checked the necklace and plucked a speck of fuzz off Marlowe's shoulder. The director of photography held a little device in front of her face, testing light quality or something else Marlowe didn't fully understand. Sound guys did a volume check and discussed ambient noise. A continuity monitor shifted the magazine on the oil drum. By the time everyone was ready to roll, at least thirty people had fussed with something in Marlowe's vicinity.

Just you and me, she recited to herself. *Just you and me.*

The world around her gradually settled into place, everyone going still and quiet. Fritz caught her eye, raising his brows, silently asking if she was ready. She checked her hands. Relatively steady, especially when anchored in her lap. Her heart rate was another matter. Thankfully, no one would see her racing pulse on camera, though the giant boom mic hanging over her head looked strong enough to pick up the sound. She took a deep breath before nodding. The woman beside Fritz stepped in front of the camera with a clapboard, announcing the scene. With a sharp snap of the boards, they were rolling.

Marlowe stared off into the distance, immediately to the left of the camera and the three guys in black tucked in beside it. Footsteps approached behind her, slow and steady. She stiffened at the sound.

"You always were one for sudden departures," Angus said.

She played with her earlobe, drawing attention to the fake freckle, giving him time to close about half of the distance toward her.

"The diner gets so stuffy," she said. "I needed fresh air."

"There are better places to find it."

She glanced around at the trash near her feet. When her gaze lifted, Angus was stepping up beside her in his dusty leather motorcycle jacket. His hair was slicked back in Jake's trademark low pompadour. His jaw was set with stony determination. His eyes were locked on hers.

"I-I shouldn't even be here," she stammered. "I've been filling in for my cousin before I have to get to . . . a family event. Just a few days. By Sunday I'll be gone."

"Then I'm glad I came by before Sunday." He barely moved, every gesture subtle, well-honed for the camera. A lift of his chin hinted at a challenge, a tilt of his shoulders brought him closer.

She turned away, pivoting on the milk crates, grateful they were glued together.

"I should get back inside before they—"

"Thirteen years, Adelaide."

Marlowe closed her eyes. She imagined herself as a twelve-year-old girl, driving away from her first love, unable to say goodbye. The gulf of loss. The trauma of aborted potential. The empty road stretching out behind the car as her parents drove away. When she had the moment clear in her mind, she gripped the crates and pivoted back around to face Angus. Although he was dressed and styled as Jake, she could easily imagine him as the one who got away, the *what if* that tugged at her heart years after parting, the biggest missed opportunity of her life.

"I thought I'd never see you again." He brushed a tendril of hair off her face and tucked it behind her ear. The gesture was cliché, seen or described in every romance, but it was referenced so often for good reason. The tenderness of an almost touch, so close to a caress without crossing a line. Affection thinly disguised as an act of assistance.

"We had no reason to see each other again," she said.

"Didn't we?" He took a step closer.

"We were kids." She fussed with the hair he'd brushed aside, echoing his gesture as though doing so might lock in the memory. "We were young. We were bored. We had no one else to play with. It was never going to last past the summer."

"You don't believe that."

"Don't I?" She risked another look in his eyes. Amber toward the centers, russet toward the edges. Dark, thick lashes that were usually much paler. She fought back a smile as she realized they'd been coated in mascara. At her change in expression, his eyes narrowed slightly, a subtle break in his performance, a glimpse of Angus hiding within Jake's darker, harder shell. Seeing the real him grounded her. *Just you and me,* she thought as she positioned her hands to push off the milk crates. "My boss is probably—"

"You just left me there!" His voice broke on the words. His posture drooped. In an instant he was a broken man, bent, buckled, a hand clutching at his chest.

She held her position, still half-seated on the crates.

"A family emergency," she said. "We left in a hurry. I didn't have a choice."

"And if you *did* have a choice? What then? What now?"

Her hand drifted to the chain around her neck. He moved closer, his eyes brimming with heartache. Even knowing it was all fake, pity swelled inside her. In that moment she ached to hold him, though whether that instinct was for his comfort or her own, she couldn't say. Her gaze traveled over his face and landed on his lips. They were full, almost plump, perfectly bowed at the top, barely parted as his breath came out, forced and fast. She leaned toward him while her hand rolled into a fist around her chain. He smelled like soap and toothpaste. Like Angus.

"We're not kids now," he murmured just above a whisper, still drawing closer.

"No," she managed. "We're not."

He reached forward, his movement tentative, tracing one of her eyebrows.

"Can you honestly say you had no idea you might find me here?"

"I told you. I've been filling in for my cousin."

"That wasn't my question." His fingertips trailed across her cheek, along her jawline, down her nose, over her earlobe. Her breath sped up with every touch. Her nails pressed into her palm as her grip tightened on the chain. His brows rose. An inquiry. A question. A choice. A blurring line between fantasy and reality. "Tell me the truth."

"I . . . I don't have to tell you anything," she said.

"You're right." He held her face between his hands. "You don't need to say another word." He leaned toward her, moving slowly, his lips parted for a kiss.

She set a palm against his chest. He halted, his face inches from hers. She drew the engagement ring from inside her uniform and held it up so he could see.

"Is that . . . ?" he started.

"Saturday. The family event I mentioned. I'll be the one in the veil."

His brow furrowed, though otherwise he remained rigid. "But we only just—"

"We were kids," she repeated. "It was never going to last."

For several seconds neither of them moved. He stared at the ring. She watched for any change in his expression. He was the first to retreat, straightening up and running his hand over his chin in a way that was so distinctly Angus, Marlowe snapped back into reality. The cameras, lights, sound gear, and people all emerged as if from a fog, though of course they'd been there all along.

As the intensity of the moment faded, she let the ring drop back into place, pressing it to her chest before pushing off the crates.

"Goodbye, Jake." She set a hand on his shoulder as she passed. Then she carried on until she disappeared around the corner of the diner.

"Cut!" Fritz called from his spot by the monitors.

A murmur erupted as the crew leapt to task, resetting gear and checking what they'd recorded. Marlowe leaned back against the side of the diner and blew out the longest breath of her life. She knew Fritz would want a zillion more takes, but at least she'd made it all the way through the scene once. More than made it through, actually. She'd lost herself in several moments, felt what her character might feel. It was wild.

Angus appeared from around the corner, grinning broadly.

"I knew you could do it!"

"Once, maybe." She rolled her head toward him. "Repeating it's another question entirely. That was exhausting. I seriously don't know how you do this every day."

"Some days are easier than others." His eyes twinkled above his brilliant smile. He was so openly proud of her, so enthusiastic about her tiny little achievement. She couldn't remember the last time a guy looked at her this way, as though her success or failure wasn't simply a reflection on his own. "You've got this. I promise. But you have to tell me what you were thinking in that moment when you twitched."

Marlowe grimaced, recalling her blunder. "I noticed your mascara. I tried to stay in character but an image popped into my head of badass Jake Hatchet finessing his makeup right before straddling his motorcycle."

Angus flicked at his lashes. "The blond doesn't show up well on camera."

"I figured." She fanned her face, even though an entire crew was on hand to help with her high-speed sweat production. "Think Fritz noticed that moment?"

"Even if he didn't, I bet the camera caught it."

As if conjured by the mention of his name, Fritz rounded the corner of the diner. Wes emerged a second later, drumming a hand on his chest.

"Good first take," Fritz said. "Better than good. But we've been talking."

"The scene's not working," Wes added. "The tension's there but it's not enough."

Marlowe stopped fanning herself, gripped by an all-too-familiar sense of failure.

"I'm sorry," she said. "Maybe with another rehearsal—"

"No, no." Wes waved his hands in front of his face. "It's not you. It's the script."

"We want to try something new on the next take," Fritz said. "Spice it up. Raise the stakes. Make that final choice at the church the biggest will-they-won't-they possible."

Marlowe looked to Angus for reassurance but he'd gone uncomfortably still.

"When Adelaide says *It was never going to last*," Wes explained, "you'll get up to leave, as before. This time, as you set your hand on his shoulder, before you say goodbye, Jake will say *Then it won't matter if I do this*."

Marlowe's eyes darted across the faces around her.

"Do what?" she asked.

"He'll kiss you, of course."

Chapter Twenty-two

Marlowe gulped back an entire bottle of water.

"I can't do it," she said when she finally came up for air, practically gasping.

"So don't." Cherry took the empty bottle from her. "It's not what you agreed to."

They were seated on a pair of folding chairs behind a generator, just out of view of the group gathered around the set. Marlowe had requested a short break, even though she knew time was money when so many people were standing around waiting for her. Angus was back with Fritz and Wes, talking through options.

"The line's terrible," Marlowe said. "I know Jake's supposed to be a take-what-he-wants kind of guy, but there's a point where it gets kind of, I don't know, aggressive, even hostile. Jake and Adelaide barely know each other and he provides no opportunity for her to give her consent. He plunges right in. It's not romantic. It's wrong." She got up to pace, too agitated to sit still. "I've spent way too much time in messed-up relationships to perpetuate this crap. Do you realize how many messages the average woman gets in a lifetime, telling her a man's role is to want and her role is to be wanted? Like why does the guy always kiss the girl while the girl 'gets kissed'? Why can't they kiss each other?"

Cherry snorted through a smile. "So you *do* want to kiss him?"

"Yes! No!" Marlowe fanned her face, hoping her anger masked her blush. "I just mean that if *Jake* and *Adelaide* are going to kiss, it should be a mutual choice, right?"

"Totally." Cherry popped her jacket button to reveal the print on her T-shirt. It had four simple outlined figures, each with a word below their feet. The first walked up stairs. *ASCENT*. The second held a gift. *PRESENT*. The third and fourth held hands, with semicircle smiles and a heart over their heads. *CONSENT*.

"Have I ever told you you're my hero?" Marlowe asked.

"We'll do karaoke one night. I'll get you to sing it."

"For you, anything." Marlowe managed a laugh before renewing her pacing, still stuck on the issue at hand. "I was up for the fake boobs and the 'girl has to be shorter than the guy' gender norms bullshit. I didn't even mind the slow lean-in. At least it gave Adelaide agency to say no or to meet Jake halfway, but I'm so sick of seeing men in control while women are only in a position of reaction. I swear it's one of the reasons I stayed with Kelvin so long. I'd been brainwashed into thinking he was more likely to be right than I was. Even though I know—trust me, I *know*—I should see past it all. But when the entire world engages in a conspiracy to make you feel like you're not even allowed to be the subject of your own story, it's hard not to buy into it."

Cherry shot her a wry look. "You do realize you're talking to a queer woman of color, right? You don't need to tell me what messages the world sends out."

"Sorry. I can't even imagine." Marlowe sank into her chair and leaned her head on Cherry's shoulder, reaching out to knit their hands together.

The conversation might've continued, but Alejandra approached, wearing tailored separates and vivid purple glasses that formed sharp angles against her soft black curls.

"Wes called me over," she said. "It amazes me that we're still having discussions like this, and that I have to argue for why we need more women in writing and directing positions, but change is slow." She blew out a sigh. "Come on, let's go talk to the boys."

For the better part of an hour, Wes, Fritz, Alejandra, Angus, and Marlowe discussed the proposed change to the scene. Some of the writing team FaceTimed in with opinions. Angus even got Sanaya on the phone to talk through contract implications. She apologetically confirmed that asking Marlowe to alter her lines or kiss her costar was within the producers' rights. Thankfully, with Alejandra's help, Marlowe's concerns were addressed and the script was tweaked until everyone agreed on the edits. Marlowe was so wrapped up in ensuring that the scene felt consensual, she didn't fully realize she'd agreed to kiss Angus until everyone dispersed to set up for another take. As the idea sank in, she took him by the hand and drew him away from the crowd.

"This is weird," she said, stating the obvious but unable to articulate anything more complex while her adrenaline was spiking and another panic attack was nigh.

"Do you want to talk to Wes again?"

"No. Yes. I don't know." She dropped Angus's hand and chewed a fingernail, continuity be damned. "You get why it's weird, right?"

"Because I asked you on a date and you turned me down?"

"Sort of. Yeah. And"—the dance, the flirtation, the meaningful conversations, the easy camaraderie, the shower, the hug, the video montage, the growing desire to be close to him in ways that would only bring her more uncomfortable attention—"and I don't think I can kiss anyone with all of those people watching. It's too intimate."

"It doesn't have to be." Angus leaned against a palm tree and tucked a thumb into the waistband of his jeans, his relaxed posture striking a sharp contrast with Marlowe's almost manic energy. "I've done this a hundred times. Think of it as blocking, the same way you grab the necklace or exit toward the diner. It's basic action. Position hands. Make eye contact. Lean in. It doesn't have to feel intimate or personal, *especially* with all of the people watching." He paused there, all easy reassurance while she fidgeted before him, unconvinced the situation was as simple as he claimed. "I'm a big boy. I can take a rejection and be grateful for a friendship. I can also keep my personal and professional lives separate. We're acting, and if I do anything you're not comfortable with, just stop."

She spat out a sliver of fingernail and started tugging at another. "What if I'm already uncomfortable?" she asked.

"It's up to you. We can give it a shot or we can demand we stick to the old script."

She perked up. "We can do that?"

"Officially, no, and I like to play the asshole card sparingly, but they're not likely to fire me two episodes from the end of the season. It'll also cost them a hell of a lot more to write you out at this point than it will to finish the scene and move on." He smiled softly, watching her with all the patience in the world. No pressure. No shaming. Just an unwavering sense of support.

"It's only blocking?" she echoed.

"Position hands, make eye contact, lean in," he repeated.

She spat out another fingernail sliver and shook out her hands. "Okay," she said. "I'll try. With the changes."

His smile widened. "I'd hug you but I have a feeling almost anything I do right now will only make the next hour feel even weirder."

Marlowe skipped a breath. "The next *hour*?!"

"You don't think we're going to get it in one take, do you?"

"We're damned well going to try."

They headed back to set and did a quick rehearsal with the new lines and blocking, minus the kiss. The higher-ups agreed that the scene worked well and they should go for it. Marlowe and Angus took their places, her on the crates, him standing before her. The hair and makeup people swept in with combs, sprays, and powders, fixing stray hairs and blotting away any hint of sweat. Marlowe held up the ring. Angus set his hands on either side of her face, as before when he'd leaned in for a kiss. The contact caused her already galloping heart to race even faster, but a continuity monitor joined them a second later, ensuring their positions matched the prior take. *Right thumb angled more. Left hand shifted down half an inch. Shoulder back. Hip forward.* Angus was right. This was all about blocking. It didn't have to feel intimate at all.

When everything was ready to go, the crew went quiet. The woman with the clapboard gave it a sharp snap, and they were rolling.

"I'll be the one in the veil," Marlowe said.

"But we only just—"

"We were kids. It was never going to last."

They held their position, each trying to read something in the other's eyes. Though Angus was fully in character as Jake—his jaw firmly set and his gaze razor sharp in its intensity—he snuck a hint of reassurance into his look. Then he stepped away, rubbing his chin and shaking his head, wrestling with his thoughts. Marlowe let the ring drop with the chain. It was cool against her skin, solid and real, something to ground her. She started to push off the crates, but Angus lowered his hand and turned her way.

"Swear you didn't come here looking for me," he demanded.

She swallowed, gripped the crate, sank back down. "I-I swear."

"Then what's your cousin's name?"

Marlowe looked toward the diner and back at Angus. "Lucy."

"There's no Lucy on the waitstaff."

"Susan?"

"No Susan, either." Angus watched her as though anticipating another denial. When no denial came, he closed the distance until he was within arm's reach. He stopped there, his hands by his sides, both rolled into loose fists.

This was it. Marlowe's moment to reach instead of being reached for. To take control. To make a choice.

She raised her hand and laid a palm against his cheek. His skin was soft, even with the stubble. His regard was unflinching. He was so close and so beautiful.

"I needed to know," she said. "If I . . . I mean if you . . ."

He cupped his hand around hers, pressing it more tightly to his face.

"If I what?" he prompted.

Heart pounding, she traced his lower lip with her thumb. He inched forward until his legs were wedged between her parted thighs. She stretched up toward him as her hand slid to the back of his neck. The tip of his tongue grazed the inside of his lip, leaving behind a hint of wetness. Her whole body tingled as shivers of anticipation danced across her skin, real shivers that told her this was never going to be impersonal, not for her.

"I needed to know if you still wondered, too," she said.

He nodded, barely. His Adam's apple rose and fell as he swallowed. She edged closer. He did the same. She let her eyelids drift down, steeling her nerves. Then she shoved aside all remaining anxieties and drew his face to hers.

As their lips met, Marlowe and Angus held for a moment, as if each of them was allowing the other an opportunity to retreat. Neither took that opportunity. Instead, his lips parted as his head tilted to the side. She countered, a peck, a nibble, a taste, drawing him closer still. His hands slid around her hips, gripping lightly, and then not so lightly. She knotted her hands in his hair. It was stiff with product but she found her way in, curling her fingers into his locks. His lips moved against hers, harder and faster. Thought fell away. Impulse took over. Her tongue pressed against his upper lip. His pressed back. Her pulse leapt. Her skin ignited. His fists yanked the fabric of her skirt into little knots. She hooked a leg around his thigh. He let out a soft moan. Acting? Accidental? Did it matter? Did anything matter? All she wanted in that moment was to be closer, to feel more of him, to shred anything that barred them from knowing each other entirely.

Someone shuffled in Marlowe's peripheral vision. She snapped to attention and pulled back, both hands laid against Angus's breastbone while she blinked at his chest and caught her breath. When she finally looked up, he was smiling at her, as Jake or as Angus, she couldn't tell. The bright lights lit up his cheekbones and brought out the golden tones in his stubble. His hair, now tousled, shone bright.

"Copper pennies," she said.

The skin beside his eyes crinkled as his smile widened.

"What about them?" he asked.

"Your hair. I finally figured it out. It's the color of brand-new copper pennies."

He tipped his forehead against hers, laughing softly.

"And cut!" Fritz called from his spot by the monitors.

Marlowe felt her entire body flush.

"I said that in front of everyone, didn't I?" she asked.

Angus beamed at her. "Easily edited out and totally worth it."

Despite Marlowe's mortification, few people around her seemed to care that she'd broken character and shared a moment of real intimacy with Angus. Maybe it wasn't as obvious as she thought, or maybe everyone was so accustomed to watching Angus kiss his costars, nothing about the scene seemed odd, even her unscripted assessment of his hair color. Wes, Fritz, and Alejandra dove into a discussion about what else they needed to capture—the end of the scene, of course, which Marlowe had completely botched, but also close-ups and transitions that would be edited together later. Makeup people scurried forward to reapply lipstick and fix any smudges. A girl with an apron full of combs and clips sat Angus down to force his waves back into submission. The lighting and sound crew was all business, rattling on about boom angles and volume settings. Angus was right. For everyone but Marlowe, capturing these last few minutes was a job. Only a job. And they were about to repeat it again, and again, and again. At least next time the kiss ended, she'd remember to stand up and say goodbye. Maybe.

Four hours later, Marlowe was back in the trailer, dressed in her own clothes and scrubbing the last of her makeup off in the sink. Cherry knocked and entered, bearing coffee and biscotti. She set them on the counter while Marlowe dried her face.

"I got you something else, too." She handed Marlowe a glittery tube of fruity lip balm. "Figured you might need this about now."

Marlowe gave Cherry a teasing shove but she opened the lip balm right away.

"That was insane," she said as she applied the gel to her burning lips.

"You got through it, though. Two scenes down. Only one more to shoot, and all you'll have to do is pine for him across the street and then duck into a church."

Marlowe sank into a chair and drew the lid off her coffee, inhaling the sweet mocha-scented steam. She was exhausted from trying to get the scene right over and over while Fritz gave her new input after every take. *The goodbye's too sudden, the kiss starts too fast, I need to sense more conflict, take a longer pause, take a shorter pause, slow down the exit, stand up faster, look over your shoulder as you leave, scratch that, get away as fast as you can.* It was all too much to process. But that very first kiss . . .

"Maria and I are grabbing drinks after work tonight," Cherry said. "Wanna come? We can make it a group thing. Invite Ravi and Patrice. And anyone else you want?" Her voice rose at the end of her question, making her implication clear.

Marlowe hid a frown against the rim of her coffee cup, her mind in turmoil about what she wanted, and what she didn't want, and how to untangle the two.

"I think I'll head home and crash early," she said. "God knows Babs will have ten days' worth of work for me to fit into the rest of the week."

"Probably, though at least we'll be on wrap by the end of next week. With the actors gone, Babs won't send you on more jealousy-induced errand marathons. Though holy shit! That bomb she dropped about her marriage? Guess she just wants the same opportunities as her ex. It's so unfair that a woman who dates a much younger man is called a cougar while a man who dates a much younger woman is called a man. Also, spinster versus bachelor? Fuck the patriarchy." Cherry's phone buzzed. She checked the screen. "Speaking of Babs, duty calls." She grabbed a cookie and backed against the trailer door. "By the way, I hope it's okay if I wait until we wrap before I ask her about hiring you on for the girls' rock camp film. I'm pretty sure she'll say yes but watching you mash faces all day with her fantasy boy toy hasn't put her in the best mood."

Marlowe conceded the point with a nod and a look of understanding.

"No rush," she said. "Besides, I'm having second thoughts about staying in L.A."

"We scared you off that fast?"

"Of course not, but today's conversation with the writers and producers cemented something I've been thinking about a lot recently. I liked having a voice, and seeing that voice affect the story being told." She glanced at the Achebe script half-buried on the makeup counter. "I might be ready to try designing again."

Cherry jammed the cookie between her teeth, stepping forward to high-five Marlowe before removing the cookie and brushing crumbs off her jacket.

"Happy to be your plan B," she said. "And I don't say that to all the girls."

Marlowe laughed while nursing a little ache in her heart. She'd miss more than the tacos and the sunshine if she left L.A. Much, *much* more.

"Thanks," she said. "And thanks again for being so awesome when I was freaking out earlier."

"I will never be anything but awesome." With another ear-to-ear smile and a few hummed bars of "Wind Beneath my Wings," Cherry headed out.

As the door closed, Marlowe pulled out the Achebe script and thumbed through the pages. Words and phrases flashed by, already embedding themselves in her memory. She grabbed a pen, marking key passages the way she used to when she was preparing for conversations with directors and design teams. *A bedraggled hem, torn and knotted over a century of sleepless nights. A deep blue sadness. Plague-pocked. She carries her voice in her hands.* The more she read, the more her excitement built. She couldn't run errands indefinitely, nor could she engage in costume work that prioritized brand recognition over character and story. Not if she could use her voice as a storyteller, telling the sorts of stories that might make fewer girls like her question the value of their desires, their ambitions, and their impulses, defaulting to a position of getting small.

She texted Chloe to let her know she loved the script and she hoped the director would call soon to chat about possibilities. Chloe replied right away with a stream of party emoticons and her usual run of exclamation points. Her excitement was infectious, even in text form, making Marlowe that much more anxious to return to New York.

She was packing up to head home a few minutes later when her phone buzzed.

Angus: You doing ok?

Marlowe: Yeah. Thanks for the support today

Angus: You rocked it. Hardest part's over now

Marlowe: That's what people always say before an even bigger challenge arises

Angus: Nah. Next time no one will tell you to kiss me

Marlowe stared at the text, not entirely loving the way it sounded in her mind. Granted, after the first few takes that day, she understood why Angus thought about kissing as basic blocking, nothing more. They shot in quick beats that lacked the emotional build of the longer takes. The cameras and crew felt more present. Fritz's direction stifled any personal instincts, smothering them with reminders to tilt her head at a certain angle or push away from Angus at a precise moment. And yet . . .

She could still feel the echo of Angus's hands gripping her hips, the sheer solidity of his body planted so near hers, the softness of his hair sliding between her fingers, the warmth and pressure of his lips against hers, the sparking sensation when their tongues touched or he let out a little moan of pleasure that made her want to—

Her phone buzzed again.

Angus: You going out to celebrate?
Marlowe: Just me and the owls
Angus: Did you kick out the dead yak?
Marlowe: Forgot about him. Also, I live across the street from dead people
Angus: Ok. Now I'm intrigued

Something fluttered in Marlowe's gut. Was he fishing for an invite? Did she want to make one? It wouldn't be a date. Just a bit of friendly companionship. They could order takeout. Watch TV. Make her apartment feel less like a pit of existential dread.

Marlowe: Know any resuscitation spells?
Angus: I once revived a dying houseplant

Marlowe: Would your tactics work on the yak?
Angus: I'm not opposed to trying

Okay. Definitely fishing for an invite . . .

Marlowe: Think you'd be followed?
Angus: I have a stealth car
Marlowe: Batmobile?
Angus: Super boring ten-year-old gray sedan. Hasn't been washed in forever. Family decals on the back window. Two moms, three kids, and a dog. Not sure why I picked those. Though I've always wanted a dog
Marlowe: You can't get a dog. You'd feed it spring rolls
Angus: Only when it looked hungry
Marlowe: Exactly

Marlowe stared at the screen, wondering if she was asking for trouble.

Marlowe: Just as friends. Okay?
Angus: I promise not to flirt
Marlowe: Right. And I promise not to breathe
Angus: Consider it character research. Bill Greg for your overtime
Marlowe: Not sure he can pay enough to make it worth my while
Angus: Now who's flirting?

Crap. Trouble confirmed.

Her thumbs hovered over her screen. The safest bet was to claim she'd forgotten a commitment or needed to get some rest. She wasn't going to date Angus. He wasn't one-night-stand material, either. He'd made that clear on Sunday. She liked that about him. She wasn't sure she was one-night-stand material, either. Besides, she was hoping to be back in New York sometime next month. Even if she and Angus were simply building a friendship, getting closer to him now would only make leaving L.A. harder.

On the other hand . . .

Marlowe's apartment was so painfully empty, so devoid of shared memories. She'd had such a good time with Angus on Sunday, and even today, laughing and chatting between takes. Besides, didn't Babs say she should seize the choices she was offered? And who was Marlowe to deny Babs's instructions?

Marlowe: Tell Jeeves he has your place to himself for the evening

Chapter Twenty-three

Quiet neighbors," Angus said.

"Old joke." Marlowe glanced past him to the cemetery across the street.

He craned around from her crumbling cement stoop, following her gaze. He'd swapped Jake's dark and dusty clothes for his usual white tee, faded jeans, and bright canvas sneakers. He also wore a red Pizza Boys windbreaker and ball cap, and he carried a pizza box to match. Marlowe wore a lightweight cotton dress with a short, flared skirt and a row of buttons that ran from the sweetheart neckline to the hem. The style lines provided the illusion of curves, which was as close as she'd get without Babs's help. She hoped the dress looked like something she'd thrown on without thought, though she'd agonized for hours about what to wear. She didn't want to imply anything remotely date-like, but she didn't need a repeat of last weekend's pinnacle of unattractiveness.

"You brought pizza?" She nodded at the box.

"Not really." He lifted the lid to reveal an array of gourmet-looking tacos, each one individually garnished and crisscrossed with a different sauce. "Got the feeling this was more your speed, but they were willing to pack the tacos in a pizza box so I could complete my ingenious disguise." His brows waggled above the rims of his aviators.

Marlowe breathed in the scents of fresh cilantro, grilled onions, and spicy mayonnaise.

"You're making it really hard for me to not like you," she said.

"Give me a few minutes. I'll say something idiotic and it'll be easy again."

Marlowe took the box, sliding him a dubious look. While she carried the tacos into the living room, he hung his hat and jacket on a hook by the door, beside the New York Yankees cap he'd loaned her on Sunday. She liked seeing his things in her space, even though she wasn't sure she should.

"Have any trouble on your way here?" she asked as he studied an owl painting. It had a distinctly vintage palette of avocado, pumpkin, and mustard yellow, with eyes made of dingy glass beads. The painting was one of four, all equally hideous.

"I called my security company. They're dusting for squatters. Those SUVs you saw on the weekend are gone. For now." He leaned away from the owl painting, and then tilted his upper-body right and left. "Do the eyes follow you everywhere?"

"Even into my nightmares."

"And the yak?"

"Come smell for yourself."

Angus joined her by the sofa, his face immediately pinching into a grimace.

"I think he's past the point of resuscitation." He set a hand under his nose as though he was blocking the smell. "Can I stick around anyway?"

"You showed up with tacos. You can stay as long as you like."

He smiled at that, and something in his eyes told her he was reading more into her statement than she meant. Something in her chest told her that was okay.

As the sun set through broken blinds, sending pink streaks across a sea of beige, Angus and Marlowe started in on the tacos while chatting about the day. They laughed about a spat that'd erupted between Fritz and Wes, and remarked on the efficiency of the hair and makeup crew, sweeping in with a comb or sponge between takes. They joked about his fake height and her fake boobs. They only flirted a little. Relatively speaking.

"What would you be doing if you didn't come over tonight?" Marlowe asked as she nudged a teetering sprig of cilantro deeper into her tortilla.

"Hanging out at Idi's probably. He runs a monthly poker game. I always lose but we have a good time." He twisted a strand of melted cheese around his finger, struggling to tame it in a way Marlowe found deeply entertaining. "I lucked out with this job. None of us knew each other when we started filming season one. Now they're five of my best friends. Crazy to think next week might be our last working together."

Marlowe lowered her taco, struck by a note of deep sadness in Angus's voice.

"You don't think *Heart's Diner* will have another season?" she asked.

"Depends how ratings are doing. It could go either way." He finally managed to sever the cheese strand, peeling it from his finger with his teeth. "Honestly, I'm hoping we get one more go, even if the material's tired. Otherwise I'll probably end up on an action film. They're pretty much all I've been offered lately. So far the top contender is a script about a wrongly convicted parolee who sets out on a path of revenge. It's super formulaic but someone else would do all the stunts so I'd just have to look pissed off and say things like, 'You really thought you could get away with that? Think again, asshole.'" He fired a finger pistol, rolling his eyes as he lowered his hand. He played the idea off as if it amused him, but the note of sadness hadn't left his voice.

Marlowe let her dinner idle. "Doesn't sound like the role of your dreams."

Angus shrugged as he prodded his cheese. "It is what it is. You spend enough years glaring at the camera as a borderline alcoholic with a sex addiction and a ready box of matches, people don't line up to put you in a rom-com about an earnest flower seller who takes in too many stray cats."

Marlowe smiled to herself as she pictured Angus surrounded by bouquets and meowing kittens. It was a nice image, and she suspected she wouldn't be the only one to think so. Funny how she'd thought someone with Angus's name recognition could pick and choose whatever roles he wanted, but apparently his situation wasn't that different from her own, even if he made a lot more money and spent a lot less time in shoe stores.

He leaned over to examine her remaining taco, extracting a few of the more offensive vegetables and adding them to his fillings, easily intuiting that she didn't want them.

"How about you?" he asked. "What's next for Marlowe Banks, costume designer, challenger of sexist producers, and lover of cute but malodorous jalopies?"

Now it was her turn to shrug. She had her hopes but so much was still unknown.

"Same," she said. "Vigilante piece. Lots of guns."

"Thought so." He circled a hand in front of her face. "You have that hardened ex-con look about you. Bet you pulled the legs off spiders as a kid."

"No, but I punched Pete Kensington in the eye when he called my best friend fat."

Angus let out a burst of surprised laughter and requested the rest of the story. Marlowe cringed in embarrassment but with further encouragement, she described her first and only foray into pugilism. She was nine years old at the time, gangly, awkward, and frustrated at the ways people used words to hurt others, especially when those people took pride in the accomplishment. The strange bridge between ego and malice.

"It's funny when I think about that day. It wasn't funny to Pete Kensington, of course, but it was the first time I realized how often we judge people based on their appearances. Rather than try to pretend that wasn't true, I started looking for ways to understand it." She got up to refill the water glasses, calling from the kitchen as she ran the tap. "It was how I got interested in costumes. If we know we're being judged by our appearance, how do we curate that appearance? How does someone choose their outfit, or hairstyle, or shoes, or tattoos? What makes a person feel brave or beautiful, and how is someone's approach to those ideas unique to their outlook and life experience?" She returned to the living room with the glasses. Two glasses, she noted. Not one.

"Then there's Halloween," she continued. "People light up when they put on clothes that make them feel like precisely who they want to be. As a kid, that often meant a princess or superhero costume. Later it meant busting through gender norms or assisting actors with body dysmorphia. Clothes are often considered trivial and superficial, but they're incredibly powerful tools of expression. And when we change the outside, sometimes we change the inside, too."

Angus took his glass from her with a smile she didn't recognize. It wasn't smug. It wasn't amused. It wasn't particularly flirtatious. It was . . .

"What?" she asked.

"Nothing." He shook his head, still smiling. "I'm just glad I'm here."

After dinner, Marlowe and Angus settled in to watch a film on her tiny TV, opting for a classic detective movie so they could stay on brand, there being a shortage of films in the not-really-a-cattle-tycoon genre. She picked out *The Thin Man*. He suggested *The Big Sleep*. They tossed a coin but he swatted it aside mid-spin and suggested a double feature instead. Anxious to retain his company as long as possible, she agreed.

They started the first film seated beside each other with their feet kicked up on the coffee table and the beige comforter blocking the worst of the sofa's odor. Gradually, awkwardly, and with very little subtlety, they scooted closer to one another. When their elbows bumped, he swung an arm over the back of the sofa and invited her in. She leaned into his side with her head tipped against his shoulder. Sweet. Friendly. Cozy.

After a few mutual yawns—maybe feigned but probably not—sitting became spooning. His body was warm and solid against her back. She also liked the weight of his arm resting on hers. She liked it even better when he eased his arm sideways and set his hand on her thigh, where his fingertips inched past the hem of her dress and drew whisper-soft circles on her skin. On the other side of the room, William Powell and Myrna Loy tossed out lively banter about martinis and murder, but Marlowe's attention was locked on that spot on her thigh where four fingers circled, circled, circled, making her toes curl and her breath catch in her throat. Did he notice? Surely he noticed.

About halfway through the film, Angus shifted behind her, gently nuzzling her neck, the contact so subtle it could almost be mistaken for an accident. Almost, but not at all. She wedged her body more tightly against his, pressing backward with her hips and adjusting the bend in her knees, almost like she was stretching. Almost, but not at all.

His fingers inched higher, barely, an unspoken question. *Is this okay?*

She closed her eyes and drew in a breath. *Yes,* she thought. *More than okay.*

They went on like this for several minutes, ostensibly watching the film while his hand made its slow climb up her thigh and she fought a growing inability to lie still. The higher those circles climbed, the greater her unrest. Her toes pressed against the tops of his feet. His feet flexed and pressed back, easing his thighs against hers. His lips rested against her neck, not forming a kiss, just . . . there. She tilted her head away from him, letting his breath curl around her neck. His soft stubble grazed her skin. She waited for him to kiss her, *willed* him to kiss her, but he didn't, wouldn't. Instead he hovered there, never crossing that line.

They might've continued in the same vein all night—playing at cuddling while not really cuddling—but as his thumb neared the edge of her underpants, her hips rolled against him in a way that could no longer be attributed to a random act of restlessness. It was pure desire.

Marlowe turned over, nearly sliding off the sofa in the process. Her stupid comforter might as well have been made of Teflon. Angus prevented her from falling with a strong, splayed hand on her back, watching her with unblinking eyes and parted lips. Those damned lips, the ones she'd become so well acquainted with earlier that day, the ones she longed to kiss again, here, now, where no one else would see. But she and Angus had agreed to a friendship, and they'd made that agreement for good reason.

"I meant what I said on Sunday." She set her hands on his chest, unsure where else to put them. The placement was a bad choice. She was already dying to explore what lay beneath the thin jersey of his T-shirt. "I don't want to mislead you."

His brow furrowed above his tiger's eyes, but only for a moment before softening.

"It gets easier," he said. "Dealing with the public."

"*Easier* isn't the same as *easy*."

"Fair point." He nudged her nose with his.

She scooted closer, stacking their knees, one of his, one of hers . . .

"What if I'd never be brave enough?" she asked.

"What if I'd never be smart enough, or interesting enough, or—?"

"What if I leave L.A.?"

He flinched at that. "Are you leaving?"

"Maybe. I don't know yet, but I feel like I don't belong here."

His smile flickered into view. "You live in a horror movie set. People have probably been murdered in this apartment. Of course you feel like you don't belong."

She gave him a little shove. "It's more than that."

"I know." He guided a few unruly strands of hair off her face. "We could list a hundred reasons I should head home right now. The press and the public. Unpredictable careers. The affair you might have with my imaginary butler. The peculiar odor radiating from every surface of this apartment." His knee slid forward as his thigh rose between her legs, making her want to rub against him. "I have at least two reasons for staying."

"And they are?" she eked out.

"I really want to touch you and I think you're not totally against the idea." Angus watched her, unmoving.

Marlowe blinked at him, breathless and addled. Her mind raced but in a hazy, pheromone-clouded way. She could step away from Angus on a dance floor. She could drive away from his house. But evicting him here? Now? Like this? While the hunger in his eyes shot fire through her bloodstream? Impossible. So she traced his lower lip with her thumb, as she'd done on set before their first kiss, only this time she had no lines to recite, no blocking to remember, no boundary to draw between performance and reality.

"You are annoyingly irresistible, Angus Gordon."

His eyes narrowed as if he was chewing on her assessment.

"It's not 'the sexiest man alive,' but I'll take it." His smile was still curling upward when she closed the distance and kissed him.

This was no chaste TV kiss. It was raw and messy and unrestrained. Tongues clashed. Teeth tugged at lips. Breath slipped out in short bursts, accompanied by unexpected little noises that said *yes, this*, and *more*. Hands slid around necks and down backs. They tangled in hair, gripped clothes, bared skin. His mouth roved over her neck. Hers explored his freckled ear, eliciting a low, rumbly moan before his lips found hers again. With a deft flick of his fingers, he popped open her top few buttons. Her chest heaved. Her hips shifted against him, circled, pushed, ground. Through his jeans, his erection pressed against her. The rush of knowing he wanted her the same way she wanted him drew a smile to her lips.

"What's so funny?" Angus mumbled between kisses.

"Nothing." Marlowe shook her head. "I just like you."

"Good thing, or this would be really awkward right now." He flashed her his dazzling grin. She pulled back far enough to look at him clearly, tracing his features with her fingertips while he toyed with the shoulder strap of her dress. His lips were swollen. His hair sprang in all directions. His lashes fluttered, back in their natural blond. She liked this version of him, flushed and disarrayed, a little less polished than what she saw on a screen. He was real and he was here, and at that moment, it was all that mattered. "I like your dress." He popped open another button. "It's cute, and I hope I don't offend it by saying this, but is there any chance it has someplace else to be tonight?"

"Alternate plans can be arranged."

"Flexibility is a highly underrated quality." Eyes locked with hers, he hooked her dress strap with his index finger and slid it off her shoulder, following suit with her bra strap so both rested against her arm. After placing a row of soft, wet, deliriously drawn-out kisses on her collarbone, he studied the scalloped edges of her bra with both his eyes and his fingertips. Slowly, gently, he drew her bra cup down to bare her breast.

"They're a lot smaller than Adelaide's," she said, bracing to be judged, a habit she hated but came by honestly.

"They're perfect." Circling her nipple with his thumb, his expression grew pensive the way it so often did when something fascinated him. Marlowe had never considered herself fascinating. She barely considered herself worth a passing glance. His attention felt good. His touch felt good, too. It echoed her steamy fantasy in his shower. As those thoughts resurfaced—and several others besides—she reached up and popped the hooks at the back of her bra, sliding the straps off from beneath her dress.

The second her bra dropped from her hand, he rolled her onto her back. As her head hit the cushions, his tongue flicked across her breast, shooting a rush of sensation straight to the spot where she most wanted him to touch her. With that, the last of her insecurities fell away. No more fear of judgment. No more comparing herself to others. This was a moment for giving in to pure, unrestrained pleasure.

With the careful pressure of his lips, tongue, teeth, and fingers, he teased out one nipple and then the other. She writhed beneath him, knotting her fists in his hair, relishing every second while silently chanting *lower, lower, lower*. Reading her body if not her mind, he popped another button on her dress. Then another, dragging his lips across her skin, pausing to look, to linger, to enjoy. She arched against his trail of kisses, her anticipation building. It was maddening. It was wonderful. It was—

Marlowe shrieked as the slippery comforter carried her off the sofa and onto the floor with Angus tumbling after. Her head hit the table leg. His hip jarred a water glass, spilling the contents onto her bare stomach. She jerked in response. Her forehead smacked his nose. He let out a low, pained moan as his hand flew to his face.

"I'm so sorry." Marlowe reached toward him.

"Fucking yak," Angus joked through a laugh. "I knew this place was cursed."

"Or unlucky?"

"Definitely cursed." He dabbed at his nose. She drew aside his hand and took a look. His skin was pink and his eyes were watering, but he wasn't bleeding.

"You going to be okay?" she asked.

"Yeah. Just give me a minute." He wedged himself beside her, lying on his back and exhaling slowly. In the background, the film continued playing, with rapid-fire dialogue and melodramatic, suspenseful music. It set a certain mood, one in which curses weren't entirely out of the question. Just in case, Marlowe snuggled into Angus's side. While he patted his nose again, she circled the freckle on his earlobe with her thumb, mimicking his earlier caress of her breast. It appeared to have a similar affect as his eyes closed, he leaned into her touch, and he let out a soft and contented, "Mmmmmm."

Taking it as a sign that Angus wasn't *totally* out of commission, Marlowe shoved the table aside and climbed onto his lap. She was all limbs and elbows, moving in a manner that resembled a teetering stick bug, but somehow she managed to straddle him. Scooting backward, she found the hem of his T-shirt and drew it upward. He took over, wrenching his shirt off and tossing it aside. She shook her head at the sight of him, all rippled contours, a high contrast to her bony limbs and lack of curves. She ran her hands down his chest and over the distinct ridges of his ab muscles. As he clenched against her touch, a laugh bubbled up and sputtered out of her without warning.

He responded with an amused smile. "What now?"

She regarded him with awe. "We clearly have the same workout routine."

He raked his hands up her thighs, following their path with an appreciative glance.

"We're different people. I enjoy exercise. And vegetables. Looking fit is also one of my job expectations. And in case you haven't noticed, I'm excessively vain."

"Oh, I've noticed." She skimmed his sides with her knuckles. The gentle bump-bump-bump of ribs that eased into a sharply defined waist and taut muscles that wrapped his hip bones. "It's unreal. You're like a Ken doll, but, you know, anatomically correct."

"I definitely have all the parts." He wiggled against her, his eyes twinkling with an unmistakable note of pride. The trait might've been off-putting, but not when he was so self-aware about it. He also worked hard on his body. He deserved to be proud of it.

She traced his hip bones toward the waistband of his jeans, wondering what it would feel like to be so used to being looked at and admired.

"Have you ever been self-conscious about anything?" she asked.

"Of course. I'm just really good at compartmentalizing."

She nudged the tail of his belt through the wide brass buckle. "Name three things you're self-conscious about."

His eyes dropped to her hands, where she continued unbuckling his belt.

"Number one, not having a college education." He sucked in a breath as she popped the button on his waistband. "Number two, an inability to make small talk or manufacture polite conversation." His grip tightened on her thighs as she drew his zipper down. "Number three"—he blinked, watched, held his breath as she slipped her hand between his legs and cupped his erection—"number three will have to wait."

Whether or not he'd completely recovered from her brutal head-butt, he pulled her toward him, his lips already parted for a kiss. Together they plunged into another tempest of reckless kisses, bared skin, gusted breath, and roving hands. He inched backward on the carpet, pushing off with his heels and thrusting against her hand as she stroked him. She grew more turned on with every ragged gasp and moan of pleasure. When their entwined bodies emerged from the valley between the sofa and the table, he flipped her onto her back and pulled her underwear down, yanking them off her ankles and flinging them toward the sofa. Seconds later he was gliding his fingers through her slick folds, murmuring in her ear about how wet she was and how much it turned him on. She'd never been into dirty talk before. It always sounded kind of ridiculous, but she loved the feel of his deep voice rumbling through her. He could've been talking about her body or the latest book he read or even kale. It would've been the sexiest thing she'd ever heard.

She was lost in the heady euphoria of deep arousal when he abruptly stopped fondling her to grip her face between his hands, his smile curling up, his eyes on fire.

"We have to relocate," he panted out. "You can't cum where someone died."

She turned her head to see a dark, blotchy stain over her shoulder.

"Let's hope that's only coffee. But the bedroom's that way." She tipped her head toward the open doorway just past the front entrance. He leapt up and hauled her to her feet, drawing her face against his for another kiss. Still lunging at each other—her with her unbuttoned dress hanging off her shoulders and him with his jeans gaping open—they stumbled toward the bedroom. They halted partway there when her back hit a wall. He pressed her against it, parting her legs with his knee. With a quick flash of his grin, he dropped to his knees. His mouth found her thigh. A kiss. A bite. A hot breath against her skin before his lips moved higher. He spread her with both hands, teasing her with the slow, deliberate pressure of his thumbs until his tongue flicked against—

Her head hit the wall, forcing an owl painting to fall from its nail. It nicked Angus's shoulder before landing face-up on the carpet, its beady eyes staring upward or maybe sideways, full of accusation. Marlowe gasped. Angus fell backward onto his heels. He sat there, startled, rubbing his shoulder while sending a punishing leer toward the owl.

"Unbelievable," he said through another strained laugh. "Your apartment is actively trying to prevent us from having sex tonight."

"It does seem somewhat opinionated on the topic." She crouched beside him, peering at his shoulder. As with his nose, the wound wasn't grave, but still . . . "At least the dead haven't risen in the cemetery across the street."

"Yet." He frowned at her window as if he expected an army of rabid corpses to push through the blinds any second.

"I did warn you. The threshold should never be crossed."

"Yeah, well, we've already established that we both suck at obeying warnings." He picked up the owl painting and flipped it over, hiding its beady eyes from view. "I don't know whether to be impressed, annoyed, or scared out of my mind."

"How about really, *really* patient?" She rose to her feet and extended a hand.

He took it and followed her into the bedroom. While he stretched out on her bed, she removed the rest of the owl paintings and hid them in her closet. She tossed the Teflon comforter in with them, just in case. Then she surveyed the space for anything else that might find a way to attack. The room was sparsely decorated, and only big enough for a full-size bed, side table, and crappy dresser, but she set her bedside lamp on the floor and made sure the blinds were securely fastened to the window frame.

"I think we're safe now," she said as she lay down beside him, sharing her one, flat, lumpy pillow and adjusting her position so a bedspring didn't dig into her hip.

"Speaking of safe . . ." He trailed the back of his hand over her shoulder and down her arm. "I took your 'just friends' request seriously and didn't bring any condoms."

"Right. Good. I mean, not good, but, yeah, it would've been weird if you showed up expecting something." Marlowe scratched her head, trying to remember if she'd seen any condoms when she unpacked six months ago. It was unlikely, since she'd left New York so quickly, and with no thoughts about dating anytime soon. "I don't have any, either. This apartment hasn't seen much action. Because of the curse, obviously."

"Obviously." He nudged her toes with his. "I can go buy some, but . . ."

"But everyone will be tweeting tomorrow about what brand you bought?"

He shook his head. "But I'd rather stay here with you. If that's okay."

"To fool around some more or—?" She didn't bother finishing the question. She could tell from the look in his eyes that he wasn't talking about fooling around. As the weight of that realization sank in, her chest seized so hard, she struggled to take a full breath.

"Even in this terrible bed with no decent bedding and the smell of rotting things everywhere and blinds that let in more sun than they keep out and the knowledge that at any second, hordes of zombies might attack from across the street?"

He kissed her forehead. Her nose. Her cheek. Her lips.

"Even then," he said.

She studied him in the dim light that seeped in from the living room, tinting his freckled cheekbones and drawing out the blond tones in his stubble. His eyes were serious. His smile was barely there. She knew what his expression meant. If he stayed, this wasn't about sex anymore. It was the beginning of something else entirely. Something that seemed totally, utterly impossible. Then again, so was asking him to leave.

"Okay," she said. "But if the zombies show, I'm letting them eat you first."

"You've got yourself a deal."

Chapter Twenty-four

Two days later, Marlowe sat in her car in a strip mall parking lot, on a phone interview with the director of the Achebe play. The director had contacted her yesterday, shortly after Marlowe left Angus asleep in her bed while she headed to work. He'd stirred with her alarm but he drifted off again while she tiptoed around her apartment. He'd looked so peaceful, his copper-penny hair tousled, his mouth ajar against her pillow. She didn't have the heart to wake him. Admittedly, she had also been avoiding an awkward "morning-after" conversation. She had a pretty clear sense of what he wanted. Her own wants were more confusing, and full of contradictions. While wrestling with those wants, she went ahead and scheduled the interview, assuming she'd be running mindless errands for the rest of the week and could sneak in a half hour call. Her assumption proved true.

The interview started off rocky. The director had seen Marlowe's last show. She also shared critics' opinions about it. However, the discussion of the new work was energetic and inspiring. Marlowe spoke passionately about the themes and the director liked her initial thoughts on the clothes. Other designers were being considered, but the offer was at least possible. Even if it didn't come through, the conversation was enough to confirm without a doubt that Marlowe should pursue design work again.

Not that jump-starting her career would be easy. Competition was fierce for every job and Marlowe despised selling herself, but she could start by reaching out to her former classmates to see if they knew of any opportunities. She might even set up some interviews in L.A. The city had several really good theaters. It also had a major opera company and countless dance troupes, ranging from small grassroots companies to internationally renowned touring groups. While she was gearing back up, anything that made use of her creativity would be a step forward.

By the time she ended the call, several texts were waiting. Three were from Babs, requesting that Marlowe pick up bulk suspenders from a formalwear place in West Hollywood, bras from a lingerie store in Culver City, and dog treats from an organic pet market in Brentwood. The fourth text was from Cherry with a simple apology for Babs's latest attempt to make Marlowe's workday last as long as possible. The fifth text was from Marlowe's dad, with a link to a "helpful" article on how arts degrees could be good stepping-stones toward business or legal careers. The sixth text was from her mom, asking if Marlowe wanted to fly out for the New York marathon next month. Marlowe wouldn't run it, of course. She'd cheer on her mom as she'd done in past years when she lived on the East Coast. Her mom even offered to cover the flight since she knew Marlowe was "struggling with all that debt."

The offer rankled. Her parents never offered to pay for things without heavy insinuations that Marlowe *should* be able to pay for them herself. Yes, her student loans had a lot of zeros. Also yes, she had attended an expensive grad school and pursued an artistic career that didn't come with a six-figure salary and a tidy benefits package. But the choices were hers. She'd made them for good reasons and she was tired of her parents waiting for her to have an epiphany about how wrong she was.

The final text was from Angus. He'd sent a group selfie with Idi and Tanareve, hanging out before the museum benefit. The guys were in tuxes, both looking predictably gorgeous. Tanareve was as stunning as ever in a vivid green Grecian gown that showed off her athletic shoulders. It was the kind of dress that practically dripped off the body, all drapey and flowy with no structure or padding, the kind of dress Marlowe could never pull off in a million years. The trio was laughing about a joke Marlowe would never hear and raising cocktails she could never afford. Below the photo were the simple but heart-wrenching words, *Wish you were here*. Marlowe sincerely doubted Angus sent the text to make her feel guilty about declining his invite. He sent it because he was thinking about her. The guilt came anyway, thick and heavy, along with a tidy side order of anxiety.

Marlowe tried to shake off her discomfort but she suspected it was only the beginning of what promised to be a swift downward spiral. Despite one fun, flirty, and surprisingly intimate night, she hadn't changed her stance on public appearances. Now red-carpet photos of the museum benefit would be popping up all over the Internet. Each photo would be a vivid reminder that Marlowe couldn't give Angus what he really wanted: not a one-night stand, but a partner, by his side. A partner who wasn't there.

With concerted effort and a *lot* of therapy, maybe Marlowe could work through her fear about public criticism, but was it really worth the effort? After all, Angus lived in a world of press ops and paparazzi, of mansions and managers, of agents, social media experts, high fashion, and adoring fans. Marlowe lived in a world of shoe repairs and shopping bags. She and Angus didn't fit together, not really. As friends? Sure. As lovers? Maybe, for a little while. But as a couple in a serious long-term relationship? Unlikely.

With that ugly thought swimming through her brain—along with Babs's extension of her workday and her parents' unique brand of disapproval-masked-as-help—Marlowe dropped off two bags of shoes at the strip mall cobbler. Her mood was still souring as she got back in her car. It soured even further when she turned the key in the ignition and her car emitted a grinding, gasping noise before going dead silent. She tried again with the same results. After several more failed attempts, she sank onto the steering wheel in despair, cursing her life. She'd barely lowered her head when a large *splat* made her jerk upright. Bird shit ran down her windshield, not the innocuous little spots dropped by sparrows and pigeons, but the disgusting multicolored ooze-balls the seagulls shat out after dumpster diving. Gross, but almost poetic, all things considered.

Remaining inside her car lest the gull return, Marlowe called AAA. Then she texted Cherry to ask what she should do about work. She still had a trunkful of returns to complete, as well as pickups at three design houses in Beverly Hills and the new errands Babs had added. Cherry suggested she find a comfortable place to wait. If the AAA guy couldn't start her car, Cherry would send someone from transport to drive Marlowe around for the rest of the day. And if her car remained out of commission for more than an afternoon, Marlowe could sort out a rental over the weekend.

The AAA guy came about half an hour later. He checked the battery and any other issues that might be solved on the spot, but ultimately he ascertained that he'd need to tow the car to a mechanic who could take a closer look. Marlowe texted Cherry back to confirm that she needed a ride. Then she emptied the trunk and hauled all the bags over to the sidewalk where she could wait for transport to show up.

Naturally, the strip mall had no benches, just dirty pavement speckled with blackened gum spots. Too deflated to stand, Marlowe sat down on the sidewalk, hoping her gray pants would hide any accumulated dinginess. The hot afternoon sun forced its way through brown smog. Out in the parking lot, an exhausted-looking mom dragged her screaming child by the hand while a guy in a faded Hawaiian shirt stuck fliers under windshield wipers. A few yards away, an overflowing trash can spilled food waste and packaging onto the sidewalk. A few miles away, a crew was unrolling a red carpet.

Shortly after 9:30 P.M., Wyatt from transport finally reached Westwood, after driving a circuitous route through the L.A. suburbs to ensure Marlowe hit every last vendor on her list while they were still open. Meanwhile, the mechanic had called with a repair estimate that was well beyond the car's worth, leaving Marlowe carless and out the cost of the donation fee.

She had also caved a few hours ago and checked a fan site that was covering the LACMA gala. Sure enough, Angus was there, his radiant smile glowing for the cameras, his arm wrapped around Tanareve, where it looked like it belonged. According to various captions, they were telling reporters that they were attending the gala as friends, but that didn't change the way they looked together. Gorgeous. Perfect. Natural in front of a camera. Fan-worthy. While obsessing about all that, Marlowe had tripped, spilled coffee down her shirt, and broken a shoelace she'd replaced with a paper clip she had on hand.

Now she felt grubby, sweaty, worn out, intensely unattractive, and incapable of stemming her growing frustrations. She was angry at her car for dying. She was angry at her parents for being right about her career choice leaving her constantly strapped for cash. She was angry at Babs for extending her workday. She was angry at the city of Los Angeles for being a massive sprawl without a central shopping district. Most of all, she was angry at herself for getting emotionally involved with a guy she couldn't actually date, or at least one she *wouldn't* date, knowing she couldn't do it privately and without humiliation. Also, her compostable takeout box was leaking, making the back seat smell like fish tacos. The back seat and the increasingly wet side of her pants.

Marlowe gave Wyatt directions to her apartment. While he drove past the UCLA campus, she pulled up another photo of the gala and tried desperately to picture herself by Angus's side. She imagined a range of couture gowns and professionally styled hairdos. Impeccable makeup. Great shoes. A manicure. Improved skincare. Repeated reminders to stand up straight. Still, she couldn't make an image stick. At all. The harder she tried, the more reality crept in. Soon she was picturing herself cowering in her coffee-stained shirt with bird shit in her hair and Edith Head tugging on a leash while Angus spread his arms in his tux, shielding her from angry fans who tossed rotten vegetables at her face. This being L.A., at least the vegetables were probably organic.

By the time Wyatt pulled up to a curb near the corner of her apartment building, Marlowe had convinced herself that sleeping with Angus was a big, fat mistake. It wasn't fair to him and it was seriously messing with her head, dredging up every insecurity and flooding her with guilt for seeding a form of intimacy she wasn't prepared to nurture. She should've stuck to the friend plan. It was simple. Achievable. Next time she and Angus had a chance to talk, she'd reinstate that plan. The thought of intentionally distancing herself made her insides twist into knots, but it was the right thing to do. Obviously. Definitely. Sort of. Maybe not. At least probably with a 10 percent chance of absolutely.

Marlowe started hauling bags out of the back seat, but Wyatt offered to deliver everything to the studio Monday morning, knowing she already had enough to deal with. Soggy takeout box in hand, she thanked him for his help and waved as he drove away.

She was so busy digging for her keys and counting the seconds until she could shower, she didn't look up until she was halfway to her door. She jumped when she noticed a guy sitting on her doorstep, his head in his hands. She was about to ask if he was looking for someone—her upstairs neighbor most likely, a UCLA student who had a steady rotation of friends over—when the guy looked up.

"Hey, Lowe," he said.

Marlowe froze. "Kelvin?"

Chapter Twenty-five

Kelvin was setting two cups of tea on the kitchen table when Marlowe emerged from the bathroom. She'd changed into sweats and an old concert tee, tied her frizzy hair up in a loose topknot, and washed her face. She would've been happier with a full shower, but a conversation was obviously more pressing. It wasn't a conversation she wanted to have. Kelvin's unexpected appearance had set her on edge. She'd considered shutting him out but she didn't have it in her. She still cared about him. She still harbored a boatload of guilt, too. If all that wasn't enough, she didn't want to risk a scene. She'd had more than enough public attention lately. While she hoped her address remained private, the last thing she needed was to read about a fight with her ex on Twitter tomorrow.

They each pulled up a chair. She jammed a wadded napkin under the front leg of her chair so it wouldn't rock. She didn't bother giving Kelvin instructions. He could figure it out or not. Thus far he didn't appear to notice that nothing in the apartment was level. He simply dropped his chin onto his hand and blew out a mournful sigh. Although half a year had passed since Marlowe last saw him, he looked much the same. He was tall and lean, but a little broader, perhaps, as though he'd started working out. His straight black hair swept sideways over his eyebrows, giving him the same almost comically emo look as always, an effect that was undercut by his ordinary jeans and hoodie. The plugs in his earlobes—his only accessory—still made Marlowe think of costuming grommets while his boxy chin remained clean-shaven and his eyes remained arrestingly blue.

"You don't seem happy to see me," he said.

"You showed up here without any warning. It's kind of stalker-y."

"We weren't getting anywhere through these stupid devices." He held up his phone, glaring at it like it was his nemesis. The look was familiar. Kelvin had always been analog. As a large-scale muralist, he preferred tangible paints to Photoshop and filters. "I took a chance. Trusted my impulses. Bought a ticket, just like you did once."

Marlowe passed the handle of her mug from one hand to the other, staring at the rise of the curling steam, wishing his words sounded more like a statement and less like an accusation. The blame in his tone was subtle, but it was there. It always was.

"How did you even know where I lived?" she asked.

"I grabbed the address off the résumé on your website last week. Sorry if that makes me sound even more stalker-y." He paused as if providing her an opportunity to contradict him. She didn't take it. Instead she cursed the irony of removing her address to avoid being harassed by strangers. Apparently strangers weren't the problem. While she tried to stem her irritation at that revelation, he slid his chair forward, twitching into a faint and sheepish smile when she finally looked up. "I wasn't trying to track you down. I swear. I checked your site because I missed you. I wanted to see what you were up to. I thought you might be designing shows out here."

"I haven't been designing."

"I noticed."

"I'm still working on the TV show."

"I noticed that, too." His smile dropped away as a subtle caginess hardened his eyes. It was a small change, almost unnoticeable, but it heightened Marlowe's already substantial defenses. "Dev showed me the photo of you and that actor out at the club. I had to look twice to believe it was you. What was *that* about?" He let out a breathy laugh that was probably meant to diffuse tension but only increased her irritation.

"We were dancing."

"Yeah, but come on." He drew back, pushing out another puff of nervous laughter. "I know you, Lowe. You don't care about all this celebrity crap." He flung a hand toward the front windows, which ironically led not east toward Hollywood but west to the Los Angeles National Cemetery. "It was a joke, right? Like a dare from your friends? I mean, why else would you throw yourself at some famous guy?"

Marlowe's fist ratcheted around the handle of her mug.

"I didn't throw myself at him," she said. "We know each other from set. We . . . work together."

"I work with a lot of people. Doesn't mean I—"

"What do you want, Kelvin?" Marlowe shoved her mug to the middle of the table. The tea was too hot to drink and she hoped Kelvin would be gone by the time it cooled. "Are you here to question that stupid photo or do you want to say something else?"

"Wow. Really?" He blinked at her, incredulous. "I fly all the way across the country to see you. I tell you I miss you and I'm interested in your career and you get bent out of shape because I ask about a photo we both know is a little out of character?"

Marlowe folded her arms, fighting the tenacious urge to wither and apologize.

"Don't do that," she said.

"Do what?"

"Don't pass off your comments as 'nothing' so if I get upset I look like I'm overreacting. I'm reacting. And I have every right to do it." She caught herself slouching down in her chair. She straightened up, determined not to get small. "I said I thought we should cut ties for a while. You showed up on my doorstep. Don't expect a thank-you."

Kelvin shoved back his chair and stepped over to the counter. He was probably trying to pace, but her kitchen wasn't big enough. All he could do was anchor himself to the peeling laminate counter and watch her from slightly further away.

"I only wanted to talk to you," he said. "Not through a screen."

"I don't have anything to say that I haven't already said."

"A text isn't a conversation." He raked a hand through his hair. When his bangs fell forward, he swept them sideways, twisting at the strands while his eyes darted around the kitchen before settling on her face. They held there, as blue as summer skies and still achingly beautiful. "You know what this weekend is."

"I do."

"But you don't care."

"I didn't say that." Marlowe locked her arms more tightly against her chest so she wouldn't play with her ring finger. She also wouldn't tell Kelvin she'd recently fainted in a wedding shop, unable to fully let go of the alternate life she might've led. She couldn't blame him for thinking about it, too, but this wasn't the way to deal with those thoughts.

While she fought the urge to fidget, he let out another sigh over by the counter.

"You took me by surprise when you gave back the ring," he said. "I didn't know what to say. Half of me wanted to beg you to reconsider and the other half was so pissed off, I wanted you to hurt as much as you'd hurt me. It wasn't fair. You dropped the bomb and left. You gave me no chance to respond in any kind of meaningful way."

Marlowe forced her jaw to loosen and her shoulders to drop, though she suspected everything would tense up again any second. Kelvin sounded so reasonable but he always did at first, and if he was truly reasonable, he would've proposed a visit they could both plan for. He wouldn't have ambushed her like this.

"All right," she said as gently as she could. "Go ahead. Respond."

He tapped his thumbs against the counter where he gripped it with both hands.

"This isn't a debate tournament," he said. "It's meant to be a dialogue."

She unfolded her arms and lowered her hands into her lap. She tried to sit still but she jabbed at her cuticles, forcing her thumbnail against her skin until it stung.

"At least help me understand," Kelvin continued, still in position by the counter. "Everything was great for three years and then all of a sudden you threw it away."

"I didn't throw anything away. I made a choice I'd been considering for a while, one I thought would be best for both of us." Blood beaded on her index finger. She sucked it off. "And everything wasn't great for three years."

"Then why didn't you say something?"

"Actually, I did. I've been thinking about this a lot, and blaming myself for not being clearer, but I've replayed our conversations over and over. Nothing happened 'all of a sudden.' I raised my concerns. Many times. You never listened."

"Are you *kidding* me?" Kelvin let out a huff before launching into an emphatic rebuttal, one that made Marlowe feel like she really was in a debate tournament, though her opponent relied on few facts and spoke with far more vitriol than the average debater. She let him rant without interruption until he finally sat down and agreed to let her speak.

While he frowned at her from across the table, she reminded him of several issues she'd raised while they were still together. The parties where he quickly vanished but allowed her no authority to make her own choices about when she came and went. The hijacked dates. The always-public gifts. This constant criticism and insidious little messages that her choices weren't as valid as his. She'd brought all of this to his attention during the relationship. He'd dismissed her every time. If she was a different person—bolder, louder, more confident, more clear-headed, or simply less fallibly human—maybe she would've realized the gravity of the problems sooner. She might've articulated her points in a more definitive tone or language, but she wasn't a different person. She'd done her best. When he rejected her concerns, she backed off. She deferred. She let him be right. Sometimes she even believed he was right, always willing to at least consider his viewpoint even though he was so quick to shut hers down. Going quiet had often seemed like her best option. Arguing didn't do much good. She'd only get accused of nagging or being needy and irrational. Better to swallow her concerns and move on.

When she finished explaining, no doubt leaving out a hundred things she'd think to say later, she reached for her now-cold tea. Kelvin hadn't touched his yet, either. He'd probably only set out the mugs so they each had something to do with their hands. For all of his faults, he was good about stuff like that, deeply perceptive about human behavior. It was one of the reasons she'd never fully trusted his supposed blindness to their relationship problems. He knew something wasn't working. He'd chosen to bury it, too.

"If it was all so awful, then why did you agree to marry me?" he asked.

"Because I loved you. And our relationship wasn't awful. So much of what we had was good. Great, even. I didn't want to lose any of that. Sometimes I didn't speak up when I was hurt or frustrated simply so we could hold on to whatever was going well. I wanted to snuggle in front of a movie, not fight again. But we got into some really bad patterns early on and nothing ever changed." She gulped back her tea and got up to put her mug in the sink. She decided to scrub it out right away. It gave her something to do.

"You're wrong," Kelvin said behind her.

Marlowe stiffened without turning around. "About what?"

"If you'd told me all that, I would've heard it."

She stifled a sigh. Then she faced Kelvin as she sagged against the counter.

"I told you now. Instead of taking it in and considering it, your first response is to tell me I'm wrong. To completely discredit me. *This* is what I've been trying to explain."

His brows pinched together, two black brushstrokes, meeting in the middle.

"So you're allowed to react, but I'm not?"

"I didn't say that. You're not listening."

"I can't sit here silently when what you've laid out with such painstaking detail is total bullshit. You've twisted everything and turned me into some kind of monster." He pivoted toward her, grinding his chair legs across the linoleum. While he struggled to level the chair, she fell into her old pattern of believing his words over her own. Doubts bubbled up. Had she called him a monster? Did she twist something? Should she retract, retreat, amend, apologize, smooth things over? As her mind spun, Kelvin's eyes flashed like blue flame, as if he sensed her wavering and now he could pounce. "You do hear yourself, right? What kind of girl complains about getting flowers? Or expects a guy to praise every little thing she does? Or flips out because he doesn't lock himself to her side at a goddamned party instead of assuming she'll talk to other people? It's not just flawed logic. It's flat-out crazy."

Marlowe swept his mug off the table and plunked it in the sink, buying herself a moment to level her voice before speaking. Kelvin wasn't here to listen and understand. He'd never understand. Some part of her knew that when she'd fled New York, knew that if she didn't run far and fast, she'd be stuck in this cycle over and over and over again. Raise a concern. Get yelled at. Question her needs. Cave and apologize. Rinse and repeat. She didn't run because she panicked. She ran because it was the only way to get out.

"I need you to leave," she said.

"What, now?"

"Yes."

"Because you don't want to hear the truth?"

"Because my truth is different from yours. And it always will be."

"That doesn't even make sense."

"It doesn't have to." She walked out of the kitchen and into the foyer.

He gaped at her from his chair. "Where am I supposed to go?"

"You're a smart guy. You'll figure it out."

"You can't be serious."

"Actually, I can. All these months I've blamed myself for not being clear, for not articulating the perfect words that would've made you understand what wasn't working so we could keep trying, but there are no perfect words. And while I've spent years apologizing to you, you never once took responsibility for your own failings. *I* was always the one who had to change, who had to do better. It's not fair. And it's not true." She picked up his backpack. One of the pockets flapped open. She wrenched the zipper shut, pinching her skin in the process. The little stab of pain felt sharp and real and gloriously uncomplicated. "No one's a monster. Some things simply don't work, no matter how hard anyone tries to force them to continue. We're not right for each other. End of story. Now, you need to go." She opened the front door and stepped back.

He stood up slowly, his face a confusing blend of anguish and fury.

"Don't do this," he said. "Don't throw me away again."

"I'm not. I'm asking you to leave."

"And you don't even care how I feel about that?"

"How you feel about that is no longer my responsibility." The words came out crisp and clear but a storm roiled in her gut. She had to lock her jaw so she wouldn't withdraw her statement and tell him how much she did care, opening the opportunity for him to hold her hostage with guilt. Cherry had nailed it last month. Kelvin was an emotional predator. With his almost Machiavellian ability to target Marlowe's lack of confidence, and to twist that deficiency into a power play, she'd been doomed to become a subservient shell of her once-outspoken self. Until she fled.

While she remained rooted to her position, he shook his head, looking at her as though he didn't even recognize her.

"When did you get so cold?" he asked.

"I'm not cold. I feel things as deeply now as I always did, but I've beat myself up about you for six months. I don't owe you more hurt or shame or whatever you came here to collect." She held out his bag. "Now go. Please."

He stared at her for what felt like forever but was probably less than a minute. Then he stepped forward and took his backpack, slinging it over a shoulder.

"If I leave now, I'm never coming back."

She nodded. "I know."

"That's all you have to say to me? After everything we've shared?"

She considered the question, replaying relationship memories on fast-forward: kisses, laughter, tears, fury, aloneness. She was about to nod and say goodbye when she realized she did want to say something else, something she *finally* understood, bone deep.

"Do you remember your last words to me in New York?" She waited as his brow furrowed and he shook his head. "You said, 'You'll never find someone else as good as me.' You were wrong. I did find someone."

Kelvin reeled, scrunching up his face in disbelief.

"Who? That guy in the club photo?"

"No." She backed up to give him plenty of room to pass. "Me."

He pursed his lips, staring long and hard into her eyes. She held her ground, standing tall, unflinching, until he walked out. As soon as he cleared the front step, she shut and locked the door. Then she sank to the floor and bawled her eyes out.

Chapter Twenty-six

Saturday morning, long after Marlowe had exhausted her snooze alarm well past any actual snoozing, she picked crusted tears from her lashes and rolled over to check her phone. Her group thread with her friends had several insistent texts urging her to call as soon as she was awake. She'd texted last night to let them know Kelvin had shown up and she'd kicked him out. Her friends were three hours ahead and all asleep at the time, but they were on stand-by now as soon as she was upright. She loved them for that, and for a hundred other things, besides. Her mom had also texted, pushing for an answer about the marathon, and her dad had texted to reschedule their next chat. Again.

She set aside her phone and squinted up at her window. Bright sunlight poured through the bent sections of her mangled blinds, as usual, forming oddly angled stripes across the beige bedding. She never thought she'd miss rain and snow, but the endless perfect weather in L.A. felt like a bar Marlowe's mood couldn't live up to. Knowing that, and feeling she'd earned the right to wallow for a day, she drew the covers over her head. She threw them off again when her phone buzzed. And didn't stop.

Cherry: Wes turned in new pages

Cherry: We have an added scene to shoot Monday

Cherry: Lola Lankarani's making a guest appearance

Cherry: She only wears pink

Cherry: She's very particular about which pink

Cherry: I have her approved Pantone color samples

Cherry: Yes, I'm serious

Cherry: Babs needs us to shop options

Cherry: It'll be faster with two of us

Cherry: How soon can you get a rental car?

Cherry: Do you need a ride?

Cherry: I'm in your neighborhood

Cherry: Just need an address

Cherry: Want coffee?

Cherry: Treats?

Marlowe watched the texts appear, one right after another. If Cherry had fit them all into a single send, Marlowe might've been able to ignore it, remaining horizontal and brain-fogged for several hours to come. Instead, Cherry continued sending questions and increasingly urgent pleas for a reply. Eventually Marlowe caved.

Marlowe: Can't work today. Sorry

Cherry: Where are you?

Marlowe: In bed

Cherry: Are you sick?

Marlowe typed *yes,* deleted it, typed it again, and decided Cherry deserved the truth. Through a rapid text exchange, Marlowe explained what had happened last night. With a few choice expletives, Cherry requested an address and promised to arrive within twenty minutes, coffee and full-gluten, full-sugar treats in hand. And so she did.

"We have half an hour," she said as she flew past Marlowe into the kitchen, goodies in hand. "You're going to tell me everything. I'm going to will seven plagues on Bench Boy. Then you're showering and getting dressed and we're going shopping."

"I *really* don't want to work today." Marlowe dropped into a chair and plunked her phone on the table. She was wearing the worn-out tank top and knit shorts she'd put on before going to bed. The shorts needed a new drawstring. The straps on the top barely hung on by a thread. Her clothes were embarrassing but thematically appropriate, which at least appeased her costume designer brain. "Can't someone else do the shopping?"

"Not someone with your design eye." Cherry popped the tops off the coffees and set the cups on the table, deliberately putting space between the cups and Marlowe's phone, as if she sensed that Marlowe's accident-prone tendencies might be especially acute at present. "You have to rally. A, I'm not letting Babs down when I still need her to recommend me for a design gig. B, that guy has sucked enough of your time and energy. So until I know you're really okay, I'm going to distract the shit out of you."

Marlowe tried to laugh but her breath came out as an awkward pant/groan. While she dropped her head into her hands, embracing her lethargy, Cherry swung open the cabinet below the sink and tossed the plastic lids into the recycling bin.

"What happened to your pajamas?" She leaned closer to the trash can. "And why are they covered in syrup?"

"They were a gift from Kelvin. I threw them away last night. Then I worried I'd change my mind. It was either syrup or hot sauce. The syrup was less gruesome."

"Makes perfect sense." Cherry sat down across from Marlowe

and spilled half a dozen muffins onto the table. "I didn't know what kind you liked so I got one of each."

"Thanks. You're a good friend. You know that?"

"Yeah, but it never hurts to hear it."

Cherry opened the button on her suit jacket and sat back with her coffee. She looked effortlessly stylish, as always, as if she'd tossed on a random tee, jacket, jeans, and pair of chunky boots and they all happened to work great together. Today's shirt said simply *SIT ON THIS* above a cartoon drawing of a basic wooden chair. Her sleek black topknot spiked upward in a way that suited her energy. Marlowe's topknot was also oddly appropriate, drooping sideways as it succumbed to gravity and extreme pathos.

She reached for the least bran-like muffin and picked at it while answering Cherry's questions about last night's conversation. Cherry was predictably quick to vilify Kelvin, but Marlowe took a more tempered view of her relationship. She knew her insecurities had played a role in establishing unhealthy patterns, even if Kelvin was at fault for exploiting those insecurities, both knowingly and unknowingly.

"A lot of the time I think I was avoiding criticism," she said. "I don't know why it gets to me so badly, or why I let other people's opinions make me feel like a failure, but the avoidance is a problem. It made me leave my career in New York. It keeps me distant from both of my parents. It didn't do my last relationship any favors." *It's also affecting my chance at a new relationship,* she thought, but she kept it to herself.

"Everyone hates criticism," Cherry said. "We find different ways to manage it, but that whole 'Don't worry what other people think' idea is bullshit. If we didn't care what other people thought, we'd be sociopaths. You know, like Bench Boy."

Marlowe rolled her eyes but inwardly she appreciated Cherry's staunch support.

"He's not a sociopath," she said. "And his name is Kelvin."

"Whatever. I'm proud of you for pouring syrup on his pants." Cherry polished off the last of her coffee as quickly as ever while Marlowe continued waiting for hers to cool. "You know you're better off without him, right?"

"We're better off without each other." Marlowe scooped up the crumbs that now covered the tabletop. She'd decimated her muffin during the conversation, though very little of it found its way to her mouth. "He was predisposed to assume he deserved more. I was predisposed to assume I deserved less. We were doomed from the outset."

As Marlowe got up and dumped her crumbs into the trash, she thought about all the things she hadn't said last night, like how much she'd missed Kelvin and how often she thought of him. She didn't want to give him any mixed messages. Her mixed feelings weren't as easily controlled. Despite what she'd just said to Cherry, a part of her might always wonder if she and Kelvin could've built a healthy relationship if either of them had handled things differently early on. Fortunately it was a small part, and one that seemed likely to continue diminishing in days to come.

"You going to be okay?" Cherry asked from the table.

"Yeah," Marlowe pushed through a sigh. "I just need some time to shake off the ick factor." She shut the cabinet door, only now noticing that she'd been staring at the syrup-soaked pajama pants. "I always wanted to be one of those girls who could flick away a problem and strut off with the perfect mic-dropping quip. No mess. No regrets."

Cherry huffed out a laugh. "That girl doesn't exist outside the movies. She's as fake as your padded butt and bra. Merely aspirational. And deeply annoying."

Marlowe smiled as a warm bubble of gratitude burst in her chest. No matter what happened over the next few months—with her career, location, or love life—she was grateful for her time in L.A. After all, it'd given her one of the best friendships of her life.

As she savored that thought, Cherry's phone pinged.

"It's the boss. Adding to the shopping list. Thank god she can't track this phone."

Marlowe washed her sticky hands while Cherry manically fired off a text.

"Why do you think she hasn't recommended you for a design job yet?"

"I don't know. Maybe the right job hasn't come up." Cherry pocketed her phone and helped tidy, tossing the extra muffins into their bag. "More likely she's avoiding competition. You've seen how she punishes you whenever Angus dares to spare a smile in your direction, and she clearly has lingering—and understandable—resentment from her divorce. She doesn't like the idea that anyone else might have something she wants." Cherry put the muffins in Marlowe's otherwise-empty fridge, pausing to look deeper into the recesses, as if something besides condiments *had* to be in there somewhere.

Marlowe wiped down the table, picturing a less jaded, less self-protective Babs while hoping her own relationship scars wouldn't harden her to the same degree.

"Resenting someone else's potential success is kind of sad," she said.

"Sad but common." Cherry shut the fridge with a bump of her hip. "This business is rife with territorialism. Everyone's afraid of handing off a job. You never know which one's going to lead to the next big-budget superhero film or epic period drama. It sucks, but I'd be pissed, too, if my assistant went on to create the next massive fantasy franchise while I was designing my umpteenth season of *Heart's Kill-Me-Now Diner*."

"Makes sense, I guess. The New York theater scene was the same. I knew designers who'd take on way more work than they could handle, farm it out to an army of assistants, keep the design credits for themselves, and openly boast about how that method kept competition minimal." Marlowe rinsed out her washcloth while wondering if theater or film was more cutthroat, or if every freelance industry had similar issues. "Speaking of the New York theater scene, I had a job interview yesterday."

Cherry's sleek brows shot up. "For a design gig?"

"Yeah. A good one. Off-Broadway. World premiere. Not sure if I'll get it. The director's interviewing other designers, but they're tight on schedule, so I'll hear soon."

"That's awesome."

"Even though it would mean bailing on you for that film?"

"Are you kidding? I'd jump the assisting ship in a heartbeat if I got a chance like that." Cherry plucked a last remaining crumb off the table. "Did the interview go okay?"

"Mostly, although—" Marlowe broke off when her phone buzzed on the table.

Cherry glanced at the screen, her expression darkening into an ice-cold glare.

"Please tell me you blocked him."

"I did. Last night. Right after he left."

"Whoa. Wait. What the—?" Cherry grabbed the phone.

Marlowe leapt forward and whisked it from Cherry's hands.

The text on the screen was from Angus. *Can I see you tonight? I need to return your spare house keys. Jeeves says it's bad manners to keep them indefinitely.* The text was followed with a winky emoticon. Gut knotting, Marlowe lowered her phone and met Cherry's stare.

"Why is Chisel MacStubble texting you?" Cherry asked.

"He only—I mean, we kind of—That is to say—"

"Holy shit." Cherry's jaw dropped open. "You had sex with him, didn't you?"

Marlowe cringed. "We didn't *technically* have sex, but . . ."

"But you sucked his face off while he put his hands down your pants?"

"Something like that?" Marlowe sank into a chair and braced herself for a diatribe. To her surprise, no diatribe came. Instead, a slow smile stretched across Cherry's face.

"Was it good?" she asked.

Marlowe's eyes drifted toward the bedroom, the sofa, the living room floor, the faint rectangle on the wall where an owl painting was still missing.

"Yeah." She nodded. "It was really good."

"Was it just for the not-technically sex?"

Marlowe hesitated before shaking her head. Cherry's smile faded. For a moment the two of them simply sat there, silently acknowledging Marlowe's reluctant admission. Then Cherry's eyes narrowed as though she'd just remembered something.

"Wasn't he at that gala thingy with Tanareve last night?" she asked.

Marlowe nodded again, sliding further down in her chair.

Cherry took her hand and gave it a squeeze.

"Oh, lord," she said. "You're fucked now."

Chapter Twenty-seven

By the time Marlowe and Cherry were sorting through pastel pantsuits at Ladies' Choice—a bland atelier that catered to women of a certain age and financial bracket—Marlowe had explained the full situation to Cherry. No, Angus wasn't dating Tanareve. No, he wasn't looking for a quick fling. Yes, he'd asked Marlowe to be his date last night. Also yes, she wanted to stay as far away from celebrity fanfare as possible. Also, *also* yes, she really liked Angus and she wasn't sure what to do about that.

"I'm such a chicken." Marlowe flipped past boring but well-tailored suits in powder blue and minty green, searching for anything pink. "Being seen with him in public shouldn't be that hard. So what if people think I'm ugly or slutty or that I don't deserve him? Why can't I focus on what *I* want and ignore what people say about me?"

Cherry scoffed from the next aisle over. "Because it would be a *lot* of people. We're talking about Angus Gordon, not some dude who's lucky to get upper-balcony seats at the Emmys. Do you really want *TMZ* reporting what you had for dinner last night? Or *Access Hollywood* putting you on a worst-dressed list?

Or *People* magazine blowing up your phone for your version of the breakup?" Cherry grimaced as Marlowe flashed her a look. "Sorry. I get it. He's beautiful and amazing and you'd never break up. Whatever. You had some fun. Now leave him to do his thing while you go do yours."

Marlowe considered the suggestion, but it didn't sit well. Despite yesterday's convictions about aborting any relationship possibilities, now that she'd slept on the idea—and on a lot of other thoughts besides—she was far less certain.

"I think I'm too attached already," she said.

"Fine, then secretly bang him for a few weeks and see how you feel after."

Marlowe considered that idea, too. While it had more appeal than Cherry's first suggestion, it didn't sit well, either, and she doubted it would sit well with Angus.

"I think that would make me even more attached." She pulled out a pink sateen jacket and compared it to her approved Pantone color chips. "I at least need to answer his text, but what do I say? *I'm pretty sure I'm falling for you but could you make all of your fans think you're going to marry Tanareve so they leave me alone?*"

"Bad plan. It'll only make them hate you more when new clickbait leaks." Cherry held out two silk blouses, turned up her nose at both, and put them back. "How about asking him if you can borrow a car?"

Marlowe balked. "So I can take gross advantage of his wealth?"

Cherry pursed her lips. "So you can open up a conversation without leaping straight to *I love you, I need you, but we're doomed.*" She nodded at the jacket Marlowe was examining. "It's too peach. Lola will hate it."

Marlowe put the jacket back, even though the color was *so* close to her sample.

"If she's this particular, shouldn't we be building custom?" she asked.

"We custom built for her last season. She even preapproved the fabric. Then she flipped out in her fitting, asking how we could've *dreamed* her complexion would work in a color so vile." Cherry rolled her eyes as she moved on to the next rack. "She demanded we rebuild her dress in a *slightly* bluer pink. We did it. Only had two days. Everyone worked around the clock. No point going through that again. Better to have multiple options on hand."

Marlowe shook her head as she assessed the color of another jacket.

"This job is crazy," she said.

"Yeah, but at least it's interesting."

With a nod of agreement, Marlowe helped Cherry search the store for pieces they could fit on Lola. As Cherry made the eventual purchase, Marlowe stepped outside and opened Angus's text. *Can I see you tonight? I need to return your spare house keys. Jeeves says it's bad manners to keep them indefinitely.* Winking emoticon. She loved that he wanted to see her again, even if she was really confused about how far to let things progress. After much debate, she opted for Cherry's Start Casual plan.

Marlowe: Jeeves has no right to meddle

Angus didn't reply right away so she checked her email. She had two messages from Yale. The first requested her student-loan payment. The other was from the alumni association, soliciting donations. The overlap in timing was ironic, but not uncommon.

Angus: Hey! You're up!

Marlowe: Would've slept all day but I had to work

Angus: Egotistical actor demanding a personal jeans shopper?

Marlowe: Not far off, but swap the jeans for tepid pink separates

Angus: Lola, right? I heard she was back. How late are you working?

Marlowe: Until we find what we need, so around the time stores close

Angus: Can I still see you? Maybe at my place this time? It's curse-free

Marlowe stared at the screen, torn between embracing whatever private time they could spend together and not wanting to make the situation harder. Then she worried she was broadcasting her indecisiveness by making Angus wait too long for a response.

Marlowe: Not sure I can make it

Angus: Conspiring with the yak?

Marlowe: I don't have transit. My car died yesterday

Angus: My deepest sympathies. May her pungent odor rest in peace

Marlowe: She seems more like the haunting type. Maybe the zombies can use her

Angus: Good call. How about I pick you up? You can take the stealth car home. Use it as long as you need it. Please say yes. Jeeves is very insistent about returning these keys

Marlowe melted against the storefront. Of course he offered her his car, and before she even asked. Just like he'd given her his

Yankees hat, recruited his agent, opened up his home, planned breakfast . . . He also made her laugh. He supported and encouraged her. He didn't autopilot to a position of entitlement or authority. He embraced words like *you're right* instead of always defaulting to *you're wrong*. He even helped her confront her problems in a kind and thoughtful way. How could she walk away from all of that?

Marlowe: I'll see if Cherry can me drop me off after work

Angus: ☺ ☺ ☺ ☺ ☺ ☺ ☺ ☺ ☺

Marlowe: You're cute. You know that?

Angus: I'm counting on it. Keep me posted. See you later

Cherry's car was packed with shopping bags by the time she drove Marlowe through the winding streets of Bel Air toward Angus's house.

"You sure you don't need anything?" Cherry asked. "A comb? A toothbrush?"

"Doubt it," Marlowe said. "He's very well stocked."

"I've been in enough of his fittings to notice." Cherry waggled her brows.

Marlowe couldn't help but laugh. "That wasn't a euphemism."

"I'm just saying, if that's what you're into . . ."

Marlowe got out her phone as a means of cutting off the conversation. She had no interest in discussing what Angus stocked in his pants. She had no complaints, either.

Three emails had come in since she last checked: a receipt for her car donation, a bill for her union dues, and . . .

"Oh, my god." She gaped at the message on her screen.

Cherry snuck her a glance before steering around an S-curve. "Everything okay?"

"Yeah. I got the job. The Off-Broadway design one I told you about this morning."

"Fuck, yeah, you did." Cherry held up a palm for Marlowe to high-five. "I'm so happy for you. I'm also insanely jealous. How soon does it start?"

"Right away, though I can join the first meetings remotely. I'd head east in four or five weeks, shortly after we finish wrap. Sneak in a few friend and family visits in late October. Use November to prep for December rehearsals and fittings." As the idea took shape, Marlowe's excitement built. After months of menial errands, she'd finally get to use her creativity again, and she'd get to dig in to a script with depth and purpose. She was surprised at how ready she felt, but her days of invisibility were behind her. Besides, if she could face her ex, she could face a few critics. "I'll move back in with my friends, cheer on my mom in her marathon, find a new excuse to avoid my dad, drag out my favorite cozy sweaters, and put myself out there for other jobs."

Cherry beamed at her. "That all sounds perfect."

"Well, almost perfect." Marlowe leaned against the door, watching the next bend in the road. As they rounded it and approached another, her excitement faded and her posture wilted. "I'll miss hanging out with you. And then there's You-Know-Who."

Cherry pulled her car onto the shoulder and put it in park.

"Maybe this is for the best," she said. "The timing's ideal. You had some fun. You didn't make each other any promises. You're already freaking out about him. Why not get out now, before you have to deal with any more clickbait bullshit?"

Marlowe frowned as she pivoted to face Cherry.

"You know why," she said.

"You guys spent one night together."

"It's about more than that night."

"Is it? How can you tell?" Cherry stared Marlowe down, the picture of skepticism, but Marlowe didn't buy it. For all of Cherry's sass, she had a mushy side, too.

"What if your next job required leaving Maria?" Marlowe asked.

Cherry shrugged but the creases by her eyes and mouth belied her indifference.

"I've put ten years into this career. I've known Maria for less than a month."

"But you guys have potential, right? You recognize that you found something unique in each other, something that fits and feels right and makes you both happy in a meaningful way. You wouldn't want to just end things?"

Cherry shrugged again but her creases only deepened. Marlowe watched her, recalling how giddy she'd been after her first night with Maria. Marlowe understood that giddiness well, even if her own feelings were mixed with a heavy dose of anxiety. How strange to fear the loss of someone whose presence had only just begun to matter. But also to know with complete certainty that the loss would be profound.

"Maybe I could become bicoastal," she said. "I can spend two or three months in New York and then fly back to pick up another gig here."

Cherry raised a brow. "You can afford to keep two apartments? Pay for the flights? Deal with being unemployed half the time because the jobs won't line up perfectly when you're not available to follow a team from one show to the next?"

Marlowe shifted uncomfortably as she considered Cherry's

points. If she left in October, even temporarily, someone else would take her spot on Babs's team. Marlowe would have to start from ground zero again if she returned, building new connections, proving herself to other designers. Rebooting her theater career also meant being present in New York, setting up interviews, attending opening nights, networking in that community. All of that was hard enough in one city. Could she really do it in two?

"Your call," Cherry said. "I can finish the drive or I can turn the car around."

Marlowe opened her phone and skimmed through past text conversations with Angus. Words flashed by: *garnish*, *cattle*, *detective*, *butler*, *luck*, *curse*, *tacos*, *disguise*, *jeans*, *dog*, *freckled ear*. Over only a couple of weeks, she and Angus had already begun building a private language, the accumulation of symbolic mementos that cemented connections between two people. It was a good language so far. It wasn't weighed down with accusations and guilt trips and power plays. It was full of laughter and joy.

She lowered her phone and looked out at the next bend in the road, lit by warm pools of light from the illuminated gates that flanked it.

"Do you still think it's possible to be in love with someone you've only known for a few days?" she asked.

Cherry took a breath, allowing the question a moment to settle. "It's definitely not impossible," she said.

"My thoughts exactly."

Chapter Twenty-eight

Cherry pulled up to Angus's gate, leaning forward and squinting toward the house.

"Nice place," she said.

"No kidding, though it's homier on the inside than it seems from the outside." Marlowe checked her makeup in the embedded visor mirror before smoothing out her skirt. Thankfully she'd put on a cute dress that morning. It was pale yellow, in a fit-and-flare style that was well suited for cycling in Paris with a baguette and a bouquet in the handlebar basket. While cycling probably wasn't on the night's agenda, she was pleased to arrive at Angus's house in something more attractive than an overwashed T-shirt covered in dog hair and congealed vanilla shake.

"Maria's meeting me for a late dinner in Santa Monica," Cherry said, "but I can be back here in about half an hour if you change your mind and need a ride."

"I doubt that will be necessary."

"Offer still stands."

Marlowe gave Cherry a big hug. Then she got out of the car, called Angus through the speaker box to let him know she'd arrived, and waited until he buzzed the gate open. She was halfway up the driveway when he stepped through his front door and jogged forward to meet her. He was wearing his usual jeans and white tee, plus the ridiculous knit ski hat he'd held on to when he gave her his Yankees cap.

"I don't think we're expecting snow," she said through a laugh.

"Doesn't matter. It got a smile out of you." He swept her into an embrace. She breathed in the smell of his soap and shampoo. The scents weren't fruity or flowery, nor did they conjure images of avalanches or waterfalls. He simply smelled clean, and while Marlowe was the furthest thing from a clean freak, she found the smell incredibly sexy.

"Thanks for inviting me over." She drew back, but only far enough to meet his eyes.

"Thanks for agreeing to come." He pulled her in for a kiss that felt so easy, so natural, Marlowe got the sense he'd already moved past all of the questions she was still wrestling with. "Did you get a chance to stop for dinner while you were working?"

"What do you think?"

He kept an arm hooked around her waist and led her toward the front door.

"Let's get you fed. Then you can tell me about your car, and your workday, and anything else you want to get off your chest."

While helping prepare a pasta dish with homemade pesto, Marlowe stopped stressing about Big Questions. She was calmed by Angus's relaxed presence and her usual enjoyment of joint creation. His determination to slowly overturn her revulsion of green food also amused her. It was sweet, and it implied he was already picturing more meals together. The idea made her smile despite all of her earlier unease. It also confirmed that they needed to clarify a few expectations before tearing off each other's clothes again.

Over dinner, they chatted about the past few days. She told him about her car, and shopping for Lola's perfect pink ensemble, and even kicking Kelvin out of her apartment. He told her about the gala, and discussions he'd been having with his PR rep, and filming a sex scene in a rose garden, which was far less romantic than it sounded, thanks to the dirt, rocks, and random thorns the greens crew hadn't fully pared away. The conversation flowed effortlessly, as though the two of them had known each other for ages. Marlowe didn't even realize almost two hours had passed until she and Angus were putting their pre-rinsed dishes in the dishwasher.

As he bent to pick up a fallen fork, his T-shirt stretched across his back and shoulders, revealing the contours of his muscles, or as Cherry had once called them: the Great Gordon Chisel-fest. The epithet had seemed like hyperbole at the time, but right now, it was apt. Also, the seams in his jeans lined up precisely where they should.

"For the record," Marlowe said, letting her gaze linger, "you don't need professional help to pick out jeans. The ones you're wearing fit you really well."

He twisted around as if he was reminding himself which jeans he had on.

"Babs let me have them. They're left over from season three, but thanks for noticing." He held up a hand. "Don't say it. I know. Occupational hazard."

"Actually, this time I was just looking." She bit her lip, flushing at her unexpected burst of candor.

As he tossed the fork into the utensil basket, his eyes lifted to hers. For a long moment he simply looked at her, reading her expression, her body language, maybe even the accelerated rate at which her chest was rising and falling. She returned the look from her spot by the sink, where she was rinsing a wine glass. He took the glass from her hand, set it aside, and turned off the tap. Then he lifted her by the waist and set her on the counter, wedging himself between her knees and cupping her face in both hands.

"I've been thinking about this since I woke up alone in your bed on Thursday." His eyes got all twinkly as he tipped his forehead against hers.

"Same," she said, forcing herself to focus. "Though I've been thinking about a lot of other things, too." She found the belt loops at his hips and pulled him closer. If she was going to have this conversation, she wanted as little distance between them as possible.

"Things like . . . ?" He nuzzled her nose, her temple, her cheek, her ear, every little bunt soft and slow.

She drew in a breath, preparing for the worst.

"Like I got a design job. In New York."

He inched away, offering her a conflicted smile, mostly happy but also sad.

"Congratulations," he said. "It's what you want to be doing, right?"

"It is, and you helped me embrace that, but . . ." She twisted one of his beautiful copper-penny cowlicks around her finger, watching it spring back into place. "It means giving up my apartment here and leaving L.A. once my job on *Heart's Diner* ends."

"Leaving for good?"

"I don't know. Not necessarily."

"Okay." His brows dipped and she could almost see him working through everything she'd talked out with Cherry, about extra expenses and opportunity costs. "And until you leave?"

"I don't know that, either." She trailed the back of her hand down his stubbled cheek, marveling yet again at how soft it was. "I'd like to keep seeing you, but you said it yourself. Casual only works if it's what both people want."

His brows dipped again. "Does this feel casual to you?"

She shook her head. "I kind of have a habit of getting attached."

"Not a habit that requires a ten-step recovery program. In fact, I believe it's often considered an end goal." His lips brushed hers as his brows finally lifted. She draped her arms around his neck and let a hand slide up into his soft waves. He kissed her again, just as featherlight, while busily studying her eyes as though he could read the complicated workings of her heart in a look, and maybe he could.

"Distance didn't work for you last time," she murmured against his lips.

"Different relationship. Different circumstances." He planted another kiss on her lips before inching away again. "I'm not going to lie and say I'm thrilled you're going back to New York, but in this industry, it's all distance. Next year I might be on location in Moscow or Mongolia. Your next TV gig could take you to Vancouver for six months. Staying connected takes effort but the question isn't *Can it work?* It's *Do you want it enough to try?*" He traced the curves of her ear without breaking eye contact. She leaned into his touch as she let his statement sink in. He was right, of course. She'd been asking the wrong questions for the past few days. This was the one that mattered. "I can't know for sure how either of us will feel by the time you catch a flight east, but right now, my answer's yes, and in a few weeks, there's a damned good chance it will still be yes."

She kissed him for that, though she couldn't quite share his certainty.

"Even if we only see each other in private?" she asked.

His kisses and caresses came to an abrupt halt. He backed out of her embrace, running a hand down his face and rubbing at his jawline in that way he had, as if motors in his mind were running fast and furious and he was trying to still them. She leaned toward him, aching to retract her question and assure him she'd adjust to his lifestyle. After all, judgment from strangers was no worse than what she'd endured from her ex, her parents, her boss, and a slew of professional critics. It was more scathing, perhaps, but also meaningless, invented, based on half-truths. Over the past few weeks, she'd built up enough confidence to excise Kelvin from her life, and to restart her design career. Surely she could leap this last hurdle. And yet . . . the assurance wouldn't come.

She was still searching for words when he held out a hand. She placed hers in his. She liked that he made a habit of offering instead of taking. She also liked that he hated small talk and he was a lot smarter than people gave him credit for. She probably even liked the third thing he was self-conscious about, the one he hadn't yet revealed.

"You can't hide from the public completely," he said. "The producers hired you to build buzz. If nothing else, they'll book you—or more likely *us*—on a few appearances in December before your episodes stream. Sanaya went over all of that with you, right?"

Marlowe nodded, running her thumb over the back of his hand.

"She also said it wasn't the official PR I had to worry about."

"And she was right." Angus gave her hand a squeeze. "What if we use the intervening time to ease you into everything? No red-carpet events. No formal interviews. Just a night out once in a while and a bit of social media engagement with those accounts I'm no longer pretending don't exist. We can make an introduction, and a direct request for privacy. So we have some control over the narrative, and so I don't have to keep explaining to reporters why I'm showing up somewhere with Tan again."

He held out his other hand. Marlowe took it as quickly as she'd taken the first.

"I know this thing between us is really new," he continued. "And I come with a lot of unusual baggage. If I was someone else, we'd be out watching a film tonight, or choosing a dessert to share at a mediocre restaurant neither of us liked but we both pretended it was great because we were trying to make a good impression."

"You eat dessert?" she teased.

"So not the point here." His words were firm but he smiled anyway, leaning in to nuzzle her nose again. "I've told you how I feel. Now you tell me. Do you want this enough to try?" Despite his affectionate little touches, his smile faded. His eyes grew wary. His shoulders went rigid, as if he knew a *no* was possible, maybe even probable.

Marlowe drew their linked hands against her chest, forcing herself to meet his amber eyes while she flashed through memories of talk show hosts joking about her, Internet trolls mocking her, angry fans throwing trash at her. Other memories flashed by, too. Laughter and kindness and a profound sense of mutual care. She had no idea how she and Angus would build a relationship that would work for both of them, but if he was willing to try, the least she could do was meet him halfway.

"Yes," she said. "I do."

"Thank god." The words rushed out of him in a gust of breath. In the next instant, his lips were on hers and his hands swept upward to hold her face close to his. Equally flooded with relief, she returned his kisses while running her hands over his back and shoulders, finding every dent, every curve, every spot that shifted against her touch. The tension that'd been building for the last several minutes detonated as she and Angus drew each other close, breathless, hungry, already clawing at clothes.

He didn't tease her with slowly opened buttons this time. He yanked down the zipper at the back of her dress and wrenched the garment over her head, laughing as it caught on her boobs, her chin, her nose, her elbows, *and* her wrists. By the time his shirt followed her dress, she was already unbuckling his belt and unzipping his fly. He shoved his jeans down and kicked them aside, laughing again as he peeled off his socks, nearly toppling in the process. Then he fell against her in another deep kiss, as though a few seconds away from her was too long. She knotted her fists in his thick waves. His mouth traveled down her neck, her chest, her stomach. She reached behind her back to unfasten her bra, struggling to find the right angle while his hands and lips continued roaming over her body, planting shivers, distracting her from her purpose, painting her with desire.

"I can't . . ." she started, too breathless to finish.

"I've got it." He made quick work of the hooks she hadn't managed. As she removed her bra and flung it aside, he lifted her off the counter. She'd never been into jocks or beefy superhero types, but goddamn, it was hot the way he could raise her up in his arms as if she weighed nothing at all. She linked her ankles behind his back while he carried her through the house to a sparsely decorated bedroom. Gray walls, sleek lamps, abstract black-and-white photographs of rippling shorelines, and fluffy white bedding that looked like it belonged in a luxury hotel. He laid her down in the center of the bed, stretching himself out above her. The light was dim, provided only by a small bedside lamp he'd flicked on with a wall switch as they'd entered. It was enough for her to see the shape of him, the highlights in his amber eyes, the upturn at the corners of his lips.

"Does your answer still hold?" he asked.

"Yes. Yes. And also, yes."

"Good. Mine, too." With a growing smile, he slipped a hand into her underwear and cupped her, exerting barely a hint of pressure.

She locked her eyes on his, waiting, her breath held and her heart pounding. When the hum of anticipation grew too strong to bear, she eased her weight against his hand, forcing his fingertips to press harder. He stroked her slowly, circling and skimming without entering. Her hands raked into his hair. Her hips rolled against his touch. Every nerve in her body seemed to coil in on itself, gathering tension. He held her gaze, reading her expression, steady, focused, aware. As she started to tremble at the impossible ache for more, his mouth found hers and two of his fingers slipped inside her.

She gasped as her eyelids fluttered closed. God, that feeling, the electric thrill of being touched in places that forced her toes to curl, her fists to roll in on themselves, and her breath to catch in her throat. His fingers pushed forward. She arched against him, releasing his hair to tug at the waistband of his boxer briefs.

"Not yet." He removed her hands. "Let me watch you first."

A prickle of self-consciousness rippled through her, but she shook it off and let herself be seen, no shrinking, no hiding, no shame. She'd always associated nakedness with the kind of vulnerability that was to be avoided at all costs, but this was different. It was about shedding the unnecessary, accepting her flawed and unadorned self as enough. It was about sharing her body with someone she trusted to treat her with care.

While she settled into that trust, he found the spots that made her writhe and moan. Soon enough she was thrusting against him, pulling at his neck and shoulders, nipping at his lips, lost in a glorious sea of skin and sweat. His fingers moved faster, deeper. She drew him against her, held on tight, reveled in the weight of his body pressing down on her, whispered *yes*es, battled her craving for more.

"Tell me what you want," he rumbled against her ear.

She almost laughed, not because his request was funny, but because it was beautiful and joyous. She couldn't remember the last time she'd been given such open permission to want. She knew she shouldn't need that permission, but she'd been denied it for so long she'd almost forgotten how to find it on her own.

"I want you inside me," she said. "Please tell me you have a condom."

He answered with dead-sexy smile. They both wriggled out of their underwear. Then it was her turn to watch as he opened a drawer in his bedside table and grabbed a foil packet. As he tore it open and put on the condom, she drank in his shoulders and back, painted by soft, warm light. She noted the little dimples that paralleled his spine, the curves of his well-toned ass, the smoothness of his tanned skin, crossed here and there by a smattering of freckles. She wondered if she'd ever get tired of looking at him. Surely at some point he'd become ordinary, just a guy who teased her about making too many assumptions or not eating enough vegetables, but that point seemed a long, *long* way off.

He leaned over her but she rolled him onto his back and straddled him, making up in enthusiasm what she lacked in grace. He smiled up at her, amused—and maybe even charmed—by her struggle to wedge her lanky legs around his hips. She kissed him again, drawn in by his smile, his warm eyes, and the giant heart he was so willing to lay bare for her. With one hand braced against his stomach and the other wrapped around his erection, she lowered herself onto him. A rush of sensation followed. A fullness. An uncoiling. A fire in her blood. His hands found her waist, his grip tender but firm. She let her head fall back and her mouth drop open as she drove her hips forward. Once. Twice. A third time. Her muscles tightened around him, already hinting at the climax to come.

"I'm not going to last very long," she said.

He pulled her into another kiss, deep and slow.

"Me, neither. But I don't think that's a problem." He nodded toward the open drawer in his bedside table. Scattered atop his books were several more condom packets.

"I like the way you think," she said, half-joking.

"I like the way you everything," he said, not joking at all.

If any Big Questions lingered after that, Marlowe couldn't recall what they were.

Chapter Twenty-nine

Marlowe awoke, spooned within Angus's arms, her head on an impossibly soft pillow, her legs tangled in impossibly soft sheets. She had been kidding last weekend when she said she'd do just about anything to finagle a way into Angus's bed again, but now the joke held new weight. As she spun to face him, his lashes fluttered open and a sleepy smile stretched across his beautiful face.

Oh, yes, she thought. *I could definitely get used to waking up like this.*

While the thought lingered, she managed a husky, "Good morning."

"Damned straight it is." He nestled closer as his eyes fell shut again. "Unless you miss the vengeful owls and the murder carpet and the rancid sofa yak."

"Definitely not the yak." She drew curlicues on Angus's collarbone while he let out a drowsy little murmur of contentment. She liked his little noises, the ways his joy or confusion or even frustration leaked past his often inscrutable demeanor.

He wrapped a leg over her hip, locking her against him.

"Tell me you don't have to work today."

"Cherry said she'd try to cover anything that comes up."

"Remind me to thank her the next time I see her."

"I'll thank her for both of us."

Angus let out another rumbly *mmmm* before his hold slackened. Marlowe enjoyed the simple closeness for several minutes but she soon grew restless, reaching past him to grab the small stack of books on his bedside table. They included a collection of essays on art and artifice, a performance artist's memoir, a pulp fiction murder mystery, and a worn-out copy of *Anna Karenina*. All had bookmarks partway through their pages.

"Are you reading all of these at once?" she asked.

He yawned as he tucked an arm behind his head and watched her skim the covers.

"I jump around a lot depending on my mood. Sometimes light and fun wins out. Other times I'm looking for a deeper read. It's nice to have options. But the books don't make it to the living room shelves until I've read every page."

Marlowe's jaw dropped open. She remembered those shelves. She remembered the hundreds of books they contained, too. Fiction, history, philosophy, artistic theory.

"You've read *all* of those? And you're self-conscious about your education?"

He shrugged as he danced his fingers over her bare shoulders.

"Assuming you've had at least some exposure to fan sites and tabloids, when was the last time you saw anyone mention my brain?" He added a light chuckle, but Marlowe knew him well enough now to recognize the hurt behind the laughter.

"I'm sorry," she said. "The world sucks sometimes."

"Yeah, but it also put this incredibly sexy woman in my bed." In a swift and unexpected move, he rolled her onto her back and pinned her underneath him. She could've wriggled away, but she was content where she was. Besides, she got called sexy as often as he got called smart. She was going to lean into it for a bit.

"Want to tell me the third thing you're self-conscious about?" she asked. "Besides your education and your aversion to small talk?"

"Yeeeaaaaah, no. I think we ended the conversation in the right place last time." He kissed her then, maybe because he was distracting her from the topic at hand, maybe because he simply wanted to kiss her. His evasion piqued Marlowe's curiosity, but she wasn't about to push. She had her own insecurities, and she didn't always want to reveal them, even when she wasn't in bed with a hot naked man whose thoughts were clearly straying in the same direction as hers.

For the better part of the morning, Marlowe and Angus let those thoughts lead where they would, in the bed, in the shower, and in his impressive walk-in closet, where getting dressed took an unusually long time. Eventually he pulled on a pair of jeans and she borrowed a crisp dress shirt. She could've retrieved her dress from the kitchen but the morning already felt like a fantasy. She might as well complete it by playing a glamorous, pampered lady who lounged around in her lover's clothes when the butler wasn't on site to notice.

The fantasy ebbed somewhat as Marlowe and Angus stopped avoiding the rest of the world and checked their phones. She'd turned hers off the night before, both to save the battery and to avoid the temptation to check messages. It was still powering up when Angus sank onto the bed with a pensive "Huh," drawing Marlowe's attention his way.

"Looks like season seven's a go," he said.

She sat down beside him. "That's good, right?"

"It's better than doing that action flick." He continued scrolling, his eyes locked on his screen. "It'll be weird, though. The producers waited too long to make a decision. Idi's heading to New York to play Macbeth on Broadway. They'll get him an understudy so he can fly back to shoot his scenes, but he won't be around much. Kamala and Meg both have film deals, so their roles will also be trimmed. Whitman's hoping to land a part on the next *Trek*. Everyone's deserting me." He laughed as though he was hyperbolizing, but Marlowe knew there was nothing funny about loneliness. She also wished she wasn't one more person deserting Angus, even if they'd work out a plan to stay connected.

She held out a hand, palm up the way he'd done for her, making a quiet offer he could accept or decline. He accepted, wrapping his fingers around hers.

"Bet Jake will finally sleep with his neighbor," he said. "Then he'll ditch the poor woman for a series of meaningless flings, burn down his childhood home, and smash up his bike in yet another drunk driving accident no one really addresses."

Marlowe gave his hand a squeeze, smiling to herself at how she'd once wished Jake's character arc would end in tragedy, and how differently she felt now.

"Or maybe he'll buy a flower shop and rescue a lot of cats," she offered.

Angus smiled as he tossed aside his phone and drew Marlowe onto his lap. She bent down to kiss him, but her phone lit up, pinging away with a backlog of texts. She snuck in a quick peck on Angus's lips before crawling across the bed to grab her phone.

"Oh, shit." She quickly scrolled through the messages. "Cherry's been trying to reach me. Apparently Babs brought Edith to work today but Lola's fitting is in an hour and she can't stand dogs. Cherry needs me to come get her. Edith. Not Lola." Marlowe scrambled up. "I'm so sorry. Is it still okay if I borrow your car?"

"Actually, I have a better idea."

By the time Marlowe stepped into the design office, Edith Head was going stir-crazy, spinning in circles and leaping on and off chairs. Cherry gave Marlowe a little sly teasing for showing up in yesterday's clothes (for obvious reasons), but mostly she was grateful she wouldn't have to deal with Babs *and* Lola *and* a skittish Weimaraner for the rest of the day. While Marlowe sorted out timing and leashed up Edith, Angus was off at a nearby deli, picking up everything they'd need for a picnic lunch. Then he swung back around to the studio lot, grabbed Marlowe and Edith, and they all headed north on Highway 1.

Half an hour later, the trio was kicking up trail dust in the hills behind the Getty Villa, setting off at a leisurely pace so Edith could smell every scraggly bush. Marlowe wasn't much of a hiker, but she was glad Angus had talked her into spending time outdoors together. It was a good first step outside the protection of his magical skybox, even if ball caps and sunglasses were required. Fortunately, only a few other hikers and joggers passed by, none of whom showed any overt signs of recognition.

About forty-five minutes into their hike, Angus steered Marlowe and Edith off the main trail onto a grassy hillside with a view of the ocean. He unrolled a blanket while Marlowe helped unpack sandwiches, chips, sodas, and a container of olives Angus hadn't had the means to properly garnish. Edith showed great interest in the food, but Marlowe convinced Angus not to feed her one of everything. As they ate, Marlowe told Angus more about her life in New York. He told her more about his life in L.A., going as far back as the time a talent agent scouted him, and how his siblings had thought it was the funniest thing ever, though of course they'd long since come around to other opinions.

Their lunch finished and Edith resting comfortably on the edge of the blanket, Marlowe clambered onto Angus's lap. Having seen no sign of potential onlookers over lunch, they removed their hats and sunglasses, freeing up opportunities for kisses and caresses, and for some of the staring that no longer made Marlowe squirm. Now the way Angus looked at her made her happy. Ridiculously so. Full-on, belly-fluttering, chest-expanding joy. The kind of joy Marlowe used to think only existed in the movies, but it was real after all. Funny how long she'd spent convincing herself to accept "fine" as good enough, when all the while, *this* was possible. This unquestionable sense of rightness. Of being precisely where she was supposed to be, free of doubts or second-guesses. Though as the quiet stretched on, a crease formed between Angus's brows.

"You really miss New York, don't you?" he asked.

"L.A.'s swiftly gaining in appeal." She bent to kiss him while he tried to tame the tendrils that kept escaping her ponytail, tucking them behind her ears as more strands slid past her cheeks. Edith stirred at the end of her leash, groaning as though she disapproved of the mild PDA she was being forced to witness. Marlowe couldn't help but laugh. "I may not get design work out here, but at least I'm experienced in last-minute dog care."

Angus smiled, but his eyes stayed serious as he caressed her cheeks.

"I know it might take a while to get your foot in the right door," he said, "but you're not alone out here. Tan did a show at the Geffen Playhouse last year. I bet she can help you get an interview.

Whitman's sister works at the opera, though I don't remember as what. Alejandra loved that you pushed back about Wes's terrible script ideas. She might put in a good word for you if she knows of an indie that's looking for a designer."

"Thank you for that." Marlowe kissed him again, because he cared and because he was beautiful and because he was smart and because he made the impossible seem possible. "What about you? When does season seven start shooting?"

"Not until after Christmas."

"Does that mean you could visit me in New York?"

"If you wouldn't mind being distracted." His caresses trailed lower, tracing her neckline and sneaking under her shoulder straps. "I could even set up some auditions. Who knows? Maybe this bi-coastal idea would open up opportunities for both—" He broke off as Edith sprang to her feet, barking her head off and yanking on the leash.

Marlowe tightened her hold, peering off in the direction of Edith's focus.

"What is it?" she asked. "A bird? A squirrel?"

Angus stiffened. "I wish."

Marlowe's nerves went taut as she realized what had caused Edith's barking fit. About twenty yards away, two teenage boys scrambled out from the underbrush and ran off, waving their phones. Angus leapt up and called after the boys to stop, but they kept running.

"I'd chase them down," he said, "but it wouldn't do any good. Either they don't know who we are and I'd draw unnecessary attention, or they do know who we are and I'd make us look like we had something to hide."

Marlowe grimaced as she watched the boys disappear around

a rolling hill. She appreciated Angus's point, but it didn't prevent her anxieties from mounting. She prayed the boys thought they'd stumbled onto a random couple making out, something to chuckle about with their friends. She kept praying as she and Angus packed up, and as they trekked the forty-five minutes back to the parking lot, barely exchanging a word. When they rounded the last bend and the lot came into view, her prayers died away.

Only a few cars had occupied the lot when Marlowe and Angus had arrived. Now the lot was full of vans and SUVs while at least two dozen people with cameras and microphones milled between vehicles. Naturally, Edith chose that moment to start barking, drawing all eyes their way. Marlowe turned to bolt back into the hills but Angus grabbed her hand.

"Running won't help," he said. "They'll spin it. Let's just get in the car and go." He stepped toward the lot but Marlowe remained rooted to her spot, utterly petrified.

"You said we'd start slow."

"It seemed like a good idea at the time."

"Minimal engagement."

"But it was stupid. Willfully ignorant."

"Control the narrative."

"Too ambitious."

"Claim some privacy."

"Ignored the obvious."

"All of those people"—she nodded toward the paparazzi as they funneled toward the trailhead—"when you were *just* at that gala with Tanareve."

"We told reporters we weren't together."

"And they believed you?"

His jaw twitched as he gave her hand a gentle tug.

"Walk right past," he said by way of answer. "Don't say a word."

With Edith straining at the leash and Angus determined to face the cameras, Marlowe let herself get led into a sea of flashing lights and overlapping voices. *How long has this been going on? Does Tanareve know?* Something vile about a casting couch. Something less vile about love. Demands for answers. *Your fans need to know.*

Angus pushed through it all with a clenched jaw, opening his passenger door for Marlowe. She climbed in and let Edith leap onto her lap. He skirted the car and got in, muttering, "No comment," before slamming the door. As he pulled out of the parking space, the crowd eased away from the car, gradually giving way while still filming and shouting questions. Marlowe clung to Edith, burying her face against the dog's neck until the car was out of the winding roads and heading south on Highway 1.

Angus kept his eyes on the road, every muscle tense. Edith climbed into the back seat with some effort. Marlowe got out her phone. It didn't take her long to find what she was looking for. A quick search for #IShipTheWaitress on Twitter pulled up a photo of her sitting on Angus's lap, his hand hovering near her breast while he toyed with her neckline, her dress spread over his hips in a way that suggested she wasn't just sitting on his lap. The original tweet was posted through a popular gossip site with the caption *Looks like this ship has sailed*. The teens must've sold their photos, and sold them fast. The retweets and comments were a mixed bag of shock, smugness for predicting what had now been "proven," a smattering of enthusiasm, and a lot of condemnation. As with the dance photo, people had all sorts of words for Marlowe, few of them kind.

"Stop reading that trash," Angus said.

"My friends can see this. My parents can see this. The people I'm trying to get work from can see this." She kept scrolling. Another photo was already up. The two of them ducking into the car, set next to a photo of Tanareve in tears. *Gordon Ditches Hughes for Secret Rendezvous with Waitress. Hughes Shattered.* "It's all so fast."

"The gossip market's competitive. Everyone wants to be first to break a story."

"But there is no story. Just two people who like each other having a picnic."

He shot her a quick sideways glance, one that reminded her how naïve that thinking was. She'd known what might happen. She just let herself forget.

By the time Angus pulled into the studio parking lot, Marlowe already had texts from her friends in New York, from Cherry, and even from her mom asking what in the hell was going on. The story must've gone especially viral if her mom had seen it, informed by whatever friend or coworker had stumbled across it. One picnic. Two hours outside a gated space. Five minutes without the armor of hats and sunglasses. That was all it took, and any hope for privacy or control was wrenched away.

Angus turned off the ignition but he didn't say anything. The sweet smiles and gentle laughter of the morning were gone, replaced by a hard edge Marlowe had seen before, during their screen test, at their first shoot when she'd questioned his intentions, and at the nightclub before their dance. She understood that edge now, the reasons he shut himself off and pushed people away. What other choice did he have? But still . . .

"It's too much," she said.

"I know."

"I can't."

"I know."

"I'm sorry."

He nodded, closed his eyes, shook his head. "I know that, too."

She bit her lip, fought back tears. "Maybe if we'd—"

"It would've happened eventually. I never should've pretended it wouldn't."

"I don't know how to—"

"You don't have to. You were clear about that. I pushed too hard."

"You didn't. We both wanted—"

"You should go." He turned the key in the ignition, locked his gaze straight ahead.

Marlowe watched him for a long moment, searching for the words that would make everything okay. When the words didn't come, she got out of the car and retrieved Edith from the back seat, peering in through the open door.

"Angus . . ."

"Don't."

"Please."

"Just. Go."

And so she did.

Chapter Thirty

The next four days passed in a blur. Thankfully Babs took pity on Marlowe, allowing her to hide in the wardrobe building and start packing up the season. Aside from Cherry—to whom Marlowe had confided everything—no one on set mentioned the media explosion. They crept around Marlowe as though she was fragile or ill, sneaking her sympathetic looks as Sunday's tweets turned into sensationalized tabloid articles and heated gossip panel discussions. What gossip reporters didn't know, they built from the scraps of her past, eager to paint a picture of the woman who'd wrecked Hollywood's It Couple. A no-name background actress trying to sleep her way to the top. A fickle girl who'd jilted her ex. A wannabe designer who'd been laughed out of the New York theater scene.

Angus didn't go ignored, but a placid "boys will be boys" tone pervaded the discussion of his supposed infidelity. If the articles of the last ten years were to be believed, he went from one girl to the next faster than Edith ate spring rolls. People weren't surprised he was sleeping around. They were surprised who he was with.

Marlowe blocked what she could, but the chatter was inescapable. When she asked her landlord about breaking her lease, he asked if she was moving in with her movie star boyfriend. The rental car clerk she met on Monday snuck in a few lofty insinuations about the value of fidelity. A trio of women at a grocery store did double-takes when they saw her, before gathering close to whisper and cast appalled looks at each other. And of course, Marlowe's parents couldn't believe she'd "let this happen."

Angus and Tanareve both denied the rumors, but they kept their statements brief and to the point, likely coached by their PR reps. The two of them were friends. They were fine. No one cheated on anyone. Neither of them offered up lengthy explanations of the various relationship dynamics at play. Nor did they mention Marlowe, possibly to keep the focus off her. As Angus had so often said, defending himself did little good. The more he said, the more he'd open himself—and everyone else involved—to further inquiry. People saw what they wanted to see. The only viable response was silence.

At least once every ten minutes, Marlowe considered texting Angus. Equally as often, she talked herself out of it. There was nothing to gain. She'd said she couldn't live in the center of public speculation. He'd said he understood. What more was there to say?

At around 5:30 A.M. on Friday, Marlowe pulled into the parking lot of a run-down strip mall in Glendale. White trailers filled one side of the lot while the other side was marked off for cast and crew parking. Half a block away, a cute adobe church was surrounded by gear as grips scurried around it like so many black ants, hauling cables and unpacking road boxes. Marveling at their energy so early in the morning, Marlowe got out of her rental car while blinking her way through a long, drawn-out yawn.

"Still can't sleep?" someone said behind her.

Marlowe spun around to see Cherry crossing the lot toward her, chunky heels clicking against the pavement, two hot beverage cups in hand. Under her black jacket, she wore a vivid magenta shirt that sparkled with the words *MORE GLITTER, LESS LITTER*.

"What's sleep?" Marlowe asked. "Also, I do mornings about as well as I date famous TV actors without getting dragged through the mud." She dropped her keys into her purse, or at least she tried to. In her tiredness, she missed completely. While bending to pick up her keys, she banged a shoulder on the rearview mirror. Straightening up, her purse slipped off her shoulder and spilled its contents. She muttered curses as she crouched and collected everything. "At least no one's filming and tweeting this."

Cherry helped gather Marlowe's goods before handing off one of the coffee cups.

"Fame is so overrated," she said.

"Thank you for not saying you told me so."

"Not my style." Cherry downed a gulp of what was probably scalding-hot coffee. Then she draped an arm around Marlowe's shoulders and pivoted her toward the trailers. "The situation sucks and I'm sorry. At least attention spans are short. People tune in but they also move on. Shake it off if you can. Don't forget. You're getting married today!"

Marlowe groaned. Yes, she was about to get dolled up like Wedding Barbie, but she was also going to see Angus for the first time since Sunday's disaster. Four days of packing and inventorying clothes hadn't dulled the sharp ache of loss that had set in when she left him in the studio parking lot. She told herself she hadn't really lost anything. She'd only known Angus for a few weeks. They didn't have a relationship, just a rush of sexual attraction that would've faded soon enough. She didn't even want a relationship. Not really.

With friends, a career, and a sense of home waiting for her in New York, she didn't need anything else to feel fulfilled. She had everything she wanted.

Of course, she knew she was lying to herself, but the lies got her by.

For the next three hours, Cherry attended to background actors while Patrice styled Marlowe's hair. Predictably, Babs's style suggestions were well beyond what the average waitress might accomplish for a small, DIY wedding. The final look was a low mass of curls, bound by velvet ribbons and sprinkled with forget-me-nots. It was sleek and modern in the front and unabashedly romantic in the back, all of which matched the dress. Though Marlowe had expressed her share of doubts about Babs's disinterest in realism, she recognized that the heightened sense of style clearly indicated that the show was a fantasy. In some ways, it was less problematic than the images that abounded on social media, where idyllic lifestyles were peddled in tidy squares while just outside the frames, a completely different story unfolded. Maybe a little glamor wasn't the worst idea, as long as Marlowe could stop using it as a bar she'd never reach.

Ravi was working on Marlowe's makeup at around 9:00 A.M. when Babs made her first appearance for the day. She wore a black linen pantsuit with a jacket that plunged in a deep V. Her lips and nails were neatly colored in a deep, brick red. Her silver jewelry was plentiful but sleek. Combined with her starkly dyed black hair, she looked like a graphic print of a woman, all sharp edges and high contrast. She dropped a large, boxy handbag on a chair while eyeing the water bottle in front of Marlowe.

"Don't worry," Marlowe said. "It's not carbonated."

Babs's face twitched into what could almost be called a smile, but not quite. She got straight to business, parking herself behind Marlowe's chair and giving her a full inspection. After due consideration, she asked Patrice to reposition a few flowers and she suggested Ravi use a darker plum tone on Marlowe's lids. The three of them discussed and finessed the details until everyone was happy with the bride-to-be.

As Ravi and Patrice tidied up, Marlowe took a good look in the mirror. Her reflection was almost unrecognizable. Sure, the bone structure and eyes were hers, as was most of the hair, but four-plus hours of professional help had otherwise transformed her. Her lips were fuller. Her lashes were thicker and longer. Her barely there cheekbones popped with a dusting of rosy blush against a miraculously smooth complexion. Her brows formed perfect slender arches atop plum-tinted lids, and her hair lacked even a hint of frizz. She felt like Cinderella preparing to go to the ball: beautiful, elegant, refined, and worthy of the kind of attention she usually felt was reserved for other people. And yet . . . the costumer in her still wished the woman in the mirror looked more like an ordinary, messy, often frazzled, always conflicted, deeply insecure, nail-chewing, hot-sauce-spilling, no-time-for-makeup-or-lunch, working-class girl.

"You still want dirt under your nails, don't you?" Babs asked beside her.

Marlowe turned her head side to side, still trying to recognize herself. "I get it. I do. This isn't realism. But representation matters. Seeing only conventionally attractive girls on-screen, or brave and strong girls, or skinny girls, or white girls, or straight girls, or girls with perfectly groomed eyebrows sends a message to all the girls who don't fit those categories." She glanced sideways at Babs, prepared for a rebuttal. The rebuttal didn't come. Instead Babs folded her arms and waited for Marlowe to continue. "I was so confident as a kid. I was stubborn and outspoken, but over time I started to feel like only certain kinds of girls deserved to be listened to, and deserved to be loved. I don't think all this . . . polish helped." She waved a hand over her face.

Babs turned toward her own reflection, dabbing at the liner around her eyes.

"I agree that a consistent 'polish,' as you call it, can be problematic, but shows with spectacle bring in viewers. People want an escape from reality. Princesses, party scenes, dances, red carpets, couture, a suggestion of the extraordinary. Yes, TV and film impacts culture, but audiences create that culture as well. It's simple market and demand."

"Then I guess we're all to blame." Marlowe slumped sideways but she paused before resting a cheek on her hand, worried she'd mess up Ravi's work.

Without responding, Babs crossed the trailer and lifted the muslin cover from the wedding gown. She ran her hands down the front where two pieces of scalloped lace formed a halter-style neckline, meeting at the bustline and carrying on to the waist where a riot of swirling organza ruffles spilled out, filling the entire rack area. Her movement was slow and careful. Her eyes were distant and the usual tightness around her lips had softened. Maybe she was considering the spectacle, or maybe she was recalling her own wedding, and the vows that were broken twenty years later.

"I'm not sure how they'll top this next year," she said through a sigh. "If season six ends with a wedding, season seven will need a death or a baby."

"It'll probably be Jake's." Ravi chuckled from the corner by the sink. "The baby, I mean, not the death. Everyone loves it when a bad boy reforms."

An awkward pause followed, filled with an exchange of uncomfortable glances. Marlowe sank lower in her seat and started chewing a nail. Ravi reminded her that her nails were sacred territory for the rest of the day. Marlowe lowered her hand, duly chastened, but a weight settled in her gut and showed no signs of leaving.

While she battled an onslaught of conflicting feelings, Patrice continued the speculation about what might be on tap in season seven, steering clear of any mention of Jake. Ravi was moving on to a sci-fi film, but Babs and Patrice planned to return.

"The design's so well established," Babs said. "No point handing it off now."

"What'll happen with the film you were going to design?" Marlowe asked.

"They'll find someone else." Babs dug through her giant handbag and pulled out a menacing-looking nail file. "Timing's tight but the demands are minimal. Small cast, fast shoot, not a lot of background. Anyone could do it, really."

"Anyone like Cherry?"

"Cherry will be on season seven with me."

"But if you recommended her for the film, would they at least consider her?"

"Maybe." Babs turned away, locking her focus on her nails. While she ran her file back and forth, Marlowe gripped the arms of her chair, steeling herself to press on.

"Cherry's so smart and she has a great eye for fit, color, and character. She works harder than anyone I know. She deserves to move up from assisting." Marlowe stopped there but when Babs continued filing, muttering only a low and noncommittal *hmm*, she inched forward. "I understand not wanting to create competition but I don't think you have to worry. Cherry would never take a job from you."

Babs glanced up, her file halted, her expression inscrutable.

"I'm not worried about competition," she said.

"Then what *are* you worried about?" Marlowe pressed.

"It's none of your business."

"She's my friend. She looks out for me. I can do the same for her."

Babs scowled, flicking her file against the side of her thumb.

"Cherry will make more money here."

"I don't think that's her top priority."

"She still has so much to learn."

"She can learn while she designs."

"The script isn't even that good."

"And *Heart's Diner* is a masterpiece of literary fiction?" Marlowe stifled a laugh.

Babs's scowl deepened, but after a moment, her face relaxed and her file stilled.

"Fine," she said. "If you must know, I don't recommend Cherry for other jobs because I don't know how I'd get by without her."

"Oh. Right." Marlowe sat back in her chair, too startled to say more. She'd watched Babs and Cherry interact for six months and she had no idea Babs placed that kind of value on Cherry's assistance. She suspected Cherry didn't know, either.

As the weight of Babs's revelation settled, she renewed her filing.

"The girls in that film would all end up in logo T-shirts," she said.

"Which wouldn't be such a bad thing," Marlowe offered.

Babs pursed her lips, the picture of annoyance. Ravi and Patrice paused their tidying. As the trailer went quiet again, Babs took in the faces around her. The annoyance faded from her face, replaced by what Marlowe could only call amusement.

"You're right," she conceded with a chuckle. "It wouldn't be bad at all."

Discounting the occasional derisive bark, this was the first time Marlowe had ever heard Babs laugh. The look of respect she sent Marlowe a second later suggested that a certain stubborn, outspoken girl was still alive and well, and her voice hadn't gone unheard.

Chapter Thirty-one

Setup on location took longer than expected, but shortly after noon, an AD escorted Marlowe toward the church to walk through her blocking before she'd get into costume and cameras would roll. As a guy from the art department hurried past with a potted shrub, and a trio of grips trudged by with thick coils of cable on their shoulders, Cherry stepped out of the background tent. Her eyes lit up when she spotted Marlowe.

"Holy shit, you look amazing."

"Better than dog spit and vanilla shake?"

"Low bar, Banks. Low bar." Cherry fell in step with Marlowe and the AD, heading toward the church. "You're never going to believe this, but Babs called the producers on the girls' rock camp film. They've agreed to meet with me tomorrow."

Marlowe grinned ear to ear while her chest could've burst with pride.

"That's fantastic!" she said. "Congratulations!"

"I don't officially have the job yet, but if Babs has anything to say about the matter, I have nothing to worry about. I know she's been hard on you, and she can be tough to work with, but I think she had to be tough to gain respect in this industry."

Marlowe nodded, smiling to herself. She had a less flattering view of Babs's "toughness," but that view didn't really matter. Babs was making a major sacrifice to help advance Cherry's career, and Marlowe kind of loved her for it.

When they reached the church, Cherry got called back to wardrobe while Marlowe met with Damon, the director of the final episode. He was a short, stocky, bald guy in his mid-to-late thirties with full tattoo sleeves that made his crisp oxford appear ironic, though maybe he simply liked oxfords.

After a brief introduction, he talked Marlowe through her blocking. She'd enter from the back of a limo, followed by her bridesmaid, as played by a slight girl named Olga with a toothy smile and a blond pixie cut. Marlowe would walk up the church steps, pause at the top, and scan the street. Seeing nothing, she'd turn to head in. The sound of the motorcycle would halt her. She'd turn again. Jake would pull up on the other side of the street. As he got off his bike, she'd step forward. A moment of indecision. Look at her flowers. Back at Jake. Behind her at the church. She'd tug her freckled ear. He'd step forward. She'd shake her head, cast him one last longing look, and enter the church. As before, they'd shoot the entire sequence through. Once they had what they needed, they'd set up for shorter takes, close-ups, etc.

Marlowe and Olga walked through the action a couple of times, stepping into the church where crewmembers were working with the lighting and sound gear that surrounded the entrance. Past the bustle of activity, the church stood empty, with about twenty rows of pews and an unadorned altar at the end of the aisle. The space had a mass-produced quality to it, from the wood paneling to the bland stained-glass windows beyond the altar. Despite Cherry's instructions to imagine a fantasy wedding, Marlowe couldn't muster enough imagination to manage the task. The lackluster church was only partly to blame, but it served as an excellent scapegoat for her heartache.

Marlowe saw no sign of Angus on set. Maybe he was avoiding her. Maybe the production staff was keeping the pair apart, hoping to prevent an altercation that could affect filming. Maybe their distance from one another was simply a product of chance. Regardless, Marlowe was grateful. Better to see Angus when they were both acting. When the only grief or confusion on display would be completely, utterly fake.

Back in the trailer, Elaine helped Marlowe into her enormous dress while Cherry stood by for moral support. The dress really was gorgeous, though its sheer quantity of ruffles made Marlowe thankful she was wearing it and not making it. As she faced the mirror, centered in a delicate ivory cloud, with her dramatic makeup and fairy-princess hair, the reality of what she was about to do finally hit her.

"How do I get through this?" she asked.

"I don't know." Cherry straightened a few errant ruffles. "Ignore the reality. Embrace the fantasy. Channel the costume. Don't forget, you're wearing fifteen thousand dollars' worth of couture. You look gorgeous, even if your boobs are, like, eighty percent synthetic materials. You're not the only one in L.A. who can make that claim."

Marlowe smiled but a lump built in her throat.

"Have you seen him?" she asked.

Cherry nodded. "He's hurting, too. That's pretty obvious. But he's a pro. He'll do his job, just like you will. At least you guys don't have to talk to each other. You just have to look angsty and unhappy. Pretty sure you'll both nail it."

Marlowe snuck in a loose hug, careful not to crush the dress. Minutes later, she was being packed into the back of a limousine with Olga while a familiar flurry ensued. The art director handed off her bouquet. Makeup and hair experts performed final checks. Crewmembers consulted lighting meters, adjusted cameras, and positioned booms. The episode director and director of photography stationed themselves by a set of monitors, competing for Most-Animated Hand Gesture. The driver started the car. With a cue from an AD, everyone settled. After a few seconds of suspended quiet, the car moved forward.

The driver pulled up to the curb about twenty yards from where he started. Marlowe swapped a quick smile of encouragement with Olga before they opened their doors and climbed out. Marlowe fussed with the explosion of featherlight ruffles that fluttered all around her while Olga skirted the car and joined her on the sidewalk. Thankfully, Babs had decided to forgo a veil. Between the bouquet, the dress, and a thousand jolts of nervous energy, Marlowe had enough to manage.

With a deep breath, she followed Olga up the half dozen steps to the landing in front of the church. Olga opened one of the doors and held it for Marlowe, beaming like an eager bridesmaid on her best friend's wedding day. Marlowe stared into the church. Beyond the crew and equipment positioned immediately on the other side of the doors, empty space stretched out before her. Empty pews. Empty aisle. Empty altar. It was all so hollow, so deserted. The aloneness swept through her like a frigid wind, reminding her of solitary nights, and of days on end without company, without the warmth of shared laughter or physical touch. The strange brittleness of being lonely. A feeling so familiar, and one she shared with the last person in the world she would've imagined being lonely. For a few brief and beautiful days, they'd been each other's remedy. But now . . .

Olga cleared her throat. Marlowe blinked herself back to task. She turned and looked both ways down the street, stepping forward, craning her neck, seeking a flash of copper-penny hair. So many people. So much gear. No Angus.

She spun toward the church and stepped onto the threshold. The rumble of the motorcycle halted her, on cue. She sucked in a breath. Braced herself. Turned around.

There he was, across the street, straddling a battered motorcycle in dusty jeans, a rumpled black T-shirt, and Jake's trademark leather jacket. His hair was darkened with product but his cowlicks curled over his forehead as though they refused to be tamed. It was a good look on him, a little bit wild and open to tousling, or so it might be if Angus's expression wasn't so impenetrable. It held no hope, no joy, no questions to be exchanged or offerings of care and affection. Gone was the Angus who'd danced with Marlowe at a club or tumbled off her sofa in a tangle of limbs and laughter. The man facing her was someone else entirely. A stranger. A cold goodbye.

She watched him dismount, her stomach churning, her breath coming short and fast. As he stood beside the bike, she started toward the stairs. Olga's hand wrapped around Marlowe's arm, reminding her to stay on the landing. Angus was the one who was supposed to step forward. But he didn't step forward. He planted himself on the sidewalk, his hands jammed in his pockets, his mouth rigid, his tiger's eyes blazing with hurt and anger that felt so real, they brought tears to Marlowe's eyes. She tried to blink away the tears but she only managed to entrap them in her stupid fake lashes.

Olga tightened her grip but Marlowe wrenched her arm free and ran down the steps, her dress billowing out behind her. As she reached the sidewalk, Angus's hand rose to his ear. She stopped, waited, watched. He gave his lobe a little yank. A reminder of the blocking she'd abandoned? Or of the secret language they'd begun building together? Freckled ears. Silly garnishes. A question for a question.

His image blurred as her tears came faster. She was about to run across the street when she noticed Damon standing by the monitors, madly waving for her to return to the church. She caught Angus's eye, holding it as she mouthed, *I'm sorry*. With a swift pinch of her ear, she turned and ran up the steps, carrying on into the church.

The door slammed behind her. Motion erupted a second later, suggesting that Damon had called *Cut* out on the street. Walkie-talkies hummed with conversations. Grips reset. Hair and makeup people scurried forward to pat down sweat and tame flyaway hairs. Marlowe swayed in place, bracing herself on the nearest pew. Someone asked if she was okay. She nodded, barely, while the crew made her camera-ready again.

Cherry soon appeared, followed by Babs and Elaine.

"How are you doing?" she asked.

"Not well." The lump in Marlowe's throat returned as more tears welled up in her eyes. "Seeing him . . . I messed up. I was a total coward. I told him I couldn't handle the pressure. I ran away. I let him think he was only worth a fling. How could I do that?"

Amid the patting, taming, and fluffing, Cherry gave Marlowe's hand a squeeze.

"You did the best you could," she said. "Some people are drawn to the spotlight. Others aren't. There's nothing wrong with either. You have to do what works for you."

"But I didn't even try. That's all he asked me to do. Try."

For several minutes, Cherry talked Marlowe back toward a

place of relative calm, which at least allowed the makeup artist to do her job without battling a steady stream of tears. The art director swapped out a few smashed roses for fresh ones. Elaine brushed dirt off the underside of the train. Babs stood by, watching. Marlowe half expected her to make a caustic dig like *You should've known what you were getting into*. Instead she displayed a sort of mentor-ly patience, observing the conversation as though she was preparing sage advice, a little like Yoda, but taller and with much better hair.

Marlowe turned to face her. "You look like you want to say something."

"Your love life is none of my business." Babs pursed her lips without any apparent awareness of her irony. "Though if you're open to a small suggestion . . ."

Marlowe stepped forward, ready for Yoda-esque wisdom to pour forth.

"I am," she said. "Please."

Babs plucked a bit of fuzz off her sleeve and flicked it to the floor, somehow managing to imply that Marlowe's distress was of similar consequence.

"If you want to steer a dialogue about realistic representations of women, having a few cameras aimed at you wouldn't be the worst idea in the world." She caught Marlowe's eye for the briefest of instants, a raise of a brow, a quirk of a lip, a hint of encouragement. Then her chin tipped up and she snapped back to business, barking at a girl with a comb about fixing a velvet ribbon before the entire lot came unraveled.

While the girl attended to the offending ribbon, Marlowe let Babs's suggestion sink in. She recalled speaking up about Wes's script changes, sharing her ideas with the theater director, standing up to Kelvin, and fighting for Cherry. She recalled Angus telling her to use her voice. Not bury it. Not modify it to be more pleasant, likable, accommodating, or fun. She also recalled walking away from him, assuming it was the end, so soon after the beginning. She'd never want the kind of attention that came with his fame, but maybe she could face that attention not as a victim, but as a voice.

An AD approached and said they were ready to reset in the limo. Marlowe requested ten minutes alone. The AD got on her walkie-talkie and sorted out Marlowe's request with the rest of the team. As the church cleared while the crewmembers headed out to the street, Marlowe sent Cherry to go find Angus.

Chapter Thirty-two

Marlowe was sitting alone in the quiet church, facing the empty altar and drowning in a mound of ivory ruffles when Angus slid onto the pew beside her. Without so much as a glance in her direction, he leaned forward to rest his forearms on his thighs, his hands laced together, his eyes downcast. Marlowe gave him a moment to settle. Then she began.

"Do you remember what you wrote on the note you gave me with the flowers?"

"I think I said I was sorry for being an asshole."

"You also said I deserved better. I spend a lot of time thinking about what I do and don't deserve, but it's not helpful thinking. Because, yeah, I do deserve better, but so do you. So do a lot of people. If that wasn't true, and if it wasn't such a universal problem, we wouldn't have so many crappy vigilante movies." She forced a smile.

He tapped a thumb against his linked fists, unamused and otherwise unmoving. His walls were up and they were *solid*.

Marlowe took a breath and continued. "All this clickbait stuff is hard. I hate seeing my life dissected and my personal choices put on display for others to judge. I hate explaining to my friends and my parents. I hate thinking up a million ways to defend myself while knowing every defense is futile against trolls and haters. But you know what makes it all harder? Knowing you're dealing with it, too, and I don't even get to be with you. Knowing I said *I can't*, when the truth is, I can. I just have to learn how."

His thumb stopped tapping but his eyes remained locked on his hands. When he still didn't respond, Marlowe gathered more nerve and carried on.

"I know we've only known each other for a few weeks. And things between us are new and unsure and complicated, but if you'll give me another chance, I'd like to tell your fans the truth. They might not believe it, but I think I can find a way to live with that. It's better than going silent. It's better than getting small."

"And what truth do you want to tell people?"

"That we haven't been sneaking around behind Tanareve's back. That we met on the show and got to know each other the way people do, by spending time together and talking and cooking and doing really ordinary things. That you made me laugh and you blew me away with how smart you are. And that I fell in love with you."

Angus finally looked up, his face clouded with disbelief.

"You what?"

"I'll deal with the publicity. I'll need some coaching. The number for Tanareve's therapist. Maybe the numbers for a lot of therapists. If Whitman and Idi have any advice, I'd take that, too. Also, a bottle of wine on hand at all times. Comfort food. Really cozy blankets. Anything that feels good because I'll probably freak out a lot and internalize things I should let bounce off, but I don't want to walk away from you again. Not like I did on Sunday. Like we let them tear us apart. I may be a coward but I'm also the girl who punched Pete Kensington in the face. So if you're open to the idea,

I'd really like a chance to go on a date with you. At least once. Not at the world's worst taco stand."

He shook his head, staring at her with wide-eyed incredulity. "Go back to that other thing you said."

She laid a hand against his cheek. The softness of his stubble was so familiar now. The sharp line of his jaw. The downward curve of his nose. The dent in his chin. Even the mascara-tinted lashes that framed the fire in his eyes.

"I love you," she said. "I know the words are big, but they're the right ones for how I feel. They're the only ones for how I feel."

He leaned into her touch as his eyes shut. A moment passed, quiet and beautiful.

"My third insecurity," he said. "I'm twenty-seven years old and no one outside of my immediate family has ever said that to me. No one who knew me."

Marlowe gaped at him, dumbfounded. She'd seen photos of him with so many women over the years. She'd watched others confess undying love online, in stores, at the studio lot. He had hundreds of thousands of fans. But that kind of love didn't take into account the way he stole a piece of spinach from a taco or read four books at the same time. The sarcasm, the patient listening, the dream of owning a grossly overfed dog.

"Is that a yes?" she asked.

"That is definitely a yes."

She kissed him then, drawing him to her with both hands, and with the words that now sat between them. He kissed her back, sweetly and tenderly.

"I'm sorry I pushed you away," he said. "Guess I still need to work on that."

"We both have things to work on." She took his hand, running her thumb over his freckled knuckles. "But I'd rather work on them with you than without you."

"I like the sound of that." He tipped his forehead against hers. Another quiet moment passed, this one a little easier, gentler, more certain. It was broken when Angus drew away to pull his phone from his back pocket. He laughed as he read the screen.

"Is someone demanding we get back to work?" Marlowe asked.

Angus shook his head. "Everyone out there knows what's going on. If you think hiding from the paparazzi is hard, trying keeping secrets from people you see fourteen hours a day for six seasons." He held out his phone for Marlowe to read the screen.

Tanareve: Did you put on your big boy pants and tell her you love her yet?

This time it was Marlowe's turn to look startled. Angus shrugged as he pocketed his phone. Then he got to his feet, drawing Marlowe with him.

"She likes you," he said. "She considers you solely responsible for the uptick in my mood lately, which is no small feat. She said if we patched things up, she'd ensure everyone saw us all getting along. She has big plans to take you shopping, and clubbing, and whatever you're up for. Prepare yourself. That girl has insane amounts of stamina."

Marlowe shook her head, still stunned.

"Go back to that other thing."

Angus drew her into his arms. As he met her eyes, he rose up onto his toes, gaining a couple of inches on her height. Then he flashed her the teasing smile she'd been longing to see all week, the one that made everything brighter and more hopeful.

"I love you," he said. "And yeah, they're big words, but they're right for me, too." He leaned in for a kiss but Marlowe set a hand on his chest and pulled back.

"Does this mean I have to stop sleeping with your butler?"

"I knew something was up. That asshole's getting fired tonight."

Whether Angus kissed Marlowe, or she kissed him, their lips met, and she knew in that moment that she was finally chasing precisely the dream she wanted.

Epilogue

In mid-December, the week before Marlowe's first official Adelaide episode was scheduled to stream, she paced the well-appointed greenroom of *The Late Show*, fanning her armpits and biting her nails, frustrated she couldn't do both at the same time. Angus sat on an overstuffed sofa, his arm slung over the back and his feet kicked up, the picture of easy confidence. On his lap was the wire fox terrier they'd recently adopted, both enamored with his resemblance to Asta from *The Thin Man*. Neither of them had paid much attention to the film on first viewing, but it became a mutual favorite in the weeks that followed. Weeks that involved challenging conversations about travel possibilities, aligning schedules for bicoastal video calls, and missed opportunities to share key moments together, none of which was easy. But the weeks also included euphoric reunions, deep discussions about the meanings of art and image, gloriously lazy days spent in bed together, and hysterical negotiations about flying a spoiled terrier first class because leaving him in L.A. while both Marlowe and Angus were in New York was completely out of the question.

"They can edit this if I vomit or pass out, right?" Marlowe asked, still pacing.

Angus offered her a reassuring smile from his seat on the sofa, where he targeted the terrier's sweet spot with a firm scratch behind the ears.

"Ignore the studio audience. Ignore the cameras. It's only a conversation."

"Easy for you to say. You've done this a zillion times." She spat out a sliver of fingernail, worried she was being gross, then decided she had enough worries already and let it go. Carpets were easily cleaned. Panic, not so much. "I should've said I couldn't make it. I had last-minute shopping errands or Very Important meetings to attend."

"At five in the morning?" He chuckled softly while the dog snorted as if equally amused at her suggestions. "It's a six-minute interview segment. In and out. It'll go by so fast, you'll be on your way to the theater before you know it."

"I should be there now, making sure the costumes are ready for fittings."

"Everything was ready when you left last night. Your fittings will go great."

"They'll at least go better than my first live TV appearance." Marlowe grabbed a wad of tissues and patted her armpits dry, unable to mirror Angus's tranquility. Three months after the ambush at their picnic—three months that included regular appointments with Tanareve's therapist—Marlowe had grown somewhat accustomed to appearing in social media posts, doing online promo for *Heart's Diner*, and summoning a credible smile for paparazzi photos with Angus, but live TV provided the opportunity for a whole new level of public humiliation. "Remind me to ask Tanareve which deodorant she uses. Also, breathing exercises. Breakfast suggestions, too, like, top ten nausea-resistant foods. Maybe I should get a second therapist. Would that be excessive? That would probably be excessive." She continued rambling as she tossed the tissues in a nearby wastebasket.

When she renewed her pacing, Angus stood and halted her, enveloping her in his arms with the dog wedged between them. He didn't say anything. He didn't need to. He simply held her while she relaxed into his embrace, burying her face against his neck.

"This is why we should've called him Taco," she said.

"I still like Kale."

"I still hope you were kidding about that."

Angus laughed as he let the terrier lick his face. A common practice.

"Totally kidding," he said. "This dog was destined to be a Jeeves."

"Even though he doesn't bark with a British accent?"

"One more visit to my parents and he'll be barking in brogue."

Marlowe joined his quiet laughter, grateful for the release. Over the past few months, Angus's family had warmly welcomed Marlowe into their fold, never letting her end a visit without an armload of food and a promise to return. Marlowe's parents had also met Angus, and vaguely disapproved of the relationship.

"Thanks for suggesting we bring him." She gave Jeeves a scratch under his chin, making his back legs wiggle as though he was pedaling an invisible bicycle. "It helps."

"I know." Angus pressed his lips to her forehead, another technique that helped with her anxiety, as though he was sending his love straight to her overactive brain. As predicted, being in the public eye had gotten easier. Also as predicted, that didn't mean it got easy. The world was full of people trying to tear others down. For anyone but the toughest of the tough, being the target of trolls and toxicity was always going to hurt. But, as Marlowe now understood, attempting to avoid mean people wasn't an effective solution. Better to focus on not facing those people alone.

"Think they'll let us take Jeeves on camera?" she asked.

"Probably. If you need him."

"I didn't mean for me."

Angus drew back and gave her a quizzical look. Marlowe smiled as she brushed a copper-penny cowlick off his forehead, a gesture she doubted she'd ever tire of. Reaching toward him had become second nature. And he never seemed to mind.

"I have a theory I want to test," she said.

"That sounds dangerous."

"If you appear on national television, cooing over our dog the way you do at home, I bet someone offers you a rom-com by year's end. A rom-com that might even involve an earnest flower seller who takes in too many stray cats."

Angus broke into a dazzling grin, one that still took her breath away. Every time.

"I don't know which I like better," he said. "Your sincere investment in improving my career options or the way you just called my house *home*."

Marlowe grimaced. "Is that okay? You can call my quarter of the Williamsburg apartment *home*, too. Even if I can only offer you a drawer."

"It's an excellent drawer." He kissed her forehead again. Her cheek. Her lips. Then Jeeves got involved and Angus stepped back, laughing while he let the dog have his way, as always. "And yes. Calling my house *home* is more than okay. It's perfect."

Marlowe watched Angus and Jeeves adore each other, her heart swelling with love for them both. Despite her current stress levels, building a life with Angus brought her profound fulfillment, especially as she learned to apply Babs's astute advice about using her new visibility. Sometimes she was careful to look her best. Other times she looked like her ordinary, messy, often frazzled, always conflicted, deeply insecure, nail-chewing, hot-sauce-spilling, no-time-for-makeup-or-lunch, working-class self, because after all, that girl deserved love, too. And so did every girl who'd see the photos.

Today Marlowe had compromised. She got a professional blow-out, but she applied her own makeup and she wore a simple shirtwaist dress Cherry had helped select, FaceTiming in from the set of the film she was designing. Cherry liked the novelty strawberry print. Marlowe liked that the dress fit her well without any padding. She also enjoyed its subtle resemblance to her waitress uniform. She had no interest in reprising her role, *ever*, but she appreciated that the costume had launched her out of invisibility and forced her to reach for the kind of life—and love—she wanted.

Funny that it all started with a costume. Or maybe it started with a look.

"They're going to play the clip, aren't they?" she asked.

Angus nodded, still smiling. "I guarantee it."

"And ask what we were thinking at the time."

"Highly likely." He stepped closer and nudged her nose with his.

She nuzzled back. "I can't tell people I wanted to pour hot coffee into your lap."

"Why not? It's real. It's funny. It's you."

"And that's okay?"

"That is everything." He drew her into another embrace, one as awkward but wonderful as the last, with a restless terrier wriggling between them. "You are a brilliant costume designer opening a world premiere next month. I am an annoyingly irresistible TV actor with a successful record of expanding my girlfriend's culinary palate. Jeeves has a promising future in sock destruction. We've got this."

Marlowe set a hand on his chest and pressed a cheek against the dog.

"Yeah," she said. "I guess we do."

Acknowledgments

Any book reaching publication is the product of countless people's efforts. I'll never know the names of everyone who has a hand in editing, designing, manufacturing, distributing, and promoting my work. But I can at least ensure I include a few essential thank-yous here.

To Rona Bird, who's been the most amazing friend for over 20 years now. She was not only my first reader for this book, but my expert consultant on all things Scottish. We met when we were both working as costumers thousands of miles from where we are now, and I'm so, *so* grateful that despite all the twists and turns our lives have taken, we've held on to our friendship.

To the brilliant and intrepid costume assistants (all of whom are amazing designers in their own rights) who gave me support and advice on how to navigate the field while I was in Los Angeles. Shannin Strom Henry, Kenneth Chu, Joel Berlin, Johann Stegmeir, and Lisa Tomczeszyn. You were all such amazing role models, and I wouldn't have made it ten minutes without you guys.

To my agent, Laura Bradford, for knowing from the first messy draft what this book needed before it would speak to a reader. And to Hannah Andrade, who does the kind of hard work that's often invisible but is so meaningful. Thank you both for slogging through the ugly drafts. And for all the unseen work you do to help writers keep writing.

To my editor, Jennie Conway, for clear and kind insight about how to strengthen Marlowe's journey so the story had emotional resonance and I didn't meander too far into ramblings about ruffles. Or dogs. I kind of always want to ramble about dogs. I've been reading your name in acknowledgments for years and it's a literal dream come true to get to work with you.

To everyone at St. Martin's. The brilliant copyeditor who I swear read this with magical eyes to have picked up on so many details that needed tiny tweaks. The art department who, as I type this, are working on cover designs. The marketing and PR folks I'll meet in months to come. I make collaborative art for a living. I know this book can't become a book without all of your creativity and hard work. I'm so glad we get to play on the same team together.

To the bloggers, bookstagrammers, booktokers, reviewers, and other bookish advocates. I know we talk about books because we love books. But that love translates into meaningful support for authors, not only building visibility for our books, but also helping us know someone's out there, beyond the keyboard, cheering us on. Your efforts do not go unnoticed or un-felt.

To the many, many friends and family members who've listened to my angst about navigating multiple careers in the arts for decades now. My friend Jen once said I needed a T-shirt that read, I CHOOSE IMPOSSIBLE CAREERS. She's right. I do. But those careers are less impossible because I have the support of people who inspire me and who care about me and who let me fail and brush myself off so I can try again. My creative community is far too large to name everyone here, but you know who you are. You're my family. I love you. So much.

To the ex who said I'd never find someone better than him. Like Marlowe, I did find that someone. You'll never read this, but it feels good to write, all the same.

To anyone and everyone who makes a conscious choice to be kind instead of lashing out, especially online in public forums, thank you for making that choice. The internet is a gift. It can also be a weapon. I'm grateful for those who remember real people will read the things that get said. It's been a rough couple of years. To those who make the effort to add kindness and compassion and joy to the world, thank you. You're my heroes.

And last but not least, to anyone who has internalized personal or societal messages that they don't deserve love. You do. I promise, with my whole heart. You do. You so very much do.

About the Author

Tallulah

Jacqueline Firkins is a writer, costume designer, and lover of beautiful things. She's on the full-time faculty in the Department of Theatre & Film at the University of British Columbia, where she also takes any writing class they'll let her into. When not obsessing about where to put the buttons or the commas, she can be found running by the ocean, eating excessive amounts of gluten, listening to earnest love songs, and pretending her dog understands every word she says.